LIVING PROOF

PETER J. THOMPSON

BERKLEY BOOKS, NEW YORK

LIVING PROOF

A Berkley Book / published by arrangement with the author

PRINTING HISTORY
Berkley edition / March 2003

Copyright © 2003 by Peter J. Thompson.
Cover illustration by Complete Artworks Ltd.
Interior text design by Julie Rogers.

ISBN: 0-425-18906-6

BERKLEY®
Berkley Books are published by The Berkley Publishing Group,
a division of Penguin Putnam Inc.,
375 Hudson Street, New York, New York 10014.
BERKLEY and the "B" design
are trademarks belonging to Penguin Putnam Inc.

PRINTED IN THE UNITED STATES OF AMERICA

10 9 8 7 6 5 4 3 2 1

Acknowledgments

I would like to thank everyone who helped me in writing this book, especially Naomi Peralta, Laura Anschicks and the writer's group, Deb Matatall, and Daniel Holt for his help in Washington. I would also like to thank Bryan, Eric, and Kyle for keeping me going, and my parents for everything.

In memory of Joyce Thompson and Greg Thompson.

Prologue

IT MUST BE the Aliens, Howard thought. He'd heard about them from a man at the shelter. The man had talked about Aliens with bug eyes that came at night to harvest bodies and take them back to their spaceship. Howard had never seen them, but it made sense to him. How else could you explain the things he'd seen? The man with the weasel's head that worked at the newsstand for example. Or the building on Market Street that breathed fire and oozed slime, though no one else seemed to notice it. There were some strange things going around and he was sure that the government was behind them; but the more he thought about it, the more he realized that it very well could be the Aliens.

Howard pushed his shopping cart through the empty street, scanning the curb for aluminum cans. He moved through a canyon of concrete and glass. Buildings and streets that bustled with life in the daytime now seemed to be inhabited by spirits. Dark ghosts that made themselves known by the occasional brightly lit office in an otherwise black expanse. Downtown Houston was deserted at this time of night, all the workers having headed home to hide in their air-conditioned suburban houses. The only people left were the street cleaners, an occasional patrol car, and those like Howard who lived on the street.

The night was hot, and the air so humid it felt like he was breathing through a sponge. Howard pulled the hood of his sweatshirt tighter over his head. It made him sweat more, but he felt safer. It protected him from the creatures of the night, possibly even the Aliens.

God, I need a drink. There was an all-night convenience store over on Rusk Street close to Tranquility Park. Maybe he could buy a bottle and head over to the park. It would be cooler at this time of night with the trees and all. Other people slept there, and the cops hardly ever came by. He could rest, maybe even sleep. Howard reached deep down into his pocket and pulled out his change, one dollar and seventy-nine cents. Not even enough to buy a pint of Thunderbird. That was a major disappointment.

He walked farther on down the street, peering into the doorways, constantly on guard against anyone, or anything, that could be lurking there. Night was dangerous. He had to be careful. As he turned the corner onto Lamar Street, he saw a figure walking rapidly toward him. He gripped the bar of his shopping cart tightly and debated about whether this figure posed a threat and if he should charge at him. As the man came closer he recognized him. It was a guy that he sometimes saw at the mission, an old black guy who called himself Carmichael. He held a bottle inside a paper bag and was excited about something.

"Man, this is your lucky day," Carmichael said as he stopped right in front of the cart. Howard wondered if this was really Carmichael or maybe some being who had taken over his body. "Man, you been living right or something, 'cause you are one lucky fool."

"Don't you call me a fool, old man," Howard replied.

"What else should I call you, fool? Anybody who gets good luck falling flat onto his head and is too damn dumb to know it, I call him a fool."

Howard loosened his grip on the cart. "What kind of luck are you yapping about?"

"You listen and I'll tell you, fool. There's a guy just around the corner there who's giving away free hooch. He just gave me this bottle and he told me he'd give me ten dollars if I brought him three more people. You the third."

"Why would he do that?" Howard asked. "Nobody gives away nothin' for nothin'."

"Then don't come, fool. You be the one missing out. They're preachers. They wants to get some folks to come to their church service."

Howard didn't like the idea of having to go to a church service, and the free booze seemed too good to be true—he'd never heard of preachers giving out liquor. Still, he was awful thirsty.

Carmichael peeled away the paper bag from the bottle, revealing a Wild Turkey label. "Look at this, he's even giving away the hard stuff."

That was enough for Howard. His thirst was now monumental and he could imagine the taste of the warm liquid streaming down his throat. Together they marched around the corner and over to the waiting van. It was just as Carmichael had said. There were three of them, dressed in black like preachers do, only they weren't wearing their collars. Probably because of the heat.

They gave Howard his bottle; he snapped open the top and took a huge swig of the fiery nectar. It tasted even better than he'd imagined. His throat burned, his eyes watered, and he felt normal for the first time all day.

The three preachers helped him into the van along with

two other vagrants that were already there. Carmichael stayed behind. The van was comfortable and the whiskey was an unexpected treat. Maybe he was lucky, Howard thought. Fortune had definitely smiled on him tonight. He could put up with a church service, he'd yell out his amens and be thankful. He took another hard pull on the bottle and fought back a yawn. He hadn't realized how tired he was. He could hardly keep his eyes open.

As the van's doors closed, Howard got a good look at the head preacher. He was tall and lean and radiated authority. But it was curious. He wore mirrored sunglasses even though it was the middle of the night. The man looked somehow familiar but Howard wasn't sure why. The answer was right on the edge of his consciousness, trying to peek through.

The reason came to Howard as the van pulled out into the street. A cold panic rose up from his stomach. The mirrored glasses shining back at him looked just like the eyes of an insect, seen up close.

1

LENA DRYER DIDN'T know what to expect; she'd never watched a man die before. She didn't think it would bother her much, though. This was a story, just like any other. And as such, a sense of detachment was necessary. In her time as a reporter she'd seen enough forms of suffering that she wasn't easily shocked. One time she was first on the scene after the drive-by shooting of a twelve-year-old boy, arriving before the detectives. Her most vivid memory of that event was of all the blood on the sidewalk. She had to watch her step to avoid tracking it. On another story, in a hospital obstetric ward, she'd held crack babies who couldn't stop crying from the pain, strung out at birth. And over the years, she'd done more than her share of interviews with grieving relatives — asking mothers how it felt to lose their sons, and husbands to describe the pain of knowing their wives had been killed. These were parts of the job she didn't like, but had learned to live with. So she didn't think this would bother her much.

Lena pulled into a parking space across the street from the redbrick prison building. The trip from Austin had been quicker than she'd expected. She was early and in no hurry to get inside. Leaving her engine on and the air-conditioning running, Lena picked up her notebook and leafed through it. For the last three months she'd been working on a series on capital punishment and the Texas prison system. So it made sense for her to witness it first-hand. It seemed logical, but what was the point?

For that matter, what was the point of the whole series? Back when Lena had first pitched the idea to her editor, she'd hoped it would be a way to encourage debate and change opinions. Maybe even alter policy. But the deeper she got into her research, the more pointless it seemed. The whole system was humming along on automatic pilot and nothing was going to change that. Lena glanced at her watch and turned off the engine. Enough stalling; it was time to go inside.

As she stepped out of her car, the heat hit her like a wave. This had to be the hottest day of the year. Just a second outside and already a sheen of sweat glazed her arms. It felt like her skin was melting. It was a mystery to Lena how people here stood the heat. After two years she still couldn't deal with it. Maybe that was the real issue. Not the weather, but that she needed a change of scene. Two years in Texas and she still felt like an outsider. It was time to get back East. Besides, she thought, she'd gone as far as she could with the *Star.*

Clutching her notebook, she scanned the area. The street dead-ended at the prison. The parking area was on one side, a vacant lot on the other. There were times at past executions, she'd heard, when the whole area over-flowed with people—though that hadn't happened any-time recently. Today the only ones here were a small group on the corner across from her—a priest and two nuns. They had to be miserable in their black robes, she thought. Lena glanced at her watch again and walked toward the prison gates. At least it would be cooler inside.

At the gate, she signed the register and walked through the metal detector. The young guard frisked her with his eyes. "This your first time for one of these?"

Lena nodded.

"It's real peaceful, I'm told." He smiled and adjusted the holster on his hip. "Just like falling asleep. I hope it don't bother you none."

Lena looked away. "I'm expected inside," she said.

"Sure. I didn't mean to keep you or anything. I really didn't mean nothin'." The guard lowered his head as he let her through.

An older guard led her into the building. It was cooler here, but not by much. The lights were dim and the air stagnant. The red bricks lining the hallway had faded to a burnt pink. It was a hallway, Lena thought, not unlike the one the prisoner would walk down later that night. She wondered how he'd feel as he walked that hall, knowing what was to come. What emotions would he feel? Fear for sure. Maybe anger, or grief. Would he be praying? Searching for a God he'd only recently found?

Lena wondered, what would she be thinking if she knew that she was about to die? And almost immediately she knew, *Is this all there is?* Here she was, twenty-nine years old, not beautiful maybe, but others considered her attractive. She was tall and slim with short ash-blond hair and cool blue eyes. Her features were plain but her lips were full and her smile golden. She had a good job with the *Austin Star* where her career was on the fast track— that was her focus. But something was missing.

Midway down the hall, the guard ushered Lena into a small room, much like a classroom. It had desks with hard plastic seats and a blackboard in the front. No one else was there yet.

"The orientation's in here, but it won't start for another twenty minutes. The execution'll be at six." The guard closed the door, leaving her alone. Lena sat down and tried to make herself comfortable. At least this room was air-conditioned.

At the orientation Lena met some of the other witnesses; mostly relatives of the condemned. Three other reporters would be at the execution later, too, but this was their regular beat and they already knew what to expect. Another group of witnesses, relatives of the victims, would also view the execution. But they'd be seated in a separate witness area. One of the prison chaplains, a Methodist minister, gave the orientation. This was his fifty-second execution in the two years he'd been there, he said quietly. He went into detail about the process and took extra time to answer questions. After the orientation the group was led down to another room to wait. Lena used the time to interview the other witnesses and plan the outline for her story.

The execution was scheduled for six, but they didn't go down to the witness booth till six-forty-five. One of the guards told Lena that the prisoner had been a substance abuser and they'd had a hard time finding a vein they could use.

In the witness booth, two rows of auditorium seats faced a large window. Lena sat in the back row. Through the glass she looked into the death chamber. It was a small room painted robin's-egg blue, giving the space a false cheer. Her gaze quickly moved to the center where a large gurney faced the window. The prisoner was already there, fastened tight with leather straps. A large man, with a huge misshapen nose, he barely fit on the gurney. IV needles stuck out from each arm.

The prisoner, Billy Dale Burke, fit the mold for death

row. High school dropout, drug addict, a long record of prior convictions. There was no question of his guilt, either. Some twelve years earlier Billy Dale had killed a customer and a clerk while robbing a gas station. He'd been convicted of robbing the same station five years before and both times he was caught on video. Appeals dragged the case out for years; now, all appeals exhausted, his sentence was to be carried out.

The warden stood at the front of the witness booth. He faced the prisoner through the glass and, by microphone, read the death decree. When he was done he asked if there were any final words.

A boom mike came down from the ceiling. "I want everyone to know how sorry I am," Billy Dale said. His voice wavered and his hands, though bound at the wrist, shook. Tears formed in his eyes. "I didn't plan on none of this happening, and I wish to God I had another chance. I hope the Lord is forgiving. That's all."

The warden paused a moment, then removed his glasses. Lena knew this was the signal to start the process. She glanced at her watch. Six-forty-nine. The fluid in the IV tubes changed color and after a few moments Billy Dale's eyes closed. A minute later he let out a long sigh, almost a snore. And then he lay still.

Lena sat back and waited. No one tried to talk. The only sound in the room was the muffled sobbing from a blonde in the front row. Though the room was air-conditioned, it still seemed stuffy. The scent of someone's aftershave filled the air. After a few minutes one of the witnesses nervously cleared his throat and shifted in his seat. The minutes dragged by.

After what seemed an eternity, the prison doctor entered the chamber through a separate door. Using a stethoscope he bent over the body and listened for a full minute. Then he announced the time of death as 6:59 P.M. The whole thing took less than fifteen minutes.

Lena took a deep breath and held it in. She still didn't know how to react. A man had died in front of her eyes. And all she felt was numb.

FORTY-FIVE MILES AWAY in the segregation section of the Terrell Unit in Livingston, Ramon Willis lay on his bunk unable to sleep. He'd tried reading, but the words on the page could have been written in Chinese for all the sense they were making. He couldn't quiet his mind to concentrate. It were as if there were a neon sign flashing in his head with the message saying, *You're next*.

One week, just seven more days, and his life would end. And there wasn't a thing he could do about it. He stood up and moved around his cell. It measured nine feet long by five feet wide — hardly enough room to turn around in, let alone pace. He was filled with nervous energy and needed some form of outlet. He felt like rattling the bars of his cage and screaming out in anxious rage, but he refused to lose control. He couldn't. He got down on the floor, and wedged between his bunk and the far wall, he pumped off one hundred push-ups. He followed this with another one hundred sit-ups. Ramon had been doing this several times a day since he'd first arrived ten years ago, although then he couldn't do more than a few at a time.

He stood up, barely panting from the exertion, and surveyed his cell. Three concrete walls with the cage in front. A stainless-steel bunk built into the wall, covered with a thin mattress and sweat-stained sheets, a concrete stool and a concrete desk, a stainless-steel toilet next to a stainless-steel wash basin with a mirror also made of polished stainless steel. There was a small shelf above his bed. Placed there were a few books, a radio, and some photographs. This small room was his life. Everything that he owned was in this small enclosure. Once he was gone, all evidence that he'd been here would disappear, too, like a stone sinking below the surface of a pond without leaving a ripple.

Ramon moved over and looked into his mirror. He thought of how he had changed in prison. Physically he hadn't changed much. He was older of course, and much stronger, even healthier-looking despite the starch and fat that served as a diet here. If someone had known him before, they'd surely be able to recognize him now. He had a distinctive look. From his Mexican mother, he'd inherited the high cheekbones, jet-black hair, and bronzed complexion. From his father he'd gotten his eyes. Deep blue eyes that caused people to do a double take. Viking eyes in an Aztec face.

But in other ways he had changed a lot. It was his attitude mostly. He felt different, he thought different, he acted different. Ramon believed that the measure of a man was how he responded to adversity; and he thought that he measured up well. Death row is the end of the line. Once a man is sent there, he might as well give up his humanity at the door. It's filled with society's ultimate losers, and being caged together doesn't bring out their finest qualities. But Ramon had responded to prison as a wakeup call, too late, saying that his life had to change. He wasn't the same person he'd been ten years ago when he first entered this prison.

Not that it mattered—they were about to kill an innocent man.

2

RAMON AWOKE EARLY on Wednesday, before the TVs went on. The unit had a series of large television sets bolted near the ceiling out in the hallway, positioned so that the inmates could watch from their cells. The authorities always turned the TVs on at 7 A.M. and they stayed on for the rest of the day. The noise blared into the cell block. Whenever new prisoners moved into the wing, they would invariably find it overwhelming. It was never quiet. After a while, though, they'd get used to it and it would seem like wallpaper. Just part of the background.

Because he'd been placed on deathwatch, the guards came by every half hour to record what he was doing in their notebooks. They wanted to make sure he was in a good frame of mind. Some inmates got depressed when their time came due; some would get suicidal. But the authorities couldn't allow that. It was important to keep the prisoners safe until the state was able to kill them.

Keeping them safe wasn't always easy. Ramon remembered one man who'd had an appendicitis attack two days before he was to be put down. They rushed him to the infirmary, performed the appendectomy, and he recovered fully. When he was once again healthy, the death decree was reinstated and they put him to death a week later.

Ramon had been in this position twice before. Both times his death date had been set, and both times he was given a stay of execution. The first time his stay didn't come through until the day before he was to be executed. The anxiety of waiting and hoping for a reprieve and not knowing if it would come felt close to unbearable. Once it had finally come through, he'd felt like he was in a dream. It didn't feel real. It took several days before he could comfortably breathe again, knowing that he had put off death. At least for a time. And then the waiting game began again.

This time he didn't feel confident at all. His appeals had all run their course and he had few avenues left to turn to. The state was on a roll. Executions were being carried out at a record pace, and they weren't granting any pardons or stays. The whole system was carrying out its mission with brutal efficiency. Ramon felt sure that this time was the real thing, so mentally he'd prepared for his death.

They'd changed his routine since his latest death date had been announced. For a time he'd worked in the prison laundry. Eight hours of work a day gave him two hours recreation time. The work gave structure to his existence and helped make the time pass more easily. It was also good socially. He was around other people then. Having someone to talk with, or even just listen to, felt good in a way that he would never have thought before. He missed that.

Now, in segregation, he was locked down twenty-three hours a day. They let him out one hour each day for a shower and a trip to the indoor recreation room where he could walk around and stretch out. Then it was back to his cell until the next day.

This week was different, though. Because it was his last week he was allowed more time to meet with visitors. Today he had two people coming to see him. His attorney, Barry Resnick, was coming by later that morning. Barry had been with him for the last eight years, taking the case for the appeal. It had been his efforts that had kept Ramon alive up till now. Later in the day he expected another visitor. A reporter from the *Austin Star* who had been writing a series on death row inmates.

At five-forty-five they came by with his breakfast. He tried to ignore everything while he ate his grits and bacon.

BARRY RESNICK PULLED his BMW through the prison gate and into an open parking space near the visitors' entrance. The trip from Houston took just over an hour and the ride up always felt good. The highway was free of traffic and his car was built for the open road. He made it a point to turn off his cell phone and use the time to relax and unwind. This morning he'd turned on the radar detector and pushed the car harder than usual. He wound through the gears, hitting a top speed of 120 miles per hour. As the sun came up, the scenery blurred past in a haze of orange. Driving fast gave him a feeling of freedom, though it never lasted long enough.

As he crossed the parking lot he looked up at the dull gray walls of the prison. A tall concrete-block wall surrounded it, with razor wire at the top and guard towers at the corners. The prison was four stories of precast concrete, no windows.

Barry walked to the visitors' entrance and presented himself to the guard at the gate. He showed his identification and signed in. The guard made a quick check of his briefcase and walked him through a metal detector. After passing the inspection, another guard escorted him into the main building.

As the doors closed behind him, he momentarily panicked. He had to force himself to keep walking forward instead of fleeing back to the sunlight. The fluorescent lights gave everything a surrealistic green tint. The sounds of his footsteps, even the smells of the building curled down and settled over him, making it difficult to breathe. He always felt claustrophobic when he entered the building. He couldn't imagine having to live there.

He followed the guard to a small waiting room and sat down in a chair by a table placed against a wire mesh fence that cut the room in half horizontally. The seat on the other side of the barrier was caged in on the remaining three sides by chain-link fencing, reminding him of a dog kennel.

It was still early. The only other person in the room was a guard on the other side of the cage who sat in a chair, leaning against the yellow wall, trying his hardest not to fall asleep. Barry opened his briefcase and pulled out a file.

Though he'd been making this trip for years, he'd never gotten used to it. At forty-four, Barry Resnick was at the top of his career trajectory. To look at him you wouldn't know it. He was short, balding, and prone to fat, with the kind of face that you could see every day and still not notice. But he'd made partner in one of the top law firms in Houston—the head of their tort division. He was well respected, had a loving wife and daughter, and last year he'd made more than two hundred and thirty thousand dollars. He held the world by the tail; he had all that he could possibly want. Except one thing.

He wanted to make a difference. Most of his clients were corporations or wealthy businessmen whom he defended from lawsuits. Some were nuisance suits but others were richly deserved. Barry was good at what he did. He saved his clients a good deal of money, and in turn made a good deal of money for the firm. But the work was routine and some of the cases made him uneasy. Moral ambiguity was par for the course in law though, and he knew it would be worse if he'd chosen criminal law; the burnout rate there was extremely high.

He hadn't planned to get involved in Ramon's case— he wasn't getting paid. In fact the case had cost him a small fortune. A friend in the anti–capital punishment movement had asked him to take it as a favor. Criminal law wasn't Barry's field, but even he could see that Ramon had gotten a raw deal. The case against him was weak at best. There were inconsistencies in the evidence and the only witness was a paid police informant. But the court-appointed lawyer at Ramon's original trial had done nothing to help his cause. A white man had been killed; a Hispanic was accused of the crime. It wasn't hard to get a conviction.

Barry tried to involve some of the criminal attorneys at his firm, but there were no takers. They said the case was a loser; it didn't matter whether Ramon was guilty or not, there was no way he was going to be granted another trial. Barry's colleagues pointed out that the original prosecutor had been J. Douglas Aarons, a legendary state's attorney who'd become a judge shortly after Ramon's conviction. Now he headed the appeals court and was ready and able to bury his mistakes. No way in hell would Judge J. Douglas Aarons grant a new trial.

Maybe it was his white liberal guilt, but as a last resort Barry took on the case himself. He'd had to teach himself the ins and outs of defending a capital case, with at least some success. And strangely he found this more fulfilling than all his other work. It felt good to think that he'd made a difference in at least one person's life. But he couldn't shake the feeling that he hadn't done enough. His lack of experience was too big a handicap. Still, he'd been able to delay the execution and keep Ramon alive. Until now anyway. After eight years they'd run out of options.

Barry snapped to attention as the door on the other side creaked open. Two guards led Ramon into the room. He was dressed in his prison whites, short-sleeve coveralls. His hair was shorter than the last time Barry had seen him, but he still looked as strong and hard as ever. He moved in a staccato rhythm forced by the chains that bound his ankles to his wrists. He smiled at Barry. The smile softened his face and made him look almost boyish, his startlingly blue eyes flashing with life. The guards herded him over to the seat in the cage across from Barry. They padlocked the cage and then retreated to the far corner where they pulled out their smokes and quietly gossiped.

"You'll never make the Cowboys moving like that," Barry said.

"Give me a chance and I'll show 'em how to run," Ramon replied.

"How they treating you, Ray?"

"I'm OK. No worse than you'd expect anyways."

Barry nodded. "I wish I had some good news to give you."

"I know. It's not like this is a surprise." Ramon spoke with a slight Spanish accent. "I thank you for the help you've given me. You've been a true friend."

"Well, I'm not quitting yet, Ray. We've still got two options to explore. I mean, don't get your hopes up but—"

"Barry, please," Ramon cut in. "You know, I was thinking. Back when I was a kid, we were living in Brownsville. Down by the border. My uncle Gustavo came to live with us. He was my mother's brother. He'd heard about all the money that you could make here in the States and wanted to get his share. He got a job at a small auto parts factory; they rebuilt generators. It was a small shop and the working conditions weren't too good, but my uncle and all the other workers were illegals. They had no choice."

Barry settled back in his chair and listened.

"He worked there for a month when they had a fire. The place was a firetrap and once it started, it went up like a torch. Burned right down to the ground. Thirteen people worked there and twelve of them died. The only one to escape was Gustavo, and he walked away untouched. Not a burn, not a scratch."

"It sounds like he was lucky," Barry said.

"That's what he thought, too," Ramon continued. "He'd looked death in the eye and lived. He felt very lucky. That night he went to a cantina to celebrate his good fortune. He drank tequila and beer and got very drunk. He left there late at night. Walking home he must've stumbled, he fell into a drainage ditch. There was very little water, only a few inches—no more than three. But he landed facedown, too drunk to move. He drowned in a puddle of water."

Barry rubbed his jaw with the back of his hand. "Huh, he drowned in three inches of water?"

"Lo que es, es que es . . . Destino. You can't change your fate."

Barry paused a moment before he spoke. "I've . . . I've filed for a stay of execution and we should have a ruling by Friday. And the governor can still step in. There's still a chance, Ray."

Ramon gave a sad smile. "No, I don't see it happening this time. The court has turned down every stay this year. They want the executions to go through. And we both know the governor is no hope at all. This is an election year. Thank you for everything, Barry, but it's time I faced facts. This is it. I can deal with that though. I'm ready. I'll face my fate like a man."

Barry nodded his head and absentmindedly played

with his watch. He felt embarrassed. Over the years they'd gotten to know each other well. He was Ramon's attorney, but it was more than that. He genuinely liked Ramon. As he thought about it now, he realized that he'd miss him and the visits up here. He suddenly felt emotional and not sure of how to handle it. He picked up his files and stuffed them back into the briefcase. "Just tell me what I can do. If there's anything else I can do to help." He clicked his case shut. "I'll be talking with you on Friday once I hear the court ruling. Don't give up hope though."

Ramon smiled. "I'm fine, Barry."

Barry stood up and made ready to leave.

Ramon stood up also. The guards saw that the meeting was over. They put out their cigarettes, opened the cage, and escorted Ramon out of the room.

Barry stared at the closed door for a minute before he, too, left the room.

MIDMORNING, THE PRISON doctor came by. The guards stood in the hallway and watched as he went into Ramon's cell for an examination. The doctor looked to be in his early fifties. He stood about five feet eight, but appeared taller with his stiff martial posture. With his potbelly hanging over his belt he gave the impression of an athlete who'd gone to seed. Ramon found himself staring at the doctor's right eye. He had a lazy eyelid that drooped down making him look as though he was half asleep.

"I'm Dr. Meeks," he said. "Just relax, I need to do a quick examination." A smoldering cigarette hung from the side of his mouth as he held Ramon's wrist and checked his pulse. He took Ramon's blood pressure and used his stethoscope to listen to the heart and lungs.

"How tall are you, about six feet?"

"Five-eleven," Ramon replied.

"And your weight is about two hundred?"

"Yeah, right around there."

"Good. You seem to be in excellent health. Let me get your temperature now, too." The doctor pulled out a thermometer and handed it to Ramon, who placed it under his tongue. "Just relax and count to sixty." He gripped Ramon's wrist with one hand and tapped his forearm with the other. "You have nice veins. That's good."

Meeks thumped on the veins again, testing them. "Flex your muscle a few times, I need to draw some blood." Ramon flexed his arm. Meeks pulled out a large rubber band and wrapped it around the bicep as a tourniquet. He rubbed an alcohol swab over the forearm and pulled a hypodermic from his bag. Then, without warning, he jabbed the needle into Ramon's arm, striking directly into the vein. He pushed in on the vein with one hand as he pulled back on the plunger with the other.

Ramon pulled back in pain. "God! What the hell did you do that for?"

Meeks calmly withdrew the hypodermic, now loaded with blood, discharged the needle into a test tube, plugged it up, and set it into his bag. He blew out a long cloud of smoke before he responded. "It's OK. Nothing to be alarmed about. Everything seems to be just fine." He shut the case and left the cage. The guards locked it back up. "Thank you for your help, Mr. Willis." He looked Ramon straight in the eye. "I'll be seeing you." He smiled as he walked down the corridor.

LENA TRIED TO control her irritation. It was forty-five minutes past the time she'd scheduled the appointment with the warden and he still hadn't even acknowledged her presence. She closed her eyes and took a deep breath. *Stay calm,* she told herself. *He's doing this to rattle me; just stay calm.* Charley Porter, one of the newspaper's staff photographers, was slumped down in the chair next to her. He stared off into space with a half-assed smile on his face as if he didn't have a care in the world. This irritated her even more.

"So how long is he going to make us wait?" Her voice came out louder than she'd intended in the stillness of the small waiting room.

Charley flinched as she spoke, interrupting his daydream. "What?"

"How much longer do you think he's going to make us wait?" Lena didn't try to hide her annoyance.

Charley pondered the question for a long time before he slowly drawled out his response. "I don't know, maybe another twenty minutes. Maybe more . . . But it could be less. Why don't you just try and relax."

Lena stood up and paced the floor. They were in a small wood-paneled room down the hallway from the warden's office in the Terrell Unit. The warden's secretary had led them to the waiting room and told them to expect the warden momentarily. Lena thought about going back to find the secretary and demand that she tell the warden that they were still waiting. But he already knew that. She decided to give him five more minutes.

Even after two years with the *Austin Star*, Texas still struck her as almost a foreign country. She liked the people, she liked the landscape, and most of the time she could even deal with the heat. But she couldn't get used to the pace; people moved so slowly here. And Lena hated to wait.

All her life she'd been on the fast track. She aimed high and always achieved her goals. Before coming to Austin she'd graduated with honors from Princeton, interned at the *New York Times*, and worked on the city desk in Boston. Each stop a step closer to her objective.

But she wondered if she'd chosen the right path. Not just on the job, but with everything. After going home to attend a friend's wedding, she'd come back in a true funk. She'd cried herself to sleep each night for over a week.

She hadn't realized how lonely she'd been. Lena had her share of opportunities, but she sometimes thought that she'd erected a kind of force field around herself just to repel eligible men. Lena knew who she was and where she was going; a lot of men found that intimidating.

Back in Boston she'd fallen into a relationship that showed real promise. Jack was a great guy and they'd gotten close. Too close. Sometimes she thought that was the reason she'd come to Texas.

When the offer from the *Austin Star* came she jumped for it. It wasn't the biggest or the most influential publication, but it was well respected and had a reputation for treating its reporters like real people. More important, they'd promised that she'd get a chance at the big stories, the important news. That was her goal, at least her short-term goal, to become a fixture on the front page.

Along with her normal reporting, she'd gained attention for a series of articles on problems facing the residents of Austin and the surrounding region. But it was her current assignment, the series on the prison system, which really made her reputation. Since the first article ran two weeks before, she'd gained national attention, including a feeler for a more prestigious job back East. Her tour of duty here was almost at an end.

But now she couldn't even get in to see the warden. Lena checked her watch again: forty-eight minutes now and still waiting. She took another deep breath. Maybe she should leave, she thought. She didn't need this interview; she had enough material to finish the story. But even as she thought of that, she knew it wasn't an option. The reality was that she'd become too interested in Ramon Willis's case.

Ramon could have been the poster boy for the anti–death penalty crowd. He'd truly rehabilitated himself while in prison. He'd been a punk with a long record of juvenile offences: breaking and entering, vandalism, and car theft. But no history of violence. After turning eighteen he seemed to change his ways, he stayed out of trouble for nearly three years. Then everything quickly unraveled. He was picked up for a bar fight, charged with assault, and released on bail. A month later a prominent businessman was murdered. They charged Ramon with the crime and he'd been imprisoned ever since. But he'd become a model prisoner. He'd gotten his GED and took correspondence courses for college. He'd even helped to tutor some of the other inmates in reading; illiteracy was shamefully high in prison.

And then there was the other thing. He said he didn't do it. Not that that was unusual; the jail was full of self-proclaimed innocent men. But his claim was believable. The evidence was circumstantial and the prosecution's case was full of holes. It was a better than even shot that he really was innocent. Not that she could change things now. Guilty or not, he was just days away from his death.

The secretary entered the room and announced that the warden was ready to see them. They'd asked permission to meet and photograph Ramon in his cell; even though it wasn't the usual procedure. The warden agreed to the interview but said no to the pictures. Then he lectured them about morality and the responsibilities of the news media. He set forth the ground rules for the interview, then called a guard in to escort her up to the segregation unit to meet with Ramon Willis in his cell.

The walk through the unit was frightening. The noise was unbearably loud. TVs blared and Lena's entrance caused a noisy outbreak among the inmates. She felt like she was walking through a gauntlet as the prisoners yelled out or whistled at her. Lena just tried to walk as straight and tall as she could, letting the calls fall down on her like rain.

When she first saw Ramon he was turned away, reading a book while sitting on his cot, seemingly unaware of all the chaos.

"Wake up, Willis, you got a visitor." The guard banged on the bars with his truncheon. Ramon put his book down, turned toward them, and looked directly at her. He was bigger than Lena had imagined him to be. Strong and darkly handsome. And the eyes, the blue eyes that were so out of place on his bronzed face. It was peculiar, just one look and she felt that she'd made some kind of connection with him. This hadn't happened before and she wasn't expecting it. If she'd seen him on the outside dressed in a business suit she'd have found him attractive; now it just seemed so sad. Such a waste.

"Hello, Ramon. I'm Lena Dryer with the *Austin Star*. I'd like to ask you some questions." She knew she'd be haunted by those eyes for a long time.

3

THE FOLLOWING DAYS passed quickly. On Friday the court denied the stay and ordered that the execution proceed as scheduled. Lena's story was a front-page feature in the *Austin Star*'s Sunday edition. It caused quite a stir, but nothing concrete developed to help Ramon.

On Tuesday, execution day, Ramon awoke long before the TVs or the rest of the cell block came to life. He used the quiet time to write a will of sorts, leaving his books, radio, and a few other pieces of property he had to other inmates. There were a few personal items that he had a hard time deciding what to do with. He didn't have any close family. His mother was dead, there were a few cousins but none that had kept in contact with him. He'd planned to leave his effects to his father, even though they hadn't been in contact for close to fourteen years. But he'd died a month before. Now there was no one, so it didn't really matter.

The guards came by just after seven and led him to the shower. He stayed in an extra long time. The hot water felt good and the steam flushed out his pores and helped him to relax, at least for a few moments. When he was finished he put on a new pair of white coveralls.

Then it was time for him to be moved to the death chamber at the Walls Unit in downtown Huntsville. They bound him with chains on his hands and feet. The chains were connected so as to hobble him and make it hard to move with any speed. Surrounded by guards, he was led down to a waiting van at the back of the building. As he walked through the doors he felt the unfiltered rays of the sun for the first time in years. He blinked and squinted at the light. He gulped in the air as if he were drowning and thought of what it would be like to really be free. From behind, a guard shoved him toward the van. Ramon stiffened in resistance, but then moved slowly inside. On the ride over he craned his neck to see the passing scenery, his last glimpses of the real world.

Once they checked him into the Walls, he was taken to a holding cell down the hall from the execution chamber. The guards checked in on him every fifteen minutes and wrote down what he was doing in their small notebooks. He was allowed to make phone calls to anyone that he wanted, only there was no one he really wanted to talk to.

Over the course of the morning Ramon's anxiety level had gone up another notch. He tried to read but he couldn't concentrate. He passed the time by watching the TV in his new cell. Around noon a news show caught his interest. Among the stories it had a brief feature on his case and the fact that his execution was scheduled for that night. It was strange watching his life being discussed on TV by strangers who knew nothing about him.

One part of the show was a surprise though. They showed videotape of a visiting politician, Randall Morgan, the senior senator from Wisconsin, addressing a

Teamster's convention in Houston. Although he hadn't declared, it was widely assumed that he was positioning himself for a run for the presidency. He was seen as a white knight by the liberal forces, a strong protector of the environment, a proponent of personal liberties, and a foe of the death penalty. He made the news that afternoon by deviating from his prepared remarks to mention Ramon's case and the series in the *Austin Star*, which called into doubt the justice of his sentence. "I'm calling for the governor of this state to step forward and do the right thing," he'd said. He asked that the governor stop the execution and personally look into the facts of the case.

Upon seeing the tape, Ramon had a moment of true hope. Here was a champion, someone with real power who was bringing his case up to the light of day. Someone who would step up to bat on his behalf and swing for the fences. Maybe this would do it, maybe the governor would step in. Maybe he would get another chance. The feeling didn't last long, though. Even if there had been a chance it was too late now. He turned off the TV after that.

Barry Resnick came by in the afternoon and they talked for over an hour, mostly small talk. Barry avoided even mentioning what was going to happen that night. He hugged Ramon as he left the cell and told him he was sorry it had to end like this.

At four-fifteen they brought Ramon his last meal: tamales, fresh tortillas with refried beans, a garden salad, and a thick T-bone steak. The food looked good, but Ramon could only swallow a mouthful or two. He just didn't have an appetite.

The prison chaplain, a Catholic priest, stopped by around five-thirty and stayed for the rest of the evening. Ramon had been raised in a religious household where his mother went to mass nearly every day. Ramon stopped going to church when he moved in with his father at the age of twelve. His father said that it was nothing but superstitious nonsense and had forbidden him to go. Ramon continued to pray for a time but after a while he stopped doing that, too. Over the last few years, as his situation became more desperate, he'd renewed his interest in religion and had read extensively on it. He now considered himself a spiritual person though he no longer considered himself a Catholic. Still he was comforted by the priest's presence and confessed his sins for the first time in years.

They came for him just before seven. The captain of the guards and two others were there to escort him down. The priest performed the last rites before leaving. He walked down to the witness station while the guards fastened the chains and prepared Ramon to be moved down to the execution chamber.

As Ramon made the long walk down the corridor, he felt as if he were moving in slow motion. It was a sudden change that left him feeling detached, as if he were in a movie, not a real person. The footfalls in the hallway blended together in long echoes. The sound of the blood surging in his head seemed like waves crashing against rocks on a beach. So loud it was deafening. After a moment he realized that he was actually grinning. He wasn't afraid now. It seemed like this was happening to someone else and he was standing above, watching.

After all the times he'd thought of this moment, the nightmares, the dark primal fears that had always been there, lurking in the back of his mind for all these years. The time that he dreaded most was now here. And it didn't seem so bad. He wasn't nervous, he wasn't anxious, he was calm and cool. He wanted to live, or at least he had up till now, but the life he'd been living in prison wasn't the life that he wanted.

It seemed to take hours to walk the twenty yards to the death chamber. The room was a small rectangular-shaped space with three powder-blue walls opening out to a huge window in the front.

The interior of the room was stark and empty except for a hospital gurney in the center of the floor and a metal cart next to it. A series of cords and tubes snaked out from a hole near the floor in the far wall and terminated at rest on the cart. The guards directed Ramon onto the bed and laid him down. His chains were removed and leather straps were pulled out and, in seconds, fastened tight around his legs, thighs, chest, and arms, attaching him securely to the gurney. Another set of straps bound his wrists to the side of the bed.

He could hardly move. His feeling of well-being abruptly left him. With a rush he was back in real time, his forehead beaded with sweat and his stomach churning. Suddenly it was all too real. He was afraid he'd lose control of his bowels.

Two technicians came into the room; one checked the straps while the other took hold of his right arm and tapped on the flesh of his forearm looking for veins. He found one that he liked.

"This will just hurt for a second," he said as he pulled an IV needle off of the cart and stuck it into the vein. Ramon winced. He tried to look out the window but the technicians were obstructing his view. One technician connected the needle to a tube on the cart and taped it in place. The tube had a shunt near the top to allow drugs to be injected directly into the vein. The technician took a hypodermic needle off of the cart and shot its contents into the shunt. "This should help you relax," he said.

While he did this, the other technician opened Ramon's shirt and placed a cold metal monitor on his chest near the heart. He taped this in place. Next he attached sensors to both wrists. When the men were done, they adjusted the gurney so that there was a slight tilt facing toward the window. They exited the room closing the door firmly behind them.

Ramon looked out at the viewing area. Sitting on the

other side of the glass in auditorium seats were the warden, Barry Resnick, Lena Dryer, the reporter from the *Star,* the chaplain, and four people that he didn't know. Many of the people were looking away from him, avoiding eye contact. Even Barry. Only Lena looked straight at him, her eyes locked in on his, as if she was trying to tell him that she wished she could help.

The warden stood up and flipped a switch near his seat. Ramon heard a brief crackle of static and realized that the room was equipped for sound. He turned his attention to the warden, who had picked up a sheet of paper and had begun to read. "Ramon Umberto Willis, you have been convicted of capital murder by the Superior Court of the State of Texas. . . ." Ramon couldn't concentrate. He was aware of his breathing, heavy and labored. He felt constrained by the straps on his chest. The needle in his arm was an irritant, not so much painful as uncomfortable. Suddenly he just wanted to get the whole thing over with.

The warden finished the reading of the death decree. "Do you have any final words before we carry out your sentence?"

Ramon stared out at them. He felt much calmer now, almost dreamy; he knew that the Valium shot was working. "This is the wrong thing," he said. "You know this is wrong what you are doing to me."

The warden waited a moment to be sure he was finished. Then he spoke again. "May God have mercy on your soul." He flipped the speaker switch off, sat back down, and removed his glasses.

In the room behind the execution chamber the lethal injection had been prepared. Now they depressed the plungers and began the process. To achieve death, precise quantities of three chemical compounds were injected directly into the veins. The first compound, sodium thiopental, caused a general paralysis and shutdown of bodily functions; the second substance, pancuronium bromide, collapsed the diaphragm and lungs; potassium chloride, the third compound, induced cardiac arrest, stopped the heart and caused the death.

Ramon heard a gentle hum and felt the cold liquid entering his veins. His muscles tensed, he wondered how long it would take. His eyes began to blur. He felt dizzy, sleepy. He tried to keep his eyes open, but couldn't. He closed his eyes — just for a moment. Then his mind turned off. Nothing more registered.

To Lena, watching from the next room, it appeared as if Ramon had simply drifted off to sleep. He didn't appear to be in pain; at least he didn't seem to suffer. She breathed in deeply, almost gasping for breath. She couldn't wait to get out of the stuffy room and get home to take a long, hot shower. She needed to wash off the dirt. Just being there made her feel unclean. She hoped it wouldn't last much longer.

At twelve-twenty-six, Dr. Conrad Meeks went into the execution chamber. He put his stethoscope to Ramon's chest, listened for a full sixty seconds, then glanced at the time on his watch. He looked out at the spectators as he spoke. "The official time of death is twelve-twenty-six A.M."

Lena felt tired. But she still had to write her story and file it by one-thirty so it would make the deadline for the morning's paper. Most of it was already written. She just had to finish it and modem it off from her hotel room. The warden said a few final words, then they all began to disburse. Lena took an extra few minutes to get quotes from Barry and the chaplain before she, too, escaped into the hot Texas night.

DR. MEEKS WAITED until after the crowd had gone. When enough time had passed, he and one of the technicians wheeled the gurney, with Ramon's body on it, out of the execution chamber and down a short hallway to a room at

the back of the building. The technician took a green canvas body bag from a shelf and together they wrestled the
inert body into it.

"We should put them in this beforehand. It wouldn't be
so hard then," wheezed the technician when they'd finally
accomplished the task.

Dr. Meeks didn't reply. He zipped the bag shut nearly
to the top, pulled out a cigarette, and lit up. After taking
two long drags he looked at his watch. It was now one-
fifteen. "We better get moving. We've got a ways to
ride."

The technician opened the back door and propped it
open. They pushed the gurney out the door and onto a
loading dock. A nondescript gray Dodge cargo van was in
position waiting for them. The technician opened the
van's rear door. The interior setup was similar to an ambulance. Most of the length of the van on one side was
taken up by a shelf wide enough for someone to lie on.
Next to it was a space, then another bench which opened
out for storage.

They pulled the gurney up close to the van and used a
straight piece of board to slide the body from the dock
onto the shelf in the van where they strapped it into place
with bungee cords. Dr. Meeks grabbed his medical bag
and hopped into the vehicle. The technician shut the van
door, walked around to the front, started the engine, and
slowly pulled away from the dock.

The streets were empty at this time of night. They
drove through the prison gate, rode through town and onto
Route 190 heading west. In the back, Dr. Meeks lit up another cigarette and settled back for the ride. It went pretty
smoothly tonight, he thought. Another scumbag bites the
dust courtesy of the great State of Texas. He looked out
the back window. Just a few minutes outside of Huntsville
and the lights of the city had already faded away. You
could see stars out here. The only other lights were the

headlights from an oncoming truck, and after it passed the darkness closed in on them completely. Meeks finished his cigarette and ground the butt out underneath his heel. He stretched out on the bench and tried to make himself comfortable. They had a long way to go. He might as well try to rest. It didn't take more than a few minutes before he fell fast asleep.

He awoke with a start when the van dipped and he nearly slid off his bench. Without even looking outside he knew they were in the hill country of central Texas. He rubbed his eyes, yawned, and sat up. While lighting a new cigarette he looked at his watch. Four-seventeen. They'd been on the road for nearly three hours and they weren't even halfway there. Still, now seemed as good a time as any.

He reached down under the bench and pulled out his black doctor's bag. He snapped it open and withdrew a small leather case. Unzipping the case, he examined the four stainless-steel scalpels it contained; each one had a different angle to the blade. He chose one with a slight curve at its tip.

He leaned over the body, down below the waistline. Keeping his cigarette between his lips, he steadied himself. Taking into account the rolling of the van, he grasped a handful of the canvas with his left hand and pulled it taut. In his right hand he gripped the scalpel. Carefully, as if he was cutting into a real live human, he made an incision into the bag, cutting away six inches of the material covering the thigh. Satisfied with that cut, he made another incision from the opposite angle. This cut made an X in the bag, exposing the corpse's leg to the open air.

Dr. Meeks leaned back and contentedly drew a long puff on his Marlboro. As he exhaled he leaned forward once again. Holding the cigarette between his thumb and forefinger, he brought it down to the area in the bag opened by his cut and pushed the red-hot ember through the sheer fabric of the corpse's pants into the muscle of his leg. There was a brief sizzle as the cigarette was extinguished in the flesh.

Dr. Meeks smiled as Ramon's leg twitched.

4

THE SUN WAS bright and halfway up in the sky by the time they left the highway and pulled onto a gravel access road. The surrounding area was desert. Scrubland, a wide, flat expanse of white sand occasionally punctuated by a splash of green mesquite. With the morning sun bearing down, it seemed barren and inhospitable.

Their tires crunched against the gravel, shooting stones up against the underbody of the van. They were getting close. Dr. Meeks sat up and smoothed out the wrinkles in his clothes with his hands. When he felt presentable enough he pulled out and lit another cigarette. Then he looked at the body on the seat next to him. He had fully unzipped the body bag hours before, opening it fully to the air. Meeks looked at the face. It showed no movement, the eyes were shut, and if he was breathing it was imperceptible. It still looked as if he were dead. Meeks knew better.

He leaned forward and banged his palm on the metal wall that separated him from the cab. The van slowly came to a stop. The situation was stable: The body was fine, not ready to wake up and certainly not going any-where. The driver opened the rear door, Meeks climbed out of the back of the van and made his way up front for the balance of the trip.

Soon they passed a warning sign: Lyndon B. Johnson Army Installation—U.S. Government Property—No Ac-cess. A mile and a half farther down the road they came to the gate. A heavy-gauge metal fence surrounded the perimeter of the property extending in both directions as far as the eye could see. The top of the fence was covered with curled razor wire; the fence itself was electrified. Twenty feet inside the perimeter another fence of the same construction was erected; it too went on to the horizon.

Two guards in U.S. Army khakis with automatic rifles at their sides manned the gate. They stood in a glass-and-metal booth that straddled the road. Video cameras were aimed at the road in either direction. The driver pulled the van in next to the enclosure. The guard was tall and lean with close-cut blond hair. He opened the window and gave a hardened look at the driver. "This is a closed in-stallation, sir. You're going to have to turn your vehicle around—"

Meeks leaned forward so that the guard could see him. "We're expected, Corporal."

The guard's attitude changed. "Good morning, sir. It's good to see you again. I didn't realize you were there—"

"You need to be more observant, Corporal."

"I'm sorry, sir. I will be more observant. I wasn't ex-pecting—"

"I can see that, Corporal. Hand him the papers, Len."

The guard tried not to look flustered. "Yes, sir, may I see your papers?" He extended a hand toward the driver.

The driver handed over a document with his and Dr.

Meeks's IDs attached. The guard closely inspected the papers before turning back to the van. "Very good, sir. One moment while I authenticate these orders." He picked up a phone and talked softly for a minute before hanging up and turning back to the van. "Thank you, sir. Everything is in order. Please proceed directly to the base, sir."

The driver nodded in reply. Meeks just sat back in the seat and stared straight ahead. They waited for the gate to be raised, then passed through. Inside the gate the road turned to asphalt. On either side the desert stretched on. They passed several army barracks. No soldiers were visible but the parking lots next to them were filled with vehicles, Humvees and personnel carriers. The driver accelerated to sixty miles per hour. It took a full eight minutes to reach the base.

As they neared the installation they had to pass through another gate with the same routine and another guard. A Humvee met them on the other side and escorted them to the main building. It was an immense concrete structure, bone white with no windows. It rose only one story above the ground, but it covered the equivalent of two city blocks in area. To Meeks it seemed that the place buzzed with activity: People moved purposely in and out of the building; Hummers circled the area. As they drove closer, a helicopter flew into view and hovered above, preparing to land atop the roof. The building reminded Meeks of a great hive, though the soldiers seemed more like menacing wasps or hornets than bees. Even with all the activity, the morning seemed quiet, but in the background there was a low but insistent humming sound, the sound of huge motors, or fans sucking in the desert air.

They were directed to a loading dock built into the side of the structure where the driver backed the van up against the bay. Their escort Humvee pulled in beside them. Its driver wore a crisp khaki uniform with captain's bars and a purple slash above the insignia. The captain stepped for-

ward to greet them. He was tall and lean, skinny almost,
or he seemed that way till you looked closer. His arms
were sinewy, his neck thick; it wasn't that he was skinny,
it was just that he had no fat on his body.

The captain moved with an air of natural confidence
and authority, the fluid grace of a predatory animal, like a
wolf or perhaps a mountain lion. His blond hair was cut
short in a military style and his nose and chin jutted out in
sharp angles. With his hair and light complexion people
might expect that his eyes were gray or ice blue, but they
were hidden by mirrored sunglasses.

"It's good to see you made it. Ya have any problems?"
He smiled as he moved over to meet them; his voice had
the hint of a country drawl.

"No, sir, Captain. Everything went just the way it was
supposed to, sir." Meeks's van driver crisply saluted the
captain who casually returned the salute. Dr. Meeks
pulled out a cigarette and bent his head down to light it. A
look of distaste briefly passed over the captain's face.

"Good, Sergeant, excellent job. I'll handle this from
here. Why don't you go get some rest?" The van driver
saluted again, nodded to Meeks, and walked away.

The captain turned his attention toward Meeks. "Is our
subject in good health, Conrad?"

"He's alive." Meeks blew out a cloud of smoke.

The captain nodded. "Well, that's just fine. Let's take a
look at him and get him moved into service." Together
they walked up the ramp. The captain opened the back of
the van, spread the doors wide open, and peered in on the
comatose body of Ramon Willis. "Sleepin' like a baby.
How much longer will he be out?" he asked.

"About two more hours," Meeks replied. "He was
starting to move around some at the end so I gave him another shot."

The captain bent over the body and pulled back on
Ramon's eyelids. "You checked him out?"

"Of course I checked him out. The test was negative," Meeks replied.

"Let's get him inside then. You have his papers?"

Meeks handed over a file. The captain walked over to the side of the dock where a gurney was waiting. He wheeled it over close to the van and together they transferred Ramon onto the cart. Carefully, they pushed it out of the van, onto the dock and near the door.

Meeks exhaled a stream of smoke and cleared his throat. "Things have changed, Parker," he said, addressing the captain. "Tell the colonel that we need to talk."

The captain continued with his work. "Talk about what, Conrad?"

"That's between me and the colonel."

"He's a busy man, Conrad. You're going to have to let me know what this is about first."

Meeks sucked on the cigarette and flicked the ash onto Ramon's body. "Two more bodies will be available next week. But I'm concerned about the risk that I'm taking. This is dangerous work. The next two are going to be double the rate. For this kind of risk I'm going to need more money."

The captain stared at him for a long moment before answering. "You're right, Conrad. This is dangerous work. We talked about that before you agreed to do it."

"That's right. And we're talking about it again now."

The captain kept his gaze fixed on Mecks without speaking for an uncomfortable length of time. "What about your patriotic duty, Conrad? This is a chance to serve your country again."

"And what would happen if I talked to the media and explained this service to my country. They might not see it quite the same way."

"That's not a threat, is it, Conrad?"

"This is a business arrangement and I'm just saying that we need to change the terms."

The captain smiled and seemed to loosen up. "Fine, Conrad, you just get your deliveries ready. I'll talk with the colonel." He pushed the body up to the loading dock door. "You gotta be tired. Ya sure had a busy night. You better go get you some sleep. I'll talk with the colonel . . . but I don't know that you're going to like his answer."

Meeks wasn't sure but felt that he had been vaguely threatened. "I'll have your deliveries next week, but you tell the colonel that it's going to cost him." As he stared back at his reflection in the captain's mirrored glasses, he realized that he felt quite tense, and he couldn't tell if it was from fear or anger.

The captain smiled and nodded his dismissal. He turned to the door, inserted a keycard and punched in an access code. The door slid open with a pneumatic swish. Pushing the body before him, he entered the building. The door closed behind, leaving Meeks alone on the dock.

THE CAPTAIN WITH the mirrored eyes wheeled the gurney down a long hallway till it dead-ended at a thick stainless-steel door. He put his keycard into the slot and swiped it through. The door slid open. He moved into a central room; it was octagonal, and three other doors opened onto other hallways going off at right angles to each other. Between each doorway was a bank of elevators, two to a side. In the center of the room was a guard station, also octagonal, equipped with rows of video monitors showing the activity of each hallway and elevator leading to or away from the room.

Four soldiers in full uniform manned the station. They saluted the captain as he presented himself. He handed over a set of papers to a young officer, Lieutenant Green, who was the officer in charge of this station. Lieutenant Green was thin and wiry with curly brown hair, thin lips, and a long, thin nose. The glasses over his deep brown

eyes usually gave his face a serious look but his eyes be-
trayed his discomfort.

The captain stared at Green for a long moment before
he smiled and broke the silence, "Lieutenant Green, I've
heard some very good things about you."

"Thank you, sir," Green stood at attention as he stared
back at his image reflected in the mirrored glasses.

"Yep. I heard some very good things. I've heard that
you are a man that can be trusted with responsibilities."

"Yes, sir. I believe I can, sir."

"Soldier, we have a new patient for quarantinc number
two. Do you know where that is?" the captain asked.

"Yes, sir, I think I do."

"Good," the captain said as he handed over a set of papers. "This fella needs to get down there pronto. I'm
passin' the responsibility on to you."

"Yes, sir," the lieutenant said crisply. "I'll arrange for
an escort to . . ."

"I don't think you understan', Lieutenant," the captain
interrupted, "He needs an escort now and I need someone
that I can count on. And I guess you're it, son. Take him
down to Q-two. They're expecting you real soon."

"Yes, sir. I'll take him down myself, sir. I'll just need a
minute to call in a replacement for my post."

"Call your replacement, soldier, but you don't have
time to wait for him. This patient is under certain time restraints. I'll watch your post till your backup comes. Do a
good job now, Lieutenant. There's some real opportunities
here for men that can be trusted."

"Yes, sir," Lieutenant Green said after a brief hesitation. "Thank you, sir." He made his call, hung up the
phone, and stepped out from behind the station. He
glanced uneasily at the other soldiers, then at the captain.
He took hold of the gurney's handles and pushed it toward
the elevator on his right.

"Say, Lieutenant," the captain called out. Green turned

back to see that the captain was holding up a black plastic access card. "You ain't going far without this." He flipped the card across to Green, who caught it on reflex.

"Thanks," Green inserted his keycard into the slot. The door opened silently. Without looking back, Green pushed the gurney onto the lift, stepped on, and the doors closed.

Inside the elevator there was a standard instrument panel with buttons for three levels below the ground floor. Above the panel a video camera was aimed at the occupants. Lieutenant Green punched the button for the third floor below ground level. A soft jolt in the pit of his stomach told him that the elevator was moving down. Packed into the tight space with the gurney, he hardly had room to move.

Green had only been in the installation for three months but he'd heard rumors of strange things that went on in the lower chambers of the building. Crazy rumors about human experiments. Things that he didn't want to know. To Green it sounded like something that the Nazis would do, not the U.S. Army. This was a top-level security installation. They recruited only career soldiers and put everyone through an extensive background check before they could serve here. They did things differently here, too. The purple slash that the captain wore was not a U.S. Army emblem but something used strictly on the installation. It was a marking of an elite group among the troops. Green knew that something sensitive was going on and there had to be a good reason for whatever it was. But he'd never encountered anything like this firsthand, and he didn't like it.

After a moment the elevator stopped and the doors slid open. Green stepped out into a bright yellow corridor that led off to the left and right, dead-ending on each side at a closed metal door. He moved to the path on the right, pushing the gurney in front. When he came to the door,

Lieutenant Green inserted the captain's keycard and the doors swooshed open.

He entered a small room. The doors closed behind him. He heard a loud hissing like air being sucked into a vacuum. Green stepped up to the other door and again slid the card through. Pushing the gurney ahead, he stepped out into another corridor; the doors behind him slid shut. Halfway down, the corridor intercepted another hall. He turned and followed that path.

The building was color coded. This floor was identified by its yellow walls. Lieutenant Green wondered how he had ever learned to navigate the building as much as he had—it was so large and mazelike. When he had first been assigned to the complex he had thought about dropping bread crumbs behind him, just so he would have some means of finding his way back. Since then he had learned to navigate his way around the parts of the building where he was allowed admittance, though this was the first time that he would go all the way down to level five.

At the end of this hall he had to pass through another metal door. On the other side was another control room with a guard station, a bank of elevators, and one door that exited out to the other side of the room. The officer on duty here was Maj. Al Stepman, one of the ranking officers on the base. He was short and cocky, quick to boast and even quicker to anger. Behind his back his men all called him Rooster. He was a regular along with Green at a low-stakes poker game that some of the men held every Thursday. Green saluted and handed over the order papers.

"I've got a delivery down to the basement, sir," he said.

"Another live one going down, huh?" Stepman casually glanced at the papers. "You playing on Thursday?"

"Yes, sir, I've got to. I need to win back some of the money you stole last week," Green replied with a grin.

"Just bring your money, soldier, 'cause I got bills to

pay." Stepman handed back the papers. "What are you doing on this run? Somebody get sick or something?"

Green shrugged. "I don't know, just at the right place at the right time I guess. I'll see you tomorrow, sir." Green saluted again and turned toward the elevator at his left.

Stepman spoke from behind him, "Wrong door, Charley. Q-two is that way." He pointed to the door on the other side of the room.

"Oh right . . . sorry. First time down." Green wasn't sure but he thought that he was close to the center of the building. The door swooshed open and he walked through. He was in a small hallway with another door directly in front of him. The door closed behind him and the next door opened. Green felt a slight breeze as they entered the new room. He was in an airlock; he could hear the sound of huge fans sucking all the air out of the room. After the rear door closed the front one opened. Green pushed the gurney out to a room with a single elevator and stepped in.

The control panel on this elevator serviced subfloors three, four, and five. He pushed the button for number five. After a brief drop the doors opened onto an orange room with a single sentry sitting at a desk facing the elevator. He wore a respirator that covered most of his head. On the wall behind his shoulder, a large red-and-white sign warned that this was the quarantine area, containment suits were required from that point on. A metal door to his right was the only other way out of the room.

The guard stepped forward. "Thank you, sir. I'll take that. We've been expecting you." He grasped the gurney and pulled it out onto the floor.

Green stayed on the elevator. He sighed with relief when the door slid shut.

EVERYTHING WAS WHITE. He turned his head around, but no matter which way he looked it was all the same, a bright, all-encompassing whiteness. He felt lost, confused. He didn't know where he was or what time it was. Not even the day, month, or year. He didn't know how long he had been there. It seemed like a long time. His sense of self was vague and indistinct; he knew who he was but he couldn't remember his name. Or how he had gotten here, in this place wherever it was. It was all so white.

He felt his hand; the fingers were cold as ice. His whole body was cold. His legs were frozen, his toes burned with pain. *Where am I?* He held his hand straight out in front of him, but couldn't see it. Just the white. As he peered out toward his hand, it seemed to him that the white was not one entity but millions of fragments of white substance blowing around and falling on top of him, so much of it that it seemed to be a single essence.

He felt slow and sluggish. He had trouble thinking. But suddenly it came to him. It was snow. A fierce snowstorm and he was standing alone taking it all in. It seemed so new, so strange.

He'd only felt snow once before and that was years ago when he was a kid. A freak snowstorm had hit Texas back when he was eight or nine years old. He had lived near Brownsville then, close to the Mexican border. It hardly ever got cold there, but this time a cold front had blown in. It was freezing cold for a week and then it snowed. The snow only amounted to about an inch but everything stopped. There was no school. Stores closed. They shut down the highway. The adults were worried, but the kids loved it. He remembered playing with his cousins, running in the snow, letting the flakes fall in their mouths and melt on their tongues. They scooped the fallen snow off of cars and benches and threw it at each other. They felt cold but alive. The next day it warmed up and the snow disappeared by the afternoon. That was his one experience with snow.

Until now. And this was different. The snow here was

falling much harder and the cold was more intense. He heard a sound. A faint sound of music somewhere far away. The song was familiar. He remembered it from a time a long way back in his past, a song from his childhood. He tried to concentrate. He could hear a guitar playing and a soft female voice singing in Spanish, words that he didn't understand. But the voice was so familiar. He listened harder. The music seemed to be coming closer. He was sure that he knew the voice but still couldn't make out the words. And then suddenly he could but they weren't just words. It was a name. His name, *"Ramon."*

And he knew the voice, it was his mother. His mother who had died when he was just ten years old. And now he could hear her as if she were standing right next to him. He peered into the raging storm trying to see her, but he could see nothing but white. He walked toward the sound, his arms outstretched, searching. He called out, *"Mama!"* But she didn't answer; the voice was gone. He thrashed about, going in one direction, then another, calling out, screaming her name. Still there was no reply. He felt a panic rising in his chest. He was going to lose her again.

Then he heard the music once more. Behind him this time and far, far away. He turned toward it and stumbled forward, trying to find its source. His heart beat like a bass drum now and he was panting from the fear and exertion. He realized that it wasn't cold anymore. Now it was hot and humid. The snowstorm had stopped. It was still a world of white but now it seemed more like fog, or steam.

He rushed forward now, trying to find the source of the music and thought that he must be getting close. He ran faster, but no matter how fast he ran, the sound stayed in front of him. But he couldn't lose her again. He ran even faster and this time it was as if he had launched himself into the air, he was off the ground and he felt like he was flying. Suddenly the whiteness dispersed and he saw where he was for the first time. He wasn't flying at all but had stepped off of a cliff and was now falling face forward into a deep canyon. The ground was far below but looming closer.

Ramon's head jerked back against the cart. He was suddenly wide-awake, his heart was pounding, his veins pulsing with adrenaline. His whole body was soaked with sweat. *It was only a dream,* he thought, *just a dream.* He let his breath out in a long sigh. *Nothing but a bad dream.*

He tried to bring his hand up to his face to wipe his forehead but he couldn't, his arms were restrained. For the first time he noticed his surroundings. He was in a bright white room. The room was empty. Three walls were bare concrete. The fourth wall contained the door. It was thick stainless steel with no doorknob, an electronic keypad built into it. Next to the door was a mirror, set at eye level, that ran the length of the wall. He turned away from his reflection.

Ramon tried to move his legs but they, too, were restrained. *Where am I?* He had to think. It wasn't familiar at all. He tried to sit up, but his entire body was bound by some kind of straps. He was on some kind of bed, fastened tight to it. His right arm felt especially uncomfortable, a needle was poked into his vein, taped securely, connected to an intravenous bag that slowly dripped some unknown fluid into his body. *What am I doing here?* Ramon tried to remember but his head was sluggish, his brain dull. This wasn't the prison. The sounds were altogether different. This room was so quiet, the only sound a soft electric hum.

He felt anxious—it was like he had awakened from one nightmare into a new one. *How did I get here?* He thought back, *What had happened last? Where was I before I went to sleep?* It seemed so long ago he couldn't recall. Then all at once he did. He had been put to death. The last thing he remembered was being in the death chamber at Walls, strapped down and ready to die.

He gripped the sides of the bed, the veins in his neck pounding, his eyes bulging. He screamed. He was gripped with a seizure and spasms contorted his body. He gasped for breath and screamed again and again. His mind shut down. All he could feel was fear, the utter terror of the situation. His screamed until his throat was raw.

After a long time, he regained control. He gripped his fingers against the sides of the bed, grasping the wet cotton sheets. He struggled for air. *There must be an explanation.* With effort he regained his normal rhythm of breathing. His heart slowed a notch then, but his eyes were frantic as they scanned the room looking for clues. *There's got to be an explanation.*

A sound came from the doorway. The door slid open with a quiet whoosh, followed by a rush of air entering the room. A figure appeared in the doorway, large and strange. He appeared to be human but Ramon couldn't tell for sure. He was dressed in a large, bulky Day-Glo yellow Mylar suit that covered his entire body including his head. The figure lumbered forward, his eyes just visible behind the clear visor of his headgear. His breath rasped out in a staticky electronic drone. A backpack peeked over his shoulder, letting out a mechanical hum. As he moved into the room, another figure, smaller but dressed in an identical outfit followed him into the room pushing a small cart. Once the second figure came all the way inside, he turned and passed a card through the keypad in the door. The door slid shut.

The two men moved the cart beside Ramon's bed. He could see it out of the corner of his eye. It held gauze, some tape, yards of tubing, and a small stainless steel cylindrical device with a plunger at one end. The men's breath rasped out rhythmically. They stepped up to Ramon. The first figure took hold of his arm and held it in a viselike grip to the side of the bed so that Ramon couldn't move at all. The second figure picked up the metal device, brought it up to Ramon's arm, and depressed the plunger. Ramon felt a jolt of pain as a needle entered his skin.

The shorter man bent over Ramon, his visor glaring with reflected light. Ramon felt as if his head were going to explode as the man began to speak. The electronic apparatus distorted his voice, but Ramon could hear the words clearly. "Welcome to hell, Mr. Willis."

5
_____

LT. CHARLES GREEN always looked forward to Thursday nights. Discipline was tight here at the installation, and Rev Tanner's poker game was one of the few chances he had to unwind. The game was for officers only, but nobody paid attention to rank. For a junior officer this was a revelation. While the game was on, they were equals; no "yes, sirs" or "no, sirs" were necessary. If Green saw them at the installation tomorrow, he'd have to salute and play the part, but tonight he was free.

The Johnson Installation was in many ways like duty on a submarine. For the officers on the base, it was often a long time between leaves off base. But their paychecks came regularly. And since all their necessities were paid, gambling was a common pastime. This was basically a friendly game though. No one ever lost too much or took it too seriously.

Green couldn't play every week. Sometimes he would

have to pull late duty, but whenever he could he made it a point to go. The players shifted each week depending on schedules, but there were a couple of constants. Rev Tanner was one; the game was held in his room in C barracks. He was only a lieutenant, but he ran the game and somehow he always was cleared of duties on Thursday nights. Rev was big and as black as asphalt. He stood over six feet tall in his bare feet and he weighed about two hundred and sixty pounds. Mostly muscle, too. He'd been a fullback for two years at the University of Georgia before quitting to enlist in the army. Green didn't know Rev's real first name, but everyone called him Rev because of his voice. He had a deep, smooth bass that would have been the envy of any Baptist preacher.

The other constant in the game was Maj. Al "Rooster" Stepman. Stepman was short and feisty with a chip on his shoulder the size of New Hampshire. He was competitive in everything that he did. He was quick to argue and quick to take offense. But he was also a born leader, the kind of guy that men would want to follow in a battle situation whether he was wearing the stripes or not. He was well up in the hierarchy of the installation but he still acted like a regular guy. It was Major Stepman who had first invited Green into the game, and Green felt indebted to him for it. He also felt honored that he had been chosen for special treatment.

Green rapped on the door. After a moment Rev Tanner opened it. The room was a haze of cigar smoke. Four players were sitting around an old card table absorbed in the game. A baseball game blared from a TV in the corner but nobody was watching it.

"Hi, Rev, how's it going tonight?" Green asked.

"Charley the Tuna! Come on in, boy. We need your money." Rev opened the door all the way and Green walked through.

"Hey, guys, who's winning?" Green asked.

Stepman tossed some change into the pot and glanced up. "Grab a beer and grab a seat," he called out. "We need some fresh blood." The other players simply nodded their heads or grunted acknowledgment as they studied their cards.

Green walked over to the refrigerator in the corner and pulled out a Lone Star. He twisted the cap off and sat down at the last open chair. He took a long pull on the bottle and prepared to wait while they finished out their hand. He was sitting to the left of Rev Tanner. Virgil Ortman was on his other side. Virgil was a lieutenant also, originally from New Jersey. He always came on like a clown, a real wise guy. He was usually the first one to fold and he rarely won, but he played so safe that he never lost much, either. Next to Ortman was Bob Durmo, a major from Indiana who took his cards and everything else seriously. His ears were about a size and a half too big and people called him Dumbo behind his back. Next to Durmo and across from Green was Rooster Stepman. The night was early but from his bloodshot eyes it looked like he'd had a head start on the drinking.

Green almost didn't recognize the last player in the group. He was a captain with short blonde hair and a fighter's body, hard and lean. His face was all angles. What threw him were the eyes—soft, and green as a lazy river. They would have been fine on a painter or a poet but not on this man. They weren't at all what Green had expected when he met him the other day—though at the time the captain had been wearing mirrored sunglasses.

"You know everyone here, Charley?" Rev asked as he returned to his seat.

"Yeah, sure. Well, not officially . . ." He looked over at the captain.

"Hey, pal, sorry if I was short with you the other day." The captain flashed a cold smile at Green as he extended his hand. "You handled yourself real good. Name's

Parker . . . Parker Cain. We appreciate people like you that can do their job and keep quiet about it."

"Yes, sir." The handshake was firm to the point of bone crushing and Green realized that he might have been wrong about the eyes. There was an intensity that he hadn't noticed at first.

"Okay, we all know each other. Let's finish the hand, fer Christ's sake," Rooster Stepman called out.

Green took a sip of his beer and settled back in his seat. He hadn't realized it before but he now saw that Durmo, Stepman, and Rev Tanner all had the same purple slash emblem that Captain Cain wore. Funny how he hadn't noticed it before.

"Pot's right, cards are coming." Virgil Ortman was the dealer. They were playing seven-card stud. The first two cards were dealt facedown, the next four were dealt out one at a time, faceup with wagers placed after each. The last card was always facedown. Ortman was dealing out the third up card, laying out a running commentary as he did so.

"Pair of bitches out front, looking good . . . eight of hearts, possible straight . . . six of hearts, that's a lot of red . . . a black jack for the black jack."

He dealt the last card to himself, the ten of diamonds, which was no help at all. "And I fold." Ortman threw his cards down. "Bitches bet."

Durmo picked up his hole cards and glanced at them, then he looked around the table. He was showing two queens and a nine of diamonds. He tugged on his right ear trying to decide. He tentatively reached into his pile. "I'll bet a dollar."

Stepman glanced at his hand, a six of diamonds, eight of hearts, and a nine of spades. He had two cards to draw to complete his straight if he didn't already have it in the hole. "Raise you two-fifty." He threw three ones and a fifty-cent piece into the pot.

Capt. Parker Cain was next. He rubbed his eyes and tossed in the three-fifty without even glancing at his cards. Then he tossed in an extra five-dollar bill. "Let's make this interesting . . . raise another five." He slipped his sunglasses out of his pocket and put them on. "Sorry, fellas, the light bothers my eyes."

Rev Tanner was showing a jack of spades, an ace of clubs, and four of diamonds. Without hesitation he threw his coins into the pot. "You gotta pay if you're gonna play. I'm in, guys."

Durmo stared at his cards, then studied the pot as if he were doing a profit-and-loss analysis in his head. Very carefully he pulled out five singles and dropped them into the pot. "I'll meet your raises and call." The pot was beginning to look quite substantial.

"Okay . . . last up card," Ortman threw the cards down on the table. "Damn, three bitches . . . a seven to help your straight . . ."

"That's right, baby!" Stepman snapped his fingers.

"You got Durmo's last queen, no help to you . . . and a jack to go along with your other jack . . . bitches bet again."

Durmo studied his cards. "I'll bet three bucks." He tossed the money onto the table.

"Meet your three and raise you the same." Stepman threw his bills onto the table.

"Meet and raise it again." Parker Cain threw the money in without any hesitation. Green looked around at what was showing on the table. Durmo had three queens, that was a given. Stepman had the makings of a straight but he was prone to stay in to the bitter end just on the hope that he would catch something on the draw. Rev Tanner had a pair of jacks showing but if he had more he would be betting more aggressively. Green didn't think he would be a factor. Cain was the wild card, he wasn't showing that much—three hearts, but he was betting like he already had the flush covered, he was playing with confidence.

Rev Tanner threw his cards down on the table with a grin. "Damn fellas, this is getting awful rich for a working man. I guess I'm going to have to pass."

Durmo tugged on his ears again, and his forehead began to sweat. "I'll meet your raises, then I call." He threw his money onto the pile. Stepman dropped three bills in to balance the pot.

"Okay, pot's right. Last card." Ortman dealt the last card facedown to the three remaining players. "Queens still got the floor."

Durmo deliberated for a moment then threw five dollars into the pot. "Okay, five to you."

Stepman threw the money in. "Let's see who's got the cards."

Parker Cain tossed a five into the pot, then glanced over at Ortman. "What's the limit on a raise here?"

"Twenty is the limit."

"Then I raise twenty." Cain threw two tens onto the pile.

Durmo had a sour look on his face. He took a long time to decide what to do. As Green looked over he felt that he could read his thoughts. For this group, this was a big pot. For Cain to throw around money so loosely it had to mean that he had his flush, a hard hand to beat. Still, Durmo had invested a lot in the hand already; he couldn't just toss it in now. That would feel like surrender. Durmo tugged hard on his ear then reached for his money. Halfway down, his hand had second thoughts. It paused in midair for a moment before courage finally won out. "Well, I might regret this . . . but . . ." He threw down the twenty dollars then added another ten of his own. "I'll meet your twenty and raise you ten."

Stepman's face reddened. "Shit." He looked at his cards, as if willing them to be something else. "Shit." He threw his cards onto the table and took a huge swig on his beer. "He's got to have a flush. I'll let you big spenders fight this one out." Green thought that he was doing a good job of controlling his temper.

Cain met the ten and bumped it up ten dollars more. Durmo tugged on his ear again.

"No more raises. That's the limit." Ortman said.

Durmo grimaced as he threw in the last ten. His voice cracked as he spoke, "Okay, I've just got the three queens, what have you got?"

Cain shrugged and flashed a smile as he threw his cards facedown on the table. "Ya got me pardner."

"God damn! I had a straight. You chased me off with nothing?" A vein was throbbing in Stepman's temple. "I don't believe it."

Cain was as cool as ice. "Relax, Rooster; it's only money. Nothin' but money, my friends."

Everyone tensed for a moment. No one called Stepman "Rooster" to his face, especially not a junior officer. Stepman's face reddened but he didn't respond. Green waited for the eruption, but it didn't come.

After a moment Durmo nervously raked the money over to his pile. "Whew, that was something."

Ortman collected the cards and passed the deck onto Durmo for his deal. He gave a short laugh. "It's only money! I like that, Captain. It's only money. You playing, Tuna?"

"Yeah, I'm in," Green replied. He pulled out his cash and asked for change.

The game continued until about one. Durmo was the first to leave, as he had to be up early in the morning. Parker Cain left soon after. He had been the big winner that night, ending up taking money from all of them. Now it was down to the last four and they were all about ready to call it a night. Green took a big gulp on his beer, not in a hurry to leave.

"It's only money. Can you believe that shit?" Stepman was more than buzzed, and irritated at losing for the night.

"He had our number tonight, that's for sure," Rev Tanner said as he looked at his watch.

"Who invited that asshole to play anyway?"

"Well, I thought . . ." Ortman was about to apologize.

"It's only money. I can't believe he said that."

Green had been thinking about his encounter with Cain from the other day. Cain had seemed so much in control then, like he owned the place. More than his captain's rank would have called for. And he had brought the body in for delivery to level five. Green had heard rumors of things like that before, but this was the first time he had seen it firsthand and he'd been thinking about it ever since. There were some things that you just didn't talk about, not if you wanted to get ahead. But tonight he was feeling good and these were friends. "Who was that guy? I mean who is he really? He had me deliver a patient down to the basement."

"Captain Cain?" Ortman responded, "He's like a straight shot to the colonel is what he is."

"He's an asshole is what he is," Stepman cut in.

"What's the deal with that anyway? I've heard that they do some kind of experiments down there," Ortman chimed in. "There's some strange shit going on down there. . . ."

"Hey. Hey! You're out of line here, soldier." Stepman's attitude had changed.

"Who are these people they're carting in? Where do they come from? It's . . ."

"Stop talking now, soldier. That's an order." Stepman stood up. He was still half drunk but his anger was mixed with fear and he suddenly seemed sober. "You're way out of line. This is crazy-assed talk. You're officers in the U.S. Army. You are paid to follow orders. You are not paid to think. If a superior officer tells you to shit, you damned well better mess your drawers right then and there." The veins in his neck were bulging and his face had turned a bright crimson. "If . . . and I mean *if*, something is going on down there, it's going on for a reason. Your superiors have reasons for what they do. We're in a god-damned forest and you pricks are getting your tits in a wringer cause you see some trees. *We are preparing for war!* It's not your decision . . . or mine . . . how we fight this god-dammed war. If something is being done it's being done for a reason. I suggest that you stop this pinko talk and let your superiors do the thinking. Do I make myself clear?"

"Yes, sir," Ortman replied, his gaze fixed on the floor.

"Absolutely, sir." Green realized that he was standing at attention.

"And I don't want to hear anymore of this talk. It's over."

The party quickly broke up and everyone left at the same time. As he walked out the door, Green realized that Rev Tanner had remained silent and detached throughout the entire exchange. He hadn't said a word.

LENA COULDN'T SLEEP. She lay in her bed, eyes wide open and her mind racing, unable to relax and let go. It seemed that her life had changed in some way. Somehow things were different. The well-ordered categories of her life had been rearranged in some subtle way, leaving her anxious and depressed. It was funny, because new opportunities were opening up. Opportunities that she had been working and planning for for years. She should have been excited—but instead, her thoughts were of dying.

Hcr series on the death penalty and the Texas prison system had ended with the story of Ramon Willis's execution. Returning from Huntsville, her story filed and printed, was a triumphant homecoming. Half the day was taken up with congratulatory phone calls; calls came in from her editors, coworkers, and past associates. It was nice to be the center of attention, but she just felt empty. The story had been her main focus for the past two months. And now it was over. The series went over well, critically acclaimed and well read, but she knew that in the end it would make no difference. The impact of the series would be as fleeting as the paper it was printed on. People were talking about it now, but they'd be talking about something else tomorrow. Long range, nothing would change. Texas wasn't about to change its policy on capital punishment because of anything she wrote.

Later in the day Lena got a call that changed her mood for the better. Allen Edwards, the associate editor of *Newsworld* magazine, called. She'd sent him a resume ages ago but never got a response. Now he was calling her about a position with the magazine. She was a rising star, he said, a bold new talent. She made an appointment to fly out to meet him in New York the following week.

After that she'd felt better. It lasted until that night when she was alone in her apartment. She was looking at a magazine and an ad for a prescription drug caught her eye. In the ad, a couple was walking contentedly through a field of summer flowers. The sky behind them was a brilliant shade of blue—the same shade as Ramon's eyes. Images of the execution flashed in her head. The needle sliding into the vein in his arm; the liquid flowing through the clear plastic tubes into his body; how he seemed to shudder once before he stopped breathing and was still. She could smell the viewing area of the death chamber: disinfectant and the warden's stale aftershave.

She closed the magazine but the images lingered. A man had died in front of her eyes. His death was peaceful; he certainly didn't appear to be in pain. But it was still a strong young man dying long before his time. It made her feel vulnerable and for the first time that she could remember, Lena truly considered her own death. If she died now, what would she have to show for her life? Some minor awards, some bylines in archived newspapers, and that was it. No lasting relationships, few people who would actually mourn her when she was gone. She'd never felt so alone.

Lena had always considered herself an independent, self-sufficient woman. Her career was the focus of her life—in order to succeed, it had to be. But at times like this she longed for the comfort of a man, a partner who shared her goals. Someone who loved her, someone she could make a life with. She'd had that before but walked away from it. She wondered if there would be another chance. She didn't sleep much that night.

Now it was three days since the execution and she still couldn't sleep. As she lay in bed, the walls of the room seemed to close in and bear down on her. Sleep wasn't an option. Lena rolled out of bed and went out to the main room. She looked out the window; the best feature of her apartment was the view. The lights of Austin's skyline were like soft candles in the distance. She sat in the dark and watched. It was comforting.

But she still couldn't sleep. She thought about turning on the TV to one of the late shows, but the idea of trivial jokes and canned laughter left her cold. She wasn't in the mood for laughing. After a while she got up, poured a cup of milk from the refrigerator, and switched on her laptop. If she couldn't sleep she might as well work.

For the last several months she'd been playing around with a story idea about the Internet. How it had opened up and legitimized behavior and ideas that in the past would have been considered eccentric at best. There were now virtual communities clustered around any oddball belief that could be imagined. What kind of people were drawn to these communities? A lot of them were probably normal people, Lena thought. Just average people in real life, who found meaning on the fringes of cyberspace.

There was one chat room that Lena had been monitor-

ing for some time. She'd found it the first time by accident
but had returned several times since. Its focus was conspiracy theories and other outlandish ideas.

Her idea was to approach one of the people in the chat
room, develop some trust, and then get an in-depth interview. What are they like in *real* life? What draws them to
the fringe? How does it affect their other relationships?
And then the big picture, what does this say about the rest
of society? Are we so cynical that we want to believe
everything is corrupt? There was a story in there somewhere. Just thinking about it helped make Lena feel better. It was good to be involved with something new.

She clicked onto the site. Voyeuristically, she monitored the conversations. Mostly it was wacko stuff: the
Trilateralist committee and the defense industry had engi-
neered the September 11 attack; Richard Nixon was behind the Kennedy assassination; there was a government
plot to implant computer chips into people to monitor and
control them. It was crazy but for some reason she found
it intriguing.

Lena took a sip of her cold milk as she scrolled through
the postings. The only light in the apartment was the glow
of the computer screen. Alone in the dark, she felt a real
connection with the people conversing on the site. As odd
as the ideas were, they were looking for connections, just
like she was. They weren't that different from her.

The participants of the chat room all went by some sort
of code name. Someone would make a statement, others
would respond, and conversations would bubble up.
Sometimes several different discussions would be running
at the same time. If two people wanted to have a confidential conversation, they could move out of the main
area and into a private space. Watching the conversations
move across her screen she felt she could get a sense of
some of the personalities behind the statements. There
was one who would come on strong with one idea and try

to bludgeon others into agreement by repeating the idea in a different form, over and over. The only ones responding to him were those new to the site. Another talker came on very wishy-washy, agreeing with everyone, even if their positions were opposed to what he had agreed to previously.

There was one though, who seemed to be a likely prospect for her story idea. He went by the name of True Believer. His ideas were just as wild as the rest, but his arguments were logically supported. He seemed to be a regular; Lena had noticed him before.

Lena finished her milk and stared at the screen. It was late. She was tired but didn't want to sleep. It was better to be communicating with someone than lying in bed alone. She paused for a moment then made her decision. She typed out a message and addressed it to True Believer, then hit the enter key and sent it over the wire and into cyberspace.

She signed it Ms. Skeptic.

RAMON WAS NO longer sure what was real and what was a dream. The white room felt real, but it seemed so strange and alien compared to what he had known of real life, that he began to convince himself that it wasn't real at all. It was a nightmare from which he would wake up if he remained calm and just gave it enough time. But it kept coming back like a recurring dream. He wondered, maybe this really was hell. An individual hell created expressly for him. Maybe this torment was how he would spend the rest of eternity, strapped to a hard bed unable to move, with needles sticking into his veins and tubes connected to every orifice.

Or maybe this wasn't Hell but purgatory. Limbo. His terror had passed and been replaced by a general anxiety, and boredom. As bad as this was, he had the feeling that it could be much worse. That this was just a way station to what was in store for him.

The spacemen, as Ramon decided to call them, came back at regular intervals. They would draw some of his blood and check the monitors, maybe hang a new IV bag. It seemed that they were waiting for something to happen, waiting for some kind of change. Waiting for the time to move on to the next stage. He tried to talk with them and ask them questions. Who were they? Why was he here? Why were they doing this to him? But they never answered him. Except for the first exchange, they never said a word.

Still, he thought that he had figured out a pattern. They would come into the room two at a time, always the same people in a pair. Although they didn't talk, he had been able to tell them apart by their size and a glimpse at their eyes that he could see through the masks in their space suits. There were three pairs. Each team would come in two times in a row before being replaced by the next team. Ramon had figured that the reason there were three teams must be because they were working in three shifts. If each team's shift was eight hours, that would mean that a full day had passed when the first team had appeared for the second time. Keeping track of their comings and goings was hard; with the monotonous sameness of the room, he would drift in and out of sleep. In order to try and keep track he had bitten into his cheek or lips each time that someone had entered the room. By playing over the sores with his tongue he could, in a way, measure time. By this reckoning he had now been in the room for three days since he had discovered the pattern.

Another way that Ramon could tell that time had passed was by the way his arm felt. Originally, his arm would begin to ache after each injection. It had started out as a low-level irritation but had increased to the point that he wished that his arm would fall off, the pain was so bad.

For a time the pain was all that he could think about. It was like a toothache in his arm that throbbed and pulsated till it had taken on a life of its own. The pain radiated downward to his fingers and up through his shoulders, eventually resonating even in his head. He thought that his arm must have gotten infected. He'd become hot and feverish. The spacemen were very interested in the arm, too. They checked the wound on every round, sometimes prodding it to check for tenderness. Still later, Ramon knew that time had passed because his arm no longer hurt. He'd gone to sleep retreating from the pain and had awakened clearheaded and pain free.

He tried to gain control of his environment in any way that he could. In his mind he had named his captors. Huey and Dewy were one team. Huey was tall and thin, Dewy was a full head shorter. The second team he called Heckle and Jeckle. They were both tall but Heckle seemed wider — the loose-fitting space suit clung to his body. Jeckle had a lumbering gait that Ramon thought was probably from back trouble. The third team was actually the first one that he had seen. In his mind he thought of them as Tom and Jerry. They were both about the same size and the way they moved, so tentatively, reminded him of cartoon mice.

To stay sane Ramon had to believe that he had some control over his situation, even if the control was just being able to move his hands and feet. He did his best to exercise his muscles but under the circumstances it was anything but a full workout. He'd start with his toes, flexing and unflexing them, just trying to move. Then he would do the same thing with the next muscle, working upward. First his calves, then his thighs, tightening, then relaxing. Upward through his body, his stomach, chest, arms, gripping his fists into tight balls. Clenching and unclenching each muscle till he was done with the muscles in his face. Then he'd rest for a moment and start again.

This morning—*was it morning?*—he'd come up with a plan. A small act of defiance. He planned to resist his captors when they came in by tensing his muscles and making it difficult for them to do their tests. Twisting his arm when they went to draw blood, maybe he could be an irritant to them anyway. Maybe he could provoke a reaction. Huey and Dewy were expected. He waited with anticipation for them to enter.

He didn't know how long he waited. It seemed like an eternity, but finally the door opened. He knew immediately that something was wrong. The pattern was broken. Huey and Dewy entered the room like they were supposed to, but Heckle and Jeckle followed them in. They silently surrounded the bed. Ramon felt his anxiety rise. There had never been four of them in the room at the same time.

A moment later the door slid open again. A short, stocky figure clad in the familiar space suit entered the room. He walked to the head of the bed. His voice was a staticky drone. "Time to get dressed, Mr. Willis. It's graduation day."

6 _____

THE SMOOTH MAHOGANY surface of the desk was always clean and clear of papers. Darkly polished to a near mirror finish, the massive desk rose up like an island in the dimly lit room. It, like everything else in the room, was there as much for its symbolic value as for its function. The room was large but sparsely furnished: just the desk, two leather chairs in front of it, one behind, and an American flag in the corner. The chairs, like the desk, were oversized, as if designed for people who were larger than life.

The figure behind the desk fit the chair like a hand fits a glove. Tall and broadly built, he stood six feet four inches tall and weighed close to three hundred pounds. His skin was dark, a deep mahogany that nearly matched the color of the desk. In the dim light of the room he seemed to blend in with his surroundings. Only the glint of light reflecting off of his glasses was proof that he was really there. Col. Lucian Pope was an intimidating figure. Most of the people under his command had never seen him in person, but his reputation was mythic.

He was alone in the office now. Pope sat as still as a stone, holding the phone to his ear, silently listening. A yellow legal pad lay within easy reach, but he had no use for it. It was said that he had a photographic memory. He never put anything down in writing unless he specifically wanted a record of the fact.

He listened to the speaker on the phone for a long time before he broke his silence. When he spoke, he spoke crisply and precisely, enunciating each word. "Yes, I am quite aware that there are budgetary constraints. . . . However, if you want me to accomplish my stated task there's no way around it. This project requires more money." Pope went silent as the party on the other end began to talk.

Colonel Pope reached into the top drawer of his desk and pulled out a brand-new deck of playing cards. Listening, he cradled the phone into his shoulder, pulled the strip on the pack of cards, and began to peel off the cellophane. He opened the package and slid the cards onto the table, cut the deck into two piles, and with a flick of his wrists, shuffled them back into a single deck. The cards were dwarfed by his huge hands. "Yes, I clearly understand that," he said into the phone.

He placed the cards facedown and drew the top two. Without looking at the cards he placed them on their sides and leaned one into the other at a ninety-degree angle. Then he placed a third card against the ends of the first two. Satisfied, he picked up the next card and placed it on top of the others as a roof. He then performed the same operation with some new cards, interconnecting them to the first structure.

"Yes, General, I entirely understand your reservations. I know you have political issues to consider. . . . Yes, that is correct. . . ." He glanced at his watch. "Excuse me, General, something has just come up. Could you hold the line a moment please?" Without waiting for a response, he put the call on hold and pressed down on the intercom button. The call was immediately answered.

"Yes, sir."

"Is Captain Cain out there yet?"

"Yes, sir, he's been waiting for you."

"Send him in."

He contemplated his card house for a long moment before punching the hold button and returning to his conversation. "Yes, General, I'm so sorry about the delay. You were saying?" He picked up two more cards and added on to the foundation of his building.

The door to the room opened and Capt. Parker Cain walked in. He glided across the carpet and quietly sank into one of the immense leather chairs, and waited.

"Yes, that is accurate." Pope didn't look up at the arrival. He placed another series of cards on the desk, connecting them with the others, broadening the base. "The bottom line, General, as we have discussed before, is the security of the United States of America." He spoke with conviction. "Will our nation prevail, sir? That is the very question that you need to ask yourself. If you cut my funding, will our nation prevail?"

Pope started on the second story of his structure, carefully placing cards slightly inside the perimeter of the first floor. "You have my report, sir. As you know, the potential impairment could be catastrophic. Are you prepared to make that decision, sir? Are you ready to take that burden on your shoulders?" There was a period of silence while he listened. He finished the second floor and began to work on the third. Then, "Very good, sir, a wise decision. You've done a great deed for the republic, sir. . . . Yes, and the best regards to your family, too." With that he hung up.

The colonel continued to build his pyramid of cards. Without looking up he spoke to the captain. "A buffoon. A complete buffoon. That's the problem with our system, Parker, the people chosen to lead us are those least equipped to do so."

"Yes, sir."

"Political considerations. This is just one more indication of how weak this country has become. The role of a leader is to lead. You make the decision, justify it after the fact if you must, but make the damn decision. History alone will say whether you were right or wrong. Remember that, Parker."

"Yes, sir. I will."

The colonel placed the cards with great care. "A leader's role is to determine the correct path. People are like sheep. Left to their own devices they'll wander aimlessly; lacking direction they will flounder. They want someone to tell them what to do and where to go. Society functions because of strong leaders."

He stopped working and looked up at Cain for the first time. "And here we have this buffoon talking about political considerations. He spends too much time in Washington." His face puckered with disgust. "They have to take a poll out there before they can decide to move their bowels. Have you studied history, Parker?"

"Well, some sir. I know a little about the Civil War and such. . . ."

"Roman history, Parker. Ancient Rome." He contemplated his tower again before placing two more cards on top. "Rome had a society much like ours, an empire that was the envy of its age. They had strong leaders who did what was necessary to build and expand their territory. They built a great society, they carved a majestic civilization out of a barbarous wilderness."

"Yes, sir. I know some about them."

"Their civilization lasted for a time, but they became

rich and decadent. Morally corrupt." He put another card
on top, "Much like our society."

Cain nodded.

"From talking with our scientists I understand that we
are very close to achieving our objective. The vaccine is
in the seventh generation and showing positive results.
They anticipate a breakthrough soon. We've come a long
way."

Colonel Pope took the last two cards off the desk and
with steady hands teepeed them onto the very top of his
tower. He had used the full deck, and the structure was tall
and well built. He leaned back in his chair and admired his
creation. "We are very near our destination. We can't afford to get careless at this juncture. . . . What I need to
know, Parker, are there any loose ends?" He looked Cain
straight in the eye and with his right hand pulled a single
card from the bottom of the structure; with that the whole
arrangement collapsed. Captain Cain watched with fascination as the cards sprayed across the table and skidded
onto the floor. "Remember, Parker, we can't afford any
loose ends."

THE FIVE MEN in space suits surrounded Ramon. They disconnected him from the monitors and machines. They
loosened his straps and he was allowed to stand up. It felt
so good to move, but his body wasn't accustomed to it. His
legs felt like rubber, his muscles quivered like Jell-O. A
thought flashed into his brain. *Now's the chance, RUN*.
This was an opportunity to escape; he could lash out at his
captors and flee. His brain told him to run but his body
was doing its best just trying not to collapse onto the floor.

"Take off your clothes," the short spaceman ordered.
Out of habit Ramon did as he was told. He peeled off his
soiled robe and dropped it to the ground. Standing naked
before them he felt even more exposed and vulnerable.

"This way." The short spaceman's voice rasped electronically as he turned toward the door. The others flanked Ramon and herded him toward the exit. The door slid open and they moved into the hallway.

His legs still felt weak. It was taking all his power and will just to walk forward. All thoughts of running had disappeared. He just wanted to cover his nakedness. He looked around. They were in a short corridor with walls of smooth orange-painted concrete. He tried to look behind him but his captors were obstructing his view. He saw that one of them was holding a small black device in his hand. It looked like an electric razor but he held it like a weapon.

They came to the end of the corridor. The door slid open and they entered a small chamber with another door directly in front of them—an air lock. The door behind them closed and the door in front opened. They moved through into a wide hallway. There was a loud rushing sound of air being sucked upward. They moved to the end of the hallway and through another door.

"Close your eyes, it won't hurt you," the short spaceman rasped. Ramon almost gagged; the air was filled with the fumes of disinfectant. A mist fell on him from all sides. He tried to hold his breath so that he didn't choke, but his nostrils burned and his lungs were on fire. Just as he reached the point where he could stand no more, the spray stopped. They stepped through another set of doors into a new room.

He opened his eyes again and gasped for breath. One of the spacemen was staring at him, the eyes barely visible through the mask. "Shower," he said, motioning to a stall off to the side of the hall. It looked like a normal shower stall but Ramon felt uneasy. He thought back to stories he had heard of the Jews being given showers in the concentration camps in Nazi Germany. *It would be so easy,* he thought, *they could kill me before I had a chance to resist.* But it didn't make sense. If they had wanted him dead they would have killed him already. He was still alive for a reason. He moved into the stall and turned on the water.

The water was hot and soothing. His muscles relaxed while seeming to firm at the same time. He washed the accumulated grime off his body. The oils, the sweat, the stench. He rubbed himself with soap from head to toe and let the hard stream of water cascade over his skin. Breathing in the steam, he felt renewed and strong again. He didn't even care that they were watching him. Something was happening, but he was here for a purpose. They wanted him alive, at least for now. All he could do was to wait and hope for the best. After a time he turned off the water.

One of the spacemen handed Ramon a towel. He dried himself off. Another of the spacemen thrust a robe at him. "Put this on." He was happy to comply. It was just a thin cotton hospital robe but being dressed made him feel better.

His captors flanked him again and herded him forward. A sign by the door said that they were entering Quarantine Number Two. They stepped through into an open rectangular area with doors on three sides and a corridor going off on the fourth side. The rooms were all numbered and had darkened windows looking into them. "Number three is open," the short man said in his electronic drone.

They moved over to the room marked number three. The short man swiped a card through and the door slid open. Ramon was pushed forward into the darkened room. He could just make out the outline of a bed, a chair, and some equipment of some sort.

One of the spacemen flipped a switch and the room was flooded with light. Ramon saw that this was an ordinary room with an ordinary bed. But there was a movement on the bed. It was only a second before the guards realized that something was wrong. Someone was in the room. The figure on the bed had sat all the way up before the spacemen reacted. "Out! Wrong room, get the hell out!" Even through the electronic crackle Ramon could sense the panic in their voices.

They tried to push him out of the room, but he resisted as he stared at the figure on the bed. It was an image from a nightmare. The man was tall but skeletally thin, his skin covered by oozing purple boils. The room had the putrid smell of waste, disinfectant and decaying flesh. "Please . . . please help me," the man croaked pleadingly. Ramon was in a state of shock. There was something about the man, something about his dead eyes and huge misshapen nose that seemed so familiar.

The spacemen shoved, Ramon stumbled out of the room, and the door slid shut behind them. They were back in the hallway. In a flash it hit Ramon why the monstrous figure had looked so familiar. Yes, he looked very different than when Ramon had last seen him, but there was no doubt. It was *him*. It was Billy Dale Burke. *But Billy Dale was dead*. He'd been executed a week before Ramon. But then *he* was supposed to be dead, too, which meant that this was to be his fate also. Adrenaline surged through his body. He snapped. All the fear and anger that he had been living with for so long exploded in his brain.

One of his captors grabbed him by the arm, trying to move him toward a different room. Ramon shook the captor off and came back hard with his elbow, hitting the guard in the stomach and emptying him of breath. Before the others could react Ramon was on him. He knocked the guard against the wall and hit his head with his fists. Fast hard shots. The first hit cracked the plastic of the visor in his helmet. The second shot knocked the headgear halfway off his head exposing the guard to the dangerous air. As the guard fell to the floor, Ramon pivoted toward the others. They had been slow to react. They weren't ex-

pecting the viciousness of the attack, and they seemed
stunned and frightened.

"Grab him!" the short one shouted. One of the guards
tried to grab Ramon from the side, but the space suit was
too bulky and he was too tentative. Ramon sidestepped
him, grabbed onto his suit, and threw him into another
guard. They both tumbled to the ground. Ramon stepped
forward to attack, hitting and kicking. For the moment
there were only two left on their feet and Ramon was a
whirlwind. He was fast and brutal. He was fighting for his
life and he was ready to destroy anything in his way. He
grabbed the short guard, hit him once on the side of the
head, then grabbed for his headgear, trying to yank it off.
His head, too, if need be.

The last standing guard quickly stepped behind
Ramon, holding the black device in his hand. He swung it
over to the small of Ramon's back and pressed the trigger.
A spark, an arc of blue electricity jumped from the small
device to Ramon, who instantly let go of his hold,
straightened up, arched his back, and dropped to the floor.

The fallen guards got to their feet and joined their com-
rades. They looked down at the floor. The last guard lay
dazed on the ground. His mask was off and he was breathing in the unfiltered air. Ramon lay next to him, shaking
with spasms on the cold cement floor, flopping like a
landed trout.

7

THE ROUTINE WAS always the same on execution nights. Dr. Meeks would arrive early and check all the equipment to make sure that it was working properly. Then he'd move the van into position near the loading dock and make sure that the exit route was clear. When that was all accomplished, he would personally prepare the chemicals for the lethal injection machine. The proportions had to be exact. Too much and he'd have a dead body on his hands; too little, and the body would show signs of life. Either outcome was unacceptable. The mixture had to be precise.

Leonard Stoats, the lead technician, was supposed to be in charge of setting up and running the machine. The machine's manufacturer had trained and certified him in its use. Stoats had only been at the Walls Unit for three months. Prior to that his resume stated that he had been on the death row staff for the State of Florida. His time was actually spent closer to home, working as a sergeant at the Lyndon B. Johnson Army Installation. Captain Parker Cain had taken a special interest in Stoats and had pegged him for special duty and accelerated advancement. As was the agreement, Stoats deferred to Meeks in all matters. This was to be their eighteenth execution together.

Tonight Meeks had finished all his tasks early. He was in his office writing out the preliminary information on the death certificate for that night's subject, when Stoats came into the room. Stoats was young, athletic, and seemed perpetually cheerful. Each of those qualities by itself was enough to irritate Meeks.

Stoats grabbed a chair, flipped it around, and sat down straddling it backward. "Hey, Doc. How're we lookin' tonight?"

Meeks ignored him and continued with his paperwork. In the week that had elapsed since the last corpse was delivered, he had given the matter a good deal of thought. He had been threatened. Looking back on the conversation with Cain, he was sure of that. Who were they to threaten him? After all he had done for them, too. Just thinking about it made him angry. He felt an involuntary twitch in his droopy eye. He steadied himself by force of will. It wouldn't do to show his emotion. That was a sign of weakness. Meeks put down his pen and shook a new cigarette out of his pack. He lit up and sucked the smoke deep into his lungs. He acknowledged Stoats for the first time by blowing the stream of smoke straight back into his face.

Stoats just smiled good-naturedly, blinking back the smoke. "What do you say, Doc? We rock and rollin' tonight?"

Meeks leaned back in his chair with a forced calm. "What time is it?"

Stoats glanced down at his watch. "Eleven o'clock. One hour to show time."

Meeks took another draw on his Marlboro before responding. "Everything's set to go. I've got some paperwork that I need to catch up on. You go down and look important. I'll be there in a little while."

Stoats shrugged. "Sure, Doc. Whatever you think." He flashed his smile again. "I'll be seein' you down there." He slid the chair back toward the corner as he got up and left the room.

Meeks seemed to be in deep thought as he finished up his cigarette. When it had burned down almost to the filter he stubbed it out and stood up. He opened his black medical bag and pulled out a hypodermic needle. He removed the safety cap and placed the needle on his desk. Above the desk was a small safe. He withdrew the key from his pocket and opened the safe. Inside there were two wire racks with several rows of small glass vials. He looked through the vials until he found the one he was looking for. He took it out and closed the safe again. Placing the vial on his desk, he picked up the needle, pushed the tip through the rubber stopper, and pulled back on the plunger to load.

When the hypodermic was full, he tossed the empty vial into the trash can and placed the safety tip back onto the needle. Meeks put the loaded needle into a compartment at the top of his bag and stuffed some papers into another compartment. He then picked up the bag and left the office, locking the door behind him.

The execution went just as planned. At twelve-thirty-two Meeks checked the body and announced the official time of death. An hour later the warden had left, the witnesses were dispersed, and Meeks and Stoats had moved the prisoner's body back to the room adjacent to the loading van. They wrestled the body into the green canvas body bag. "God damn, Doc, there's got to be a better way to do this," Stoats said.

Meeks was silent as he lit up another cigarette. He took a few long puffs before speaking. "Go check out the van; make sure we're ready to go."

"I thought you did that already."

"Do it again. You need to make sure it's clear before we just wheel him out."

Stoats nodded his head, opened the door, and stepped outside. Meeks opened his medical bag and withdrew the loaded hypodermic. He took off the safety cap and slipped the needle into his side pocket.

A moment later Stoats came back in. "No problem. It's all clear." Meeks took a last puff on his cigarette, threw his butt down, and crushed it under his heel. "Let's do it then."

They propped the door open, and together wheeled the gurney through the door and out onto the loading dock. The doors to the van were spread wide open. The van had one long shelf on the left side for placing the body, a space in between and then another bench that opened up for storage underneath. They moved the gurney alongside the shelf in the van and used a board to position the body on the shelf. When they were finished they moved the board out of the way. Meeks picked up a handful of bungee cords and tossed them over to Stoats. "Strap him in."

Stoats bent over the body near the head and began to connect a cord from the side of the shelf to the van wall, holding the body in place. Dr. Meeks reached into his pocket and withdrew the hypodermic. Quickly, he stepped in close behind Stoats and jammed the needle into the muscle at the back of his neck. He hit the plunger in with his other hand releasing the contents.

Stoats cried out. He grabbed his neck and began to turn, an expression of shock on his face. Meeks stepped backward. Stoats pulled the empty needle from his neck and looked at it as if it was some strange kind of bug. Then he dropped it and stepped toward Meeks with his hands out as if to throttle him. He managed one step forward before he dropped to the ground unconscious.

Meeks stepped forward again and gave Stoats a vicious kick to the ribs. Stoats didn't move. Meeks kicked out again, this time connecting with the head, which flopped over to the side and bounced off the van floor. Meeks bent down and checked to make sure Stoats was still breathing, then he grabbed on to his feet, pivoted him, and pulled the body to the back of the van. He reached into his medical bag and pulled out a roll of duct tape. He yanked Stoats's arms behind his back and wrapped the wrists tight with the tape. Then he wrapped some more tape around Stoats's ankles and knees.

Satisfied that Stoats was not a problem, he took the bungee cords and finished strapping the other body into place. When that body was secured, Meeks stepped out of the van and glanced around the area to make sure it was clear. Everything was still as death. He closed the van doors, grabbed his medical bag, and hopped down from the dock and climbed into the cab. The keys were already in the ignition. He started the engine and slowly pulled away. He signed out with the guard at the gate then slowly made his way through town taking Route 35 heading north.

He didn't speed up once he was on the highway. He checked the side-view mirrors regularly, looking to see if he was being followed. The traffic was light, nothing but trucks speeding through; they shook the van as they blew past. He crept along at just past forty miles per hour. About fifteen miles out of Huntsville there was nothing behind him but the night sky. He pulled off at a country road heading toward the east. He drove about two hundred feet then pulled off the road, facing the highway. He situated the van so that he had a full view of anyone going past or pulling off the main road. He cut the engine, turned off the lights, and rolled down his window.

Meeks lit up a new cigarette and silently smoked. The air was filled with the sound of crickets. Every now and then a truck zoomed past on the highway. Meeks lit up another cigarette from the glow of his last and waited. After about fifteen minutes a car pulled off the highway onto the country road. Meeks tensed, staring at the car. He reached under the seat and pulled out his pistol. But as the car barreled past him he saw that it was a pickup truck pulling a horse trailer. Nothing to worry about. It didn't even slow down. Meeks waited another five minutes before he started up the van and pulled back on the road heading east.

He drove through the night, meandering down mostly two-lane country roads, steadily heading toward the northeast. It was still dark when he pulled off a country road and onto a main highway. He drove another twelve miles till the road intersected with another highway. There, he pulled off the exit and into a large truck stop. He moved past huge Navistars and Peterbilts with their diesel engines idling roughly. He drove the van up a long ramp to the auto bay.

By the gas pumps, he stopped the van and turned off the engine. Getting out of the van he stretched his legs and shook his arms, trying to shake off the fatigue of the long ride. He listened by the back door, but all was quiet. Meeks lit up a fresh cigarette as he filled the gas tank.

When he was finished, he locked up the van, walked into the truck stop, paid the bill in cash, and went into the trucker's lounge. Along one wall was a row of booths. Each was enclosed with a stool to sit on, a pay phone, and a glass door for privacy. Meeks went into a booth at the end and closed the door behind him. He pulled some change out of his pocket and fed several coins into the slot.

He punched in a number and waited for the line to be connected. A moment later he heard a male voice at the other end: "Unit 803."

"I need to talk with Colonel Pope," Meeks said.

There was a long pause before the voice answered, "Colonel Pope is unavailable. Who is calling please?"

"It doesn't matter who is calling. The colonel will want to talk with me. Why don't you stop being irritating and go wake him up."

There was another long pause before the voice spoke again, "I'm sorry, sir, but that isn't possible. Who is calling?"

"Tell him that waking the sleeping is better than waking the dead. He'll want to talk with me."

There was another long pause, then the voice said, "One moment, sir. I'll connect you."

Meeks was put on hold for over two minutes. He was sure that they were trying to trace his call. A new voice came on the line; this one was thick from being wakened from a sleep but still spoke with precise enunciation. "Who is this?"

"Hello, Lucian. I hope I didn't wake you."

"Meeks? Is that you?"

"Who else would it be?"

"Why are you calling, Conrad? Is something wrong?"

Meeks pulled out a cigarette and rolled it between his fingers. "On the contrary, Lucian, nothing is wrong at all. Everything is just . . . rosy. You contracted for one body and I'm bringing you two."

There was silence on the other end for a long moment, "I don't know what you're talking about, Meeks. You are wasting my time."

"Then let me help you to understand. I have some pictures, two live subjects, and the documents that link them to you. This could make for some very interesting reading. . . ."

"What are you saying, Meeks?"

"I'm saying that the price has just gone up considerably. I'll be talking with you soon to let you know how to handle the payoff. I plan to live to enjoy it."

"Wait, Conrad . . ."

Meeks hung up the phone. He smiled as he popped the cigarette into his mouth. He looked both ways down the hallway, then left the booth and made his way back outside to the van. He again listened by the rear door, it was still quiet inside. He was feeling good as he got back in the van and pulled out onto the interstate. They'd be looking for him now, he knew that. Maybe they'd even traced the call, but it didn't matter. Everything was planned out. If they were going to search for him they'd have a lot of ground to cover and before they even got close he'd be on to phase two.

He drove on, moving from road to road, always northeast. Dawn was breaking when he pulled off the highway onto a two-lane access road. He was now in the lake district near the Louisiana border. He drove for a while before turning off on a small blacktop road. A faded sign for cabins to rent pointed the way. A mile farther he turned onto a dirt road. It wound through some pine woods for another quarter of a mile before coming to a clearing.

In the clearing was an old dilapidated cabin with a corrugated tin roof and an ancient Coke machine on the front porch. Meeks stopped the van and got out. As he was walking toward the front door, a grizzled old man came out of the cabin. He was wearing coveralls with no shirt and was missing two front teeth. "You that city guy that called?" he said as he scratched himself.

"That's right." Meeks pulled some cash out of his pocket. "How much do I owe you?"

The old man looked him over. "You here for the fishin'?"

"No, I'm just here for the peace and quiet." He peeled two hundred dollars off and handed the cash to the old man who looked at it greedily.

"It's too damn hot to be fishin' no how." He took the bills and crumpled them into his pocket. "You can have the cabin down by the end of the road. It's real quiet down that away." He nodded toward the woods. "Nobody else is about this time anyways." He pulled a key out of his pocket and flipped it over to Meeks.

"Good." Meeks pocketed the key and turned back to the van.

"You gonna be here long? If you gonna be here longer'n a week, I need some more money."

Meeks opened the van door without turning back. "I'll be gone in a couple of days."

He drove the van past the clearing, around a curve, and down a dirt track, passing two branches of the trail that led up to other cabins. A little farther on the road dead-ended at another run-down cabin. Meeks parked the van between the house and a large tree. He got out and looked around. All was still and quiet. He went to the house, unlocked the door, and glanced inside. It was a one-room shack that smelled of mildew and damp earth. It looked as if it hadn't seen use since the 1930s. Meeks smiled. This would be fine for his purposes.

He walked back to the van and fished the keys out of his pocket. Everything was going just as planned. In two days he would have enough money to live out the rest of his life in luxury, and a new identity to enjoy it with. He unlocked the back of the van and pulled the right door open.

As he opened the door he saw that the bench on the

passenger side had been raised, exposing the empty storage section. Meeks paused. Had he lifted the bench? He didn't think so, but he must have.

He was reaching down to flip the latch on the facing door when he felt the pressure on his neck. There was a jolt to his shoulder and suddenly he was spun around with his back to the van. Something was around his neck, pulling, cutting into the skin and choking off his air supply. He grabbed for his throat but couldn't grip anything. He tried to reach behind him but he only grabbed air. He felt the first edge of panic. He couldn't breathe. No matter how hard he struggled it was no use, his attacker was too strong. He felt his life slipping away. Struggling, he managed to turn a little. And then he understood. The last thing he saw before his eyes closed for the final time was his own face, reflected back in the mirrored sunglasses.

LENA DRYER USUALLY got what she wanted in due time. A week after the execution, she had flown to New York to interview for a job with *Newsworld* magazine. The meeting went just as well as she could have hoped for. She met with Allen Edwards, the assistant editor, in his office overlooking the Manhattan skyline and they talked for more than three hours. It turned out that they had some mutual acquaintances in the business. He was enthusiastic about her work and felt that Lena would be a good fit for the magazine. The job would initially be background reporting in the lifestyle section—in time there would be opportunities to move up front into hard news. But after all this was the big time, and with her talent, he assured her that it wouldn't take long.

This job was everything that she had been working toward, but Lena surprised herself by telling Edwards that she needed some time to think about it. He told her that he'd hold the job for a few days but he needed an answer soon.

On the plane ride home she replayed the interview in her mind and tried to figure out why she hadn't committed. The money was great, the job was prestigious, she'd be back East again, and future prospects were far better than they could ever be in Texas. If it wasn't a dream job, it was close to it.

But she felt a vague sense of unease. A feeling that her work was incomplete. In the week since the execution she had yet to get a full night's sleep. After a long day's work, sleep usually came easy. But now, she would lie in bed tossing and turning as images of the execution played over in her mind. The hands of the technician strapping the prisoner onto the gurney, the hum of the machinery, the doctor coming in to the room to pronounce the death. And most of all the memory of Ramon—his haunting eyes staring at her.

Lena knew that she'd get over it. One of her first news assignments had been a traffic accident where a semi truck had rear-ended a car containing a family on their way to a beach vacation. It was a fiery wreck and everyone in the car died. Lena had arrived on the scene just as the bodies of the children were being loaded into the ambulances. It took her a long time to get over that, but she did. It was just one of the perils of the job. You either learned to deal with it or you got out. Only this felt different. It felt like unfinished business. Ramon was dead but maybe the story wasn't. And if he was innocent it was still news. Maybe.

She went over her options as the jet carried her back to Austin. By the time they landed she had made up her mind. The only reason for staying was emotional, and that would surely pass. This job was a true opportunity. It was what she had been waiting for. She made up her mind to call Edwards and accept the next day.

The next morning, Lena had a bounce to her step as she entered the *Star* building. "Good morning, Mike," she greeted the guard in the lobby before taking the elevator to the offices on the eleventh floor. The elevators in the building always moved in slow motion. Normally that was a source of irritation, but today it just made her smile. She got off on her floor, walked past the receptionist, and made her way through the sea of cubicles to her unit in the middle of the floor. As she settled in, she listened to the sounds around her. The low hum of the computers, the chattering of fingers on keyboards, the buzz of conversations. Someone in a cube nearby was on the phone having a muted argument with her husband. Just the normal sounds of a busy office. In a way Lena was going to miss the place.

She looked at her watch. It was after nine o'clock in New York. Would Edwards be in yet? She picked up the phone but immediately put it back down. She didn't feel comfortable calling from work. It was probably too early anyway. It would be better to call later; she didn't want to appear anxious. Instead, Lena decided to get a cup of coffee.

The newsroom ran on caffeine. There were coffee stations located at strategic areas around the floor. As she was walking toward the nearest station, Jack Van Russell, the managing editor of the paper, stepped into the passageway. Van Russell was tall and lanky with a full head of thick white hair. A transplanted Midwesterner, he had comfortably adjusted to being a Texan. The suits he wore were fashionable but always accompanied by cowboy boots and a bolo tie. A huge pair of horns from a longhorn steer dominated the wall behind the desk in his office. "Lena, I was just about to come looking for you. I've got something I wanted to run by you," he greeted her.

"Well . . . I need to talk with you, too, Jack."

"Good, let's walk back to my office." He took Lena's elbow and steered her down the hall. "I just got some bad news. You know Bill Wentworth?"

"Our Washington correspondent? Sure."

"Right, of course you do. He's run into some kind of personal situation and he's going to be taking a leave of absence. He'll be leaving at the end of next month. The plan is that he'll be off for six months, maybe more—to tell the truth, I'm not sure that he'll even be back."

"Really?"

"Anyway, I've talked it over with the board and we all agree, you're the person we want there."

"The Washington bureau?" Lena stopped in the hall-way, her eyes registering her surprise. It had never crossed her mind that there could be a real future here at the *Star*. The Washington assignment was a jewel—an opportunity that she'd never thought possible. It was definitely a step up, but it was still with the *Star*—and the *Star* would never have the prestige of any of the bigger East Coast publications. Logic said that New York was still the way to go—in the long run the news magazine would be the better move. Logic told her to go, but her intuition said no.

"I'm not saying this is permanent. But it is high pro-file. I know you were hoping for more ink," Van Russell went on.

"Great, that sounds just great."

"You'll be doing some campaign coverage, too. Election season is just around the corner and I'd like to do some profiles of the candidates." They came to the end of the corridor. The executive offices were all at the perimeter of the building, with window access. They turned right and headed toward his office. "We'll need you to get out there pretty quick," Van Russell continued.

"Right, of course."

He opened the door to his office. "Now it's your turn, what did you want to talk with me about?"

"Nothing. Nothing at all." Lena was already making plans. Washington would be a nice change of scene.

8

THE OFFICERS' CLUB was a small room in a spare Quonset hut located near the center of the base about half a mile away from the main building. It wasn't much to look at, an empty room with a bar on one side, a jukebox in the corner, a pool table on the other side, and several clusters of tables scattered throughout. The club was popular. Base leaves had been scarce and this was an accepted way to pass the free time. Fridays were always the busiest time and tonight the club was packed.

Charley Green leaned against the wall by the pool table waiting for his turn to play. He took a gulp of his Lone Star. He was on edge. It seemed like everyone was. Stir-crazy. They'd been cooped up on the base for too long. He looked around the room; out of about one hundred people gathered, there were only about five women. And two of them were majors' wives. Too much time without female companionship was bound to take its toll; it was no wonder that he was tense. He hadn't been there nearly as long as most of them, but it felt like ages since he'd been anywhere else.

Green distractedly peeled the label off of his bottle as his mind wandered. Not that long ago his life had looked very different. In some ways he'd had a hard life. His parents had died when he was twelve and his grandparents had raised him. They were old and set in their ways and he had chaffed at their control, couldn't wait for the chance to escape. He joined the army right after high school. It was a good fit. For the first time in his life he felt at home. He quickly advanced to the rank of sergeant. He showed leadership ability and was chosen for Officers' Candidate School. His career path was set. He was a lifer in the service.

Before coming to the Johnson Installation, he was stationed in San Diego, California. His job was a breeze and he had lots of opportunities to enjoy the fresh air and sunshine. His social life was set, too. Ellen Chantras, his girlfriend for over four years, had followed him out from New Jersey. It had long been assumed that they would be married. When she came out they made it official and even set a date. But even as they planned for their future together, he was looking for ways to get out. His life was quiet and orderly—too quiet. He was bored out of his mind. Without saying anything to Ellen, he had begun to explore his options, checking out postings overseas, looking for something that promised at least a change. Maybe even danger and excitement.

When the opportunity for a transfer to the Johnson Installation had come, he jumped for it. The assignment required a top security clearance, and several interviews as well as a full psychological examination. But the word was that it was looked at favorably on career evaluations and the pay was set at combat levels. And it promised mystery and excitement. Ellen was devastated by the breakup, but the truth was that the relationship had been over for a long time before he made it official.

It had been more than four months since he left Ellen and California behind. At the time it had been a relief. His early days at the base had been exciting; it seemed that he was part of a great undertaking, something historic. Even the secrecy was appealing. At first. Later it began to gnaw at him. What exactly were they doing there? There were plenty of rumors, each one wilder than the last. Green didn't buy into them. He felt that they were here for a reason. The army knew what it was doing and whatever was going on was intended for the greater good. Or at least he hoped so. But even if it wasn't, what did it matter to him? He was after all an officer in the United States Army. His job was to follow orders. He was in no position to question a superior's order. After all, *they* were seeing the forests and he was stuck down at tree level. Still, he had to admit that it did bother him.

And lately he had been getting pulled into it deeper and deeper. The night after the poker game he had received a call from Captain Cain. There was a special job lined up for him. It was another delivery, another body that had to go down to the fifth level quarantine area. The next day there were three more. And there were four more the week after that. Green didn't know where the people were coming from, but in each case they were sedated at the time of arrival. They all appeared healthy though some seemed to be bloated and reeking of alcohol. The subjects—that's how they were referred to—were a mixed group, ranging in age from young to old and mostly male, though there were two women in the last group. What happened to the subjects after he delivered them he didn't know. He tried to tell himself that he didn't care what happened. It wasn't his problem. But it was never far from his thoughts. Whatever was happening to them, he was now involved.

For some reason he had been chosen and it was too late

to have second thoughts. He was part of it. There was no way that he could transfer out now. He was here for the long run. Cain had given Green an access card of his own, so he was now granted admittance to many areas that had previously been restricted. When Green wasn't delivering subjects, he acted as a courier, delivering sealed envelopes and packages from one section of the building to another. By now he knew most of the complex so well that he could get around it easily. Nevertheless, there were a few areas that were still closed to him. That added to his uneasiness. Half in, half out. It made his imagination spin in overdrive, wondering what was really happening in these closed-off areas.

Green finished his beer and set down the empty bottle. There were still two other games before it was his turn to play pool. Rev Tanner was playing now, and the way he was shooting it was a sure bet he'd be holding the table for a long time. Green looked around the room again. Rooster Stepman was sitting alone at a table near the bar. It looked like he'd been drinking heavy for some time; empty glasses littered his table. Green was careful not to make eye contact. He'd been doing his best to avoid Stepman over the past few weeks, even going so far as to skip the last two poker games.

"Hey, Tuna," Rev Tanner called out. He held his empty beer bottle up in the air with one hand, and his pool stick in the other. "How 'bout a refill my man? It's your round."

Green nodded his head, moved toward the bar, and waited at the end of the line for the lone bartender to get to him. He felt like calling it a night, one more beer and it was time to go. The smoke was beginning to bother his eyes and he was bored. There was really nothing going on worth sticking around for, and if he stayed he'd end up getting drunk and feeling sick in the morning. He tried to relax as he waited. The bar was noisy with the chatter of dozens of conversations competing with the sound of a crooner on the jukebox.

He glanced around the bar as he waited in line. He was now nearly next to Stepman's table. He tried to turn so that he wouldn't make eye contact, but it was too late.

Stepman stood up and stared straight at Green, his face set in anger. "What's a matter, Green, you afraid to look at me?" Stepman spit the words out.

Green was caught by surprise, "Who, me?" he looked around to see if someone else was behind him. There wasn't. Stepman was talking to him.

"Yeah, you, ya asshole! You got some nerve, pal. I'll bet you been talking about me, saying things behind my back." Stepman was about six inches shorter than Green, but with his chin and chest jutting forward and his hands clenching into fists he was intimidating.

"No, sir, you've got the wrong guy. I haven't said a word about you, sir." Green stood his ground.

Stepman swayed slightly. "The wrong guy, my ass. You were always a little weasel. I could tell that when I first met you. I don't know why I thought we could bring you in."

Green realized that Stepman was drunker than he had at first thought. His eyes were red dots and although he was talking clearly, it seemed that he was having trouble standing up straight. "I'm sorry if there's been a misunderstanding, sir. Maybe we could discuss it tomorrow when we're both sober." Green turned away, back toward the bar.

At that, Stepman exploded. He launched himself at Green, his head down as he charged forward trying to tackle the taller man. Green saw the movement out of the corner of his eye. He pivoted toward Stepman and stepped back. By pure reaction he caught Stepman by the shoulder as he was coming by and shoved him downward, sticking his leg out to trip him at the same time. Rooster Stepman fell to the floor with a thud, grunting as he hit the concrete.

Green reached down to help Stepman to his feet. Stepman slapped Green's hand away and tried to push himself up from the floor. It seemed that all the conversation in the room had stopped and everyone was looking over to see what had happened.

Stepman pushed himself to his knees, and he had one hand in his pocket as if searching for car keys. "I'll tell ya, pal." He looked as if he was about to fall back to the ground. "I'll tell ya, you couldn't do that again if you had a million years." Stepman staggered to his feet. He seemed more subdued now, and his hand was still fumbling around in his right pocket.

Stepman swayed as if to the music. He spoke quietly. "I'll tell ya, I'm so sick of this place I could puke." Some of the people standing nearby moved back farther just in case he was true to his word. He took another step toward Green, then seemed to lose his footing and started to lurch forward. Green caught him just as it appeared that he would hit the floor.

Green put his arm around Stepman's shoulders and steadied him. "Are you all right, sir?"

"God, I hate this place," Stepman mumbled to himself as he shook Green's arm away. He suddenly yanked his hand out of his pocket triumphantly holding a single key, but in the process everything in his pocket seemed to spring out and hit the floor. Coins, crumpled bills, and match packs skated across the floor.

Green and several other people bent down and began to pick the objects up. Green had picked up several coins when he saw the flash of light reflecting off of something near the edge of the bar. At first he thought it was a credit card. As he reached for it he realized that the shiny black plastic card was an access card. Green knew that Stepman wore the purple slash emblem, a sign that he had clear-

ance for entry in the most restricted areas of the base.
Green glanced behind him. No one was paying him any
attention. Instinctively he slid the card into his pocket and
switched it with his own.

THE DOOR WAS marked with a large red sign stating Restricted Entry. Lt. Charley Green looked behind him; the
hall was empty. He slipped the stolen access card from his
pocket, looked at it for a moment, then slid it through the
scanner. The door opened with a *swoosh* and Green
walked through.

Green had never been in this section of the complex
before. He was on the fourth level underground at the
northeast quadrant of the building. His heart was pounding. He had no authority to be where he was, in an unauthorized section of the installation with a stolen access
card. If he was caught, the best he could hope for would
to be thrown in the brig. If he wasn't so lucky there would
be a court-martial followed by an execution for espionage.
And all for a vague uneasiness that he couldn't shake. A
compulsion over which he had no control. He had no idea
what he was looking for or what he would do if he did find
something.

The sweat welled up under his arms as he walked.
Upon first waking in the morning, Green had had second
thoughts about keeping Stepman's card. His half-baked
plan of investigating the unauthorized sections of the
complex seemed dangerous and stupid now that he was
completely sober. That morning, the first thing he had
done was to search out Rooster Stepman and try to give
him back his card. He intended to explain that it had been
picked up by mistake. That would have ended everything
right there. However, when he had reached Stepman's
post, Green was surprised to learn that Stepman wasn't
there. He had left the base that morning for a few days of
R and R. The captain manning his booth had confided that

Stepman had been under a lot of pressure recently. Green walked away with mixed feelings. Whether he wanted it or not, he would have the card for the next few days.

The hallway walls on this level were painted yellow. He walked cautiously through the corridor, looking in every direction for any sign of movement. The hallway turned to the right. His heart was beating hard as he poked his head around the corner. The hall was empty. Green made the turn and continued walking. The only sounds were the click of his boots against the tile and the hum of the ventilation system. His stomach churned as he moved forward. At the end of the hallway he had two choices— the hallway teed off with entrances to the right and to the left. He paused for a moment trying to decide which route to take, then arbitrarily picked the door on the right. He glanced behind him one more time and then turned back to the door.

"Open sesame." He passed the card through the scanner. The door slid open and he moved through onto an observation deck. Green quickly surveyed the room. It was just a narrow platform that ran down the perimeter of the adjoining room. There was a single row of seats looking down on a large white room below. He was cut off from the room below by a thick sheet of glass, a window that extended the length of the room. He turned to look out the window, and with a shock he realized that there were people down in the room below. He dropped down out of sight, his heart thumping so loudly he was sure they could hear it.

After a moment he poked his head back up and looked down. No one below had noticed him. He scrunched down in the corner so that he could look down without showing himself. The room below was white and brightly lit. There were three figures there—two men wearing yellow rubber biohazard suits were standing over a table on which the third figure lay.

The third figure was naked and unmistakably dead. His lifeless body was covered with purple sores and had a long incision down the middle of his torso exposing the body cavity. The internal organs were open to view. They appeared blackish and swollen. The face was so bloated that Green could hardly make out the features. One of the men in the rubber suits reached into the cavity with one hand and grabbed on to one of the organs, and it seemed to shift in his hand, more liquid than solid. With his other hand the man went underneath the organ and carefully cut it away, disconnecting it from the body. The man pulled out what looked like the liver. Green turned away at this point. He felt bile rising into his throat and he had to cover his mouth as he fought back the urge to retch.

Green stayed a little longer. Long enough to be unmistakably sure that what he was watching was an autopsy — and that the corpse below him was one of the men that he had wheeled down to quarantine, or someone like him. The men working on the corpse were wearing the rubber suits for a reason: The man must have died of some kind of contagious disease. Could he have had the disease before they brought him here? Green supposed it was possible, but he didn't think so. If he had, and they knew it, they would have isolated him when they brought him in. Anyone who came in contact with him would have had to wear the full hazmat suits, and that hadn't happened.

It seemed so bizarre yet it had to be true. He wondered, who was the corpse? What kind of man had he been? And where were they getting these . . . subjects? And most important of all, why were they doing it? And what if he was wrong? He didn't know any of the answers, but if it was what he thought, he didn't want to have anything to do with it. By the time he slipped out from the deck and back into the nonrestricted area, he had made his decision. He knew that he had to find out more.

•   •   •

THE COLORS ON the TV were wrong. On the monitor, Ramon's flesh appeared to be the color of lime Jell-O with orange slices for contrast. He paced across his room, walking from one wall past his bed to the other side. Then he'd turn around and do it again. The image came from a video monitor in the corner of a white lab room.

A short white-coated scientist reached over and tried to adjust the color but the best he could get was a fluorescent shade of pink with yellow undertones. He gave up and sat back down next to Colonel Pope, who watched with fascination, as if this was grand entertainment.

"He does this every day?" Pope asked as he steepled his fingers to his chin. He was sitting on a plastic and metal frame chair that was dwarfed by his immense bulk.

"Constantly, he's moving all the time. Walking, exercising . . . when he's not sleeping he's always moving," the scientist replied.

"And he appears healthy?"

"Yes, sir, very healthy. We try to check his vital signs several times a day . . . he doesn't cooperate so we have a hard time, but he's very healthy. I wish I had his energy."

"Has he actively resisted you again?" Pope shifted his weight; the small chair creaked in protest.

"No, not actively. We go in with a full security detail. I think he's waiting for an opportunity though. He's very dangerous."

"Yes, yes, he is." Pope crossed his legs. "It was a shame about Jenkins." They were both silent for a moment as they thought about Jenkins, who had been exposed to the air in the quarantine when Ramon had fought back. Jenkins had been placed in a quarantine unit for observation. Within two days of exposure he had begun to exhibit symptoms of the disease. Within a week he was dead.

On the television screen Ramon stopped his pacing, dropped to the floor, and began to do push-ups, his body moving up and down with the regularity of a machine. Colonel Pope uncrossed his legs and shifted again, clearly uncomfortable in the flimsy chair. "Is it safe to have him unrestrained?"

"We take every precaution," the scientist replied. "From a scientific standpoint, it's important to allow him normal movement. We want this to be as close to a real situation as possible considering the limitations of the experiment."

"Yes, I can understand that." Pope watched the monitor with fascination. Ramon was now doing sit-ups. "But put the straps back on anyway. He makes me nervous."

The scientist nodded his assent "Yes, sir."

"How long has it been now?" Pope asked.

"He was signed into the facility twenty-one days ago. He was given the vaccine at that time. Three days later he was inoculated with the virus."

"So it's been eighteen days. And there have been no symptoms?"

"No, sir. Nothing visible. Before this, the longest that a subject has gone has been ten days, but in that case he was exhibiting symptoms within four days. It just took longer till termination."

"I see. What do the blood tests show?" The chair creaked again as Pope leaned in toward the TV.

"Positive for antibodies."

"Is he contagious?"

"No, sir. He has the antibodies but he's not producing any live virus."

Pope pushed himself to his feet and stretched out to his full height. "Tell me, Doctor, do you think this is it?"

The scientist thought for a moment before replying. "With one subject it's too early to tell . . . but I think we may be onto something. I think this may be it."

Colonel Pope nodded. "Good. We have three more subjects coming in tomorrow. Give them the same batch so we can compare results." He stared at the TV monitor. Ramon had now returned to pacing the room. "Give this subject another forty-eight hours to see if he develops any symptoms. If not, terminate him and give me the results of the autopsy." Pope reached over and shut the TV off. The picture faded to darkness.

AS HE WENT through his duties over the course of the day, Charley Green felt like a traitor. These men that he worked with were friends; they shared the same hopes and fears that he did. Living together day in and day out, experiencing the same hardships, forged a certain kind of closeness. It was an "us against them" mentality that helped strengthen their bond.

As he made his rounds, Green smiled and made small talk with the other soldiers but inside he felt cold. If his suspicions were correct, they were all involved in a criminal enterprise. A man would have to be blind not to see the signs. This was clearly an abnormal operation.

Each soldier had to deal with the situation in his own way. Some chose to ignore the irregularities of the base and pretend that it was routine to have unconscious bodies entering a military establishment. Others went along with the peculiarities because that was their assignment and they were just following orders. But the "good soldier" defense could only go so far. In the end a man was accountable for the decisions that he made. And Green knew that he couldn't go along if they were engaged in corruption.

But what if he was wrong? If there was a legitimate reason for the things that he had seen, then he was the one in the wrong. In his gut Green was sure he was right. But he needed proof. The proof would be found in the network computer system.

Green always had a knack with computers; they ran on a pure form of logic, which he appreciated. His first experience with computers was back in high school. It happened when he was in school after hours serving a detention. Students on detention were normally placed in the school lunchroom. But on this particular day the lunchroom was being painted, so the students were put into the computer lab. The computer lab was actually just a large room with two ancient Apple II E computers, but it was all his school could afford. About fifteen minutes into the detention, the teacher charged with monitoring the group left the room. Some of the students began to act up. Charley Green had other ideas.

Using a tool set left in the room, he dismantled one of the computers. He wasn't trying to break it, he just wanted to see what made it work. When the teacher returned, the computer was disemboweled. Wires and circuits were scattered over the desk and Green was hunched over the remains, totally absorbed.

That stunt had gotten Green suspended for two weeks, but he thought it was a small price to pay. Up till then he had thought of technology as magic. A mystery beyond understanding. This experience taught him that computers were merely machines. Just electronic boxes that needed explicit instructions to perform the simplest task. In Officers' Candidate School Green had his first chance to work extensively with computers. The modern army was technologically advanced and expected its officers to be conversant with computers and their applications. He'd even learned the basics of programming there. He'd learned his lessons well: When the other officers had problems with their units they would often turn to Green for advice. Still, he was no expert.

The Johnson Installation computer system was a local network that linked all of the base's computers to a central processing unit. It had firewalls in place to prevent access from unauthorized entry from the outside. Internally, security was dependent on access cards and passwords.

Each user had to pass his access card through a slot in the terminal, then verify his identity by typing in a password.

The passwords, an irregular combination of letters and numbers, were changed weekly. The level of system access was keyed to the individual; junior officers were able to access only those areas necessary for the completion of their duties. More senior officers had greater access. Major Stepman, befitting his position, would have a very high level of access. Green had Stepman's card, but he knew that he didn't possess the hacking ability to circumvent the password system.

But there was another possibility. A couple of months back, at one of the Thursday night poker games, Stepman had made a comment that stuck in Green's mind. During the course of the game, complaining about the installation was normal and acceptable, up to a point. Green remembered the night because it had seemed that Stepman had crossed beyond that point.

It was late in the evening and they had all been drinking. They were discussing some mundane item when the conversation had turned to the level of security at the installation and how bothersome it was to comply. Somebody complained about the passwords and how difficult they were to memorize. Someone else complained about having to memorize a new one each week. That's when Stepman had spoken. "I never have that problem," he'd said quite smugly, "I just write 'em down." Green remembered being shocked by the statement. It defeated the whole idea of having passwords. It seemed an amazing confession. But nobody said anything about it either then or later.

But now it was very important indeed. Earlier in the week, Stepman had been working out of a station on the third level down. Today there were some documents that needed to be picked up at that station. Green tried to time his arrival for late in the afternoon, when they normally changed shifts. He entered the room just as the guards were making the change and positioned himself at the counter near where Stepman had been posted. Green waited till the soldiers were occupied at the other end of the station, then dropped his pen over the counter. He quickly stepped over to retrieve it. One guard glanced over, but then returned to his paperwork. Green searched the desk with his eyes as he bent over to pick up his pen. He could see nothing written down. He glanced back one more time, then quickly snaked his hand back along the surface of the desk running his fingers over the base of the computer. He felt something. A slip of paper was taped to the underside of the monitor. Green quickly unpeeled and pocketed the paper.

Later that night, Green went down to a room on the second level. The room was just off the main hallway. The room adjoined a laboratory and had a full computer system. Green had passed the room dozens of times and had never seen it occupied. He entered the room, put a sheet of cardboard over the window to darken it to the outside, and sat down at the computer. He passed the stolen access card through the slot. A window immediately appeared on the monitor screen—

Good evening, Major Stepman. Please enter your password.

Green hesitated a moment, he looked down at the slip of paper he had taken earlier. He'd come this far; it was too late for second thoughts. He took a deep breath, then typed out the characters shown on the paper, 2E#8nq*A@-4l.

The screen image momentarily went black, then changed to a menu page. Green let his breath out in a whistle of relief—he was in. The program was the same one that he worked with every day but now it listed options that he had never seen before, a list of commands that covered every facet of the installation's day-to-day operation. Green wasn't sure where to start. At random, he chose the command marked *Vaccines*. He scrolled through the file.

It was a long document filled with notes and comments written by several different scientists. The file was filled with medical and scientific terminology that was way over Green's head. But he could make out enough to understand the general concept. They were developing a vaccine to be used against an especially virulent breed of virus. According to the notes, the project had been in effect for over two years and the vaccine was in the seventh generation of development. No smoking gun, but this information validated Green's suspicions.

He closed out the file and opened a new one. The next one he chose was marked *Subject log*. This file consisted of a spreadsheet. Across the top it contained columns marked: *subject #, room #, enter date, inoculation date, vaccine #, first symptoms date, expiration date, autopsy,* and *comments*. Green scanned the columns.

The first subject had been entered over two years ago. It showed that symptoms had occurred on the same day that he had been inoculated and his expiration was listed as two days later. Further down the page the results showed a longer period between the onset of symptoms and the expiration date, but it followed the same pattern. The symptoms would first appear within the first two days, and expiration—death—would occur within the first two weeks.

The pattern was the same until the third entry from the bottom, subject number 236. It showed that this subject had been inoculated nearly three weeks previously and there were still no symptoms of disease. Green stared hard at the comments section for that entry: "Subject is healthy with no adverse signs. Tests show positive for antibodies.

Scheduled for forced expiration and autopsy." The date listed in the comments was the next day.

Green sat back, shaken. They were about to kill a man as part of some bizarre science experiment. He'd heard a quote one time about the banality of evil, how easy it was to be sucked into the worst of behavior when the evil was considered to be normal behavior. So many times he'd heard of atrocities committed in other parts of the world and thought, *That can't happen here*. But now it had.

Green took his time and pored over a number of the files. He examined files dealing with the video surveillance system, subject acquisition, the building layout, and the scheduling of security—nearly every facet of the operation of the complex. He printed out several of the files and copied as much information as he could onto a computer tape cartridge. Before leaving for the night he made some adjustments to one of the programs. He knew what he had to do, and a plan was beginning to form.

9

RAMON WAS SURE he was losing it when he began to see faces in the white walls of his room. Images seemed to appear like a slide show projected on the blank walls, like dreaming with his eyes open. It had started after he had been strapped back in to the bed. When he could no longer move, his mind had begun to spin into overdrive. At first there were shadows in the corner that, if you looked at them just the right way, would form into the image of some kind of object; at first he saw the outline of a dog and then a bird. Soon his mind was filling in the blanks and he was seeing objects all over the walls, complicated things like a leopard, spots and all, and a fire truck. The wall would be blank and then like magic he would suddenly see the picture so clearly that he would wonder how he had missed it before. It was the isolation. Cooped up by himself in an empty room with nothing to look at and nothing to do, he knew that his mind was playing tricks on him.

Then he began to notice the faces. Faces of people whom he had known before. The details seemed so real and vivid that it was like they were physically there. The first face that he saw was that of his attorney, Barry Resnick. With a sad expression he looked just like he had when Ramon had last seen him on the day of the execution.

He saw other faces, people that he had known while in prison over the long ordeal of waiting. He saw inmates who had gone on to meet their fate before him, guards from the prison, and others who had worked on the ward. Sometimes the image would just be a flash on the wall and other times it would linger, staying for minutes at a time.

Then he saw the face of J. Douglas Aarons, the state's attorney who had prosecuted him at his trial, and Ramon's eyes clouded with anger. He was the wrong guy—he didn't do it. The D.A. and the police had lied and suppressed evidence in order to get the conviction. They knew he was innocent, or at least not guilty of murder, but it didn't matter. He'd fit the bill fine.

After his conviction Ramon had spent his early years on death row in a haze of hate and self-pity. His days were spent concocting ways that he would enact his revenge. Violent fantasies that could never happen. Eventually he changed. He tried to make the most of whatever time he had left. He continued with his education, became more spiritually aware, and tried to put his past behind him. But now, seeing the face on the wall, it was as if nothing had changed. His anger welled up and he pushed against his restraints.

But then the face on the wall changed again. This time he saw his mother. She looked like she did right before she had died back when he was just a kid. He usually remembered her smiling or laughing but now she had tears in her eyes. And Ramon was sure that she was crying about him. He had thought of her often as he waited in his prison cell, wondering how she would have dealt with his situation. No mother would want to see her son end up as he had. It was better that she hadn't lived to see it.

Whether it was just or not, he had been convicted as a murderer and executed by the state. The pain and humiliation—it would have broken her heart. Ramon looked back on all the things he would have done differently. Hindsight made everything so clear. He had made so many mistakes when he was young. He'd give the world for a second chance.

Lost in his thoughts, Ramon didn't notice the door opening and the lone figure entering the room. It seemed like another of his hallucinations at first, blending in with the faces on the wall. The man in the yellow space suit was almost to the bed before Ramon reacted. He strained against his straps and clenched his teeth. If he had been free of the restraints he would have attacked. This was the first time that one of his captors had come in alone.

The man took a step backward and put his hands up in the air. "Calm down buddy," his voice came out in the electronic rasp. "Just calm down. I'm here to help."

Ramon stopped struggling and watched the spaceman. It was hard to tell in the bulky space suit, but he didn't look like any of his regular captors. The man held his hands out. "We're getting out of here but we need to hurry. Okay?"

Ramon looked beyond the visor into the man's eyes, then nodded in agreement. The spaceman bent down and undid the restraints and disconnected the tubes. Ramon sat up and stretched. It felt good to be up and moving. He stared up at the man, "Who are you? What's going on?"

"My name's Green but we don't have time to go into it. We need to get moving." Charley Green turned toward the door. "Follow me, do what I do, and no matter what happens, don't say a thing." Ramon hesitated for a moment, then followed. Green took out the keycard and swiped it through. The door opened. They stepped into the hallway. Green glanced quickly in both directions. The corridor was empty.

They moved to the right toward the door at the end of the hall. To Ramon it was all so unreal. Ever since the night of the execution Ramon had been on the verge of madness. Had he truly died and was this his own private hell? It all seemed so dreamlike that he still wasn't sure. And if he was still alive, where was he? And where were they going?

At least he was out of the room and moving again. Maybe this spaceman was really going to help him to escape—*if not,* Ramon thought, *I'll be ready for that, too.* Whichever way it worked out, when the opportunity came he was prepared to make a move. He felt a rush of excitement. Maybe this was a real chance at freedom. He hoped that he wasn't setting himself up for another fall.

Green led Ramon through the hallways of the lower level, through a series of air locks and containment chambers. They went through the disinfectant showers and the soap showers, emerging free of surface microbes. They dried off and Green led them around a corner to a small locker room.

There was a bank of lockers against the wall and Green scanned them quickly till he found the one he was looking for in the corner of the room. Ramon noticed that there were beads of sweat on his forehead. Green reached in and pulled out two full army uniforms. He handed one uniform to Ramon and began to put the other on himself.

"I don't know that this is going to be the best fit. It might be big, but it's what we got." He strapped on his watch and checked the time. "They won't notice that you're gone for a while; I've doctored the video display. Our first test will be right outside of here. If everything is the way it's supposed to be, the guard for this section will be off his post. If he's there, we've got a problem."

Green handed Ramon a pair of shoes about two sizes too big. "If we get past this post clean, we're taking the back way out. We shouldn't run into much traffic, but if we do, don't say a word. Just follow my lead."

They quickly finished dressing. Green helped Ramon properly adjust his uniform then took a small duffel bag out of the locker. He opened the bag and checked its contents. Then he pulled out a small black device and stuffed it into his pocket before closing the case. "All right, let's go."

They passed through another air lock into the main corridor where they stopped. Green checked his watch. They waited for two long minutes before he was ready to go again. After a short walk they were at the checkpoint at the entrance to the quarantine area. The post was abandoned—there was nothing there but an empty chair. Green stepped forward and quickly surveyed the area. "Let's move. We've only got a minute before he's back."

Ramon quickly followed Green across the room. Facing the guard's station was a bank of two elevators. Green passed his card through the sensor of the car to the far left. A moment later the doors slid open and they stepped on. Green punched the button for the fourth floor. The doors slid shut and the elevator smoothly moved upward. "You knew he wouldn't be there?" Ramon asked.

Green gave a tight nod. "I'm just glad he sticks to schedule."

The elevator stopped at the fourth floor. They exited into a small chamber with doors leading out from the opposing three sides. They took the door to the left, which opened into a long empty hallway, then walked to the end of the corridor where it dead-ended at a bank of elevators. The highest these cars would go was the third floor. They got off on three and moved down a short corridor, to a new set of sliding doors. Green stopped for a moment and looked over at Ramon. "Okay, be ready. We're on now."

They walked through into a large rectangular room with doors opening out from each side. A guard station was in the middle. There were two guards; one was a tall, skinny corporal with rounded shoulders. The other guard was Lt. Virgil Ortman, his skin pale and his eyes bloodshot.

Ortman looked up from a book as Green and Ramon entered the room. They all exchanged casual salutes, then Green handed over his order papers to Ortman. The corporal stayed in the background looking bored. "How's it going, Virge? Getting any action down here?"

Ortman took a quick glance at the papers. "Nah, nothing much happening. Just trying to stay awake. Where have you been? I haven't seen you at the poker game recently."

"Been working. I'll try to be there next week, though. How about you? You have a late one last night?"

"Nothing outrageous, just a few beers. You stay in last night?"

"Yeah, had to be up early today."

Ramon's stomach churned as he listened to them talk. He tried to stand straight and look bored while he waited for them to finish. Everything seemed so casual, so low-key. Like nothing unusual was happening. Green was acting friendly and nonchalant, but Ramon could see the sweat running down the back of his neck.

"I'll tell ya, I'm going to die of boredom down here. This place gives you the creeps after a while, it's so quiet." Ortman handed the papers back to Green. "Nothing ever happens."

"Yeah, I know what you mean."

"So they got you chasing around again, huh?"

"Oh yeah, there's always something." Green took back the papers and backed up a step, getting ready to move on.

"So who's the new guy?" Ortman looked directly at Ramon for the first time.

"Oh, he just got his transfer in here, came from back East. Captain Cain wanted me to show him the ropes."

Ortman stared at Ramon for a moment. "You know, you look familiar. I know you from somewhere. Where were you stationed before?"

Ramon's heart thumped so loud that he was sure that it would give him away. He started to open his mouth but no sound came out. His body froze. He could feel the panic welling up inside him. He had to fight the urge to run.

Ortman had a perplexed look on his face, and the corporal behind him moved forward to take a closer look. Green hurriedly filled in the void, "He was back at Norfolk, he was stationed at Camp . . ."

"No, that's not it." Just then the phone rang. Ortman put up his hand to pause the conversation as he picked up the phone. "Lieutenant Ortman, station six."

Green reached into his pocket and grasped something. He looked over at Ramon, his eyes showing the tension.

"Yes, sir . . .uh-huh . . . " As Ortman talked into the phone, he rolled his eyes at Green and gave a wave of dismissal. Green nodded back and with Ramon following behind they exited the room.

As they moved into a new corridor, Green leaned in toward Ramon and whispered, "God, we almost got toasted there. Why didn't you answer him?"

"You told me not to say anything."

"Yeah, well, next time just say, 'yes, sir'—do something."

They continued on, hurrying through the back ways and least traveled sections of the building. They came to another bank of elevators and took one all the way up to the first floor. At the end of another hallway they stopped.

Green looked at Ramon, "Okay, this is the last checkpoint. Once we get past this we're out of the building. It should be easier then."

Ramon nodded his head. Green continued, "Just be ready—follow my lead."

The door slid open. They moved into a rectangular room with a guard station in the center. Two guards manned the station. Both were sergeants, one was short and dark, the other was taller with fair hair and wire-rimmed glasses. They saluted as Green moved to the desk. "Good morning, sir. May I see your papers?" The taller sergeant stood straight and held out his hand expectantly.

"Yeah, sure thing, Sergeant." Green handed the passes over. "So how's the world treating you here?"

"Very good, sir." The guard took the papers and began to read through them.

"Have you guys been out recently? I'll tell you I'm raring to get outside—it's been so long since I've seen a real girl that I'm not sure I'll recognize one." Green forced out a chuckle but Ramon could see the sweat pooling up on his collar.

"Yes, sir." The tall guard continued to study the papers.

Green shifted his weight from foot to foot "Where you from, Sergeant?"

"Hackensack, sir." He turned the papers over and peered at them closely, not being drawn into a conversation. He took his time, reading the papers closely. The other sergeant moved in closer to see what was going on.

Green tried a new tactic. "Come on, soldier, let's hurry this up, we're on a tight schedule." His voice had an edge of apprehension. Ramon moved in close.

The sergeant turned the paper back over and looked directly at Green. "I'm sorry, sir, this pass doesn't appear to be valid." He motioned to the side of the room. "Please stand here while I call the watch commander for authentication."

Green looked dumbfounded. "What do you mean it's

not valid? Hell yeah, call the watch commander, and tell him you're wasting my time with this bullshit!" Green slipped his right hand into his pocket.

The tall sergeant reached down toward his hip where he had his sidearm holstered. "Sir, please step to the side while I make the call." His voice was stern and authoritative. The shorter sergeant reacted to the tone and moved out of the desk area with his hand on his pistol, too.

"I sure as hell won't step to the side, Sergeant!" Green leaned in so that his face was just inches away from the guards. "Unless you want to have a personal talk with Colonel Pope about why you detained me for no god damned reason I suggest you let us go right now!"

"Sir, please step over right now. This is your final warning," the tall sergeant barked. He held his ground and tightened the grip on his gun.

Ramon felt the adrenaline surge through his body. His chest tightened and his breath came short. The dark sergeant started to pull the pistol from his holster. Green made his move. He swung his hand out of his pocket holding a small black Taser device. He connected with the small of the tall sergeant's back and pulled the trigger. A spark came out and the sergeant's back went into an extended arc. The shorter sergeant ripped the gun out of his holster. Ramon jumped in and grabbed him in a bear hug; squeezing tight, he pinned the sergeant's arms to his side. The taller sergeant fell to the ground, his body jerking frantically.

The shorter sergeant screamed as he struggled violently, but Ramon was too strong. Green stepped over the body of the taller sergeant as he went to help Ramon. The guard was holding his gun by the butt of the handle, but with Ramon squeezing the breath out of him, he couldn't move it any closer. Green grabbed the guard's wrist with one hand and pried the gun out with the other. Green looked up at Ramon. "Let go," he yelled.

Ramon stared into the guard's eyes. All he could see was fear and hate. He released his grip. Green hit the trigger on the Taser and the second guard arched forward, then hit the floor.

"Shit! God damn!" Green was panting as he stared at the two prone men. "God damn shit!" He hit the top of the desk with his open hand. "Now we're dead." He bent over and cradled his head in his hands.

Ramon's heart was racing as he put his hand on Green's shoulder. "Come on, man, what do we do now?"

Green stood straight, took two quick deep breaths, and regained his composure. "Okay." He looked around the room. "First we need to keep these guys out of action. Then we need to buy us some time. If anybody comes through here before we make it out, then it's all over."

Green reached into his bag and riffled through the contents. He came up with a spool of copper wire, some wire cutters, and a large roll of duct tape. He tossed the tape to Ramon. "Work on these two. Make it so they can't move." Ramon nodded and went to work wrapping the tape around the two guards.

Green took the copper wire and cut four pieces, each about six inches in length. He took the first piece and fed it down into the slot for the keycards. When it was in as far as it could go, he propped it up so that a few inches were still sticking out of the top. He then picked up the Taser and pressed the trigger sending an electrical current through the wire. There was a loud pop and a puff of smoke. He knocked the charred wire out of the slot and passed his keycard through. Nothing happened. The door remained shut. Satisfied, he repeated the process at each doorway except for their exit.

By the time Green was done, Ramon had the guards taped up like mummies. "Let's move," Green said, "we've got to get out of here quick." He picked up the duffel bag and headed for the exit.

The sergeant's guns were sitting on top of the counter. Ramon grabbed one and slipped it into his waistband before following Green out the door. Green used the last piece of wire on the door after they left the room. They went down a short corridor, through a final door and out into the bright midday sun.

Ramon stopped for a moment, squinting against the light. He sucked in the fresh air and felt tears come to his eyes. So much of his life, his freedom, was wasted. He had come so close to losing it all for good. Now he'd been given another chance. As warped as this all was, he was still alive. And he wasn't going to give that up easily. He wiped his eyes on his sleeve and hurried after Green.

A Humvee was waiting for them in the loading bay near the exit. Green put the bag down between the seats and started up the engine. They eased out into the roadway and circled around the front of the building to the main road. Traffic around the center was moderate, just the normal comings and goings of people moving from place to place and supplies being delivered. Nothing seemed out of the ordinary. No MPs searching or alarms sounding. Green took the main road out to the gate, the first checkpoint before leaving the installation proper. There was a double fence enclosing the perimeter of the compound. The gate was electrified and topped with razor wire. It appeared formidable but getting through was easy. Green handed over the papers while he laid out a smooth chatter. The guards gave a quick check of the documents before waving them on.

Ramon gave a sigh of relief as they went past the gate. "That was it? We're out of there?"

Green stepped on the accelerator, bringing the speed up past sixty before he responded, "No. No, that was just the first step. We're still on the base. This road goes on for another eight miles before we leave the complex. Let's just hope that they don't find out what happened before that. We've been lucky so far. I hope our luck holds."

They rode on in silence. Ramon's mind was spinning. There was just too much happening. The smell of fresh air; the warmth of the sun on his face and the flow of the wind through his hair; the feeling of motion and the blur of colors rushing past. After years of the drab gray prison, and his time here in the flat white of the room, this was overload. He had lived so long with fear, anger, and boredom. The fear was still there but now it was mixed with exhilaration and hope. But what was going on? There were so many things that he needed to know.

After a minute Green broke the silence. "You know, I've never disobeyed an order before. I just hope I'm right. If not, what I just did is treason." He gave a humorless laugh. "God, I better be right."

Ramon stared at him. "Tell me, what's going on? Until you came in I was starting to think that I'd lost my mind."

"Yeah? That fits right in. Everything about this place is crazy." He glanced around. They were passing a row of narrow concrete barracks, their metal roofs gleaming in the sun. The parking lot in front was filled with military vehicles. On the other side of the road two personnel carriers sped past, heading in toward the complex.

"I don't know," Green continued. "I've got part of the picture but I'm missing a lot. Here's what I do know. This is a top-secret base, everyone who works here has to have the highest level of clearance. They've been bringing people in—people like you. Some of them seem to be bums or derelicts, but they're healthy enough when they first come in. The people—they're referred to as subjects—are transported down to the quarantine area. None of them leave alive."

Ramon nodded his head. "I guessed that. I knew that they were planning to kill me. I just didn't know when. But what are they doing?"

"I don't know all of it. It's biological though, something to do with germ warfare. They're testing toxins and trying to find some kind of a cure, a vaccine. From what I've found out, you're the first one that has survived and remained healthy."

"But if it's the army that's behind this, the government knows what's going on. What happens when we get out?"

"I don't know. I haven't gotten that far." Green thought for a moment before going on. A convoy of trucks rumbled past on their way in to the camp. "All I know is that what I've seen is a violation of every law on the books. I guess I'll go to the top brass. I think this is a renegade project. I go to the brass and they'll be in a position to stop it. Hell, they'll have to stop it. I've got documentation of what's been going on here, I've got enough data to blow this whole place inside out. This shows names, dates, all the specifics. And besides that, I got my ace in the hole." He paused a moment before looking back at Ramon. "I've got you."

Ramon felt like he'd been punched in the stomach. The thought hadn't occurred to him—he was evidence. Walking, talking proof. Things were moving so fast, until now his only thoughts had been on being free. What would he do once he was outside? He wanted to bear witness against the installation and the people who had tormented him. If he could bring the place crashing down, he would do it. But was he prepared to give up his freedom to do so? He had already been executed once. After the state realized their mistake would they want to do it again? He wanted to do the right thing but there were other things that he wanted, too. Other things that he needed to prove. They rode the rest of the way in silence.

THE GUARD STATION was a glass-and-metal enclosure that straddled the road into and out of the base. It was the only opening in a long stretch of heavy-gauge electric fencing that surrounded the entire perimeter of the property. Access into or out of the installation was regulated by metal gates that swung down from the station like windshield wipers, blocking or granting access at the guard's command. Two guards were inside the enclosure. Seemingly clones, they were both young, lean, and blond. Each was armed with an automatic rifle.

The Hummer pulled to a stop at the side of the enclosure. Green reached down, pulled out his order papers, and handed them up to the guard. "How's it going, Sergeant?"

"Not bad, sir. Not bad at all." The guard quickly flipped through the papers. "How long do you intend to be off base, sir?"

"I'd expect we'll be back within forty-eight hours. But if we finish our chores early, we might cut loose with a night of R and R. Being around nothing but guys so long I think a goat would look mighty attractive now, if you know what I mean."

The guard laughed. "Yeah, I hear ya, sir, it's been quite a while." He glanced at the papers again. "Just give me a minute, sir. We need to put everything in the log and stamp your papers. I promise I won't keep you away from those women any longer than I have to." He stepped back, fully inside the enclosure as he worked on the papers.

Green glanced over at Ramon and gave a slight nod. On the other side of the roadway a small tanker truck pulled up, winding its engine down as it came to a stop at the opposite side of the guardhouse. The second guard stepped over to check the papers. "Hey, Willie, what's up?"

"The usual. Got me runnin' diesel all day. Figure I'll be makin' three trips at least." The driver handed over his papers. He was wearing a khaki army shirt with sergeant's stripes.

It took an uncomfortably long time, but finally the first

guard returned. He handed back the papers. "You're all set, sir. Say hey to all those single women out there."

Green took back the papers and slipped them into a folder in his bag. "You got a deal, Sergeant." He put the Hummer into gear and waited for the gate to be raised. Inside the booth a phone began to ring. Ramon's muscles tensed. The gate wasn't rising. The phone rang again. The second guard looked up from the papers he was working on and picked up the phone. The gate started to move up; it seemed like it was in slow motion.

Suddenly, from inside the guardhouse, the second guard shouted, "Stop them!"

Green didn't hesitate. He popped the clutch on the Humvee and, with the accelerator jammed to the floor, shot forward. They hit the gate head-on. The metal pole was ripped off its hinges, flew into the air then clattered down on the asphalt road.

It seemed as if everything happened at the same time, so fast but it felt like slow motion. Ramon looked back. The guards grabbed their rifles and rushed outside. The first guard tripped, fell to the ground, and picked himself back up. The truck driver saw the situation, jammed the gearshift into reverse, and accelerated, racing the tanker backward attempting to cut the Hummer off. The Hummer raced forward, past the gate and on toward the gravel road that led out to the interstate.

The two guards scrambled out onto the road, raised their rifles and without fully aiming each fired a burst at the Hummer. Green shifted the gears frantically, trying to push the Hummer to its maximum speed. Ramon slumped down in his seat as the bullets whistled past. One bullet slammed into the windshield, shattering the glass and sending fragments flying.

The tanker truck, rushing backward, moving faster than Ramon would have thought possible, pulled even with the Hummer. The driver cut the wheel and the tanker body veered in toward the Hummer, forcing it off the road. The Hummer was forced over, but Green kept the gas pedal full down as he tried to outrun the tanker. He couldn't do it. The tanker had the angle, if the Hummer didn't slow down it would crash into the rear of the tanker. Green swerved hard, downshifted, hit the brakes, and cut the wheel as hard as it would go in the opposite direction.

They went into a skid, the momentum pulling them forward. The Hummer turned, nearly parallel to the tanker but still sliding. It was as if they were being pulled into the side of the truck by magnetic force. Just before impact, Green popped the clutch again, hit the gas and they shot forward running alongside the truck, which was now going in the opposite direction.

The guards sprayed the air with their automatic rifles. The bullets came in a flurry. Some slammed into the body of the Hummer, others ricocheted off the hull of the tanker. The truck driver slammed on the brakes and shifted forward trying to reverse his momentum. A stream of errant bullets hit his front tires. The cab skidded in one direction as the tanker jackknifed in the other. The Hummer sailed past and cut back onto the road as the tanker slowly teetered, tipped up until the weight shifted and the momentum took it down. It hit the ground hard and slid on the asphalt, sparks shooting up like a roman candle. The smell of spilled diesel was heavy in the air.

The Hummer was back on the road and racing outward. Another burst of gunfire rang out. The sand on the side of the road seemed to dance as the bullets screamed past the Hummer and tore into the ground. Ramon felt a flash of exhilaration. They were outside the base and headed toward freedom. Against all odds they had made it. He almost felt joyful, then he looked at Green. Green was slumped forward, a neat red hole at the base of his skull. There was no doubt that he was dead.

The Hummer began to drift. Ramon grabbed the wheel and jerked it back toward the road. The change in direction caused Green's body to shift. He fell out of the seat, tilting toward the ground. Ramon grabbed on to his arm and tried to drag the body in but he felt the Hummer slowing down, its engine sputtering. Ramon let go of the arm as he grabbed the steering wheel and reached his leg over to stomp hard on the gas. Green's body fell onto the roadway as Ramon stepped all the way over into the driver's seat and regained control. The Hummer sped away and turned onto the gravel road. Ramon glanced behind him in the rearview mirror. The guards were running back as the diesel fuel began to burn.

10

THE INSTALLATION'S COMMAND center was abuzz with activity. The room was a gleaming enclave of glass and stainless steel, computers and telephones. There were six officers in the room, all talking on the phone at the same time. For all the activity, the center was a haven of relative tranquility compared to what was happening outside. Out in the adjoining hallway the maddening on-and-off shriek of a siren could be faintly heard. It was enough to put everyone's nerves on edge.

Maj. Bob Durmo sat in the center of the room. He was on the phone when Colonel Pope entered. As soon as he saw the colonel he cut his conversation short. "Listen, I'll call you back." Durmo hung up the phone, quickly stood up, and saluted the colonel. "Hello, sir . . ."

"Major, we need privacy. Relocate your officers for the time being."

"Yes, sir." Durmo called out the command. The other

officers quickly finished their conversations and left the room leaving Durmo alone with the colonel.

Colonel Pope sat down. He leaned his huge frame back in a swivel chair and closed his eyes. It almost looked as if he was napping. "Tell me the situation as you perceive it, Major."

"Well, sir." The major cleared his throat and spoke slowly and cautiously. "It appears that two men breached security in an attempt to escape the installation. One was killed, the other is still unaccounted for."

"You aren't telling me anything that I don't know, Major. What I want you to tell me is who these perpetrators were, and how were they able to escape this facility."

"I don't know that, sir. We've identified one of them— it was Green. Lt. Charles Green's name was on all the papers and we believe he was the one that was killed."

"Hmmm. It appears that a grave error was made with Lieutenant Green."

"Yes, sir."

"Who was the second perpetrator?" Colonel Pope pulled a handkerchief from his pocket, removed his glasses, and began to clean them.

"I don't know, sir. As you instructed, we put a lockdown in place for the building and have accounted for all of our men. Green is the only one missing." Durmo tugged on his right ear nervously.

"Could it be one of the subjects?"

"That would be quite impossible, sir, our guards have been watching the monitors and . . ."

"Have you physically inventoried the subjects?"

Durmo paused a moment before answering. "No, sir. No, sir, I haven't. Let me do that now." Durmo started to reach for a phone but Colonel Pope waved him back down.

"I've already ordered a count, Major. We should have the results presently."

"Yes, sir." Durmo tugged on his ear again.

"What actions have been taken to apprehend this fugitive?" Colonel Pope put his glasses back on, carefully folded the handkerchief, and stood up to his full height. He towered over Durmo.

"We've dispatched several units to search and apprehend. There was an accident at the main gate, however, so I understand that the search has been delayed temporarily while they clear the debris. The helicopters will be in the air shortly, though. As a precaution, we have also contacted the local and state police. They are setting up roadblocks, just in case he somehow is able to evade us."

"Good. I trust that won't be necessary. How many—" the colonel's pocket phone buzzed. He stopped in midsentence and picked up the phone. "Yes . . . I see . . . Bring me the full file." He hung up the phone and closed his eyes for a moment, pausing before speaking. "Perhaps impossible was too strong of a word, Major. One of the subjects is indeed missing."

"But, sir, the monitors—"

"Had been tampered with. Previously taped sections were being replayed on a series of monitors. Do you realize the implication of this, Major?"

"I'm not sure. . . ."

"Our Lieutenant Green had access to the computer system. Our security has been compromised."

"Yes, sir." Durmo stopped tugging on his ear and his arm fell limply to his side.

The colonel began to pace as he talked. "I want a full report on how they were able to breach our systems. I also want a complete investigation as to the identity of any potential coconspirators. I want a list of anyone who had the means and opportunity to be involved in this. Do this quickly and discreetly, Major. If there is a Judas among us we need to know who it is." The colonel paused and stopped his pacing for a moment before he continued.

"Bring me any files we have on our missing subject. You will notify me as soon as he has been apprehended. If he is alive, I want to question him personally. Our project is so close to fruition, this lapse has put everything we've worked for in jeopardy."

"Yes, sir."

"Get to work, Major. You are dismissed." Durmo saluted as Pope turned to go. Colonel Pope had his hand on the doorknob when he turned back to Durmo. "One more thing. Where is Captain Cain?"

"He's on assignment off base, sir."

"Contact him and bring him back immediately. He's needed here now." As Pope opened the door, the discordant blare of the alarm filled the room. When the door shut behind him the room seemed strangely silent.

RAMON DROVE THE Hummer to the end of the gravel road and turned onto the main highway. In the course of an hour his world had changed. He'd actually escaped—he was outside, alive and free. Running for his life, but still free. It didn't seem real; it was like a fever dream. Everything was so vivid, so achingly beautiful. The sky was a fairy-tale blue, the sun reflected off the sand in blinding splashes of white. The blacktop ahead shimmered from the heat.

It was all so real—hyper-real—but it felt like it was happening to someone else. Or it was happening to him, but he was in a movie theater watching it unfold in Technicolor. In a way he was happy. Ecstatic almost. Or at least a part of him felt that way. The other part was a step away from a full-blown panic and just wanted to find a place to hide.

It had to be morning—the sun was still rising toward its peak. But it was hot already. Ramon's shirt was wet, nearly drenched with sweat. He glanced behind in the rearview mirror. There were no vehicles behind him, just a column of black smoke from the burning tanker. With any luck, that would buy some time. Ramon took a deep breath and tried to relax and think rationally. But he couldn't. His head felt like a balloon that had been blown too big. It was too strange to believe. He had been executed, brought back to life, used as a human guinea pig by the United States Army, escaped, and was now running for his life. He needed some time to let this all sink in.

He needed time to figure out his options, too. Where would he go? What would he do? Everything was moving too fast. From the moment that Green had walked into the room, Ramon had been reacting. There was no time to think. It was all instinct and following Green's lead. He owed his life to Green. He was a good man, a true hero — but now he was gone. And it was all because of him. Green had sacrificed his life to save him. Ramon gripped the steering wheel and tried not to think about it, but he couldn't help picturing Green's face right before his body slipped out of the Hummer and landed on the road.

Even though Ramon had known Green less than an hour, he felt a sense of grief. Here was a man who didn't even know him, and he risked everything to save him, all because he knew it was the right thing to do. Ramon wondered if he would have done the same thing if he were in Green's shoes. That and the certainty that if Green were here, *he* would know what to do next. Now Ramon was alone with God-only-knew-what behind him. He took another deep breath and tried to contain the panic. He was free, but none of this would matter if he made a mistake now. He forced a deep breath and focused on the task at hand.

He glanced down at the gas gauge. It was much lower now than just a few minutes before. The tank had to be leaking — probably the result of a stray bullet. At the rate that the gauge was going down Ramon knew that he wouldn't get far before the engine sputtered to a stop, leaving him stranded and vulnerable. He checked the rearview mirror again. He didn't think they were after him yet but he couldn't tell for sure. There was traffic going in both directions on the highway. But if they weren't after him now they would be soon. He had to do something fast.

The terrain surrounding the road was flat and barren, the only vegetation being brushwood and scrub — stunted plants that could survive the long periods between rainfalls. Ramon scanned the horizon. There was one exception. About a half mile down, just off the road, a stand of trees towered over the surrounding ground. For the trees to grow that high had to mean that there was water. He headed toward them.

When he was close, Ramon pulled off the road and drove over the sand and through the scrub, making a beeline for the trees. Eight ironwoods were clustered together along the banks of what must have been an old riverbed. It was baked dry now, but the ground sloped downward and it looked like it was the course that the water took when the rains came. The path of the river would have run across the road if not for a large culvert built underneath. Ramon drove the Humvee past the grove of trees, down to the riverbed, and into the culvert. The engine was coughing as he pulled to a stop. The Hummer fit with room to spare.

Ramon turned off the Hummer and tore off his uniform shirt, leaving his undershirt. He was hidden for now, but if he didn't move he was as good as dead. He checked the gun he'd taken from the guard at the base, and pushed it down in his waistband, covering it with his T-shirt. He picked up Green's duffel bag, walked out of the culvert, and scrambled up to the side of the road.

Hugging the ground he looked over the guardrail. There were some cars coming but they were still in the distance. Ramon ducked down until he was sure that the

oncoming car wasn't an army vehicle. It was a red con-
vertible. Ramon jumped up, stepped into the road and
waved, trying to force the car to a stop—but the car sped
up as it blew past him.

He moved back to the side of the road. A semi truck
was approaching. Ramon put out his thumb, signaling he
needed a ride. He tried to smile and look calm, but his
heart was pounding like a jackhammer. The truck rushed
past him but then downshifted and braked, coming to a
stop a few hundred feet down the road. Ramon raced
down to reach it.

The driver reached over to open the door. "Hey, amigo,
what the hell you doing out here in the middle of
nowhere?" The driver was a middle-aged Hispanic with a
cowboy hat and a friendly expression.

Ramon forced a smile. "It's a long story."

He climbed up and settled into the seat with a sense of
relief. The truck pulled back onto the highway and
reached cruising speed. Ramon suddenly had a strong
feeling that he was going to be all right. Not long after, he
saw the first of the helicopters, crossing back and forth
along the road, searching.

THE SUN WAS on its way back down as the black Chinook
helicopter touched ground in the dry riverbed near the culvert. The whirling twin blades raised a cloud of dust that
hung in the air. A squad of soldiers was gathered there.
Most were engrossed in tasks, but some were relaxing,
leaning aimlessly against their vehicles. When they saw
the helicopter, they quickly found things to do that would
make them look busy.

Captain Cain was inside the culvert examining the
abandoned Humvee. Once the helicopter landed, he
walked out of the culvert and approached the aircraft. He
had been finishing up some business in the eastern part of
the state when he received the call. He'd come straight

away and joined in the search, but it seemed to dead-end here.

The whole sector was crawling with troops. It looked as if half the camp was involved in the search, helicopters as well as ground troops. But so far they'd come up empty. It was beginning to look as if the subject really had escaped.

The side door of the chopper opened and a ramp telescoped down to the ground. Colonel Pope bent low to avoid the blades as he stepped out of the doorway and motioned for Cain to come on board. He held a file folder in his right hand. "Come quickly, Parker."

"Yes, sir." Cain adjusted his sunglasses, walked up the ramp and went inside. The interior of the helicopter was divided into two portions. The pilot and copilot occupied the front. The rear portion was set up as a command center for Colonel Pope. The space was laid out for maximum efficiency. It contained a table with a built-in computer and a full communication system. On each side of the table were two oversized leather captain's chairs.

Colonel Pope settled into his chair and dropped the file folder onto the table. "We are faced with an unpleasant situation, Parker."

Cain sat in a chair opposite the colonel, took off his sunglasses, and picked up the folder. "How bad is it, sir?"

Pope sat stiffly in his chair. He paused for a moment before answering, "It appears that the subject has made it through the roadblocks. We've combed through every inch of land in between; I have no doubt that he has escaped."

Cain shook his head then opened the file. The first page contained a picture of Ramon. "Who is he?"

"One of our acquisitions from Dr. Meeks. A convict by the name of Ramon Willis. He appears to be a most unusual subject."

"How's that, sir?" Cain stared hard at the picture.

"It's all there, Parker. Our Mr. Willis was a convicted murderer. He executed a businessman in Bay City. The court assumed that it was all drug related. The case was circumstantial. As one would expect, he claimed his innocence. As point of fact, he maintained his innocence right to the end. He was, according to our information, a model prisoner. He obtained an education while inside. He appears to be an intelligent and willful subject. This is the same subject that compromised Corporal Jenkins."

"He had the virus? Is he contagious?"

"I'm assured that he is not. All indications are that he is completely healthy and physically sound. However, he does have knowledge of our operation. His very existence is proof against us. Also, there is the possibility that he may have evidence of some form in his possession."

"What kind of evidence?"

"We don't know, Parker. This is pure conjecture, but our security was compromised. It's entirely possible that he has documentation in his possession."

Cain leafed through the dossier. The sound of the blades spinning above them made conversation difficult. He raised his voice, "What do you think he's planning on doin', sir?"

"What would you do if you were in his shoes, Parker?"

Cain thought for a moment before answering, "I might just chuck the whole thing and head for Mexico. It's not far away. He's Mex; he'd blend right in. He could forget the whole thing and start himself a new life. That's what I think I'd do."

Colonel Pope shook his head. "No. No, you wouldn't. I know you too well, Parker. You would not avoid a confrontation."

"I guess you're right about that, sir. So you think this guy might have some kind of hard-on for us?"

"In all likelihood he will run as far from here as possible and hide. If he does try to go against us, he won't dare go to the authorities. He's a convicted murderer. And if he did, chances are no one would believe him. Odds are that he will disappear quietly. But what if he doesn't? We can't take that risk."

"How about contacts, sir? Any close relatives?"

"The prison visitation log is in there. There was no wife or girlfriend. There were some cousins that visited when he was first incarcerated, but they haven't come in years. He had contact with a number of people in the anti–death penalty movement, but his closest contact seemed to be his attorney, Barry Resnick."

Cain turned to the section on Barry Resnick. "Right. I see that mentioned here." He set the file down and looked back at the colonel. "What's our plan goin' to be?"

"As I remember, you like to hunt, Parker?"

"Yes, sir. Back in Tennessee I was huntin' rabbit an' coon with my daddy before I could talk—"

"Yes, and what did you do when you hunted for rabbits?" Pope shifted in his chair and leaned forward.

"First you got to go where the rabbits are."

"Exactly, Parker." Pope stood up to signal the end of the meeting. "Pick your team. Use whatever resources you require. Find this subject and dispose of him. We can't afford the risk."

Cain smiled. He hadn't been on a good hunt in ages.

11

AFTER THREE WEEKS in the fields, Ramon had turned dark from working in the hot sun. The days were hard and long. His knees ached and his back hurt like hell from stooping down to pick the beans. But he couldn't remember when he felt better. All he had to do was look around and he'd feel a rush. The sky was so big here. So big and so blue. He didn't know how he'd survived all those years in prison without it. Just breathing the outside air made him feel alive. Even the pain felt good.

Life was starting to feel normal again. When he first escaped, Ramon was sure that they would find him quickly. He was constantly checking behind his back, jumping at any sudden movement. Fearing the shadows. Now, it was amazing how much he'd changed in these few short weeks. His confidence had returned.

"Quiere usted agua?" Juan Marin, a slender young

Mexican, stood up in the next row and offered his canteen. He'd come into the camp at the same time as Ramon.

"Si." Ramon reached for the canteen. He took a long sip before handing it back. *"Gracias."*

"De nada." Juan bent down and returned to his work. Ramon stretched his arms as he stared out at the mountains in the distance. Somehow he had made it. He was finally free. Ramon bent back down and grabbed a fistful of beans as he thought back to all that had happened over the last weeks to bring him here.

Standing on the side of the road, waiting for the helicopters to show up, he had been prepared to die. When the truck stopped it felt like a new beginning. It was like someone was watching out for him, that God was telling him that it was all going to be all right. The truck driver seemed lonely and happy for the company. He started talking as soon as Ramon got in. About fifteen miles down the road, the traffic came to a halt. The flashing lights of a squad car up ahead indicated either an accident or a roadblock. With the helicopters buzzing around, a roadblock was more likely. The driver noticed Ramon's apprehension. "There's a space behind the sleeper," he'd said, "It's a little tight but they'll never find you there."

He was right. They made it through the roadblock without any trouble. Later, when Ramon had crawled back into the seat, the driver continued talking as if nothing had happened. They rode together for several hours but the driver never asked for any kind of explanation. He dropped Ramon off in McAllen, Texas, a town just across from the Mexican border.

The road where Ramon had gotten out was at the top of a ridge. As he looked down, past the trailer parks and factories, he could see a diamond of light reflecting off of water far below. The Rio Grande. And on the other side was Mexico.

It would be evening soon, he'd thought. He could easily make his way down to the river. There were spots where he could cross. The Border Patrol monitored the area but they wouldn't be expecting someone to be sneaking out. Once he was in Mexico he could blend in and disappear. That would be the end. The end of this life anyway, but an opportunity for a whole new existence on the other side. He was still young. And things were looser in Mexico—he could start all over, make himself into the person that he wanted to be. Find a girl, start a family, live the life of a free man.

But if he crossed the border it would mean that he was running away. He would be alive, but for what? The hope of proving his innocence had kept him going throughout all the long years in prison. When he had nothing else he still had his self-respect. Running away now would mean that it was all a sham. Ramon looked down at the bag he had taken from the Hummer. And whatever was going on at the army base would continue to go on. People would die, innocent people. It would mean that Green had thrown his life away for nothing. Ramon picked up the bag, turned, and walked toward the center of town.

Walking through the streets of McAllen, Ramon had felt out of place. It was strange to be walking out in the open in broad daylight—he seemed so exposed and vulnerable. But nobody else appeared to notice. He was just another man of Mexican descent on a street filled with the same. Nobody looked, nobody stared. He blended in naturally. In a way he was an invisible man—and it's hard to find an invisible man.

After a little while he relaxed. The danger didn't seem so close. He was safe enough for now. But how would he survive? His stomach was already growling with hunger. He had no money, no change of clothes, and no form of identification. There was no one he could go to for help. The flip side of invisibility was helplessness.

Ramon had wandered through the town most of the

day. That first night he had slept by a Dumpster in an alley behind a grocery store. At one point he had been so hungry that he rummaged through the Dumpster for his meal.

The next morning he woke up before dawn to the sound of trucks rumbling by. He staggered up and followed them around to the front of the building. A group of men were waiting by the corner. Two large trucks with open beds, the kind used to transport produce, pulled to a stop in front of the crowd.

Ramon walked over to see what was going on. A stocky man with a cowboy hat and a gray mustache that covered his lips got out of the lead truck and walked over to inspect the assemblage. All were men of Hispanic descent, ranging in age from young to middle aged, most with the frightened-eyed look of strangers in a strange land. The man scratched his gut as he walked around the crowd. "All right," he called out in a deep Texas drawl, "ah need forty—*cuarenta*. Any uh you *habla ingles?*"

Ramon stayed silent. A short young man with a thin mustache stepped forward. *"Si, senor. I speak ingles."*

The cowboy-hatted man pulled on his mustache and looked skeptical. He called out again, "Anybody else *habla ingles?*"

No one in the crowd responded. The older man shrugged. "Okay, Frenchy, I guess that makes you my foreman. Here's the deal. Ah need forty men for a solid month. Ya get room and board. We pay at the end of each week. It's hard work, we need sturdy men. Who'd you come with?"

"My brudder and my cousin."

"Bring 'em along. Let's pick out the rest." He walked through the crowd, pointing at people that he wanted, the youngest and strongest of the group. As they were called they would move over to take their places on the trucks. When he saw Ramon he stopped. "We got a big mule here." The man checked Ramon up and down. "This'n don't look like the others. You speak English?"

Ramon didn't respond.

"Habla ingles?" the man tried again.

"No. No ingles." Ramon looked down at the ground.

The cowboy-hatted man shrugged. "Well, get him on the truck anyway."

And that was how he had come to the farm. He'd been there three weeks now and he felt safe. The farm was an hour and a half north of McAllen, off the beaten path. No one was looking for him here. For all they knew he was just another migrant worker. At first it was strange to speak nothing but Spanish. But that didn't last long. Spanish was his first language and returning to it was like riding a bicycle.

Ramon kept mostly to himself but was accepted by the other workers as one of their own. Now he had some money in his pocket and a taste of what freedom was like. He was finally starting to make plans for the future. Maybe another week on the farm and he could risk the outside. Maybe he could even risk phoning his old attorney, Barry Resnick.

Lost in thought, he had reached the end of the row and his sack was filled to the top with beans. With a jolt his mind returned to the present. Ramon wiped the sweat off his forehead and hefted the bag onto his shoulder. He walked along the edge of the field toward the center aisle where the boss had parked the truck. As he came up, he saw that several other workers were in front of him, ready to empty their bags into the truck.

Two field bosses were leaning against the truck, watching. They both had beers in their hands and their eyes were bloodshot—it looked like they had been drinking for a while. One of the men Ramon knew as Slim. He was in his late thirties or early forties, thin as a rail, and missing one of his front teeth. He spoke Spanish fluently and didn't ride the workers too much.

Ramon didn't know the other one. He was younger, probably in his twenties, and big. He had the look of a linebacker—strong and mean-looking with a big, square face and unevenly cut hair. Ramon could hear their conversation as he came closer to the truck.

"Whadaya think makes 'em so skinny? I think it's 'cause their women eat all the food before they get a fuckin' chance." The big one paused to spit out a stream of tobacco juice. "I was down in Reynosa the other week, some of the whores down there were so fat they could swallow two ah these beaners whole."

Slim giggled as he swigged on his beer.

"Shit, it's a mystery to me. We let these skinny fucks come up here—they never even bother to learn the fuckin' language and pretty soon they're gonna be takin' all our jobs."

Ramon tried to stare straight ahead and ignore the conversation.

"Well, you don't really wanna be pickin' them beans down there, do you, Duane? I say let 'em have it. It's sure not a job I'd want," Slim responded.

"Hell no, but that's how it starts. It won't be long 'fore they got your job. Why pay you when they'll work for less? Mark my words, pard, it's happenin'." He drained his beer, crumpled the can in his hand, and dropped it to the ground along with all the other empties. He looked over at the workers unloading their bags into the truck. "Ya gotta keep 'em in line or they'll push us right out. Watch this." He walked over to the worker in front of Ramon. "Hey, Chico, you want my job?"

The worker tried to smile. *"No se, senor. No ingles."*

Ramon felt apprehensive. He didn't want trouble. He'd seen Duane's type before—a bully picking on those who couldn't fight back. But this wasn't his battle. If he just kept quiet it would blow over soon. He looked around him. The other workers were staring at the ground, trying their best to be invisible.

Duane looked over his shoulder at Slim. "See what I mean?" He turned back and gave an open-handed punch to the worker's shoulder, sending the smaller man backward. "Talk English, ya little monkey."

Slim giggled nervously. "Come on, Duane, you're gonna get us in trouble."

The worker regained his balance and put his hands in front of his face defensively. "*No, senor . . .*"

Duane wasn't listening. He slammed his fist into the worker's stomach, dropping the man to his knees. Duane then kicked the worker in the chest, knocking him into the dirt.

Ramon dropped his bag. He couldn't keep quiet. He'd been passive long enough. If he didn't make a stand, no one would. "That's enough," he said.

Duane spun around to face Ramon. "Well, I'll be damned. This monkey talks American." Duane stared at Ramon in surprise and did a double take. "God damn, Slim, now I've seen everything. A blue-eyed wetback."

"Come on, Duane, that's about enough. . . ." Slim crossed his arms nervously.

"Shit, Slim, I'm just havin' some fun." Duane sneered at Ramon. "This monkey wants to play." He smacked Ramon's shoulder with his open palm. Ramon uncoiled like a set spring. He exploded. The energy of his body converged into an uppercut that connected with Duane's jaw, dropping him like a stone, unconscious on the ground.

Ramon's body swelled with adrenaline. He balled his hands into fists and tensed his body for combat. Duane lay motionless on the ground. Ramon spun around to face Slim, who backed up against the truck holding his hands out fearfully. "I didn't do nothin', man. I tried to stop him, you saw it. . . ."

Ramon dropped his arms and looked around him. The Mexican workers were as frightened as Slim was. So much for invisibility. Now he had to leave. Ramon turned away and walked with slow deliberation toward the workers' quarters. He needed to gather his things and go.

IT WAS MID-JULY when Lena flew out to Washington. Most of her belongings were already packed and she'd even found someone to sublet her apartment. Her affairs were in order from the Austin side but she still had no idea where she would be living once she moved to D.C. The Internet had provided some possibilities, but it was shocking how much higher the rents were than in Texas. Then again, with the move, her salary was going up and there was a cost of living adjustment on top; so she knew that everything would work out fine.

Finding an apartment was easier than expected. The second one she visited was a studio in a converted brownstone in the Georgetown section. It was smaller than she would have liked, but the location was perfect. It was right in the middle of all the activity, close to the government administration buildings and some of the trendiest restaurants and clubs. It seemed that everyone in the neighborhood was young, successful, and involved in some way with the government. It was all that she had hoped for. She wrote out a check for the security deposit on the spot.

Lena had expected it to take longer to find an apartment. She was scheduled to be in Washington for three full days, and already her biggest task was behind her. Now there was time to explore and get acclimated to her new surroundings.

She drove around the capital the rest of the day. With a guidebook and a list, she checked off each place as she

found it: the White House, the Pentagon, the House and
Senate, each of the cabinet buildings and the Watergate
Hotel. All of the places that made up such a big part of the
nation's news. It was exciting being so near the center of
things.

She finished the tour and made it back to her hotel just
before rush hour. A message was waiting for her to call
Bill Wentworth, the senior correspondent whose position
she would be filling. She made the call.

He answered on the first ring and came right to the
point. "Lena, I thought you might like a glimpse of how
the real Washington works."

There was a function that night put on by the Com-
merce Department on behalf of a Chilean trade delegation. Wentworth had gotten Lena's name on the list for
press credentials. It was at these parties, he assured her,
that contacts were formed, rumors exchanged, and the
truly powerful made their alliances. Lena made arrange-
ments to meet him at the party at nine o'clock.

The affair was held in the grand ballroom of a downtown hotel. She arrived early, feeling underdressed. She'd
worn her best blue suit and a string of pearls. But as she
entered the hotel, she followed a couple in formal attire—
he in a tuxedo, she in an evening dress—and knew that
she had guessed wrong. The hotel staff checked to verify
that her name was on the list before allowing her to go in.

The room was a large space, with red carpets, high
ceilings, and opulent fixtures that were probably new at
the turn of the last century. Waiters in tuxedos moved
around the room, distributing canapés and flutes of wine.
Tables were set around the perimeter of the room, but it
seemed that most of the people were cruising the interior.

Lena slowly moved through the crowd looking for
Wentworth. She made a full circuit of the room; there had
to be several hundred people there. Some of the faces
were familiar from TV news shows—but no sign of

Wentworth. As she walked, she heard fragments of dozens of conversations: the prospects for passage of the new gun-control bill; whether the new budget would hamstring the EPA; the effects of a proposed house bill on economic development. The same issues, over and over.

This was not going at all like she had expected. It reminded her of a high school party where everyone else knew what was going on and she didn't—a club where all the others belonged and she wasn't included. She didn't know a soul in the room and didn't suspect that that would change soon.

Lena cut through the crowd and headed over to the sidelines where she found a spot across from the bar. If this was how things worked in Washington, maybe it wasn't what she wanted after all. By nature she tended to go in her own direction. The stories that interested her most were those with a strong human angle. Here, it seemed that everyone was recirculating the same news, taking the spin and reporting it as fact. Pure pack reporting. She checked her watch. She'd had about as much of the Washington scene as she wanted for that night.

As she turned toward the door, Lena bumped into a man next to her, spilling his drink across the front of his tuxedo.

"Oh God, I'm sorry." Lena touched him on the shoulder. "Are you all right?"

He dabbed at the wet spot with a paper napkin. "No, it's fine. Don't worry about it. It was only soda water anyway—it won't stain." He looked up and smiled. He was short and slim, with thick dark hair and a wispy goatee. He appeared to be in his late twenties, but the effect of the tuxedo was of a young boy playing dress up. He stuck out his hand. "Jason Ulmer, I'm with Defense."

"Lena Dryer, I'm with the *Austin Star.*"

"You're a reporter? That's great. How long have you been in Washington?"

"Well, actually I'm not really here yet. I'll be transferred here at the end of the month. I'm just in for a few days now."

"Really? You're going to love it. This city is spectacular."

As Jason was talking, an elegant couple passed by. Jason turned his attention away from Lena toward the couple, gave a small wave, and called out, "Excellent showing on the budget compromise, Langston. You came out very nicely."

The man gave a tight smile and a nod of his head as he continued walking. Jason turned back to Lena. "That was Langston Dwyer, he's an undersecretary at Interior. The talk was that their appropriations were going to be axed, but they came out pretty much intact."

Lena nodded. Jason continued, "This is a nice party tonight. A lot of the major players are here." He motioned over to a pair of white-haired men standing by the buffet table. "That's Charles Norton over there, right next to Congressman Macafee. Norton's the main lobbyist for the NRA. Chances are that new gun-control bill won't go through."

"You seem to know a lot of people here."

Jason beamed. "Oh, sure. Washington is really a closed system. There's some kind of function nearly every night of the week. You get around and you get to know people."

A tall, distinguished man with chiseled features and silver hair passed by. "Good evening, Senator. Great to see you again." Jason called out.

The man flashed a smile and gave a quick wave as he proceeded on to the bar.

"Wasn't that—"

"That's right. Randall Morgan, from Wisconsin. A true class act if you ask me. There's talk he'll be running for president, and I hope he does. They say he has no chance, but it's rare to see a man with true integrity."

Lena noticed another man, wearing a tuxedo and carrying a clipboard, walking directly toward them. As he came closer, Jason glanced around nervously.

The man stopped in front of Jason. "Excuse me, sir. Can I have your name? I need to make sure you're on our list."

"Uh, well . . ."

Lena could see that there was a problem. Jason had seemed too enthusiastic, too happy to be there. He was clearly some kind of political groupie. Her first instinct was to step back and distance herself from the situation. If he wasn't on the list, that was his problem. But he seemed so harmless — and she had felt much better after talking with him. Against her better judgment she broke in, "I'm sorry, he's with me. I didn't realize that would be a problem."

"I'm sorry, ma'am, but we can't allow unauthorized people here. It's a clear violation of our policy."

"I understand, and I can see how that could be a problem. But I thought it was okay to bring a date. Can we make an exception — just this time?"

The man looked at them skeptically. "Look, ma'am, we've gotten complaints. This happens all the time, you get gate-crashers who want to be part of the scene —"

Lena moved in a little closer and softened her voice. "Couldn't we make an exception? Just this one time?"

The man sighed. Then turned to face Jason. "I'll let you go this time, buddy. But if I hear you so much as breathe on one of our guests, I'll have you thrown out and arrested for trespassing." He gave a polite nod to Lena. "Good night, ma'am." He turned and walked back the way that he'd come.

Jason sheepishly smiled. "I guess my secret is out. Thank you for that. That was very nice of you."

"No, no problem at all."

Jason reached into his pocket and removed a business

card, which he handed to Lena. "If I can ever help you with anything, just let me know. I'd better mingle before he changes his mind." A moment later he was in the crowd.

Lena studied the card; it said:

Jason Ulmer
G8 Systems Analyst
Department of Defense

She smiled as she placed it in her purse.

She was heading toward the door when a heavyset bald man stepped out of the crowd and waved her over. "Lena, over here." It was Wentworth. "I've been looking all over for you," he said. "So, did you make any big connections yet?"

Lena just smiled.

CAPTAIN PARKER CAIN had spent a nervous three weeks looking for clues to Ramon's whereabouts. The search had started with the surveillance photographs taken from the helicopters. In the initial search, as the choppers criss-crossed the road, pictures were taken of each vehicle traveling through. Once the film was developed they had narrowed the search down to a total of fifty-seven vehicles that had been on that stretch of road in the time frame directly after Ramon had fled the compound. The images of the fifty-seven vehicles had been enlarged to the point where they could isolate the license plates. It took another day to run the license numbers through the national computer and locate the addresses and phone numbers of all the owners.

The next step was to find and interrogate all the drivers and passengers in the hope of finding someone who had information that could lead them to their prey. Cain had taken forty of his most trusted men and designated

them as field agents. Their directive was to find and apprehend Ramon by whatever means necessary. They made
their approach in civilian clothes, and under a variety of
guises. Over the next few days these agents spread out
across the country following up leads and interrogating
the drivers.

By the fourth day they had found two eyewitnesses
who had seen a black semi truck pick up a hitchhiker on
the road at about the right time. Checking back with the
surveillance photos, the list of suspects was filtered down
to two. But at that point their luck went south.

Of the two trucks, one was licensed to a small outfit out
of Flagstaff, Arizona. The driver was carrying a load of
electronics across the border to Mexico City. It seemed
logical that that would be the route the fugitive would
take. Cain assigned half his force to finding the truck. But
the driver hadn't followed his itinerary. When the trucker
didn't arrive at his destination on time, there was a bit of
panic. The agents eventually picked up the trail by back-
tracking and following the fuel receipts. It took them the
better part of the week but they finally found the driver.
He was passed out, drunk in a whorehouse outside of
Guadalajara. After a full day of physical interrogation, the
agents were convinced that the driver hadn't picked up
any hitchhikers and had no knowledge of the fugitive.
And they had wasted too much time.

Meanwhile, another team had been working on finding
the other black truck. This one was registered to an owner-
operator from Barstow. He was a freelancer so it was difficult to determine who he was working for and where he
was going. Eventually they learned that the driver had
picked up a load in Brownsville and was driving it to the
East Coast. They called the company that he was delivering to and found they were too late. He had dropped the
load there two days before. It was assumed that the driver
had picked up another load in that area but finding the

right place quickly would be a matter of luck. It was impossible to know where he was now. Too much time had passed.

Cain had hoped to avoid attracting attention from outside, but he had no choice. Colonel Pope used his contacts in the Office of Homeland Security to issue an all-points bulletin through the state police network for the driver of the truck, implying that he was somehow involved in terrorism. The Indiana State Police intercepted the truck near Fort Wayne. Captain Cain personally flew out for the interrogation. The driver initially claimed ignorance; but after four hours alone with Cain in a soundproof basement room, he told them everything he knew.

Cain and his search team quickly moved out to McAllen, Texas, to set up shop. By now the trail was ice cold. The subject could just as easily have gone across the border into Mexico or caught a ride and be in hiding halfway across the country. It didn't matter. This was their only lead and they needed to work it. If he'd gone into Mexico, he was gone for good. The chances of finding him there were from slim to none. So the search would stay on this side of the border. If the subject had stayed here, without money or identification he would have limited options. Cain had his agents check the homeless shelters, immigrant centers, and sweatshops of the town, any place that a man could hide by blending in. They showed Ramon's picture around and offered a reward for any good information. They came up empty.

Next, Cain sent his men into the surrounding areas, the farms and ranches. At first it looked like this too was a dead end. But then, three weeks after they had first started the hunt, they got lucky. One of Cain's agents was in the farm country north of McAllen when he heard a story about a very peculiar "wetback."

The agent heard how this Mexican worker had attacked a foreman for no reason, hurting him so badly that the foreman had to be hospitalized. The incident happened just a day before. The worker had fled but the other foreman and the police were actively searching for him. The story sounded worth checking out, but the next statement sealed the deal. The Mexican had blue eyes.

When he heard the news, Parker Cain smiled for the first time in weeks. Their prey was still nearby. Cain took a helicopter back to the installation to meet with Colonel Pope. The colonel was going through some papers when Cain entered the office.

Colonel Pope looked up and gestured for Cain to sit. "Have a seat, Parker. I trust you have good news to report." Pope pushed aside the papers and sat expectantly awaiting the account.

"Well, sir, in a way I do. . . ."

"In a way? Have you located our rabbit yet?"

"No, sir, not exactly. But we know he's still in the area. Just yesterday he ran away from a work farm up in Duval County." Captain Cain leaned forward in his seat.

"So, you know where he was yesterday, but you do not know where he is today? Is that correct?"

"Well, sir, that is the long and short of it."

"Then whether we know that he is still in this vicinity or not is really immaterial." Pope shook his head with irritation. "Where we are is exactly where we were three weeks ago when this fiasco started."

"Well, sir, I wouldn't put it quite like that." Cain calmly leaned back in his chair. "I think we're a whole lot closer now. What I'd like to do, sir, we're goin' to need some help from our friends on the national scene. . . . I think I know how to catch this guy."

Pope gestured. "Go on."

"When I go huntin', sir, sometimes you can take your prey and just track 'em down. Just follow the signs, find 'em and take 'em down. Other times the prey takes to hiding. 'Specially if you're tracking small game— rabbit and such. They'll hide down in a bramble patch and you won't have a clue where they're at. At a time like that what you gotta do is flush 'em out."

Colonel Pope nodded. "I see. And with our rabbit? This is what you are proposing?"

Cain sat back in his chair and folded his hands on his lap, quite relaxed. "That's right, sir. We need to flush him out."

12

BARRY RESNICK'S OFFICE was on the forty-seventh floor of the Sunoco building. It was a large corner office, befitting his position with the firm. There were full-length windows on two sides, and the view of the Houston skyline was spectacular. But today Barry was getting no enjoyment from the view. He leaned forward in his chair as he stared vacantly out the window, totally engrossed in his phone call.

"OK, Richard, we agree that there is a fiduciary responsibility on the part of my clients. The total compensation you proposed in your last correspondence is acceptable, but my clients cannot accept a lump-sum distribution. We propose to pay it out over a ten-year period. . . ."

He listened intently to the voice on the other end of the line before speaking again. "Sure, but if they take it in one payment the taxes are going to kill them. Taking it in installments means that they'll keep more in their pocket. . . ." Barry smiled as the other attorney responded. This settlement was going better than he'd expected. He tried to keep satisfaction from his voice. "Well"—he paused for effect—"I think I can convince them to accept a five-year payout. But that's the absolute best we can do." Barry noticed the red light on his phone glowing to show he had a call on the second line. He ignored it.

"Great, Richard, that will be quite acceptable. There's one more thing we need to discuss. . . ."

Barry was cut off by the intercom. It was his secretary's voice. "Barry, I hate to disturb you . . ."

"Richard, can I put you on hold for a moment? . . . Thank you." Barry put the call on hold and spoke to his secretary over the intercom. "What is it, Maria?" He didn't try to hide his irritation. She was new, but this was inexcusable. She should have known better.

"I'm sorry to disturb you but there's a man on the line who insists on speaking to you."

"Who is it?"

"I don't know. He wouldn't give me his name; he just keeps saying he has to talk with you."

Barry sighed. "Look, Maria, I'm in the middle of a negotiation on the Lamson file. Until I'm done, I don't want to be bothered unless someone has died. Understand?"

"Yes, sir."

"Just put him in to my voice mail. I'll call him back as soon as I get a chance." Barry cut off the intercom and punched the button on his phone to return to his conversation. "Hello, Richard? I'm sorry about that. What I was saying is that I can get my clients to accept this deal, but we're going to need to have a confidentiality agreement. No details of the settlement will be released and your clients will be banned from disclosing any of the details. . . ." The conversation continued for several more minutes. When they were finished, the deal was substantially to Barry's satisfaction. "Great, Richard, I'll work up the changes and have them couriered over for signatures. Talk with you soon."

Barry hung up the phone and leaned back contentedly. The agreement would allow his client to settle the lawsuit at a much lower cost than they'd budgeted for, and without the negative publicity that a trial would have brought—an altogether satisfying solution. As he reached for the phone to inform his client, he saw that the red light was flashing to show that he had voice mail. Remembering the phone call, he went into the system to retrieve the message.

He froze as he heard the voice—a familiar voice with a slight Hispanic accent. "Barry, *como esta, amigo*. I really need to talk with you, man. You're not going to believe what happened. I'm still not sure that I do. I'll get back to you soon."

Barry realized he was shaking—his forehead was damp with sweat. Could it be? The voice sounded so familiar but it wasn't possible. He reached down to replay the message but in his confusion he hit the wrong command and deleted the message. "Shit!" He hit the intercom button. "Maria?"

There was no answer. He tried again, this time nearly shouting into the intercom, "Maria!"

"Yes, Barry. I just stepped away for a second."

"That call? Did he leave a name or a phone number?"

"The one I put in your voice mail?"

"Yes." Barry tried not to sound frantic. "Did he leave a number?"

"No, I just put him in to your voice mail."

"Did he say when he would call back?"

"No, he just said that he needed to speak with you. Is something wrong?"

Barry hesitated before answering, "No . . . no, it's

nothing." He hit the intercom button to end the conversation.

Barry took a deep breath, slowly exhaled, and tried to regain his composure. It was just a voice on the phone. It sounded like Ramon but that was impossible. He'd seen Ramon die with his own eyes. The body was pronounced dead and taken out for cremation. Ramon was dead. It had to be a mistake. There had to be another explanation.

The man on the message hadn't identified himself. It sounded like Ramon, but that could have been coincidence. Lots of people sound similar. It could have been anyone. Or maybe it really was Ramon's voice but it was a tape—someone had taped an earlier message and put it on his voice mail as a form of sick joke. But that didn't make sense. It was more likely that it was someone who just sounded like Ramon. Barry remembered a contractor who had done some work on his home and talked the same way. It was probably him.

Barry relaxed a little. He hadn't realized how stressed he'd been. The long hours were bound to take their toll. It had been ages since he'd taken any time off. Your mind could play strange tricks when stressed. Stress and maybe guilt. It wasn't his fault, but Barry wondered if Ramon would still be alive if a more experienced criminal attorney had handled the case. It wasn't logical. He took the case because no one else would, but it's a hard thing to deal with when a client dies.

The phone on the desk rang again. Barry hesitated. Was it the same man calling back? What if it really was Ramon? His heart racing, he picked up the phone on the third ring. "Hello?"

He relaxed when he heard the voice on the other end of the line. It was another associate calling to ask about a project involving a mutual client. Barry cut the call short. *This is ridiculous,* he thought, *acting like a kid afraid of the dark.* The problem was that he'd been working too

hard. He packed his briefcase and told Maria to hold all
his calls. He quickly left the office before having a chance
to change his mind.

Outside the building he felt better. The air was hot and
thick—sweating weather. But it was real. In the BMW on
his way home, Barry cranked the air-conditioning on high
and opened the windows just to feel a connection to the
outside world. That was the problem, he thought. His
whole life was artificial. He always left for work early.
Drove his air-conditioned car to his air-conditioned office,
where he stayed late working under fluorescent lights.
Long hours were expected of a partner and that was what
paid for their lifestyle. But was this really how he wanted
to live? His daughters hardly knew him—his relationship
with his wife was mostly through phone calls. The man
that called wasn't Ramon—it couldn't be—but it *was* a
wake-up call. What he needed was a good vacation, some
time off alone with his family. Someplace real, a place
with no phones or faxes or fluorescent lights. A quiet
place where he could rediscover what was really important.

By the time he pulled into his driveway he was excited
about the possibility of getting away. Barry pulled the car
into the garage next to his wife's van. The house was a
sprawling brick Georgian on a large lot in a gated community. The homes were beautiful, but the neighborhood
always seemed deserted. Lawn-care workers and deliv-
erymen were the only people ever outside. Barry entered
his home through the garage, shutting the door behind
him.

"Hello?" he called out. "Anybody home?" He walked
through the kitchen into the family room. The house was
quiet. Some toys were scattered on the family room floor;
otherwise there were no signs that anyone had recently
been there. His wife's car was in the garage, and she
hadn't told him of any reason that she would be gone.

Barry felt a tinge of apprehension in the pit of his stomach. The ground floor was empty. He glanced out the back window into the backyard. No one was there.

He went upstairs to check out the bedrooms, but they, too, were deserted. It was probably nothing, he thought. But it was irritating that he made the effort to come home early and no one was there. The thought occurred that they might have left a note. He hurried back down to the kitchen, but there was no note. Then again, why should there be? Who could have expected him to come home so early?

Barry opened the refrigerator and took out a diet Coke. He'd resigned himself to waiting till his family came back from wherever they'd been, when he heard the noise. It sounded like talking and it was coming from the other side of the house. He walked toward the noise. Suddenly he was feeling nervous again; it was so quiet just a minute ago.

As he approached the source of the sound, he realized that it was coming from his den. It sounded like the TV was on. The den was off limits to the kids but they must have been inside and left the set on with the volume blaring. Barry opened the den door. He was right; it was the TV. He strode across the room to turn the set off. The return to silence was jarring.

It wasn't until Barry turned to leave that he saw he wasn't alone. A tall, hard-angled man wearing mirrored sunglasses was sitting in Barry's favorite chair.

And the gun in his hand was all too real.

NORMA'S CAFÉ WAS a little diner near an industrial park just south of Houston. It was a local institution that had survived, under a series of owners, since the fifties. Norma was long gone from the picture, but no one had ever bothered to replace the sign. When it first opened, Norma's was a shiny beacon of future promise. Now, the décor was the same but the Formica had faded and the chrome long since lost its sheen. The latest owner had added one modern touch, a twenty-seven-inch color TV that sat on a shelf overlooking the counter and was always turned on.

Ramon had discovered Norma's a week before, when he had first come to Houston. Upon leaving the farm he had hitched a ride most of the way and taken a bus at the end. Some of the workers back at the farm had talked about places they knew about where a man could find work without documentation. This area was high on the list. There were hundreds of factories and warehouses here that hired workers off the books at less than minimum wage. Ramon had found a job within hours of arriving. And he had wandered into Norma's soon after that. To conserve money, Ramon was eating only one meal a day. The food here was filling and cheap—a taco with a plate piled high with beans and rice cost less than two bucks. He'd stopped in every day since his arrival a week before.

Ramon sat at the counter eating his dinner. It was just after a shift change at the local factories and the room was full. The diner echoed with the sounds of a dozen different conversations, all competing with the TV, which was set to full volume for the benefit of the hearing-impaired owner. The set was tuned in to a game show, but it could have been anything. No one was paying any attention.

The room was noisy and chaotic, yet Ramon found it comforting—it was strange. It reminded him of his time in the prison. TVs there were turned on first thing in the morning and blared out all day long. Wall-to-wall noise, just part of the background. Ramon had waited so long to be free. Now, when he finally was, he was thinking back to his jail time with nostalgia.

He glanced up at the TV. A blonde was on the screen, turning letters on a board. He was free now, he thought, but for how long? The men who were chasing him were surely still after him. What he knew was too critical for them to take chances. Maybe they were even closing in on him now. Ramon fought the urge to look behind him. He knew he was safe here. In this place he was just another laborer, invisible. But he couldn't hide out forever. He had to tell someone what had happened to him. What was still going on at the installation. It was important enough that Green had given his life trying to expose the conspiracy. What it was they were planning to do, Ramon had no idea, but he knew that it was dead wrong. Lives were at stake.

But what could he do? He couldn't just walk into the nearest police station and turn himself in. Who would believe him? "Excuse me, sir, my name is Ramon Willis and I was executed recently but they brought me back to life so they could run fiendish experiments on me." The men in the white coats would take him away, and the army men would be following right behind. Then again, it didn't matter what he did, *they* would be alerted and move in for the kill. Still, he had to do something.

Whichever way he played it, it all came out the same way. His only real chance would be through his old attorney, Barry Resnick. Barry would believe the story—after all, he'd seen Ramon die. He'd know what to do and who to contact. *It would be good to see Barry again,* Ramon thought, *I just hope he doesn't have a heart attack when he sees me.* The call to his office earlier should help, at least he was warned.

Suddenly Ramon felt that something was wrong. Was it a sound or just a feeling? He nervously looked behind him but there was no reason for concern. Everything was as it was before, people eating and joking around. No one noticed Ramon. It was paranoia pure and simple.

Ramon glanced back up at the TV. The game show was over and the local news was about to start. The news anchor was talking but with all the noise in the room Ramon couldn't make out the words he was saying. Behind the anchorman's left shoulder a graphic held the words Home

Invasion and Murder. Ramon had finished his dinner and
was ready to go. He scanned the room looking for his
waitress. He tried to signal her for the check but she was
occupied with some customers that had just walked in. He
resigned himself to waiting.

Ramon took another sip of his coffee and glanced back
at the TV. The image on the screen was such a shock that
he nearly fell off his stool. It felt like a shot of adrenaline
had been injected straight into his spine. Barry Resnick's
face was full screen on the TV—a photograph from some
social function. Ramon's heart threatened to leap out of
his chest. He stood up and quickly moved closer to the
TV, trying to hear the sound.

He moved in as close as he could. A man was sitting at
the counter directly below the TV, and Ramon crowded in
behind him. The man turned back and shot a glance at
Ramon, but Ramon didn't notice. His attention was turned
to the television.

The image on the screen was now showing a video clip
of a large suburban home with yellow police tape cordon-
ing off the perimeter. Straining, he could just make out
what they were saying—"Mr. Resnick was an attorney respected in the community for his work on behalf of local
charities. Mr. Resnick was killed in his home this afternoon in a home invasion that appears to be a botched robbery attempt. He is survived by his wife and two
daughters, all of whom were away from the house at the
time of the crime. . . ."

Ramon felt his knees go weak. Barry was dead. It was
such a shock to hear that he was gone. Another day and
they would have made contact.

The image on the TV changed again and Ramon's
shock changed to near panic. The new picture on the
screen was a police drawing of a Hispanic man—but this
picture looked amazingly like himself. He focused in on
the announcer's voice: "Police are searching for a possi-

ble suspect who was seen near the scene of the crime. He is described as a large Hispanic male, thirty to thirty-five years of age, approximately six feet tall and very muscular. The suspect is very recognizable by his eyes, blue eyes that are inconsistent with his ethnic background. He is thought to be armed and is considered extremely dangerous."

Ramon stood frozen. They were saying that he had killed Barry. Or was it just a strange coincidence that the killer looked so much like him? No, that was too much to believe. It was a setup. It was connected to the installation in some way. It had to be.

Ramon's thoughts were broken as the man that he was standing behind turned full around to face Ramon. The man looked straight into his eyes—his blue eyes. "Say, pal, can you move? I'm tryin' to eat and you're crowdin' me."

Ramon backed away like a scared rabbit. He took a quick glance around the room. Everything seemed the same. No one was staring at him or paying him any attention. Still, there was a buzzing in his ears and the walls seemed to be closing in. He wanted to scream and run out of the room—either that or hit somebody.

Instead, he moved as casually as he could back to his seat. He pulled out some money, laid it down to pay the bill, then headed out the door. He kept his eyes on the floor the whole way.

13 _____

LENA HADN'T PLANNED on working so late. It was her last night in Austin and her intention was to go out with some friends. A quiet dinner and then home early. Something low-key and relaxing, but it hadn't worked out as she had planned. That afternoon she had packed up everything in her desk to be shipped to her new office in Washington. All the personal belongings from her apartment had already been loaded up on the truck earlier that day. For the next few days she'd be living out of a suitcase as she drove out to D.C.

Lena was set to walk out the door at five, when she got the call from Jack Van Russell, her managing editor. He had gotten a call from an old friend with a story about a married congressman who was rumored to have been arrested for drunken driving in Tijuana while in the company of a transvestite prostitute. Lena jumped in to try to verify the story. She called sources and searched databases trying to find someone who could substantiate the rumor. The more she found out, the more she was convinced that the story was bogus. By the time she finished running down the story it was after nine o'clock and the evening was shot.

For the first time, Lena realized how quiet the office was. There were pockets of activity in the building at all times, day or night. But now her section was nearly deserted. Everyone was either home for the night, on assignment, or elsewhere in the building. There was usually a steady hum of activity, phones ringing, people talking, the electronic buzz of computers. Busy, comforting sounds. Tonight it seemed unnaturally silent. Lena had packed up her briefcase and was preparing to leave, when the ringing of the telephone at her desk broke the stillness of the room.

She picked it up on the second ring. "Hello, Lena Dryer."

There was no answer. "Hello . . . Hello?" Still no answer. She hung up the phone. *Strange,* she thought, *probably just a wrong number.* Still, it set her on edge. When the series she wrote on the death penalty had first been printed, Lena had gotten a number of angry calls and letters from readers who didn't share her views. The calls had died down after a couple of weeks. Perhaps this was another indignant reader with a long memory. She took a last glance at her desk, then picked up her briefcase, hung her purse on her shoulder, and headed for the elevator.

The elevator doors slid open; the car was empty. She entered and pushed the button for the lower level. Slowly, she descended through the building. She'd never noticed it before, but the dim fluorescent lighting cast sinister shadows across the inside of the car. On the third floor, the elevator stopped and the doors opened. But no one was waiting and no one got on. As the doors again closed and the car resumed moving, Lena realized that her whole body was tense. She took a deep breath and willed herself to relax. This was so unlike her, she thought, seeing danger where none existed. She'd ridden the elevator hundreds of times before without giving it a second thought. Why was she so spooked now?

It had to have something to do with her new job and the move to Washington. It was what she wanted, what she had been working so hard to achieve. But maybe that was the problem. Maybe this was her subconscious mind telling her that she was making a mistake. Maybe the dread she felt was really fear of the unknown, fear of making the wrong decision. Her whole life was being turned upside down. She was up on a high wire and they'd taken away the net. It was normal to feel anxiety in a situation like that. Time would tell if she was making the right decision, she reminded herself, and she was still young; there was plenty of time to change. Sometime in the future she would slow down and get her life in balance. Sometime, but not yet.

When the elevator door opened, depositing her on the lower level of the building, she had rationalized her fear but hadn't conquered it. Lena walked out into a short foyer that opened into the entrance to the parking garage. As she walked into the parking structure the door closed behind her with a thud. The echo of her footsteps against the hard cement resonated through the empty deck. There was a sour smell, like old urine mixed with dust. It hung in the dry air.

Her car was parked on the first level at the end of the aisle. Most of the cars were gone by this time of night, but those that were still there threw out shadows that hinted at the presence of something unseen. Lena glanced behind her; there was nothing. She picked up her pace and hurried faster toward her car.

Upon reaching the car she fumbled in her purse for the keys. Her hands were shaking. *This is absurd,* she thought. Like whistling past a graveyard as a schoolgirl, terrified of the dark. She set down her briefcase and riffled through her purse. Her hand grazed against a can of mace before gripping onto the keys. *It's all right,* she thought, *just calm down.* Then she heard the footsteps come up behind her.

A surge of adrenaline rushed through her body. Keeping her hand inside her purse she grasped for the can of mace as she spun around toward the source of the sound. "Don't move," she shouted. "I've got a gun!"

A tall, muscular Hispanic man was standing about six feet in front of her. He calmly raised his hands to show that he wasn't carrying a weapon. "It's okay. I'm not going to hurt you," he spoke quietly. "Do you remember me?"

Lena's head suddenly felt cloudy. Everything seemed so dreamlike and unreal. She stared at his eyes—his clear blue eyes. Her purse dropped out of her hands and landed on the hard cement floor. "Yes," she said. "Yes, I do."

"HOW DO I know you're really him?" They were in Lena's car now. It had seemed wise to get away from the parking deck as quickly as they could. If someone were looking for them, they would be sitting ducks out in the open. Lena drove through the outskirts of Austin, heading north, no clear destination in mind. She constantly checked her rearview mirror for any signs that they were being followed. Ramon had poured out the basics of the story as she drove. It was so bizarre and unbelievable—but how else could she explain his being there? She glanced over at Ramon. Even as she asked the question she knew that it was really him. Still, Lena repeated her question. "I mean how do I know you are who you say you are?"

Ramon looked away from the window and into her eyes. When they had first started out, he had slumped down in the passenger seat, crunched down below the window line trying to appear invisible. Now he sat tall and straight in the seat. Something about his look caused her to flush. Lena turned back to the road. "You met me before," he said. "Who else could I be?"

"I don't know. Maybe you're his twin or something. For all I know this could be a scam of some kind. There must be some other explanation. I saw you . . . or him, die."

"You saw what you saw. I know how weird this is. I've had a hard time believing it myself." Ramon turned back to the window. He spoke so quietly that she had to strain to hear him.

"I keep thinking the same thing, that this is some kind of dream. That I'm going to wake up and it'll all be over," he said. "But then I do wake up and it's all the same. This ain't no dream. This is real, and I'm real, too."

They were both quiet for a time. Lena continued driving north, past the suburbs and into the thinly populated expanse of central Texas. Where would they go now? What could she do? One thing was for certain, Washington was out of the question. That would have to wait. If this really was Ramon Willis—and in her heart she knew that it was—then they were in deep trouble. If the story was true, he was being pursued by dangerous men who would use any means necessary to silence him. And now her, too. But there was really no choice. He'd come to her for help. She had to help. And besides, if it was true, this was one hell of a story.

"Are you hungry or anything?" Her voice cut through the droning of the engine and the hum of the tires against the road.

"No. Thank you, I'm fine." Silence returned.

Lena kept quiet for a minute before speaking again, "What was it like?"

Ramon had been staring out the window seemingly lost in thought. The question startled him. "What?"

"What was it like? Dying, I mean."

Ramon thought for a moment before answering. "I don't know. I don't think I was ever really dead. . . . It was a setup. I just remember a dream about snow, and then I woke up. It wasn't peaceful. It wasn't going toward the light or anything. When I first woke up, I was sure I was in hell."

Lena kept her eyes on the road and listened.

"It's kind of funny," Ramon continued, "I've spent a big part of my life in jail for a crime that I didn't do. Sitting in a cage waiting for them to kill me. Then this thing happens and I'm a prisoner again but this time they use me like some human lab rat. And I know that if I'd stayed in there I'd be dead for real. Now I'm out, but I'm not free. They're still trying to pull my strings and make me dance. You know what I mean? I'm running and hiding and I didn't do anything wrong."

Lena nodded her head but didn't respond. She checked the rearview mirror again. No one was behind them. It was a long time before he spoke again.

"Do you believe in fate?" Ramon asked.

"How do you mean?"

"*Destino*, fate. That you're born the way you are, you can't change who you are or what's meant to be."

"No, I don't accept that at all. If I thought that, life would be pointless."

Ramon considered the thought. "Maybe. Maybe not. You still have to play it out. I think I got out for a reason. Maybe this is my fate. Either way, I don't want to keep running."

Lena nodded again. "If your story checks out they're the ones that will need to run."

Ramon stared out at the night. The headlights cut a small swath of light into the sea of darkness. "Maybe," he said. "We'll see."

"Yes, I guess we will at that." Lena focused on the

road. Did she know what she was getting into? If it was as Ramon had said it was, they were in way over her head. It was one thing to investigate corruption in local government. Even on a national level, Nixon hadn't killed the people on his enemies list. But this was different. The army, if that's who it was, would kill to protect their secrets. What kind of project was worth that kind of risk?

They passed a sign announcing an exit for the towns of Cedar Park and Hutto. The first thing they needed to do was to find a place to hide. Somewhere that she would have some time to sort things out. She needed to find out what was real and what wasn't. Till now she'd been driving more or less by instinct. Lena had known that she had to leave the city, but she didn't have an idea of where to go. But she needed to go somewhere. Some months back she had spent a weekend with friends up near Cedar Park. There was an old motel there, just off the main road but secluded. It would be a place to rest and plan their next move. Lena took the exit.

THE MOTEL WAS a relic from the fifties, consisting of a series of small whitewashed bungalows set far back and below the main road. The neon sign in front was permanently affixed to Vacancy. Lena pulled in back of the building that served as the office. Ramon stayed in the car while she went to check them in. He looked around. Except for the glow of the sign, everything was black. All the other cabins were dark, either empty or their occupants in bed. He could hear the buzz of cars going by on the road above, but none of the light filtered down.

Was this a mistake? When he'd found out that Barry was dead he knew that he needed to tell someone, but why her? He hardly knew her at all. Just general impressions from a short talk. And she was with the press, the media—her allegiance was to getting the story. Why would she care about him or his situation? Once the story broke, who could tell what would happen? He'd be at the center of a circus with a spotlight focused on him—a spotlight that would put him in the sights of both the legal authorities and the army men who were pursuing him. It was guaranteed to bring trouble. The options weren't good. Either *they* would kill him or the authorities would put him back in jail and reset the date of execution.

Either way he was a dead man.

He'd done his part by contacting her and telling what had happened at the installation. Now was the time to pass the torch. She and her newspaper could do the investigation and stand in the spotlight. Ramon would move off into the shadows and disappear.

He was lost in thought when Lena returned. She gave him a strange look as she got in. "There was only one unit left. We got the last one." She pulled the car along the side of their cabin, out of view from the road. She unlocked the door to the room and they quickly went inside.

It was a small room wallpapered in a dingy yellow floral pattern with a dirty rust-colored shag carpet, the kind that had been popular years before. The dim light from the overhead fixture cast long shadows on the far wall. There was a large water stain on the ceiling and a strong smell of mothballs. The only furniture was a small nightstand and one double bed.

Ramon strode across the room. It was hardly bigger than his old jail cell. He opened the bathroom door and glanced inside. More water stains on the ceiling and a blotch of mildew on the shower curtain. *What was he doing here?* The cramped room made him uncomfortable, but it was more than that. It felt so strange being alone with this woman. He hardly knew her, yet he felt a sense of security and closeness. He'd felt it the first time that they'd met. A chemistry maybe. In the car, so close he could smell her scent, he'd thought of how long it had been since he'd been with a woman. But she was so different from him and his background, so unattainable. Sitting so close to her it had felt like a fire burned in his chest. Sexual attraction, lust, whatever you want to call it, that was part of it—but not everything. It seemed like she understood who he was without passing judgment.

Ramon caught his reflection in the bathroom mirror. He was unshaven and dirty. Wild looking. She'd have to have been scared but she'd still taken him in. That showed courage. And what would happen to her now? That spotlight shone two ways. By approaching her he had made sure that his pursuers—his enemies—would now turn their sights on her. It wouldn't have mattered who he had approached, the results would have been the same. But by contacting her, he'd made Lena a target.

Looking in the mirror, Ramon knew that as much as he wanted to be done with the whole mess he couldn't just leave. It wasn't a game of tag—from Green, to him, to Lena. He owed it to Green—no, he owed it to himself to follow this thing through. What they were doing at the installation was dead wrong. But it wasn't his choice anyway. There was no way that they would let him walk away after what he had been through. Not with what he knew. He'd never be free till the whole operation had been brought down.

As he turned back toward the main room he realized that Lena was still standing in the doorway. By the look on her face he could tell that something was wrong. "Are you all right?" he asked.

She didn't reply. But she didn't have to. He could see it in her eyes and the expression on his face. He was the problem. They were being pursued by professional killers. There was a conspiracy that included parts of the U.S. government itself. But from her viewpoint, right now he was the threat, or at least a potential threat. He would never hurt her, but in a way she was right. He did want her. He could picture them together, quick, hot images flashed in his mind. His pulse quickened. He took a deep breath and slowly let it out. "I'm not going to hurt you," he said.

Lena stared at him hard without speaking.

"I know what you're thinking, and it's not true. I've never killed anyone. If there were a way I could prove it, I would." Ramon stepped forward into the room and Lena backed away. He stopped. "I haven't always been the best person, but . . ." He spread his hands, palms out. "I'm not a murderer."

He looked back at her, trying to get a clue of what she was thinking. It was like she was trying to read him, too. There was fear there, but also a kind of openness, as if she wanted to believe him, but needed to find a way. But how could he show her? How could he prove it to her when he couldn't prove it to a judge or jury? He knew the truth, but in the end, the truth didn't matter. People believed what they wanted to believe. He dropped his hands to his side. "Maybe I made a mistake," he said. "I shouldn't have come to you. I didn't know where else to go."

Lena looked into his eyes for a long time. Then she nodded her head. "I believe you."

14

BY ALL ACCOUNTS, Captain Pearson of the Houston police department was not having a good day. The temperature outside was near the century mark and the station's air-conditioning was on the fritz. Hot weather always increased tensions in the neighborhoods, but with vacations and sick days he was critically short on officers even as the crime rate was moving up. And now, to make matters worse the police superintendent had just confirmed the bad news that the two men sitting across from him had announced.

"This is bullshit!" He slammed the phone down. "I've never heard a bigger crock in my whole life."

The air-conditioning was blowing hard but it just moved warm air around the room. Parker Cain, sitting across the desk from Pearson, didn't mind. He was used to the heat. Hot or cold, it didn't matter. Through training and discipline he had learned not to let variations in the environment affect his state of mind. He could endure whatever was necessary when he was in pursuit of a goal. And today he was very close to accomplishing his objective.

Cain tried not to smile. It seemed almost too easy. The rabbit had been flushed out and ran straight into the net. Now all that Cain had to do was step forward and claim his prize.

Today he wore a uniform of a different sort. A long-sleeved white shirt with a maroon tie and navy pants, the required dress for the part he played. Cain adjusted his sunglasses and glanced back at Pearson, a burly man with thick blond hair, a mustache, and crooked teeth. He looked like he'd be more at home in northern Minnesota than south Texas. His shirt was soaked through with sweat and his face was crimson with anger.

"Your dissatisfaction has been noted, Captain," Cain replied coolly.

"Bullshit!" Pearson snorted as he gripped the arms of his chair to control his anger.

Cain shrugged. The world was filled with sore losers. It didn't matter. This oaf was about to help him, like it or not. With the rabbit flushed out, they'd needed to be in position to finish the hunt. For this assignment he wanted to come in small. This pickup would be a two-man job. He'd only brought along Rev Tanner, a lieutenant at the installation who had proved that he could be trusted.

It had taken a few phone calls to arrange for credentials from the Office of Homeland Security. A federal warrant for the subject—now identified as Hector Ramerez—hadn't taken much longer. Getting the subject's fingerprints changed over to his new identity and refiled in the national archives was harder. The FBI kept the directory and they weren't known to cooperate. But when the need arose, Colonel Pope always had the connections to get things done.

"I sure can appreciate how frustratin' this must be for you, Captain. . . ."

"No, you don't. This is pure bull. We track this creep down and you Feds come in to steal all the glory." Pearson groused as he mopped his forehead with a paper towel. "You bastards . . ."

"Calm down there, Captain." Cain cut in. His voice was calm and he spoke slowly and softly, "It's awful hot in here and that puts us all a little out of sorts. You might want to be careful you don't say somethin' that you might regret."

Pearson grunted again. "This is a crock."

Cain shrugged. Let him rant and get it out of his system. It wouldn't change anything. He sat back in his chair and listened.

"This blows. We got a suspect for murder and you want to take this guy down on some bullshit charge and you won't even tell me the specifics. It freakin' blows."

"It's already been established that we have jurisdiction," Cain said. "The Office of Homeland Security has been after this guy for over six months—it's confidential, but this could be a security issue. We've got the federal warrant and your boss has already told ya to give him up. This boy is ours."

"Bullshit!"

Cain suddenly leaned forward in his chair. "Let's cut the crap, Bubba. This guy's face has been flashed all over the TV for the last two days. So you took the call and picked him up at some motel—just where the desk clerk said he'd be. Sherlock Holmes couldn't a done it better. Congratulations, but quit the whining and do your job. Why don't you take us on down and let us have a look." He sat back in his chair, "Or would you rather call your superintendent one more time?"

A short time later Pearson was leading them through the hallways to the main lockup. As they walked, Cain looked over at Rev Tanner. He was big and black as jet. He walked with the grace of a natural athlete, but was now bathed in sweat.

"You okay there, Rev?" Cain asked.

Rev nodded his head. "I'm fine, sir. I like the hot weather." He wiped his brow with an already saturated handkerchief. "I once worked a summer in a bakery in Jackson, Mississippi. Now that was hot. This? This ain't nothin'. I like it." Rev grinned. He was built like a coke machine, big and rock solid. As big as he was, he looked like he would be slow; but Cain had been with him in situations before. He knew that Rev would do what was necessary, whatever it took to get the job done. He was the kind of man that Cain could depend on.

They moved through a doorway into the cell block. Pearson had a quick conversation with one of the officers on duty who then led them over to the cell where they were keeping the prisoner.

The jailer unlocked the cell and Cain walked in. The prisoner was lying on his bunk facing away from the door. He didn't move until Cain was within an arm's length of him. The prisoner rolled on his elbow, facing Cain. The first thing Cain noticed was the scar along the jawline. The second thing he noticed were the eyes.

Something wasn't right. There was a resemblance here—a close resemblance but this wasn't his rabbit. Suddenly Cain felt a wave of anger. A rage inside him came to a quick boil and he fought the urge to strike out.

It would be so easy. Just one step forward and he could grab the man's neck. A quick twist and it would snap like a chicken's. Or he could throw the moron to the ground and stomp his head like a ripe pumpkin. It would feel so good, it would be a release—but it would bring so many new problems, too.

Discipline, he had to maintain control.

Cain took a deep breath and let the wave pass before he

turned back toward the others. "I guess you can keep him after all, Cap'n. This ain't the guy."

LENA DIDN'T SLEEP well that night. Her head was spinning with the possibilities. Her initial shock and fear had given way to a sense of almost joy. One of the biggest stories in decades had dropped right into her lap. A dead man was alive and the government was recycling death row inmates to use as guinea pigs in some bizarre experiment.

It was inconceivable — but strange things had happened before. There were other times when the impossible had turned out to be true. It had taken years for the government to admit that they had used poor black men in experiments with syphilis; or that the CIA had used drug dealing to finance the Contras. Or Waco. If the ends would justify the means most anything was possible, and this was strange enough to be true. Lena knew that if she could find proof, her career was made.

That morning she sat down across from Ramon, got out her notepad and turned on the tape recorder. "Okay, tell me what happened again. This time I want you to describe it in as much detail as you can."

Ramon talked for over two hours. He started with his time in prison, his final week, and the preparations for the execution. She stopped and asked more questions when he mentioned that the prison doctor had examined him the last week.

"Had you ever seen him before?"

"No, that was the only time."

"And he took a blood sample? What was that for?"

"I don't know. He just jammed the needle in. He didn't say why."

Ramon went on to describe what it felt like in the death chamber when he went under the drugs, and how it was when he woke up in the white room. He told her about the men in the space suits who came by in regular shifts to check on his condition, and how he had tried to escape when he had seen what they had done with Billy Dale Burke. He told her all about Green; how they had escaped from the building; about the disinfectant showers, the checkpoints, and the guard stations.

"You were being kept underground?"

"Yes, we had to take elevators up twice."

"Did Green know who you were?"

"I don't think so. He didn't say anyway."

"Right . . . What was his first name? Green's."

"Um, I'm not sure I remember." Ramon paused for a moment. "Wait, I think it was Charley. Yeah, it was on the papers, it was Charley."

"Charley Green?"

"Yeah, I'm sure that was it."

Ramon continued with how he had managed to get away after Green had died. How the truck driver had helped him get past the roadblocks and his time working at the farm. He ended with his trying to contact Barry just before Barry had been killed, supposedly by a man meeting Ramon's description. "After that happened I knew they were still after me. I thought of you. I knew that you would believe me and maybe you could do something about it."

Ramon brought out his bag and showed her the items that he had taken out of the installation—the order papers, the gun, and the computer tape cartridge. The papers were important because they were documentation from the LBJ Installation that supported his claims. But it was the tape cartridge that excited her. What could be on there? She couldn't use the cartridge with her laptop but thought that someone at the paper might have the equipment to do it. That would be for later, though. There were a lot of other things that she needed to check first.

It was still early but the small motel room was already getting hot and the window air conditioner was doing little to keep up. Ramon stepped outside to get some air while Lena looked over her notes.

When investigating a story, Lena had been taught to start with the information given and question everything. There were several avenues to explore. First she needed to check all the facts she had been given about Green and the Johnson Installation. What kind of facility was it? Who was in charge? Had an officer named Charley Green been posted there? Had he been listed as killed recently? Then there was the prison angle—how do they dispose of bodies after the executions? Who handled the task? How did they do it and what documentation did they have?

Lena got her laptop computer from the trunk and set it up. She was surprised that the phone connection worked; it appeared that the phone system was the only thing in the room that had been updated in recent years. She logged on to the Internet and went into the government archives, punching in the Lyndon B. Johnson Installation as a keyword.

A moment later several options appeared on the screen. The first was a list of army bases throughout the country. There was indeed a Johnson Installation in west Texas. She clicked on the name and the screen showed the homepage for the Johnson Installation. The information it gave was minimal at best. It stated that the camp was used for training and as a supply depot. It also stated that the commanding officer of the facility was a Colonel Lucian Pope. Lena made notes, then looked for the next connection. There were several other mentions of the base but nothing that gave her any information that was in any way helpful.

Lena then backed out of the government site and used Google to do a wider search on the web. Here again there was precious little information. She tried again using Pope's name as a keyword in several databases. This brought a slightly better result. There was a listing in

Who's Who that gave a thumbnail description of his background. Pope had graduated at the top of his West Point class in 1964. He saw action in Vietnam, Granada, and Desert Storm, and had taught strategy and tactics at the War College at West Point.

She went to the next hit on the list. It was one of a number of newspaper articles that related his fast rise up through the ranks. He had been one of the youngest officers to be commissioned as a colonel; being black, it was even rarer. She skimmed through all the articles and references. The themes of all of them were the same: Great things were expected of Pope. But the last mention was from over ten years ago and according to the Johnson Installation home page he was still a colonel.

Lena tried several related searches with no luck. The information on Pope was curious but it didn't bring any insight. What she really needed was a directory of soldiers stationed at the installation. If there was any information on Charley Green, that would be a first layer of proof. She thought a moment, then opened her phone list, found the name she was looking for and made the call.

After a moment a voice answered, "Department of Defense, Mrs. Hamilton speaking."

"Yes, I'd like to speak with Jason Ulmer please."

"One moment. I'll transfer you."

Lena tried to think of what she would say when he answered, but he was on the line too quickly.

"Jason Ulmer," he answered.

"Hello, Jason, this is Lena, Lena Dryer."

"Lena? . . . Um . . ."

"We met a couple of weeks back, at the affair for the Chilean delegation."

His voice came back with enthusiasm. "Oh God, I'm sorry. Lena, of course. Lena from Texas. How are you? Have you moved up yet?"

"Not yet, but soon. Listen, Jason, I wonder if I can ask

you a favor. I'm trying to track down an old friend. He's in the army and I've kind of lost track. I'm trying to find out where he's stationed. Can you get that kind of information?"

"Sure. Probably. I'll punch it into the computer—you don't have his service number do you?"

"No . . ."

"Well, no problem. That would have been too easy. What's his name?"

Lena could hear him working the keyboard in the background. "Charley Green," she said.

"Charley Green, okay . . . we'll try it as Charles . . . Wow. I'm going to need some more information. I just got one hundred forty-two matches."

"He was stationed at the Lyndon Johnson Installation."

"In Texas?"

"Yes, that's right."

Lena heard the clatter of fingers hitting keys. "Hmmm, that's funny, I'm not showing that." He paused for a moment but the keyboard clatter didn't slow down. "I'll tell you what, let me do some checking and I'll get back to you shortly. Where can I call you?"

Lena gave him the number for the motel and hung up the phone. She glanced out the window. Ramon was outside leaning against the car, visible only from her cabin. She turned back to her notes. The morning was nearly gone and she was hardly further than where she started. And she still needed to run down the prison angle. She went through her notes again looking for discrepancies and hoping that Jason would call back soon.

It was about forty-five minutes later when the phone did ring. Lena snatched it up. "Hello?"

"Lena, it's me." Jason's voice was just more than a whisper, like he was afraid someone might be listening. "You know, I shouldn't really be telling you this, but— how well did you know this guy?"

"Why? What's wrong?"

"I had to do some checking. Everything about the Johnson Installation is classified and—well, I'm sorry but your friend is dead. He died in a training accident about a month ago."

Lena felt a rush of excitement. She couldn't wait to get off the phone and call Jack Van Russell, her editor. The story was real. It was checking out.

PARKER CAIN WASN'T used to failure. When the rabbit had first escaped, Cain assumed that it would be quick work to catch him. But now, weeks later, he was again back to square one. The longer the subject was out, the more dangerous it was for all of them. If he told his story—if someone believed him—all their work could be brought down.

The last few days had been especially frustrating. With all the publicity on the killing of the attorney, there had been numerous calls claiming knowledge of the killer. But without fail they were a waste of time. Each call had to be checked out. Some were from people obviously holding grudges. Others were sincere calls that just didn't check out. Investigating one lead from a factory foreman down in south Houston, the tip appeared to be real. A temporary worker at the factory matched the description of the killer. Everything checked out, the dates he worked matched up and the worker's description was corroborated by other employees. But the worker hadn't shown up the last two days and the addresses he had left were all bogus. Another dead end.

Maybe he had underestimated this rabbit, Cain thought. To have evaded detection this long he had to be intelligent, or at least resourceful. Cain's experience with convicts was that they were impulsive and prone to mistakes. In almost all cases they lacked discipline. That's how they'd wound up in prison in the first place. With the

pressure this rabbit was under, it was a wonder that he
hadn't done something to call attention to himself. But so
far he hadn't.

The rabbit wasn't the only one feeling the pressure.
Colonel Pope made it quite clear that he was not pleased
with the progress of the search. If Cain didn't perform
soon, he would be replaced. And that wasn't an acceptable
outcome.

Today looked like more of the same. There was a reported sighting down by Galveston and they were on the
way to investigate. Cain glanced over at Rev Tanner in
the seat next to him, both hands on the wheel and his
eyes focused on the road. When they first came down,
Rev had talked all the time. Now he wouldn't say a word
until he was spoken to. People handled stress in different
ways.

The pager on his belt began to beep. Cain hit the button and read the number. They were passing a sign for an
upcoming rest station. Cain motioned with his hand. "Pull
in there, I need to check in."

Tanner nodded and eased the car off the exit, down a
short road into the parking area. There were a few picnic
tables, two old brown restrooms and a telephone booth.

"Wait here." Cain got out of the car, headed to the
phone booth, dropped a quarter in the slot, and punched in
a number. Moments later it was answered by a robotic
voice demanding that he enter his access code. He hit the
numbers and waited till his call was put through. He
waited patiently till he heard the voice on the other end.

"Can I have your password, please?"

Cain recognized the voice of Major Bob Durmo.
"What's shakin', Bob?"

"Parker?"

"Yeah, who're you expectin'?"

"I'm sorry, Parker, I still need to hear the password."

"Jesus . . ."

"I'm sorry, Parker, it's the colonel's orders."

"Shit. Tomcat alley forthright. Okay?"

"Sorry, Parker. It wasn't my idea."

"Right. What'd you call me for?" Cain let his irritation slip out. He'd always thought that Durmo was proof that brownnosing was good for career advancement.

"I think we've got a break. I wanted to let you know."

"What's going on?" Cain felt a touch of apprehension. After all he had been through was someone else going to snare his rabbit?

"Someone's been asking questions about the base. Specific questions, asking about Green, too."

"Yeah?"

"Well, word got back. We traced it down to some schlep in the Defense Department. He was picked up by two of our men an hour ago. It didn't take him long to tell his story. He was checking it out for a friend of his. A reporter."

"Shit!"

"Her name's Lena Dryer. We got the phone number for the place she called him from. It's a motel just north of Austin."

"I'm on my way."

"I've got a detail heading there now." Cain detected a note of triumph in Durmo's voice. "I'm sending another over to her home address."

Cain got the rest of the details and quickly went back to the car. They changed directions, making a beeline toward Austin. Cain made some calls on his cell phone to get the background on the reporter, Lena Dryer. At top speed it took them nearly two hours, but somehow, they still beat the contingent from the base.

But it didn't matter. They were too late. The girl had left earlier that day. The desk clerk didn't know where they were going and though he thought that she was with

someone, he hadn't seen the person and couldn't give a
description.

Cain made a quick search of the cabin where they had
stayed, but found nothing that would be of help. They'd
missed the rabbit again. But this time they were close. He
was still in the area, still within striking distance. And it
looked like he'd made a mistake. The reporter was
naïve—the phone call was a big mistake. The rabbit must
have linked up with the reporter recently, since she was
just checking out his story that day. That meant she was
still trying to put the details together.

Cain looked over at Rev Tanner and smiled. He felt
better than he had all day. "If she's going to do this as a
story she'll have to run it by her editor. The editor is the
key."

15

THE PLAZA ACROSS from the *Austin Star* building contained a series of fountains. Almost a block square, it was surrounded by office buildings on all sides. Concrete benches encircled the fountains, and the area in between was an open landscaped terrace. The workers from the nearby buildings often ate lunch there, or walked among the fountains during breaks. That day the weather was the coolest that it had been in weeks. The sky was clear and the temperature a comfortable seventy-four degrees. So the plaza was busier than normal.

Jack Van Russell checked his watch as he exited the *Star* building and made his way across to the plaza. Twelve twenty-five—five minutes to spare. Tall and lanky, with a full head of snow-white hair, he wore a navy-blue Brooks Brothers suit with his signature cowboy boots, bolo tie, and oversized belt buckle. He knew that he cut a striking figure for a man of his age.

It was a beautiful day for a walk, and a nice change of pace to leave the office during the day. His normal routine called for a spartan lunch served at his desk while he worked on assignments for the next day's edition. His job called for long hours and a single-minded commitment to the final result. Getting out of the office was a luxury that he couldn't often afford.

The paper was his life—had been for nearly forty years. Like the old-timers used to say, ink ran through his veins. The single thing he was proudest of in the entire world, above his wife, above his kids, above everything— was that he put out a damned fine newspaper.

It was a treat to be outside on such a wonderful day. Though he'd enjoy it more, he thought, if he wasn't so concerned with his problems with Lena. It sure looked like he'd made a mistake. She had all the attributes—intelligence, ambition, and instinct, the ability to find the overlooked story—the angle that everyone else had missed. She was still young. She needed seasoning, but her work had been exceptional. If he hadn't offered her the job, he knew it would have only been a matter of time before he lost her. She was too ambitious to stay put.

But the Washington assignment was a plum, the most coveted position the *Star* had to offer. Maybe it was immaturity, but her recent behavior really had him worried. Over the last several days she had missed two planned conference calls and had failed to check in with the Washington bureau as agreed.

And then this. Lena had called yesterday and told him she'd come across something astounding. It was something she couldn't tell over the phone. She had to meet in person, but it couldn't be at the office. It had to be someplace in the open—the office might be bugged or something. The paranoia was surprising; it didn't seem like her. But change did funny things to people. Maybe the advice columnist in the paper was right in saying that sometimes people had a fear of success. Getting too close to achieving her goals, maybe Lena needed to sabotage them in order to maintain her self-image. It was a shame, but one way or another, he'd have to deal with the problem today.

Jack scanned the plaza but didn't see any sign of Lena. It looked like he was there first. He made his way over to an empty bench near a fountain in the center. He straightened his bolo tie and sat down with his back to the fountain, positioned so it would be easy for her to find him, and he could observe the people going by while he waited.

Hopefully she wouldn't be too late. But then again, it felt good being outside. He nodded a silent hello to a young woman in a mini dress and high heels who reminded him of his granddaughter. Looking around, he noticed a tourist taking the whole scene in with a video camera. A couple walked by holding hands and talking quietly. A tall businessman with mirrored sunglasses strolled past talking on a cellular phone. Jack checked his watch again: twelve-thirty-one. In a way he hoped she was late; it was too nice of a day for a confrontation.

CAPTAIN PARKER CAIN walked past the old man and positioned himself at the next fountain over. He turned back so that he had an unobstructed view of the bench where the old man sat. It wouldn't be long now. If the editor — the old man — was here, that meant they were coming.

He tapped a button on his phone and spoke quietly into the mouthpiece. "Sighting confirmed. We got one target. You boys in position? Sound off in order."

There was a burst of static, then he listened as each man called out his position.

"This is North, I got him dead-on."

"East here, I'm in position."

"South, I got the backside."

"West here, Rover. My position is covered."

Cain tapped the button on his phone again, "That's

good, fellas. Call out if you see our primaries. No one shoots till I give the order."

Cain signed off but kept the phone in his hand, ready to respond to any new developments. This was the perfect cover. A man talking on a cell phone wouldn't attract a second glance—though in this case the cell phone was actually a networked line set to an encrypted channel. He had full communication with the four men stationed in the buildings surrounding the plaza. These men, with their high-powered rifles and telescopic sights, were positioned so that no matter where in the plaza the targets were, they would be in the sights of at least two of the snipers.

Cain sat down on the bench and turned at an angle so that he could keep an eye on his prey without staring. He reached into his pocket and removed a small device resembling a Sony Walkman. It was connected by a slim wire to an earplug, which he placed in his left ear. He pointed the device toward the old man's bench. He could hear the babble of background sounds and dozens of unconnected conversations. He slowly twisted the knobs, bringing the sound into focus. He saw the old man smile and nod to a young woman passing by. Through the earplug Cain heard the old man's greeting with perfect clarity. Now he was set.

After missing the rabbit at the motel, Cain knew he was close. But hooking up with the reporter was a surprising move—one that should have been anticipated. She wasn't on the visitor's list at the prison because she had been cleared directly through the warden. If she'd been on the list, she would have been tagged for observation. There was no doubt that they had blown an opportunity. Cain was relieved to be getting a second chance.

As soon as he found out about the reporter, he had arranged for phone taps on all of the *Star*'s managerial staff. It was the logical thing to do. Having the rabbit run to her must have seemed like a gift from heaven, a big boost for her career. Her self-interest was in breaking the story, and she'd have to get it cleared through management before she could pursue it. But what if he was wrong? What if she didn't go after the story? If she decided to go to the authorities instead—*if* she found someone who believed her—then Cain and his men would have to retreat. And if she really had the evidence, there would be hell to pay.

But she didn't disappoint him. Human nature always won out. It was less than an hour after the taps were placed when the call had come through to set up the meeting. That gave Cain more than enough time to set the trap. It looked like he'd been saved by luck. Or fate. Cain adjusted his earplug and casually glanced around the plaza. No sign yet but it would be soon.

The chase had gone on much too long. The information was like a virus—it had already spread from the rabbit to the reporter, and now her editor was in line. It was a contagion that had to be stopped. Having information about what was going on at the installation leaked to the public was unacceptable. Cain was going to make sure that the infection ended today, as soon as the other two arrived.

The plan was to wait and listen. Let them talk. He needed to find out what they knew and what proof they had. If his luck held, they would bring the evidence with them, and he could take care of everything at once. When the time was right, Cain would give the order to the snipers. Then, amid the panic and confusion, pick up the evidence and make his way out. Cain could imagine how pleased Colonel Pope would be when he found out that the mission was accomplished.

A burst of static came from Cain's cell phone. He raised it to his right ear. "This is Rover."

"Sir, we got a problem." The voice on the phone spoke with disaffection. "This is West, Rover. I've got a sighting, but she's comin' in solo."

"Shit!" Cain sat up a little straighter as his muscles tensed. He could see her now. She matched up well to her photographs—medium build, short blond hair, long legs, attractive. Today she was wearing a navy-blue skirt and a white top. And she was definitely alone. He took a deep breath and let it out slowly. "Okay, just hold tight fellas. Let's see how this develops."

Cain reached into his jacket and ran his fingers along the base of his Glock handgun. Loaded with hollow-point bullets and fitted with a silencer, it would be devastating and silent at close range. The job would be simple enough to handle. A few steps forward, two shots for each of them, drop the gun in the fountain, and calmly walk away. But that wasn't the plan—he was still missing his primary target, the rabbit.

Cain lowered the cell phone and adjusted the tuning on his listening device. The reporter—Lena—was making a beeline for the bench where the old man sat. The old man didn't notice her until she was almost next to him. Cain could hear them clearly when they spoke.

"Jack, you're not going to believe what's happened."

"We've been worried about you, Lena. You were supposed to be in Washington yesterday."

"Forget about Washington, Jack. I've got a story that's going to make us both famous."

"Settle down now. What are you talking about?"

"There's someone I want you to meet."

"Okay, who is it?"

Lena glanced around. Cain quickly looked away.

"Not here. Someone could be listening. Come with me." She turned away and started heading back the way that she had come. The old man fell in step alongside her.

"This paranoia is not like you, Lena."

"Just wait, you'll see. This is a story to die for."

Cain waited a moment, then stood up and followed. He raised the cell phone, pushed the button and spoke again.

"This is Rover. I'm goin' mobile. Hang loose and prepare to follow once I know where they're headin'."

As he walked, Cain tried to adjust the listening device so that it could pick up his target's conversation, but they were facing away from him and there was too much ambient noise. He couldn't hear them at all. He hung back and let a group of office workers move in front of him. He didn't want to get close enough to be noticed.

Lena walked to the edge of the plaza where a set of steps led underground. She looked backward, then seemingly satisfied, continued on. At a discreet distance Cain followed. The stairway connected to a concrete walkway that passed beneath the office building, linking the plaza to the garage entrance and access to the lower level of the building. It looked like it was a popular shortcut; there were a handful of office workers between him and his prey. Cain tried to adjust the listening device to monitor his target's conversation, but the echoes off the cement walls made listening impossible.

About halfway down the tunnel on one side was an entrance to the office building. On the other side, the garage entrance. Lena and the old man were well past the entrance when the office workers in between went into the building. Cain was now alone in the passageway with his targets. He couldn't let them see him. He stepped into the entranceway to the garage, away from the hallway and out of sight.

Cain waited patiently until their footsteps receded in the distance, then stepped out as they were disappearing up the stairway at the far end of the hall. He quietly sprinted the twenty yards to the stairway and watched as they turned left at the top of the stairs.

Cain pushed the button on the cell phone. "I'm stepping out on the street to the east of the plaza. They're heading north. Get your asses out here, A-sap." He clicked off, scaled the stairs at a run, and stepped out at street level.

At the top of the stairs the office building opened out onto a city street. He was in a concrete canyon, flanked by tall buildings. Shops and restaurants were at street level, office space on the higher floors. Cain turned left. Up ahead, among a crowd of pedestrians, he caught a glimpse of the back of the old man's head, bobbing along higher than those around him. Cain walked briskly to reduce the space between them.

He was still several yards back when they came to an intersection. The prey crossed over. The light changed as Cain came to the corner. He started to cross but a taxi cut him off and he had to jump back on the curb. After that he didn't have a chance. The flow of traffic was uninterrupted. He tried to keep track of his targets, but a bus obscured his vision when it stopped at his corner. By the time it pulled away, they were gone.

Cain ran across the street as soon as the light changed. He rushed down the sidewalk, pushing people out of the way, scanning those in front for any signs of his targets. He saw a blonde, wearing navy and white. He was almost next to her before he realized she was the wrong one. It was a long block and he covered it quickly, but without success.

For the first time Cain felt a sinking feeling in his stomach. He was so close, but they had gotten away. Now the contagion would spread. He could imagine the look on the old man's face as he grasped the importance of the story. Cain imagined the printing presses working overtime with the rabbit's face on the cover.

The colonel was going to be very disappointed.

Cain turned around and slowly walked back the way he had come, scanning the faces. They couldn't have turned onto the other street—he'd gotten there too quickly; they didn't have time. Somehow they still had to be on this block. But that could mean any of the buildings on either side of the street. Each building had several possible exits, there was no way he could cover them all.

He was about to call his men with his position, when out of the corner of his eye, he saw a flash of navy and white. Off the sidewalk in a recessed area near the entrance to a bank, was a long-legged blonde—wearing navy and white. Cain sighed with relief. It was her—it was Lena. And next to her, with an angry look on his face, was the old man, in a deep conversation with a muscular Hispanic wearing a baseball cap.

He'd found the rabbit.

RAMON LEANED AGAINST a wall in the small courtyard outside the bank building and tried to relax. After Barry was murdered, he had felt that a rope was being tightened around his neck. Ramon had seen his own face flashed on the TV and staring from the front pages of the Houston newspapers. His description was attached to a false name—but there was no doubt that it was *him* they were after. It was *him* they had accused of murder.

He'd expected to be discovered at any time. But now, just a few days later, he was standing on a busy city street. Scores of people were passing by and no one gave him so much as a second glance. Of course he didn't look quite the same. Sunglasses hid his eyes and a baseball cap concealed his hair. Also the news of Barry's murder wasn't as big in Austin as it had been in Houston. He wasn't exactly on the street, either. The courtyard was just far enough off the sidewalk to be discreet. The bank's main doors were behind him and the ATM machine was off to the side.

It was a Wednesday and the bank was closed, so the area was a small oasis in the hectic city. Still, he was out in the open and no one noticed. He was starting to feel invisible again.

They had killed Barry—Ramon was sure of that. It

was to force him out in the open. If he were easily recognized, there would be no place to hide. But the plan hadn't worked. It seemed almost an act of desperation on their part. If they really thought they were close to catching him, they wouldn't have made the search so public.

Ramon examined the faces of the people walking by on the street—nothing unusual. Was it really possible that he was close to being home free? He hoped that Lena was right. She was sure that the *Star* would be able to protect them. And once the story was made public, they would be safe. *They* wouldn't dare do anything when the truth was out in the open. He still wasn't completely convinced, but he'd agreed. There was no turning back now.

Ramon checked his watch. It had been nearly twenty minutes since they had parked and Lena had gone the long way around the block to find the editor. Ramon had insisted that they meet outside of the *Star* offices; he was feeling safer but it was still better to be cautious. He knew what *they* were capable of. Twenty minutes. Lena had been gone longer than expected. Ramon felt a nervous sensation in his stomach. What if something had gone wrong? What if she had somehow walked into a trap? If something happened it would be his fault. He hoped she would return soon.

He continued to look at the faces of the people going by. It wasn't long before he saw her. He let his breath escape slowly. She looked good in her navy skirt and white top, her long legs striding purposefully. Her ash-blond hair was cut short in a serious business style, but there was a softness in her face. Ramon was surprised how good it felt to see her again.

Lena glanced behind her as she led the editor in to meet Ramon. The editor looked different than Ramon had expected. He was a tall older man who looked like he had seen too many John Wayne movies. Ramon checked the faces of the people behind them. It looked clear. No one was following them.

"Ramon, this is Jack Van Russell. Jack, Ramon Willis." Lena made the introductions as if it was a normal encounter.

Ramon took off his sunglasses and nodded acknowledgment to the editor. "Lena's told you what's been going on?"

"She's told me what you're claiming. But, I don't know, son. That's quite a tale you're spinning."

"I know how it sounds. But it's true. You can check it out."

"I guess we will. But if you think you're going to make any money off of this, you're mistaken—"

"Wait, Jack." Lena tried to interrupt.

"If this is some kind of hoax, you've picked the wrong guy. You're not dealing with fools here. I've been around long enough to know a put-on when I see one."

Ramon looked Van Russell straight in the eyes. He knew the story sounded crazy, but it hurt to be called a liar. "I'm not looking for no money—"

Lena cut in again. "Jack, I told you, his story checks out. At least part of it. We need to do a lot more investigating, but . . ."

"If we print this story we'll be the laughingstock of the whole damn county. If this isn't a scam, then I'm Teddy Roosevelt."

Lena reached down to pick up the canvas bag at Ramon's feet. "We're nowhere near putting together the story yet, Jack. But there's some documentation in here. And we have a computer tape that may have the proof we need. I know how outrageous this sounds. But if it checks out, this is as big a story as there's ever been. And I've promised him, Jack, I've promised that we can keep him safe. . . ."

As Lena continued talking, Ramon noticed a tall man

in a business suit and mirrored sunglasses approach from
the street. He walked past the ATM machine and toward
the entrance to the closed bank. He moved forward several paces when suddenly, he turned and stepped in their
direction.

Ramon knew something was wrong before he saw the
gun in the man's hand. But his reaction too slow. It all
happened in an instant. The man quickly stepped behind
Van Russell, who was the closest to him, and pulled the
trigger two times. Lena screamed. The gun made a soft
smack—not the explosion a gun should make—but Van
Russell's chest exploded in a haze of red. The bullets
seemed to burst after impact, leaving a gaping hole as they
exited. He was dead before he hit the ground.

Ramon didn't wait to see the results. He was already
moving. He launched himself at the attacker and connected—a diving tackle that drove his shoulder into the
man's midsection and knocked the man's gun arm to the
side, just as he was aiming at Ramon. The man fired
again. There was a small smacking sound and the bullet
ricocheted off the brick wall.

Ramon's momentum carried him through. He knocked
the attacker off his feet. The man grabbed at Ramon's
throat with one hand while trying to swing the gun around
with the other. Hands engaged, there was nothing to break
the fall. They hit the ground hard, the attacker taking the
brunt of the impact. His head bounced off of the concrete
floor with a sickening thud.

That should have been enough, but as Ramon pushed
himself up from the ground, the man opened his eyes, and
unsteadily moved his gun arm up and into position.
Ramon kicked his wrist, knocking the gun out of his hand.

Ramon kicked again, connecting hard with the attacker's ribs. There was a crack of breaking bones. He
quickly bent over and picked up the gun. His heart was
ready to explode. The sound of rushing blood roared in his

ears. He extended his arm and aimed the gun at the attacker's face. He felt the tension of his finger on the trigger, a slight pressure—just a little more and the gun would respond, and it would all be over.

Ramon stared down at the man. The attacker's face remained stoic, betraying no sign of pain, fear, or anger. The mirrored glasses covered his eyes, reflecting back Ramon's image. Ramon and the gun. He stared down for a long moment. He didn't pull the trigger. Instead, he used the gun as a club, lashing it across the attacker's nose—blood spurted out like a fountain.

Lena was in shock, kneeling over Van Russell's body and clutching the canvas bag. Ramon turned to her and grabbed her wrist. "Let's go!"

He tugged and she responded. They ran. They were passing the ATM machine when the attacker managed to yell, "Stop him! He has a gun, he just killed a man!"

Ramon turned back, gun ready. The attacker was struggling, trying to get to his feet. Pulling Lena along, Ramon ran out of the courtyard, around the corner, and toward their waiting car.

THAT NIGHT, EACH of the three local newscasts led with the same story. Jack Van Russell, the longtime editor of the *Austin Star*, was murdered that day. Shot down in cold blood on a downtown street. The suspect in this murder matched the description of the suspect in the killing of a prominent Houston attorney just days ago. The suspect, going by the name of Hector Ramerez, was accompanied by an allegedly disgruntled former employee of the *Star*, who had been observed arguing with the victim earlier.

The most intriguing element of the story was the video footage. The ATM machine outside the bank had a security camera. It operated by a motion detector, which was set off when the suspects fled the scene. The tape was short and the image was grainy, but when slowed down to a frame-by-frame study, it was compelling. One frame showed the suspect, his gun in one hand and holding his accomplice's hand with the other, turning back and appearing to look directly into the camera.

The combination of a possible serial killer and video footage from the scene of the crime guaranteed publicity. The story went national immediately.

16

THE ROOM WAS nearly dark. A pole lamp beside the desk cast a pale yellow glow that reflected off the colonel's glasses, making them appear as if they were floating, disembodied. The air was cold. The office was chilled to a constant sixty-six degrees, a full six degrees cooler than the outside rooms of the complex. With the dim lighting and the chill in the air, it reminded Major Durmo of a cave. And if the room was like a cave, its occupant was surely a bear—a huge and lethal black bear.

Behind his desk, Colonel Pope stirred slightly. "I'm disappointed, Parker. I expected more of you." He spoke clearly, enunciating each word.

Durmo sat across the room from the colonel, separated by the large mahogany desk. He turned slightly in his seat to have a better look at the other occupant of the room. Captain Parker Cain sat in the chair next to him, looking unnaturally humble. His nose was taped down. A spot on the back of his head was newly shaved, highlighting the gash with its fine stitches. Cain sat up even straighter than normal. A result, Durmo was sure, of the tape that held his cracked ribs together.

"It was a freak deal, sir. I was sure I had him. You replay the same situation a hundred more times and I'd be the only one walkin' away," Cain replied softly.

"The only time that matters, Parker, is the opportunity that you had and wasted."

"Yes, sir."

"Tell me, Parker. Your men had left their positions in the buildings, and were coming down to assist you on the street. Is that correct?"

"Yes, sir."

"Your targets were contained in an area with only one escape route, which you had covered. Was that not the situation?"

"Yes, sir. That's how it was."

"Understanding the importance of silencing these targets, why did you choose to attempt this action by yourself?"

"Well, sir, I'd just found out that they had the documentation with them. I thought I could clean up the whole mess at one time. At the time, I thought waiting for backup would be counterproductive."

"That was a grave error in judgment, Parker."

Cain stoically stared straight ahead. "It was a freak thing, sir. The rabbit got lucky."

Colonel Pope leaned forward, exposing his dark face to the light. His voice was still steady, his words precise, but his features were contorted with anger. "We could have finished this sorry spectacle once and for all. It should have been over." Suddenly he pounded the desk with his huge fist, and his voice came out in a growl. "They're still out there and we are dangerously exposed."

"Yes, sir. I fucked up, sir."

Durmo leaned back in his chair. This was one for the records. Normally, Cain was difficult to be around. Arrogant and cocksure, he'd always acted like he knew the score. Though Durmo outranked him, Cain had never deferred to him as a superior officer. In fact it had seemed that Cain would go out of his way to subvert Durmo's authority. And he'd gotten away with it because he was the colonel's favorite. Durmo had fantasized about something like this happening, something that would put Cain back in his place. Now that it had, he almost felt sorry for Cain.

"This situation has already cost us dearly." Colonel Pope regained his composure. He sat back in his chair heavily. "Now, we have two subjects to chase. With the addition of this reporter, our troubles have multiplied. I'm relieving you of your assignment, Parker."

"No—please, sir—"

"We need to prepare for the worst. Whether it is with her paper or another, this reporter is going to publish the story."

"No, sir. I don't think she's goin' to be any trouble. She's been compromised."

"Compromised? How so?"

"Well, sir, I admit it was a matter of luck that we got those pictures off the ATM machine. But those pictures clearly show that she's with the rabbit. And the media's really bought that serial killer angle. As far as anybody knows, the guy in the pictures is a killer named Hector Ramerez. The bureau's got a file on 'im now—they even have fingerprints." Cain leaned forward in his chair. "And now she's with him. When she tells her wild-assed story, who's gonna believe it? She's compromised and contained."

Pope took a long time before he replied. "The video was extremely lucky. As bad of a situation as we are in, without it we would be the worse."

"The way I see it, sir. We've just increased our search team to the nth degree. Their pictures are all over the news. All it'll take is a suspicious store clerk to see 'em, she makes a call, and that's it. Or you get some two-bit tin star with an itchy finger and it's all over. Either way, we just go in and pick up the pieces." Cain played his finger over the tape on the bridge of his nose as he stared intensely at the colonel.

"Surely they'll go underground."

"Sure, but for how long? They can't stay down. They got no support system. They'll have to show up somewhere, and in the meantime they've been contained." Cain leaned in further. "I know how he thinks, sir. Let me stay on him. I swear I'll get the job done."

The colonel took his time before answering. "Failure is not an option. We are in a vulnerable position. I expect that you will clear this matter up quickly, Parker. Continue on for now. You're dismissed."

Cain had the faintest of smiles as he stood up and headed for the door.

After he was gone, Pope addressed Durmo directly. "Do not underestimate the motivating power of revenge. Our captain is not accustomed to defeat. I trust he will secure positive results." He moved forward into the light. "Now it's your turn, Major. You have the papers I requested?"

"Yes, sir." Durmo handed over a file folder, then sat back in his chair. "The results of this generation of vaccine are the best we've seen by far. There have been fourteen subjects who have received this vaccine—all are still alive and so far none of them are showing any symptoms."

"How long has it been?"

Durmo nervously tugged on his earlobe. "For the longest survivor it's been over a month."

"Our runaway subject still appears to be healthy and he's had it significantly longer."

"Yes, sir. That's true. There are, however, some concerns regarding the animal studies."

"Concerns? In what way?"

"Nothing concrete, I guess. The scientists just have some concerns as to the long-term health of the subjects. A few of the animals died earlier than expected. It was more complicated than that, but that was the problem in a nutshell, I'm told. They, the scientists that is, want some more time to make sure the vaccine is safe for humans long-term."

Pope sat back in his chair. His voice took on a dreamy quality. "Time is a luxury we can no longer afford, Major. This escape has forced our hand. Whether the vaccine is completely safe or not, we'll have to make do. It's time to ramp up to full production."

Durmo's breath caught in his throat; he tugged on his earlobe with renewed desperation. "Full production, sir?"

"Yes, Major. We are moving into full production. It is time to prepare for our true mission." Colonel Pope removed his glasses and leaned back in his chair. His face seemed to disappear in the darkness.

THE RHYTHM OF the wheels rolling over the rails was hypnotic; it was the steady music of motion. The train had been moving for hours, through the daylight and into night. Outside, the light of a half-moon gave feature to the landscape rushing past. Through the open door of the freight car there was a sense of movement, but the only colors Lena could see were the occasional flashes of red light from a railway gate as they passed.

She leaned against the side of the car. The rough wood rubbed against her back like splintery fingers, punctuating each movement of the train. *What had she gotten herself into?* After getting over the shock of seeing Ramon alive, her thoughts had been on the story that had fallen into her lap. It was a fantasy then, dreaming of what would happen when she broke the story. She saw herself afterward, accepting awards and handling the acclaim. Then it was an adventure. She knew there was danger but it hadn't seemed real—it was a game. That ended when Jack died. One moment they were talking. The next moment he was dead on the ground, covered with blood.

They were lucky, she supposed, or at least she was lucky that Ramon had reacted so quickly. Their assailant was obviously a professional who'd intended to kill the three of them. If things had been slightly different, her body would have been on the ground alongside Jack's. Lena pulled her knees up to her chest, hugging herself tight. Ramon had saved her life. While she was in shock, he had subdued the gunman and shown the presence of mind to get them out of harm's way. It was Ramon who had taken charge. She'd blindly followed, going along even when he had abandoned her car. She'd gone along even when he'd hopped into the vacant car of a northbound freight train.

Ramon had saved her life. At the time, that was enough. And he was moving. He seemed to make up the plan as he went along, reacting and improvising to get by. Then, while her body was still wired with adrenaline and her mind reeling, Ramon's plan made sense. It was a relief to have someone else to rely on. Now, after long hours with nothing to do but think, she was convinced they'd made a mistake.

Why had they run? She should have thought it through. Once the gunman was neutralized, they could have called for the authorities. With Jack dead and the gunman down, the authorities would have had to do something. She could have explained how they'd been attacked and Ramon had fought back and taken away the gun. She could have just explained the whole story—surely they'd believe her. It could have ended right there.

Lena looked over to the other side of the car. Her eyes had adjusted to the dark and she could see well enough. Ramon had his legs stretched out, relaxed. He looked so calm. What was he thinking? They'd talked before but had avoided the central issue. What were they going to do now? She shifted her position and cleared her throat. "Ramon, are you awake?"

Ramon turned toward her. She couldn't see his eyes. "Sure," he said.

"We need to decide what we're going to do. We can't just run away. I think we made a mistake by leaving."

Ramon spoke softly and she had to strain to hear him over the sounds of the train. "What do you think we should have done?"

Looking at him she felt self-conscious. "I'm not sure. But I think we need to go to the authorities now."

Ramon shrugged. "I don't know. I don't know who to trust. I don't know who's in on this."

Lena nodded. Who could blame him for his fear? The whole series of events was all so bizarre and frightening. And maybe he was right. Who could they trust? If the government was behind this, then anyone could be the enemy—not just the army—it could be the police, the press, anyone. Still they had to do something. And they had to do it fast. "I'd like to find out more. Maybe find out what's on that computer tape. But no matter what, we need to trust someone. We have to. We can't just run away."

Ramon didn't answer. For a long time they sat alone in the dark, silently listening to the sounds of the train.

After a time, Lena broke the silence. "Why didn't you shoot? You had the chance. Why didn't you?"

Ramon seemed to think about it. "I don't know. I was going to, but I couldn't. It wasn't for me."

Silence returned. At some point Lena dozed off. It was

hours later when she awoke to the sound of brakes grinding against the wheels. She felt a jolt as the train lurched to a halt. Disoriented, she opened her eyes. Ramon was already standing up, looking out the open door of the train.

Lena rubbed her eyes. "What's going on?"

"It looks like we're in some kind of freight yard."

Lena pulled herself to her feet, stretched, and walked over to the open door. From their vantage point she could see the shadowy forms of other freight cars parked nearby. The smell of diesel smoke and creosote were heavy in the air. Another train was coming through nearby; she could hear the muffled roar of its engine. Closer by, the sounds of a bell ringing and someone shouting could be heard over the clamor. She looked up the track toward the engine. About twenty cars up, she saw a moving light. It looked like a flashlight.

"They're coming this way. We better get going." Ramon grabbed his bag and jumped out the door and down to the ground. He held out his hand to help Lena. She picked up the bag that she had brought, turned around, and slowly lowered herself down without accepting his help.

Ramon shrugged. "We better stick close together. You can't tell what's out here in the dark."

Lena followed as Ramon started off. She kept a distance between them. They moved across the adjoining tracks, away from the men with the flashlight. Lena had to watch the ground as she walked. The tracks nearly came up to her shins; she had to carefully step over each section as they moved along. After they went across for a way, a stalled train blocked their path. They had to move parallel to it, down the track for what seemed like forever before they could get around it.

At one time they heard voices again and froze in the shadows. It was just some workers walking past. When they were gone, Ramon and Lena continued on. As they went on, she moved in closer to Ramon. It was much scarier in the dark than she had expected. It felt good to be close to him. By the time they had reached the perimeter of the yard, she was nearly holding on to his sleeve so they wouldn't get separated.

Lena looked at her watch. She could just make out the numbers in the pale moonlight. It was after 3:30. It had taken them nearly an hour to get across the railway yard. They were at the edge of a road that ran along the side of the yard. It was empty at this time of night. Up the road at the far corner of the yard was a small building with bright yellow lights that cut through the darkness.

"Let's head over there. Maybe we can figure out where we are," Ramon said as he turned toward the building. As they got closer, they saw that the building was a small concrete block restaurant. A sign in the window claimed that they "dozed but never closed."

Lena felt a tinge of anticipation. It would feel so good to be in the light, to be able to clean herself with running water, to sit and drink coffee like a normal person.

Ramon stopped short. "Maybe we shouldn't go in."

"We're hundreds of miles away. There's no way they'd know where we are." She stepped in front of Ramon and went to the door. He paused a moment before following.

Inside, the harsh glare of the fluorescent lights hurt her eyes. She blinked while adjusting to the light. It was a small room with dull gray tile and yellow plastic booths. At full capacity, the room might have held thirty people, but now there were only two customers—two men in railroad coveralls were drinking coffee in a booth by the window. They looked up from their newspapers, turned, and stared at Lena and Ramon as they came into the room.

Lena felt uncomfortable but tried to ignore it. "I'll be back in a minute. I need to wash up." She turned away from Ramon and walked across the room toward the washrooms, her eyes straight ahead as if she was in a tunnel.

In the bathroom she leaned against the sink, turned on the water, and tried to think. She felt so numb—everything was all so unreal. She needed a plan, but all she could think of was Jack dying. Her hands were shaking and she felt like she was losing control. Lena closed her eyes for a moment and took a deep breath, concentrating. As bad as this was, she'd get through it. She just needed to keep her head and think things through. With effort, she pulled herself together and relaxed.

She glanced in the mirror and saw that she looked as bad as she felt. Her hair was disheveled, her makeup and clothes a mess, and there were dark circles under her eyes. The image staring back at her was more like a street person than a hotshot reporter. She splashed some cold water on her face, quickly washed up, and did her best to make herself presentable.

Walking back to her seat she saw that the railroad men were gone, but someone new had come inside. He was turned away from her, standing near the door talking to the waitress behind the counter. He wore a blue shirt and black pants. It wasn't until he turned around that she realized that he was a policeman, a trooper of some sort. She stopped in the middle of the floor, her heart pounding. This was an opportunity to stop the insanity; she could walk up to him and explain everything. She glanced over at Ramon, who was sitting at a table pretending to read a newspaper that the previous customer had left. When she caught his eye he gave a small shake of his head and quickly looked back down to his newspaper.

"You better make that to go, Gloria. I'll be right back." The trooper walked away from the counter and right toward Lena. She was rooted to the ground; she couldn't move. She wanted to say something but couldn't. She just felt numb.

The trooper smiled at her. "Mornin' ma'am." He nodded and walked past her to the men's room.

Lena quickly went back to the table. She leaned in toward Ramon and whispered, "This is our chance. We need to tell him when he gets out. He can help us."

Ramon shook his head. "No. We need to get out of here right away." He picked the newspaper up off the table and reached down to pick up his bag. He stood up to go but Lena stepped in front.

"This is crazy. We need to stop this now before we get in more trouble than we're already in."

Ramon looked over at the men's room door. The trooper was still inside. He gazed into Lena's eyes as he pulled the newspaper out from under his arm, unfolded it and slapped it down on the table. Lena gasped. The picture was fuzzy and in black and white but there was no doubt as to who it was—Ramon was in front holding the gun, she a step behind, staring into the camera.

THE SAME THOUGHT kept going through Cain's mind, *How in hell did I fuck up?* He kept playing the scene over. Why didn't he move in a little quicker? Did he telegraph his intentions? Why didn't he take out the rabbit first? The rabbit was the most dangerous of the three—he should have taken him out first. But he'd been too anxious and had underestimated the rabbit. It should have been a cakewalk: They were unarmed in a contained environment; he had the right angle and the element of surprise working to his advantage. It should have been easy—but it turned into a royal fuckup. And he couldn't get it out of his mind.

The images wouldn't go away. First he was in control, calmly firing at his target. Then, suddenly, he was knocked off his feet and looking up at the sky—the rabbit standing above him, pointing Cain's own gun at him. By all rights he should have been dead. The rabbit had the shot but didn't take it. It was a sign of weakness. But he still winced in pain as he pictured the gun coming down and breaking his nose. Each time he thought about it, he had an overpowering urge to hit someone—it didn't matter who—it just seemed that if he hit someone hard enough, he'd be able to forget. It took all the willpower he could muster to maintain control. He needed to focus his anger and use it effectively.

The whole situation could have all been over. But now he had to start fresh with no idea where his targets were or where they were going. Cain looked down at the reports on his desk, trying to see some pattern. It had been two days since the two had gotten away and there still was no reliable clue as to where they were.

Not that there weren't sightings. The problem was that there were too many. It had seemed like pure luck that they were caught on videotape. But now it was a mixed blessing. The media had loved the story; they'd played it like the second coming of Bonnie and Clyde. Through the Office of Homeland Security, Cain had made sure that all information gathered from the press or police would be relayed back to him. As soon as the tape had aired, calls had started to come in. There were now sightings everywhere from Portland to Cleveland. One lady even swore that she had seen the fugitives waiting in line for tickets at Disneyland.

Cain didn't have the manpower to check out each lead. He had to prioritize and hope that he didn't miss something important. In a way his job was easy—every cop in the country was watching for the two runaways. All he had to do was wait and eventually they'd turn up. Then he'd need to make sure that he moved in fast to take control before they talked to the wrong person. If they talked to the wrong person, someone who believed them, then he had real troubles. That was why he needed to get to them first.

Cain was temporarily set up in a Homeland Security office in Austin. He wasn't working out of the installation, but he was still too close for comfort. He could practically feel the colonel's hot breath on his neck. As he stood to walk over to the window, he felt a flash of pain in his side. He moved his hand over his ribs. There was still pain, but in a way that felt right. It cleared his mind and kept him focused on what he had to do. There would be a second chance with the rabbit, and this time nothing would go wrong. Vengeance would feel good, and then the memories would fade.

Still, at the moment nothing felt right. All he could see from the window were other office buildings. Just concrete and glass. He was up so high and so far removed from what was happening outside that he felt detached and out of touch. This was a hell of a way to stage a hunt. He crossed back to his desk and called for Rev Tanner on the intercom. A few minutes later Tanner entered the room.

"Wha's up, Captain?" Tanner said with a smile. Despite his bulk he moved softly over the carpet. He sat down across from Cain.

"Let's go over this again. I'm tryin' to see what we missed. Go through what we've been doing one more time."

"Yes, sir. After the subject over . . . that is, after the subjects fled the scene, they used the reporter's car to vacate the area." Tanner's voice was a smooth baritone. "The vehicle was recovered later in the day, but when recovered it was being driven by some teenagers who had found the car abandoned with the keys in the ignition. It was parked just across from the railway switching yard. It is assumed that the subjects left town on board one of the freights but we've been unable to verify that. A number of

trains went through the yard over the course of the afternoon bound for different destinations. If the subjects were
aboard they could have gotten on any of the trains and
gotten off at any point between here and the trains' final
destinations. We've tried to check out the possibilities but
have so far come up blank."

Cain leaned back in his chair and nodded. "Go on."

"Well, we've been checking out the sightings that have
come from the videotape. But so far there's been nothing
there. We've met with the reporter's family and friends.
None of them can believe she's gotten involved in this
kind of situation. We're projecting it as a love affair with
the wrong guy. He's obsessive and abusive and her life
may be in danger—if she contacts them I'm pretty confident that they'll get back to us."

"I can't see her callin' 'em. This is the rabbit's game.
She's in shock and he's callin' the shots."

"Yes, sir. For now anyway." Tanner smoothed the
crease in his pants leg. "And that's about it, sir."

Cain leaned forward and put his elbows on the table.
"If you were in their place, what would you do?"

"If I were in their place? Hell, I don't know." He
laughed. "I think I'd shit."

Cain ignored the comment. He was caught up in his
train of thought. "If I were them, I'd be real interested in
that computer tape. The story they're tellin' is pretty
bizarre. If they expect anyone to believe it, they're going
to need some proof. That's the tape. It's going to take some
special equipment to get a look at that. We need to do some
checkin' and see if we can run 'em down that way."

Rev Tanner nodded.

Cain was silent for a long time. When he spoke again
it was as if he were talking to himself. "They're going to
be tryin' to check out all sorts of stuff. We got onto 'em
the last time after they called that pipsqueak over in Defense. I'll lay you odds they'll try it again."

17

LOOKING IN THE mirror, Lena could hardly recognize herself. Her short blond hair was now dyed flame red. It looked like it was on fire. She normally wore very little makeup, but now she'd applied it extravagantly, with a heavy hand on the lipstick and eye shadow. She'd bought a halter top off a rack at a truck stop and it completed the look. You could hide by blending in, she thought, or you could hide by standing out. She stood out like a weed in a flower bed, but anyone seeing her would take one look and make a quick assumption as to what kind of person she was. And after that they might look, but they wouldn't see.

Ramon's appearance was harder to alter. With his dark Hispanic features, there were definite limitations. If he changed his hair color it would be like putting a sign on his back saying he was in disguise. But his most recognizable features were his eyes, and sunglasses covered them nicely. It was now safe enough for them to go out in public.

They were the subjects of a huge manhunt — she'd heard the reports on the radio. They were saying that Ramon was a serial killer named Hector Ramerez and that she was his deluded lover. It was all pure fiction, but the media had bought it all. Lena felt angry just thinking about it. The news was supposed to be something you could trust, not something to be manipulated by those in control. It was so twisted. In one radio story the reporter had interviewed people Lena had worked with at the *Star*. Sally Ferguson from accounting, with whom Lena hardly ever talked, had said that *she* wasn't surprised that Lena had turned out like this — "She'd always seemed a little odd." It burned Lena up to hear the distortions.

In the last two days her whole world had turned upside down. The sight of a police car was a source of anxiety. Since the close call with the trooper in the diner, she'd had a mind shift. Lena was starting to think like a fugitive. She'd quickly come around to Ramon's perspective. Now she didn't know who to trust. She was more aware of her surroundings then ever before; it was like something had clicked on in her mind that was fine-tuned to signs of danger. The story she was going to write didn't seem so important anymore. Now her thoughts were of mere survival.

That night, after hurriedly leaving the diner, they had walked farther down the road to a parking lot near the switching yard. Ramon walked through the rows of vehicles, checking till he found an old car with its door unlocked. It took him less than a minute to hot-wire the car. Lena got in without a second thought. It didn't matter who owned the car; they needed it. Before they left the lot, Ramon stopped again and switched license plates with another car. The rail yard was near Springfield, Missouri. That night they made their way out of town to the inter-

state. Not knowing where to go, they took the exit east
just because it was going away from Texas.

They drove on into the daylight. They stopped at a
Wal-Mart along the way to get the hair dye and sunglasses
and at a truck stop for gas later. It was late afternoon when
they came into St. Louis. They were tired and needed to
find a place to lie low and regroup. Lena knew that she
couldn't use her credit cards; she had to use cash. She had
gotten extra cash for her trip to Washington, but at the rate
they were spending it would be gone soon. They still had
enough for a few days, but that was all.

They found an old motel in a run-down area on the east
side of town. She went into the office alone and paid for
two days. The attendant hardly glanced at her. They
grabbed some food from a vending machine, then hid out
in the small room.

They slept straight through to the next afternoon. They
watched all the news shows on the TV and there was no
mention of them, or that a search was going on. Maybe,
they thought, they were far enough from Texas, that and
with no new sightings, they had become old news. Maybe
the pressure was off—for now anyway. But they had to
do something soon.

Lena turned from the mirror and sat down on the bed.
Ramon had gone out to scrounge some food, so she was
alone. There was no way they could get out of this by
themselves, but who could they trust? They needed someone who would believe them and help them. But who? If
their pursuers were from the army, who had given the
order to pursue them? And who else was involved? The
information coming from the media was being reported as
truth. Fingerprints and false history—these things were
beyond the scope of the military. There had to be other
branches of the government involved in the conspiracy.

They needed help from someone. *Why not Jason?*
Jason Ulmer worked in the Department of Defense. He

wasn't high enough to truly help them but he could at least give them some information. She pulled out his number and dialed the phone.

It was picked up on the third ring. "Department of Defense." The voice was flat and toneless.

"Yes, Jason Ulmer, please."

"One moment, I'll connect you." The voice cut out, replaced by recorded music.

What would she say when he answered? Suddenly she felt apprehensive, she realized her palms were sweating. She had no right to involve him—this was too dangerous. She hung up the phone.

She checked her phonebook again and dialed Allen Edwards at *Newsworld.* The media was still the answer. She would tell them the real story.

A female voice on the line answered, "Mr. Edwards's office."

"Yes, I need to talk with him right away."

"Mr. Edwards is in a conference now and can't be disturbed. Would you like to leave a message, or can I connect you to his voice mail?"

Lena took a deep breath. "This is Lena Dryer. He'll want to talk with me now. I'm in the news."

The secretary's voice changed. "One moment. I'll see if I can get him."

The phone was picked up almost immediately. "Lena?"

"Hello, Allen."

"My God. I can't believe you're calling."

"It's not like they're portraying it, Allen. They've got the story all wrong."

There was a long pause. "OK, why don't you tell me what did happen."

Lena poured out the story. She started with when Ramon approached her in the parking lot and how she knew it was him; she told about her conversation with Jason and how that corroborated the story; then she talked about their meeting with Jack Van Russell, and how he had been killed and they were lucky to get away alive.

After she was done, there was a long silence on the other end. It sounded like he was conferring with someone else. When he came back on the line, his tone had a hint of condescension. "So this whole thing is a conspiracy?"

"That's right. I know this is hard to believe, but it is."

"Right. And this *Ramon* was able to overpower the man with the gun?"

"Yes, that's exactly how it happened."

There was a silence again before he came back on the line. "That's a real interesting story, Lena. I think the best way to handle this is . . . well, you need to turn yourself in, but we can be there to cover it. We can arrange everything. And we'll give you an exclusive forum where you can tell your side of the story."

"I can't do that."

"I don't see that you have any other choice. They're going to find you, Lena. My guess is it won't take long. At least this way you can control how it happens."

"If we turn ourselves in, they'll kill us. . . ."

"Do you realize how paranoid you sound? This whole story is crazy." He paused for a moment and again seemed to be talking with someone else. "How about this, Lena. We'll meet somewhere and we can discuss your options. No risk, what do you say?"

Lena's heart was beating fast. It did sound paranoid but it was the truth. Edwards clearly didn't believe her, but did it matter? Then again, what if he was with *them*? He was talking to someone. Who was there? Was he involved? Had he somehow been bought out?

"So how about it, Lena. Where can we meet?"

Her pulse was racing. She didn't know what to think. "I've got to go." She slammed the phone down on the receiver and sat back, exhausted.

That night Lena lay awake, her nerves on edge. Their

options had run out. They were nearly out of money, defenseless, and vulnerable. They couldn't trust the media. They couldn't trust the government. They were all alone. But there was no way they could make it on their own. They had to trust someone.

Lena took out her laptop, unplugged the phone, and plugged her modem cord into the wall jack. She waited while the computer made the connection, then logged into the conspiracy chat room. She signed in as Ms. Skeptic and sent out a call for TRUE BELIEVER.

THE BUILDING THAT served as a gym at the Johnson Installation was a cavernous sheet-metal structure that could, if needed, double as an airplane hangar. At its peak, the ceiling was over thirty feet high. Two full-length basketball courts were set next to each other, running the width of the building. They were surrounded by an oval jogging track. Basketball rims hung down from the rafters connected by lengths of metal tubing. The floor was covered in a texturized rubber that had been laid directly on top of the cement. It was soft on the eyes but murder on the legs.

No athletic activities were scheduled for today. Near the center of the gym two tables were set up, spaced apart, to serve as stations. In front of the tables stood a long straight line of soldiers, waiting their turn.

There were two men at each table. At one, a pair of officers handled the paperwork, looking through reams of computer printouts and marking off each man by name, rank, and company. Two white-coated technicians worked at the other table. As each man was checked off the computer list, he would walk over to whichever technician was free, roll up his sleeve and put his arm into position. Each technician controlled a stainless-steel cylindrical machine; the machine was loaded with premeasured doses of vaccine. At the push of a button, the dose shot out in a high pressure burst into the arm of the waiting serviceman. The equipment worked without needles and could immunize hundreds of people per hour.

Maj. Bob Durmo sat in the front row of a set of bleachers just off court, across from the technicians. He was close enough to hear the conversations of the soldiers as they came up to the station. They all asked variations of the same questions: "Is this going to hurt, Doc?" or, "What's this for? I've already got all my shots." Durmo knew what they were going to say before they said it. He'd been watching all morning. It had started out slow and disorganized, but as the day went on the workers had found a rhythm and the pace had picked up. Now the system was working like clockwork. They'd already processed over three thousand men — nearly half the residents of the base. It wouldn't take long for the rest.

There was no reason for Durmo to stay here, but he couldn't leave. He'd never thought it would come this far. He'd been at the base for three years, and under Pope's command for two more years before that. He was one of the few who really knew what was going on, what they were doing, and why they were doing it. The development of the vaccine was a slow and frustrating process. It had taken a full three years to come up with a beta formula, but now, the rollout was moving surprisingly fast. The vaccine was only half the equation. The first part, the toxin, was already in place. When used together they had the potential to change the entire course of world history. And it looked like they were rapidly approaching show time; it was starting to make him nervous.

Durmo tugged on his ear as he watched a skinny private take his hit and move across the gym to the exit door. *What now?* It had come this far, he thought; would they take the final step? Durmo tensed as he heard footsteps approach from behind. Even on the rubber floor the footsteps were distinct — the hard, regular steps of a large man walking with total confidence. He knew who it was without turning.

"There you are, Major. It is a sight, is it not? Just six months ago this would have seemed a fantasy." Colonel Pope came alongside Durmo and lowered himself onto the bleacher seat.

"Yes, sir." Durmo glanced quickly at the colonel. He was surprised to see that the colonel was smiling. In the five years he'd served with Pope, smiles were as rare as rubies.

"Do you remember when we first began our mission? The obstacles appeared nearly insurmountable. Our scientists were running into dead ends; the problems we had with our containment system; how difficult it was to procure the quantity of subjects necessary to keep our mission viable." Pope sat straight in his seat, eyes locked on the technicians in the middle of the floor. "Seeing how far we have come is quite satisfying."

"Yes, sir. We sure have made some progress."

"In a way we owe a debt to our rabbit. If he hadn't forced our hand we would still be cautiously rerunning the same set of experiments. This has easily shaved a year off our timetable."

"Yes, sir."

They were both quiet for a time. Durmo shifted uncomfortably in his seat. The silence was nerve-wracking. He wished he was alone somewhere, away from everyone—especially the colonel. He didn't want to hear any more; he didn't want to know any more. He just wanted to forget about everything and start all over. He'd give anything for a second chance.

Pope broke the silence. "Yes, we are far ahead of our timetable. Unfortunately, we're still under considerable constraints."

"How's that, sir?"

"We need to be prepared to move forward with our

mission at any time. If the rabbit is not snared quickly we'll have no choice."

"Yes, sir. I understand."

Pope stood up and stretched out to his full height. "Now, Major, we have come as far as possible under laboratory conditions. Before we can move into the final phase we need to make certain that everything behaves as expected in a real-life situation."

"Real life? I'm not sure I follow you, sir."

Pope took off his glasses and carefully inspected them before he put them back on. "It's quite simple, Major. I need you to prepare a test. A field test. We need a trial run with real subjects, outside the laboratory." Pope stared straight into Durmo's eyes. There was still the hint of a smile.

RAMON HAD FORGOTTEN how good it felt to drive. It was strange at first, but that didn't last long. He was amazed at how automatic it seemed, how natural. Before breaking out, he hadn't driven a car in over ten years. But as soon as he got behind the wheel he was in control. Free and in control. It was a joy to be moving, to feel the power of the car on the road. He had an urge to punch the accelerator and see what the car could do. He wanted to speed along like he was strapped to a rocket. He wanted to fly—but he didn't. Instead, he checked his mirrors and kept his speed down to sixty, making sure to stay right in the flow of traffic. The last thing they needed was to get stopped for a traffic violation in a stolen car.

They'd needed to change cars and license plates before they started out again. This time Ramon picked an old Chevy Caprice from a shopping mall near the motel they'd stayed in. The Caprice was a good road car with a strong engine and comfortable seats, but it gulped down the gas. And money was tight. They were nearly broke— Lena was down to her last ten dollars and Ramon had only coins. It was a good thing they were close to their destination.

It was a long drive from St. Louis. The road north through Illinois was long and flat. The only scenery for hours was corn and soybean fields, grain silos, and road signs. When they got closer to Chicago, the view changed to a suburban mix, housing developments and fast-food franchises. They took the interstate north, all the way past Milwaukee into semirural Wisconsin.

"That's it. Turn here." Lena pointed to the exit sign.

"The first one?"

"Right, this is the way."

Ramon took the exit onto a two-lane blacktop road. The countryside was a mixture of farmland and subdivisions at the far edge of the suburbs. Ramon drove another ten miles, making several turns in the process before arriving at their destination. The neighborhood was made up of a hodgepodge of styles and sizes, from double-wide trailers to larger brick homes, all on oversized lots.

Lena looked at the paper where she'd written her notes. "There it is." There was excitement in her voice as they pulled into the driveway.

The house was an old cape cod with yellow aluminum siding. There were two cars in the driveway; an old Ford rusting through the body, and a newer Toyota with an *X-Files* bumper sticker. They walked up to the front door. Lena stepped in front and rang the bell. Ramon looked around the surrounding area. No one was outside and the houses were spaced far enough apart to assure privacy. They seemed safe enough, but it was all so crazy. *What the hell were they doing here?*

A moment later the door opened a crack. The chain was still on from the inside. A sliver of a face looked out. All they could tell was that it was a man with glasses. "Yes?" he asked.

"Philip? It's me, Lena . . . Ms. Skeptic."

The chain came off and the door opened a little wider. "You look different than in the pictures I've seen."

"I dyed my hair. It's a disguise."

The door opened all the way. Philip was in his mid-twenties, average height and thinly built with shaggy brown hair and a goatee. He had a thin face and round-framed glasses covered his soft brown eyes. He wore jeans and a flannel shirt. He looked straight at Ramon and then he was suddenly excited. "My God, it *is* you!" He stepped outside and quickly looked both ways up and down the street. "You better get inside. Someone could see you out here."

Inside, the hall was dark. It was near dusk and the only interior light was from a room down the hall. Ramon could hear music blaring from the room.

"I can't believe you're really here. This is awesome," Philip whispered excitedly. "I stayed home from work today just in case you got here. God, I can't believe you're here!"

"We appreciate your help, Philip. There was no one we could turn to," Lena said.

"This just proves what I've been saying all along. The government's controlling everything. They've got the media in their pocket—that's why the only stories that come out are the ones they want the people to hear. The media's in on it—along with all the big businesses." Philip's voice rose along with his excitement, he flapped his arms around as he talked. "The corporations, the media, and the government are all facets of the same . . ."

Someone suddenly yelled from the room down the hall. "What the hell's going on out there, dweeb?"

Philip stopped short. "Uh . . . nothing," he called back. He turned toward Ramon and Lena. "Um, I've got room-mates. They don't know what's going on. I'll introduce you as my . . . uh, cousins." He looked at Ramon, "Or maybe she's just my cousin. It won't be a problem." He gave a weak smile and started down the hall.

Ramon looked at Lena. Was this what she had expected? Did she feel good about this situation? Lena shrugged and followed Philip down the hall. Ramon took a deep breath; if this was their best hope, they were in worse shape than he'd thought. Reluctantly, he fell in behind Lena as they walked into the room.

The room was meant to be a living room, but the only furniture it contained were an old plaid couch, a small coffee table, and a big-screen TV. Loud metal music was coming from the TV; the screen was split down the middle with dual images of futuristic cars flying over the road through a surrealistic landscape. It took Ramon a second to realize it was a video game.

On the couch, intensely manipulating their game controllers, were two large men. They both appeared to be in their mid-twenties. One was athletic, tall, and broad shouldered with short dark hair, thick eyebrows, and a dark tan that helped to hide the acne scars on his face. The other one looked like a professional wrestler. He had curly red hair, a pasty white complexion, and a crooked nose. He slouched on the couch like a mountain, mounds of fat covered his huge frame. He was one of the biggest men Ramon had ever seen.

Philip was hanging back at the corner of the room. He spoke tentatively. "Um . . . guys, Frank and uh . . . Jelly, this is my cousin . . . uh . . . Linda and her friend . . . uh, Roy. . . ."

Without looking up the dark roommate barked out, "Speak up, Dweeb. Can't you see we're playing?"

"Yeah, um, sorry, Frank." Philip spoke louder. "This is my cousin Linda and, uh, Roy. They're going to be staying here for a few days."

Frank leaned into a curve, turning his controller like a wheel. "No skin off my ass. Just don't let me hear you talking none of that conspiracy shit again. I hate that crap."

Jelly, the bigger one, grunted in agreement.

"Yeah, sure. Well, we'll see you later." Philip seemed relieved as he backed toward the door.

Frank looked up for the first time and saw Lena. His eyes widened with interest. "Hey, wow. You don't have to leave so quick." He smiled at her. "Why don't you stick around for a while?"

Jelly howled with laughter as a loud crashing sound came from the TV. Frank pivoted back to the screen with a shocked look on his face. "Hey, that's no fair! I wasn't paying attention."

"You should have been playing, jagwad. Ah'm gonna kick your ass!"

Frank elbowed him in the ribs as he grabbed his controller and punched the buttons. "Shit, you're cheatin'."

Philip backed all the way out of the room. "Come on, let's go." Ramon and Lena followed him down the hallway as the two roommates continued to fight in the background. "Don't worry about them. They're like that all the time." Philip switched on a light as they came to a stairway.

The stairs were steep and in the dim light Ramon had to be careful as they climbed. Coming here was starting to look like a real bad idea, he thought. Staying with these three was crazy—two morons and a weirdo. He wanted to talk with Lena, to see how she felt—she'd had the contact with Philip before. It didn't feel right to him. In order to survive they needed money and a place to stay, but he liked his chances out in the open better than this.

A landing at the top of the stairs opened onto two rooms. Philip motioned to one room; the door was open. A full computer system sat on a desk. "That's my room." He gestured to the other door. "This is my spare room. You can stay here."

The room was small but comfortable. It held two single beds and two dressers. A window looked out at the street below.

"Thank you, Philip," Lena said. "Are you going to get in trouble with your roommates for having us here?"

"Oh, no. I own the house. They're just staying here for a while. I knew Frank from high school. He got kicked out by his parents . . . and uh, Jelly's a friend of his, he just kind of moved in, too. I know they seem kind of crude, but they're all right, really." He laughed nervously.

Lena nodded her head.

Philip glanced at his watch. "You know, I'm dying to hear your whole story. But I need to go to work. You see, I didn't go in today but I've got a project that I need to check up on. I really should go in tonight."

"What kind of work do you do, man?" Ramon asked.

"I work at the power company. I'm a systems designer. I run their computer network."

Ramon caught a spark of excitement in Lena's eyes. Maybe this would work out after all.

THE FIRST PROBLEM was that the country was too big. Too damned big. And the bigger problem was the freedom. People were free to go across the country, from one coast to the other, across state lines, without ever having to show identification or state their purpose. As long as they had money and kept their noses clean, people could go most anywhere. And the authorities had no way to keep track, no way to monitor who was out there and what they were doing. It was a hell of a way to run a nation. It was no wonder the terrorists found it an easy target.

Cain walked slowly around the vehicle. It was a 1986 Oldsmobile Regency—a big boat of a car, gunmetal blue with specks of rust showing through like pockmarks. The interior was a gray woven cloth with rips in the upholstery where the foam stuck out. It had once been a luxury car; now it was transportation but nothing more.

But it had served its purpose. The car had somehow gotten the rabbit—both rabbits—out of danger and into open territory. Out of his grasp. Cain was on their trail; he could now reconstruct where they had been for the forty-eight hours after fleeing Austin. But it wasn't enough. He still had no idea where they were now or where they were going. The country was too damned big.

The break had come when a Missouri state trooper realized, after the fact, that he'd seen the fugitives when he stopped for some coffee the night before. It burned Cain to think about it. Their pictures were all over the media—there was a regional manhunt in progress. And this trooper runs in to them, smiles, and wishes them a good day. The next day in roll call, the desk sergeant circulated their pictures and the trooper realized he'd just blown any chance he'd ever have for a promotion beyond traffic patrol. But by then it was too late.

The Oldsmobile had been stolen that same night from the employee's parking lot at the switching yard. It had taken another day before someone put two and two together and figured that these events were somehow connected. That's when Cain finally got the call. His men were spread out checking on other leads and he was going stir-crazy sitting in his office fielding phone calls. He flew up and got to work. He interviewed the waitress and he interviewed the trooper; he walked through the switching yard searching for some kind of insight. It felt good to be back on the trail. Even though the trail was ice cold.

They'd put out an APB for the Oldsmobile. It was another lost day before it turned up, abandoned in a shopping mall parking lot outside St. Louis. The forensic team had transported it to a clean garage and done a quick run through. Analysis of hair samples found inside were proof that the subjects had been in the car. But that's all they could say with any certainty. It looked like the car had been abandoned for a day, maybe two. No one at the mall could say one way or the other.

Cain could feel the tension in his neck. The pain in his ribs was beginning to throb. They'd done it again. A god damned spick jailbird and a bitch of a reporter were making him look like a fool. He'd missed them again. And now they could be anywhere—it was a big country. He closed his hand into a fist and visualized hitting someone. Instead, he shut his eyes took a deep breath and willed himself to relax. He had to stay in control.

The technicians stood outside drinking coffee and smoking cigarettes when Cain approached them. "Listen, fellas, I need you to go over that vehicle again with a fine-tooth comb. Tear it apart if you have to. It's all we got. If there's any more information to be got, we need to get it."

While they went inside to continue working, Cain used a pay phone to make some calls. First he checked in with the office. Nothing new there. Next he called in to the installation to give his report. Colonel Pope was away at the time, so Cain left a message, happy that he didn't have to deal with the colonel. Not yet anyway.

His last call was to a number in Washington, D.C. "This is Cain. Any luck?"

"No sir," the voice on the other end replied. "Just the normal calls, work related and such. Nothing out of the ordinary."

"Damn. I was sure they'd call again. Anybody notice anything about the voice being different?"

"No, sir. Well, one guy said something but I said I had a cold, and that was it."

"Okay, well, let me know if you get any bites." Cain hung up the phone and went back inside. As he walked through the door, the chief tech headed right for him; he had something in his hand.

"Maybe we got something, Captain. I don't know if

it'll do you any good." He handed over a piece of scrunched-up white paper. "This was wadded up and wedged between the seats. I don't know how we missed it the first time. It looks like this was underneath a paper that someone wrote something on. We could only make out a little of it now. We'll see if we can get anymore of it back at the lab, we got a lot more to work with there."

Cain looked at the paper; the words came clearly through. Maybe the paper came from his subjects, maybe it was something that the car's owner had thrown away weeks ago. Either way it didn't mean a thing to him. "Yeah, check it out. You never know." He looked at the words again. Nothing. They were spelled out in bold print: TRUE BELIEVER.

18 _____

THE BUILDING WAS one of several smoked-glass structures that circled a pond in the suburban office park. It stood four stories high, a clean, simple design. Set among the trees and on the water, it seemed more like a college campus than a corporate headquarters. The large sign in front was sculpted out of polished chrome and stainless steel. Spotlights hit it from several angles illuminating the company logo, WPCO, the Wisconsin Power Company.

They parked in the lot at the side of the building and crossed over to the front entrance. The night was clear with a slight chill to the air. Lena crossed her arms to conserve her warmth. It was too early to be this cold. But the weather here was like that, hot and muggy one day and cold and rainy the next. She missed the sunny predictability of Texas.

She tried to pick up her pace to keep up with Philip. He was walking at nearly a trot, his head down, clutching his briefcase like he was afraid it would fly away. She could tell he was nervous. She was, too. It'd been over a week since they'd come to Wisconsin—one of the worst weeks of her life. Philip left for work early each morning, leaving her and Ramon alone with Philip's roommates, who didn't have steady jobs. Most of the time they'd be watching TV, playing video games, or sleeping. That and drinking beer and eating. They had no interest in Ramon but every time they saw her they would leer, then, when she turned away, they'd elbow each other and laugh like donkeys. It reminded her of sixth grade. Lena spent most of her time upstairs, working on Philip's computer, searching for information, trying to make sense of their situation.

They'd talked with Philip about their plan the night they arrived, but he could only help if he had access to his company's computer system when no one was around. Tonight was a Saturday and he was sure that no one else would be working, so he thought it was the best time to try. Lena was nervous but excited, too. She was anxious to know what was on the tape. If it contained the proof she thought it did, then their run was nearly over. With proof she could buy freedom. With proof, the authorities would have to listen—she'd even call a press conference if she had to.

They came to the front door and stepped into the atrium. The first thing she saw was the guard station right across from the door. The guard was young, even younger than Philip. He was stocky and had short brown hair; there was a small earring in one ear. He looked up from the book he was reading, surprised to be disturbed. "Hey, Mr. B. You're working awful late tonight."

"Hi, Bart. What are you reading?" Philip asked, trying to hide his nervousness.

Bart held up a textbook. "Statistics. It's brutal. I got a test on Tuesday and I'm history if I don't get at least a C.

It's usually so quiet here I can get a lot of my studying done." He looked at Lena curiously as they talked.

Philip signed in at the register. "Good luck with that, I'm sure you'll do fine." He put down the pen and started to move away. Lena moved with him. "I'll see you on the way out. I need to work on a project myself."

"Hey, Mr. B., I don't want to be a Barney Fife or anything, but I'm afraid you can't go back there with her." Bart nodded toward Lena. "Company rules."

Philip stopped. He fidgeted nervously. "Come on, man, can't you make an exception? We were out in the area and I need to get this done before Monday. Otherwise I'll have to come back tomorrow."

"I can't. I could lose my job if anyone found out."

Philip's shoulders sagged with defeat. He looked down at the ground.

Lena felt their opportunity slipping away. She smiled at Bart, a flirting, sexy smile.

There was an awkward silence, then Bart asked, "Is this Mrs. B?"

Philip looked up. "No, not exactly. This is uh . . . Linda."

Bart wasn't really listening. He stared hungrily back at Lena. After a moment he looked away. "I'll tell you what, man. Go on back this time. But nobody better find out about this. And you can't put me in a position like this again."

Philip's face lit up; his body came to life. "Thanks, man. I owe you." He stepped forward and Lena moved in step with him. "If you need any help with those statistics, let me know. I'm your guy."

They took the elevator to the second floor and went down a short hallway. The building was deserted. Walking through the hallways, past office areas with warrens of cubicles, Lena was reminded of her office at the *Star*. It felt strange to be in a space that on a weekday would be bustling with activity but was now so empty. It made her feel alone. It was more than that though. Since the whole ordeal started, since she'd first hooked up with Ramon, they'd been together almost constantly. She'd grown accustomed to his mannerisms, the way he moved, even his long silences. Now, just being away from him, she realized how much she relied on him. In a strange way she felt more alone because he wasn't there.

The hall ended at a set of double doors. Philip took out his keycard and ran it through a scanner on the side. He waited for the light to flash green, then opened the door. "Here we are."

They were in a large room filled with computer equipment. One whole wall was taken up by a row of massive gray metal boxes, their amber and green lights blinking on and off in a lazy pattern. In the middle of the room was another row of smaller cabinets, with monitors interspersed throughout. There were layers of sound in the air; some of the machines gave off a high-pitched whirring sound, others a low hum. Philip opened his briefcase and took out the tape. He slipped it into the slot near one of the servers, then sat down by a monitor. "All right now. Let's see what this sucker's got."

It seemed to Lena that there had been a transformation. Outside in the hallway and in the car coming over, he'd been like a scared kid. Now, in front of the monitor he was in his element. He tapped out quick commands and read the responses on the screen as he mumbled a running commentary. "Let's try scan . . ." Tap, tap, tap. "No, then we try . . . That's better."

It went on like that for about twenty minutes but ended in frustration. Philip leaned back in his chair and stroked his goatee. "This is a trick setup here. They programmed it on a UNIX platform, which is good. What I was thinking was we could isolate the program and reconstruct it under a new platform. But that leads us into our main problem. I can bring up the code but I can't make anything of it. It's encrypted."

"Encrypted?"

"Yeah, all computer code is based on numbers—it's all digital. But this is sensitive stuff, with the shit that they're doing, they wouldn't want anybody else to see it. I mean, you're proof of that. So what they do is they change all the numbers in the code based on a common algorithm so that the code is all still there but it's in a different form. Did you ever have a decoder ring when you were a kid?"

Lena shook her head. "No, not that I remember."

"Well, I did. When I was a kid, I made up my own code and—well, that doesn't matter. It's the same thing though. If your computer has the key built in, it reads the program like it was intended to run. If not, then it goes like this." He motioned to the screen. "Nothing."

"So we can't get into it? This is a dead end?" Lena felt a wave of dejection. So much had been riding on that tape. The tape was going to explain everything, it was going to be the proof they needed. Without it they were lost.

Philip stared intently at the computer screen. "Not necessarily. There might be a way." He was lost in thought for a long time. "There are programs out there, I can download 'em from the Net. They're designed to act as decoders. But it's not that simple. It's almost a trial-and-error system. Encryption is digitally based, so the possibilities are nearly infinite. What the program does is use the patterns that the encrypted code shows, to try and narrow down the options."

Lena nodded her head, trying to take it all in.

Philip's voice rose; he was getting more excited. He started to pace across the room, waving his arms around as he talked. "The problem is that even after the options are narrowed down, there's still a hell of a lot of numbers to plow through. But we've got a lot of computing power here. Our mainframe handles all the power transmission, our network does most of the internal functions. They're linked together. Sometimes the computers are running near capacity; other times we have dead time where they're very underutilized. What I'm thinking is, I could write a program that, when the computers are underutilized, they would be redirected to work on the encryption program. That might do it."

"That would work? How long would it take?"

Philip thought for a moment. "Yeah, I *think* it would work. As to the time, I could write the program over the weekend; that's no problem. But breaking the code? Who knows, maybe a week, maybe a month. If we don't catch a break it could take a lot longer."

Lena nodded, but her spirits fell. She hoped they had enough time.

THE VALLEY SAT at the base of the Davis Mountains near the Pecos River in Loving County, Texas, just across from the New Mexico border. It was flat, dry land, and its soil was thin and poor. From an agricultural standpoint, the land was worthless. There wasn't much value from any other standpoint, either—the official population of the entire county was only ninety-one people.

Back in the early eighties, at the height of the Texas oil boom, a developer from San Antonio had bought the land cheaply and gotten a huge loan to put up vacation homes. The land was near the river and the view of the mountains was striking; the view was the selling point. But it didn't really matter because he was working with borrowed money. By 1984 he'd built an access road, laid a couple of dozen concrete pads, and erected a beautiful carved wood sign at the entrance to the development. The sign read Shangri-La Estates.

Sales never materialized, and the developer stopped. A year later the savings and loan that lent him the money foreclosed and took title. But that company was a victim of the S and L debacle and the land soon reverted to the Resolution Trust Corporation, which was charged with selling the property. There were no takers. It had been government land ever since.

For commercial purposes the land had no value, too remote for recreational land and not suited for anything else. But the view was nice, and for some people the remoteness held an attraction. These were individuals who for one reason or another wanted to step away from the outside world. There were ex-hippies, retirees living on fixed incomes, and some just unable to get along in modern society.

Over time, a small village of squatters had sprung up on the site of the failed development. A few had brought in trailers, set them on the pads and propped them up with concrete blocks. Others arrived with small mobile homes or recreation vehicles; some had even erected makeshift structures. The year-round population fluctuated. Most of the time there were less than fifty people in the development. But in the winter, when the snowbirds came down in their RVs, the population could swell to over one hundred.

Loving County had been waging war with the squatters over numerous violations, ranging from access to zoning. But the real battle was over health. The community had no electrical power, running water or sewage disposal system. These amenities were handled separately by each individual. Some had generators and their own disposal units. Others lived much more primitively. The place was a public health nightmare waiting to happen. And now it looked like the nightmare had begun.

Rev Tanner looked up at the weathered wooden sign — Shangri-La Estates. *This was too fuckin' strange.* This wasn't the drill he'd been told about. This was way beyond the edge. The sign said Shangri-La, but it might as well have said never-never land, or Oz. This was a whole new planet.

He glanced back. They were at a roadblock positioned at the entrance to the old development, right where the road cut through a small canyon. His men were all in position, guns ready, staggered out in an arc over the high ground and covering the road below. Tanner stepped out into the dirt roadway. The dust rose up and settled on the back of his neck, caking to the sweat on his skin. He put his hand on his pistol as he called out, "Turn your vehicle around and return to your homes. You are under quarantine."

Facing him in the roadway was an old rusted RV. It belched smoke as it came to a stop. A grizzled old man jumped out from the driver's side. He was thin and wiry with long white hair and a full beard. His eyes were wild with fear. "What in hell is goin' on? You got to let me through here. My Mary's sick. I need to get her to the hospital!" he shouted.

Tanner stood still and spoke calmly. "I'm sorry, sir. But that's not possible. We've been alerted by the county health department that there's been an outbreak of encephalitis. It's highly contagious. This valley is under full quarantine. We can't allow this disease to spread. We do have medical personnel on the way though, sir. Everything's going to be all right."

The old man sniffled and wiped his nose. "This ain't right. This is a free country. I want to get out of here. You can't keep us inside."

"Yes, sir, we can. This is a public emergency and we're charged with maintaining the public health. Do yourself a favor, sir. Just turn that truck around and head on back home. We've got the situation under control." His deep voice resonated with confidence and authority.

The old man sneezed and doubled over in pain. After a few seconds he straightened up but he was wheezing.

"Mary's in a bad way. And I'm not doin' so well myself. People are talking about some chemical spill—or some kind a bug or something. I don't know what this is, but something's going on."

"You can't keep people from talking, sir. Now please turn around and return to your home. It's for your own good."

It took some more convincing, but the man finally left. But he wouldn't be the last. People had been trying to get through all day. Tanner had been in the desert three days now. The first day they'd come in the late afternoon, waiting until night to set their positions. By morning the roadblock was up, soldiers were placed in the hilly area around the perimeter of the development, and the quarantine was in place. His orders were clear: Under no circumstances was anyone allowed outside of the valley.

The first day of the roadblock, it started out slow. The first car didn't come by until mid-morning. After it was turned back, the word spread and it seemed that everyone inside had to come by to take a look at what was going on. They grumbled about being turned back—some yelled and cursed the government and the army. They'd been coming back ever since, but there was no real trouble at first.

The trouble came that evening. A caravan of vehicles, eleven old cars, trucks, and RVs, approached the roadblock. An old red pickup truck was in front. It stormed up and screeched to a stop just feet before hitting the barricade. The others pulled to a stop right behind him. A big man with greasy black hair and a wild beard jumped out of the lead truck clutching a shotgun. Men clambered out of the other vehicles, everyone with some kind of weapon in their hands. One man had a long-barreled hunting rifle, but most of the men had simpler weapons; there were baseball bats, farm implements, and one man held a pair of kung fu nunchakus.

Tanner's men were in position above and behind the barricade. "Don't do anything unless I give you the signal," Tanner told them as he took out his .45 and moved in to confront the mob. "I'm sorry, people. But you have to turn around and return to your homes. I can't let you out."

The big man with the beard pumped the shotgun and pointed it at Tanner. "We're going through and you can't stop us."

Tanner could see the sweat rolling off the man's face. There was a rash on his skin, light bumps that covered most of his exposed flesh. He wheezed as he talked. Tanner spread his legs and stood his ground. "Just back on down, now. Our orders are that no one leaves till a release is signed off by the medical authorities. The medivacs should be here any time now."

"Well, where are they? You've been promising them all day and we haven't seen anyone." The man sneezed and wiped his nose on his forearm.

"I'm sorry, but you're just going to have to be patient a little longer—"

"Don't give me that bullshit, boy! This is a free coun try; we demand that you let us through." Someone in the crowd shouted encouragement.

Tanner bristled. His adrenaline was surging, but he had to stay calm. The other squatters were moving forward. He let his deep voice rumble. "Get back in your cars and turn around now. This is your final warning—"

The bearded guy cut in, yelling, "*No*—*You* listen to me. *You* back down! You got till the count of ten to back down or we're gonna ride right over your body." He raised the shotgun, leveling it on Tanner. "One . . . two . . ."

All he had to do was give the order and his men would open fire, Tanner thought. It would be no match. But he was in the line of fire, not the safest place to be. And the big question—would his men shoot? They were good men and well trained, but would they shoot? Could they fire on American citizens? These weren't enemies who spoke another language. These weren't enemies who had been demonized and made subhuman. Could his men fire on people who weren't all that different from themselves? He didn't want to risk it. Tanner was nearly close enough to reach out and touch the barrel of the gun.

"Three . . . four . . . ah . . ." The man raised his forearm as he stifled a sneeze.

Tanner stepped forward, amazingly fast for such a large man. With his left hand, he shoved down on the shotgun, misdirecting the aim. With his right hand, in one smooth motion he brought his gun up, swung it against the bearded man's temple, and squeezed off a shot. It sounded like thunder as it echoed against the canyon walls. The big man dropped to the road, a look of shock in his lifeless eyes, a small red flower of blood blossoming above his ear.

Tanner swung the gun around to the crowd. "Who's next?" he yelled. It happened so fast that no one had moved. He stepped over the body and advanced toward the crowd. "Get back in your cars and turn around. *Now!*"

There was a pause, a long moment when it could have gone either way. Then the people backed away and got in their cars. Their engines raced as they maneuvered to turn around and started to drive back toward the development. As they were leaving, someone yelled out the window, "We'll be back."

Tanner watched the dust rise up as they receded. Then he turned back to his men on the ridge. The closest to him was a young corporal named Conway. He looked pale and shaken. "Get the body and the damn truck out of the road. Burn 'em both."

Tanner walked beyond the barricade to the back of his troop's position. He sat down, took a deep breath, and closed his eyes. *How could they put me in that position?*

He'd proved himself before. He'd done what had to be done—he always had. He was purple slash after all, part of the inner circle. He was supposed to be in the know—but lately they'd frozen him out.

They put him into this assignment without telling him what was really going on. It was Durmo, the maggot. Durmo had called him back to the base, away from the rabbit hunt. It was supposed to be a drill—the orders didn't change until after he'd arrived and gotten his men in position. Even then he wasn't given the true story. Now, he knew this wasn't a drill. For some reason they were using live toxin; there was no mistaking the symptoms.

This was the first major assignment where he was in full command. Tanner had joined the army midway through his second year of college. He was in school on a football scholarship but a hamstring injury had cut his season short. Not having the games to look forward to, he began to drift. He started skipping classes. He backed off on his training and spent his time partying. It was fun for a while but he quickly got bored. He craved excitement. Football was great—game days anyway—on the field, running and hitting, it was pure power. The rest of the time was a drag. Inevitably, he'd been put on academic probation. The coach gave him a month to get his grades up and show his commitment to the team; otherwise he'd lose his scholarship. Tanner didn't wait. Instead he joined the army as an enlisted man. There he showed promise and found the discipline that he needed.

And it was there that he met the colonel, and his life changed. It was at the colonel's recommendation that he went to officers' training school, and he'd been with the colonel ever since. Tanner believed in the colonel, he was a man of vision—*he* saw the big picture. If *he* was doing something there was a reason for it.

Tanner was ready to do whatever he had to. He'd do

the dirty work; it was the end result that counted. But this
assignment still steamed him. They had no right to treat
him like this, like some field nigger, out of the loop and in
the line of fire. He was going to have to have a talk with
Durmo when they got back. It was a mystery what the
colonel saw in the creep.

Someone cleared their throat, disturbing his thoughts.
"Excuse me, sir. The men have been talking." It was Corporal Conway. He was thin and pale.

Tanner looked up. "Sure. What's up?"

"Well, um, there's a lot of talk. If those people have
something, some kind of disease, and it's contagious . . .
that means we could get it, too. . . ."

"No, no, man, that's not how it works. They should
have briefed us on that before we left, but you remember
those shots you got the other week?"

"Yeah, sure. The vaccination?"

"Right. That's what this is. No matter what happens to
those people, nothing's going to happen to you. We've all
been through it, tested and approved. There's no way that
we can get that shit."

Conway seemed to relax. "So we're OK?"

"Yeah, you're gonna be fine. Let's go on back to the
roadblock. I'll have a quick meeting to dispel these rumors. And we got to get ready. Those yokels will be coming back soon."

But they didn't. They waited through the night and into
the next day, but no one came back. Tanner checked with
his positions around the perimeter. There was no activity
there, either. A radioman was in place to monitor and jam
any outbound communication. But this was quiet, too.

It was near twilight when he took a patrol down to investigate. In the orange glow of the setting sun, the land
seemed surreal, like a Martian landscape. At the entrance
to the valley, Tanner stopped his Humvee, turned off the
engine, and scanned the horizon. There were clusters of

vehicles, old trailers, and some shacks that seemed to be made of plywood and corrugated tin. But there was no movement. It was quiet. The only sound was the whistle of the wind.

"Let's check it out." They started up again and moved forward.

The first thing they came to was an ancient, pastel-blue house trailer. It was propped up on concrete blocks and set on a cement pad. The shades on the windows were down. Tanner took out his pistol and used the butt end to rap on the door. "Anyone home?" he called.

There was no answer.

He tried again. There was still no response. He tried the door, but it was locked. He turned back to his men in the Hummer. "Cover me. I'm going in."

Tanner leaned down in a crouch, then shot forward sending his shoulder into the door. The door broke off at the hinges and fell inward, his momentum carried him inside. The smell hit him right away, ripe, fetid—the smell of rotting meat. He covered his nose with his arm and fought the urge to gag. Quickly, he glanced around. It took a second for his eyes to adjust to the dim light, but he already knew what was there. And he knew where it was before he saw it. The flies pointed the direction. The body was draped halfway on and halfway off a ratty old couch. The skin was covered with oozing black boils.

Tanner backed away as fast as he could. He nearly fell as he rushed out of the trailer, gasping for air. Outside, he knelt in the dust and retched as his men hung back uncomfortably. When he'd recovered, he wiped his mouth on his arm, took a deep, cleansing breath, and gave the order. "Burn it down."

They sloshed the trailer with gasoline and set it ablaze with a long burst from a flamethrower. The blast of heat singed the hair on Tanner's arms. He called back to the encampment and ordered the rest of the company down, leaving only a small group to guard the entrance. They went through the development checking each vehicle and structure. It was the same scene throughout.

"Burn it all," Tanner ordered. "I don't want anything left but melted metal."

By nightfall the valley was ablaze with dozens of fires. Tanner moved up to the top of a ridge and sat by himself, watching it all burn. As the fires exhausted their fuel and burned down to embers, they blinked like fireflies in the warm desert air. When the last fire had burned out, the only light was from a thousand stars in the sky above. Tanner sat alone. He felt like he was the last man alive on Earth.

19

RUNNING DOWN THE road, the gravel crunching beneath his feet, his legs moving like pistons, his breath exploding in rhythmic bursts, Ramon truly was free. It was early evening, but the sun was still on the way down. The air was cool and comfortable, perfect running weather. The sweat on his skin dried quickly, leaving a film of salt. As he ran, he'd pick something in the distance, a billboard, sign, or building, and use it as a goal to run to. Once he was past it, he'd pick a new goal and aim for that.

It had become a routine in the two weeks since they'd been with Philip. Each evening he would slip out of the house, run out of the subdivision and down to the main road where he'd run on the shoulder. He'd never run regularly before. Starting out was hard, he felt the pain in his lungs after just a few blocks. But he kept going and soon he ran through the pain. After that he could run for miles. Ramon saw a billboard a couple of hundred yards ahead advertising Castrol motor oil. *Cas-trol-oil, Cas-trol-oil, Cas-trol-oil.* He repeated the phrase in his mind like a mantra, fitting it into the rhythm of his breath.

It felt good to be outside and moving. It made sense to stay inside, but it felt like a jail cell. The roommates, Jelly and Frank, were always there, hanging around, drinking and fighting. They reminded Ramon of people he'd known in prison—slow and stupid, but dangerous just the same. They weren't causing him trouble. They didn't know who he was and they didn't seem to care. Still, he had to be on guard whenever he was around them. It was draining.

Being outside was chancy, but if he stayed inside he'd go crazy. It was worth the risk. He knew *they* were still hunting him but they didn't seem close. How could they be? There was nothing that pointed in this direction.

And the pressure was off in other ways, too. He and Lena weren't in the news anymore. With no recent sightings, the coverage had died down. The most recent article was a sidebar in *Newsworld* the week before. Written by Allen Edwards, it related Lena's phone call to him. It didn't give specifics but implied that she was paranoid and unstable, obsessed with conspiracies. But that was the worst of it. New stories had captured center stage and he and Lena were old news. So Ramon felt safe outside.

It was a relief having someplace to hide, at least for a time. They couldn't stay here forever, but for now it was a godsend. And it looked like they were making progress. Philip went to work every day and put time into unlocking the secrets on the computer tape, and Lena was on the home computer constantly, trying to find information that would help their cause. If they found proof, someone would have to listen to them.

Ramon passed the Castrol oil billboard. Two cars whizzed by going in the opposite direction. Commuters making their way home. The last car had its lights on. If he wasn't careful he'd be running back in the dark, he thought. He scanned ahead, looking for his next target. There was another billboard a few hundred yards ahead. This one was old and faded from the weather. It showed the image of a distinguished-looking silver-haired man pictured against a wooded backdrop. The slogan read Protect Our Environment—Vote Randall Morgan.

Morgan. That name was familiar, Ramon thought. Where was it from? Then he remembered. He'd seen the man on TV while in his jail cell—the day he was supposed to be executed. Involuntarily he shuddered. By all rights he should have been dead. He tried to put the thought out of his mind as he set his sights on the billboard. This would be the turnaround point, he decided. That would make it about three miles out and another three back home. Then a hot shower and time to relax. *Ran-dall-Mor-gan, Ran-dall-Mor-gan.* He fit the name into his rhythm and kept his pace steady.

IN THE TWO weeks that they had been there, Lena had spent most of her time in Philip's room working on the computer. With his help she had gained access to archives and databases she never knew existed. The pieces of the puzzle were coming together. Her research was starting to bear fruit. And she'd never been so scared.

The central question—what was going on at the installation? From the beginning they had assumed that the installation was dealing with some kind of biological warfare agent. And *they* were using Ramon and the others as human guinea pigs to develop a vaccine.

Lena started out with a keyword search for *biological warfare.* She scanned through the hits, not sure where to go next. To get some broad background, she picked a site on the history of germ warfare. It was surprising how far back it went. The Romans dumped dead animals into their enemy's water supply in order to spread disease; in the

Middle Ages, attackers spread the plague by catapulting diseased bodies over castle or city walls; in the French and Indian Wars, the British decimated the Indian population by handing out smallpox infected blankets as "peace offerings." More recently, there were an overwhelming amount of hits relating to the September 11 terrorist attacks and the anthrax letters.

Over the course of the first week Lena read everything she could on biological warfare, or BW, as it was referred to. By treaty it was an international crime, yet every major international power had some form of program—including the United States. There were scholarly papers filed by think tanks that stated the best ways to wage, and win, a germ war. For something that was so taboo and unthinkable, it was discussed in an amazingly matter-of-fact way—terms like "acceptable losses" and "maximum kill rates" were routinely used as simply part of the vocabulary.

Lena learned the characteristics of an effective biological warfare agent. She made notes as she went through her source and found there were seven.

1. Efficient replication—it had to be something that could be easily reproduced.

2. Adequate stability—it had to be safe to handle and have the ability to hold up while being transported and set into action.

3. High infection rates.

4. Short incubation periods—the disease had to come on quickly once induced.

5. Consistent induction of desired disease—the toxin had to be something that was stable and wouldn't mutate into a new form.

6. Efficient method of delivery—for the agent to be most effective it had to be easily passed throughout the population after the initial induction. Ideally, that meant something that could be passed from person to person through their respiratory systems, through breathing or sneezing.

And the seventh and last characteristic, the toxin had to be amenable to vaccination.

Had *they* found some super toxin and were they now racing to develop the vaccine? The fact that Ramon was still alive and not infectious, that *she* was still alive, meant that somehow they had succeeded. But why? For what purpose? What was the master plan?

The characteristics all pointed to the toxin being a virus. Lena focused her research there. She scanned through medical journals and archives looking for anything that would help it all make sense. Viruses were so commonly discussed in popular culture: The flu, the common cold, and HIV were all viral in nature. But beyond that she knew little. She threw herself into the research. The amount of information was overwhelming.

In a way viruses were more like machines than living creatures—they weren't alive in any normal sense of the word. Made up of just a tiny bit of protein and genetic material, they lie dormant for years at a time, waiting for the proper conditions to arise. Once they find a host—someone or something to infect—they go into action. Using the host's body as a factory, they use all of its chemicals and nutrients as building blocks for new viruses. Like a copying machine, they replicate themselves over and over until they overwhelm their host. Once they've used up everything in one host, they break out in search of a new host to infect.

Each virus was different in its effects and gestation period. Some like the common cold or flu were passed easily by respiration, breathing. The symptoms came on fast and the infection passed quickly from person to person, but its effects were usually mild. Others like HIV could be deadly. But HIV was relatively hard to pass and it took years for any symptoms to appear. Then there were those like Ebola and Marburg, the African killer viruses, that were deadly and fast acting. But even these weren't as contagious as people had feared. It usually took blood contact for the disease to spread.

Lena tried to put herself in the position of the army. For this new weapon to be suitable as a warfare agent, it had to be a killer bug that hit quickly and spread through a population easily. The Centers for Disease Control and Prevention in Atlanta had compiled a list of every known virus. Lena spent days going through the list, comparing each against the list of BW characteristics and the symptoms that Ramon had observed on the man in the quarantine. Nothing fit.

There was one other possibility. There were hybrids—designer viruses. The installation's scientists could have designed a germ from scratch that fit all the characteristics of the perfect toxin. And this was the truly scary part. Viruses could be designed, but could they be controlled? If *they* had a super virus that could kill quickly and efficiently, it would be like controlling fire. If it were put out into a population, it would kill enemy and friend alike. History showed more empires had been destroyed by disease than by armies. That's why they would need a vaccine, a dependable vaccine. But who would get this protection? And was the installation really prepared to use the virus?

By the time she had reached this point, Lena had enough information to write a book. But she'd learned nothing that really helped Ramon and herself. The other focus of her search was to find out as much as she could about the Johnson Installation. Her results weren't much better there. The only thing that seemed unusual was the amount of money that was allocated to it — more than triple the amount of any other training base of its size.

After she ran out of options with the installation, she turned to an examination of its commander, Col. Lucian Pope. She'd been checking out that angle for the last two days but wasn't making much headway.

Lena's concentration was broken when she suddenly heard a loud noise from one of the rooms below. She took her hands off the keyboard and sat back to listen. She heard another thud and then shouting. She relaxed. It was the roommates, Frank and Jelly. At least once a day they'd get into some kind of fight where they would wrestle around and knock over furniture — it usually happened in the afternoon after they'd been drinking. They were loud and obnoxious. She felt sorry for Philip, who had to put up with them. But they appeared harmless. She avoided them as best she could, although the house was feeling awfully cramped by now. She glanced at her watch. Ramon would still be out on his run for another half hour or so. The two roommates seemed harmless but she always felt better when Ramon was nearby.

Wearily, Lena returned to her work. At first she couldn't find much more about Pope than she'd known before. He'd been advancing on the fast track until about twelve years ago when his career stalled out. She couldn't find any incident in the records to explain it. What had happened then? The timeline coincided with the Gulf War — Desert Storm. But Pope wasn't in a combat unit. There was no notation of what his position had been at the time. And there was no listing of Pope after the war. It looked like a dead end.

Philip had shown her how to gain access to a number of normally restricted archives, including one from the Defense Department. She'd already run through it once but this time she tried a different tack. This time she isolated the period between 1985 and the start of the Gulf War in 1991. Nothing new came up. She tried the search again but this time she rephrased the command. She got a hit.

She found a transcript of a lecture given by Pope at the War College in December of 1989. The title was: *Defensive Strategies to BW Initiatives in Regional Conflicts.* The text of the speech read like a doctoral dissertation, the language precise and filled with jargon. In the speech Pope called for a new focus in military preparedness. With the fall of the Berlin Wall and the breakdown of communism, the threat of a full-scale nuclear war had declined tremendously. But instead of ushering in a new era of world peace, it increased the probability of regional conflicts. The status quo was broken. Without the countervailing pressures of two superpowers, the possibilities of flare-ups of ethnic and religious conflicts, or opportunism by a regional strongman, were now greater than ever. That, Pope said, would define the role of U.S. military policy for the decades to come.

The thesis of the speech was that the enemy would not be able to compete in a battle using conventional warfare. So they would press the battle using nonconventional means—BW gives the most bang for the buck. The only way to rebalance the power would be to develop a defense against BW so that it was no longer something to fear. Pope proposed a comprehensive series of vaccines targeted toward every possible toxin. He called for the setup of a dedicated group to develop the technology for these vaccines.

Lena sat back in her chair. That explained a lot. This had to be the start of what eventually became the Johnson Installation. And now, after so much of what he'd predicted had come to pass, with the threat of terrorism so real, there was an even greater need for vaccines. But this didn't explain why Pope was still a colonel, or what had happened since. And the virus that they were dealing with was unlike anything in the listings. That had to mean something. There had to be more.

At the bottom of the page was a link to another document, this one from the Senate archives. She wrote down the document number then clicked on the link. The screen blinked as it moved to the new site. As the new location flashed onto the screen, Lena read the message identifying the document as a transcript from a meeting of the Strategic Arms Subcommittee of the Armed Services Committee dated October of 1991. The link on this showed there was no electronic file available. The file could only be accessed physically through the Senate archives.

Lena stared hard at the screen. Something in this document would explain it all. But she couldn't get it. The file was locked up somewhere in Washington.

PHILIP ALWAYS FELT safe in the computer room. It was a sanctuary. The hum of the equipment, the coolness in the air, even the glare of the florescent lights was comforting. Here, he was in control. This was his domain and he was the master. By the clock on the wall, it was past quitting time. All his staff had already left and he was ready to follow. But Leo Stern, the vice president of power transmission, had made the trip down and needed his wizard's touch.

Stern was a heavyset man in his fifties. He scratched his head as he handed the papers over. "I got to admit, Phil, this stuff's all Greek to me. But we're having some real problems with our emergency contingency plans. I've been told that there's going to be zero tolerance for brownouts — we got too much heat on it this summer — so to speak. But the real problem is they don't want it to impact the bottom line. They want it to be fully cost-effective."

Philip took off his glasses as he looked over the print-out, which showed times and areas affected by that summer's brownouts. "So increasing overall capacity's out?"

"Yeah, we can't do that. They want a solution where we only pull the power when we really need it."

"So it's got to be predictive? That's going to be hard to do."

"Yeah, tell me about it. My guys have been drawing blanks."

Philip scanned the paper. "Maybe something like . . . well, I could do a historical analysis. Say, over the last ten or twelve years, see when we've had the problems and what areas have been most affected." He stroked his goatee as he thought. "That could show patterns and we could arrange to pull from the grid at the projected peak times. But, you can't predict weather that well."

"No, you're right. But this would help."

"When do you need this?"

"When can you get it?"

"There are some other projects that I'm working on. But I'll take a run at it. Maybe we can get you something next week?"

"That would be great. That would do real good, Phil. I knew I could count on you."

After Stern left, Philip felt like kicking himself. He was already carrying more than he could handle. The three programmers under his supervision were complaining of overwork and he'd taken on some of their work to pick up the slack. His plate was already too full, and now he had another commitment to worry about. He wished he knew how to say no.

Philip looked at the printout one more time. It wouldn't be too hard. He could put something together, he thought. He'd just have to work a little harder. It would just take some more time. But not tonight. He'd already worked longer than he'd planned to. He laid the paper down as he sat at his terminal. There were just a couple of things he needed to check and then he could call it a day.

There were six new e-mail messages—but nothing that he needed to respond to immediately. He felt exhausted and his mind was zoning out. He couldn't think as clearly as normal. For a moment he wondered if it was something in the air, or maybe in the drinking water. Some conspiracy to take over by wearing down people's defenses. Or maybe it was just in the corporate water supply and the company was using it as a way to manipulate their employees. It could be possible, he thought, but it wasn't rational. If anything they'd want them more revved up. He was overworked, pure and simple. It was time to call it a day.

He'd logged out of the system and was about to turn out the lights when he remembered his other project. He'd been so busy he hadn't checked it all day. He logged back on and called up the program he'd designed to unscramble the tape cartridge. The last time he'd checked, the screen showed lines of numbers flashing across the screen, scrolling down in search of a match. It took a moment for the screen to come to life. He blinked his eyes; the screen had stabilized. Now there was a menu.

The heading read: *Johnson Installation Operations.*

He'd broken the code.

THE AIR IN the room was ripe with the smell of spilled beer, sweaty socks, and old food. The big-screen TV was blaring at full volume but nobody paid any attention. Frank had Jelly in a headlock, and they were sprawled out on the couch, fighting for position. They'd already kicked over the coffee table, knocking their beers and a bag of chips onto the carpet. "You give? Say you give, dude, or I'll twist your head off."

Jelly arched his back and twisted in, trying to use his

great bulk to its best advantage. "You're dead meat, bro. I'll kick your ass!"

They rolled off the couch and tumbled around on the floor. Jelly moved on top; he had his arms around Frank, squeezing the air out in a great bear hug, crushing him with his weight. Frank hung on to the head with all his strength, moving his forearm in for a choke hold. They stayed in that position for nearly a minute, stalemated, both wheezing from the effort. Frank made the first overture. "OK, I'll let go if you do."

Jelly grunted his agreement.

"Ok, on the count of three we both let go. . . . One . . . two . . . three, let go." They both started to tentatively let go, neither one fully trusting the other. They staggered to their feet, still maintaining their grips. "Come on, let go."

Jelly let go completely. Frank started to, but then clamped on tight again when he had the advantage. He stepped in back while he squeezed hard on the head. "You give?"

Jelly's voice was weak from the pressure on his windpipe. "You cheated!"

"You give up, dude?"

"Yeah, I give."

Frank let him go with a laugh. "I got you, dude."

Jelly brushed off his clothes and picked up what was left of his can of beer. "That wasn't fair. You cheated," he pouted.

"You're just mad cause I got you." Frank uprighted his beer and flopped down on the couch. "Come on, you wanna play a video game?"

"No." Jelly settled down on his side of the couch. He was still breathing heavily and his face was nearly as red as his hair. The heaving of his chest started a wave that rippled through the fat on his massive stomach. "You're dog meat next time."

"Quit pouting, man. I got you." He tipped his can up and finished the beer. "How we doing with the brew?"

"This is it. We've only got a six-pack left after we're done with these."

"Damn. Well, I'll call the dweeb and have him pick some up then."

"Yeah."

Frank got up and kicked around the spilled chips looking for the remote control. He found it, sat back down, and started to flip through the channels, hardly pausing to see what was on each. While staring at the TV he motioned up the stairs with his hand. "Don't you wonder what she does up there all day?"

"The Ice Queen?"

"Yeah. What's her problem? She thinks she's better than us."

"She's a bitch." Jelly leaned back in his seat; his breathing was just returning to normal.

"Yeah, she's a stone bitch." Frank continued flipping through the stations, stopping occasionally to watch something for a second then moving on. He scratched behind his ear. "Someone needs to put her in her place."

"Yeah." Suddenly Jelly got excited. "Hey, stop. Go back."

Frank stopped and flipped back a channel. "What, here?"

"No, back one more."

He backed up another channel. On the screen, a man was standing in the middle of a set that looked like a modern broadcasting studio. Workers were hunched over tables, talking on phones or staring at monitors. The man walked through the studio, talking as he went. "Tonight we feature a case that is fresh from the headlines but no closer to being solved than when the killer first struck months ago. On the night of . . . "

"Let's watch something else."

"No. This show's cool." Jelly leaned forward to watch.

Back on the screen, a man was walking through a kitchen. At the bottom of the screen a caption flashed: *Reenactment*. The man from the studio was talking in voice-over. "Attorney Barry Resnick left work early that day with the idea of taking some time off from his busy schedule. It was his misfortune to cross paths with the notorious killer Hector Ramerez." The actor on the screen walked down a hallway to a closed door. He opened the door; there were two quick bursts from a pistol and the actor dropped to the ground. "Was it a botched robbery? Was simple greed the motive? Or was it something more sinister? Only Ramerez can tell us. . . ." The show continued on. It showed the video from the ATM and gave background on both suspects, Hector Ramerez and Lena Dryer.

"Dude, do they look familiar to you?" Frank squinted at the TV.

Jelly just grunted.

"Look at those faces, man. Look close. Look at the dude."

As the show was winding down they played the video again.

". . . It's been several weeks since the last sighting. If you have any information on these fugitives please call our toll-free number. . . ." The number flashed across the bottom of the screen. "A reward of fifty thousand dollars for any information leading to their apprehension."

Frank's eyes were bulging as he stared at the screen.

The screen changed again to show still pictures of both Hector and Lena. The toll-free number continued to flash below.

"Fifty thousand dollars." Frank smiled as he tried to contain his excitement. He slapped Jelly on the shoulder. "Dude, we're going to make us some money!"

•   •   •

LENA STARED AT the screen as she tried to process the information. Somehow the answer to their problem was in Washington. This was the proof. But the documents were classified. How could they get access? Somehow they had to find out what was really happening.

Suddenly Lena felt uneasy. She moved away from the keyboard and listened. It took her a minute to figure out what it was. It was too quiet. The TV downstairs had been blaring away for hours and now it had been turned off. She'd gotten so used to the noise that the quiet seemed strange. She focused again. That was it. They'd just turned off the TV. It wasn't anything to worry about, but she still wished that Ramon was back. She'd feel safer when he was.

She turned back to the computer and was about to type in a new command, when she heard a noise. It was the creaking of the stairs. She felt a surge of adrenaline. Something wasn't right. She pushed back her chair, stood up, and moved toward the door, putting her ear close to listen. She heard it again. Another creak. The roommates never came upstairs, it couldn't be them. Maybe it was Ramon, back from his run.

"Ramon?" She called out his name but no one answered. "Is anybody there?" Still no answer.

Lena's heart was thumping wildly. It was probably nothing, she told herself. But she felt on edge. It just didn't feel right. She quickly locked the door, just in case. She was about to sit back down when she heard the floor creak from someone heavy stepping onto the landing. Then another creak—it was like someone was trying to sneak up. And they were whispering something. She couldn't hear the words but someone was definitely whispering.

Frantically she scanned the room, looking for something to use as a weapon. Her purse, with her can of mace, was in the bedroom.

Someone outside grabbed on to the doorknob and twisted, but it didn't move. "Shit! She locked it."

"Then break it!"

It was the roommates. What were they doing? Why were they out there? What was going on? She couldn't see anything in the room that could be used as a weapon.

The door thudded. They were banging their shoulders against it. On the desk next to the computer was a tin can filled with pens and pencils. A brass letter opener with an anchor shaped handle stood up above the other the other items in the can. Lena grabbed hold of the letter opener, gripped it in her fist and faced the door. It thudded again but this time the lock broke. The door crashed inward and the two roommates tumbled in.

Lena stepped backward, holding the opener. "Stay away from me!"

Frank, the dark one, was in front. Jelly, the pasty, red-haired one was a step behind. Their eyes were wild. Frank grabbed for her arm. Lena jabbed at him with the opener, and the tip pierced the flesh of his forearm.

"You bitch!" Frank grabbed her arm with one hand and twisted it while he used his weight to push her against the wall. He pried the opener out of her hand and threw it on the floor. Then he stepped back and smacked her hard with his open palm. She cried out in pain and slid down the wall. Frank looked down at her and screamed, "You gonna get nasty? I'll show you nasty. We own you, bitch!"

Lena looked up from the floor; they were towering over her. Her face hurt. Her lip was bleeding; she could taste the blood inside her mouth. She'd felt so secure before but now that was gone. She bit the inside of her lip and willed herself not to cry.

"The geaser's going to be back soon. Go check out the other room and see what you can find," Frank ordered. Jelly sauntered out of the room.

Frank stood over her, licked his lips, and grinned.

"We're gonna have some fun tonight, bitch. You can bet on it."

She could hear Jelly thrashing around in the room next door, throwing things on the floor, and kicking around. What would happen if Ramon came back now? Would he be any match against these two? She prayed that he would be.

From next door, Jelly suddenly yelled. It was a whoop, a victory call. A moment later he rushed back into the room. "Hey, Frank. Look what I found." Grinning from ear to ear, he looked like Yosemite Sam, holding a gun in each hand.

RAMON HAD RUN longer than he intended. It was dark when he turned onto the block to Philip's house. The air was cool and still, and his sweat dried on contact. He was tired but it felt good. He touched his finger to his neck and checked his pulse as he slowed to a walk. It was racing but he knew he'd recover quickly.

As he walked, cooling down, he listened to the night sounds of crickets and cicadas. The run was refreshing. It was good to be outside in the fresh air, his muscles moving, his head clear. He wondered how he'd survived so long in prison. He needed the space of the outdoors, the sunlight, the smell of clean air. It was freedom, something he'd taken for granted until he'd lost it. Now, he knew he'd rather die than go back.

By the time he'd reached the house his pulse was nearly back to normal. Philip's car wasn't there yet. It looked like another late night at the office. Ramon took the key off of the cord on his neck and unlocked the door.

Something seemed wrong as soon as he stepped through the door. It was too quiet. Normally the TV was blaring. Tonight it was still.

He closed the screen door. His muscles tensed, he listened for any other sign but he couldn't hear a thing. As he closed the door behind him, Ramon sensed movement from behind him. Adrenaline shot through his body— someone was behind the door.

He started to react but it was too late. Frank stepped out from behind the door and shoved the pistol barrel up against Ramon's skull, right behind his ear. The metal felt cold against his skin.

"It's time to party, dude."

Suddenly there was a flash of white light. Ramon saw starbursts and felt himself slipping. It was all an explosion of white. And then there was nothing.

20

CAIN KNEW HIS stock was dropping. Back at the base, everyone had feared and respected him. Rank was irrelevant, he was The Man. He was the power, the colonel's law. If something had to be done, he did it. No questions asked, no excuses given. He'd get it done. He did the hard jobs, quickly and professionally, leaving no loose ends. But this project was not going well and it was costing him in too many ways.

He'd started the hunt confident that it would just be a matter of time before the rabbit was found and neutralized. But from the start there had been setbacks. Then, when he had finally found his prey, he botched the job. It was inexcusable. Now instead of one rabbit, there were two. And the trail had gone cold. Now, it had been two weeks without a reliable sighting. They'd completely dropped off the radar. With the whole country looking for them, somehow they'd just disappeared. There was no way that they could have done this on their own, which meant that someone, somewhere, was hiding them. The contagion had spread again.

Living with the failure was bad enough, but what really set Cain's teeth on edge was that the colonel seemed to have lost interest. After the fuckup in Austin, the colonel was ready to pull the plug and start over with a new team. He'd stayed with Cain, but now it looked like he was working with different options. Cain's calls to the colonel were now being passed through to Major Durmo. Something was going on and he was so out of the loop that he didn't know what it was. Priorities had changed and his resources were being cut. First they'd pulled Rev Tanner, his top aide, off the detail. Then they'd cut the rest of his team to the bone, leaving him with no more than a skeleton crew.

So now it had come to this. He was staying in a Holiday Inn in the Chicago suburbs, a double room no less. He glanced over at the other bed, where his roommate for the night, Virgil Ortman, a tall, lanky lieutenant from New Jersey, was sprawled out. Ortman was OK, but it irritated him that he had to share a room. And besides, it was partly Ortman's fault that they were here. If he'd done his job back at the base, the rabbit never would have escaped in the first place.

Cain took a deep breath and closed his eyes. He felt a headache coming on. He could feel a band of pressure ratcheting tighter on his skull. He sat up straight and rubbed his temples as he turned his gaze to the TV on top of the dresser. The theme music for *America's Most Wanted* was beginning to play. This was his last gamble. He'd pushed hard to allocate reward money and get the show on the air. In the end he'd had to nearly get down on his knees and beg. The colonel finally agreed; he interceded with the network and pulled in some favors to make it work. This was desperation. If the targets didn't show up after this, it was all over. If he failed now, Cain would be called back to the base and the rabbit would win.

Cain had two men at the studio manning the 800 line. They were screening the calls; the most promising leads were then to be relayed directly to him on his mobile line so he could decide how to proceed. If this didn't pay off Cain was out of options.

The lab had analyzed the paper found in the stolen car. Lena's fingerprints were on it, so there was no doubt that it was linked to his prey. When Cain had first looked at the paper, he could make out the imprint of the words TRUE BELIEVER. The lab had detected more writing underneath. It appeared to be directions. Starting in St Louis, it described a route northwest into Illinois. The last notation was 294-North heading toward Wisconsin. They couldn't make anything out after that.

They were obviously directions to this TRUE BE-LIEVER. But from what was written, the location could be anywhere in northern Illinois or Wisconsin. And the paper was two weeks old so by this time the targets could have left and gone anywhere. But it was all they had to go by. This Holiday Inn, in the suburbs north of Chicago, was as good a spot to set up operations as any. They'd been working out of the motel for the last week and a half.

All the other lines of inquiry were coming up empty. He'd tried to trace down places where they would have computer tape readers compatible with the stolen computer tape. But the number was too high to follow through. It was a popular model with the corporate and in-stitutional market. Besides, he was assured that the tape was encrypted and could not be unscrambled.

Cain had found out that his targets had been in St. Louis because that's where they recovered the stolen car. But they hadn't made that mistake this time. No car had been found that could be linked to them.

He still had a man in place at the Defense Department

in Washington, but so far his targets hadn't tried to reach their contact there again. Everything was coming up blank.

The last lead left was the name TRUE BELIEVER. Believer in what? Cain thought it had to be some kind of religious association. But looking into the reporter's past there was nothing that would suggest a strong connection to any organized religious movement. Nothing for the rabbit either. They checked through all her known contacts looking for some connection, still nothing. The only listing they could find in the area with the name, was the True Believer African Methodist Church in Waukegan, Illinois. It was a storefront church in a run-down section of town. They checked it out—he even put two men on surveillance there. But again this lead came up empty.

So now his only hope was that another shot of publicity and a big reward would be enough to flush them out into the open. Cain stared at the TV but it didn't hold his interest. He'd seen it all before. He felt the blood surging inside his head. The dull ache was starting to spread, the pressure was growing. He forced his concentration back onto the TV. Neither he nor Ortman spoke as the show went on. He watched the reenactment of the shooting of the attorney—it didn't look at all like he remembered it. He cringed as they replayed the video from the ATM machine. Unconsciously he brought his hand to his nose, touching the damaged area. The show ended with the toll-free number flashing on the bottom of the screen.

Cain got up, turned off the television, then paced across the room, willing his phone to ring. Ortman sat up on the other bed and looked at Cain. He seemed like he was about to speak but Cain glared at him and he remained silent.

The quiet was unnerving. Cain continued pacing back and forth across the room as the time passed. He had to be moving. He wanted to do something and it hurt to be in such a passive role. The room was quiet. The only sounds were from the hiss of the air conditioner and the occasional clunking of the ice machine down the hall.

Cain's head was pounding now. The pain was intense, it magnified his feelings of frustration. As he continued pacing he could feel his rage grow. This was his last chance. He'd gambled everything on the show and nothing was happening. If someone was going to respond, he'd expect it to happen quickly. The longer it took the less chance there was that something would pan out. He knew that calls had to be coming in, but his men were screening everything. They'd have to follow up on whatever they found later, but he was hoping for a breakthrough. Something so big it would require his attention now. He glanced down at his watch; the show had ended nearly an hour ago. It was too damn quiet.

Ortman sat up on his bed and cleared his throat. "It don't look like anything's happening tonight, Captain."

Cain spun around. "What did you say?"

"Well, I'm just saying, it's been awful quiet, sir. Maybe nothing's going to happen tonight. Maybe you should just chill out and relax a little."

Cain's muscles tensed. It was bad enough that he had to share his room with a subordinate. But now this loser was telling him what to do. The pressure in Cain's head was too much. He felt like a bomb about to explode. He'd kept his discipline. He'd maintained control. But this was too much—he needed relief.

His eyes bored into Ortman; he wanted to hit him. He wanted to beat him hard, to rip him apart with his bare hands. He wanted to smell fresh blood and feel the crack of snapping bones. Consequences be damned, he clenched his fists and stepped forward.

Then the phone rang.

• • •

WHEN RAMON OPENED his eyes all he could see was white. His first thought was that he was back in the base, tied to the bed in the white room. But that wasn't right. He was restrained somehow; he couldn't move his arms. But he was sitting up, propped against something. And the white wasn't from the room but the color of something covering his face. It was a loose fabric that covered his entire head. His breath was trapped there, it came back hot on his face. His breathing sounded so loud. There was a ringing in his ears and his head hurt like hell.

He wanted to move his hand up to check his head, but he couldn't. His hands were tied together somehow. He felt disoriented, not sure what had happened, but it came back quickly. The roommates had jumped him as he came in the door after a run. Frank had his gun. Ramon couldn't tell for sure but he didn't think he'd been shot. With the pain in his head he thought that he'd been hit hard and knocked unconscious. He didn't know where he was but it had to be somewhere inside the house. But what was going on? Why had they attacked him? And where was Lena? He hoped she was all right.

He stopped moving, tried to slow down his breathing and listen. He knew he was still in the house when he heard the compressor on the refrigerator kick on. It seemed so quiet otherwise. There usually was loud music playing and the sounds of the two roommates yelling or fighting. What was going on? He held his breath and strained to hear. It was hard to concentrate with the ringing in his head, but with effort he could. There was a rumbling, banging sound in another part of the house. Was it upstairs? He thought it was.

He took another deep breath, held it and listened again. He thought he heard something closer by. It sounded like breathing.

"Is anybody there?" He spoke just over a whisper.

There was a muffled reply, almost a groan. Ramon's

breath caught in his throat. He couldn't be sure but it sounded like Lena. What had they done to her? He had to help her.

He struggled against his restraints—they were tight, but he was determined. He tried to get to his feet. He leaned back, leveraging himself against the wall, and pushed up off the floor. He was starting to get his feet in position, when he heard the voices. It was Frank and Jelly. The sound was coming from above—a room at the top of the stairs. Ramon dropped back into a sitting position. It wouldn't do to have them come down when he was on his feet but still restrained. They'd just club him again and then he'd be useless. He tried to relax, slump over, and sit as still as he could.

They sounded like thunder as they crashed down the stairs and into the room. As he heard the footsteps, Ramon had the urge to tense his muscles but he tried to loosen up and sit as motionless as possible. The footsteps came right to him. Without warning, he felt a jolt of pain in his thigh; one of them had kicked him. He clenched his mouth tight so he wouldn't cry out, and let his body go limp. He flopped over to the side. He felt so vulnerable. There was nothing he could do to protect himself—he wished that he could see what they were doing. He lay still and tried not to breathe.

"Maybe you hit him too hard. I think he's dead." It was Jelly's voice.

"He's not dead. And even if he is, we were just protecting ourselves. He's a killer. We'll still get the reward." Frank had a smug edge to his voice.

The footsteps moved away. "What are we going to do with her, Frank?"

"I've got some ideas." He laughed.

Ramon heard a low moan. Now he was sure it was Lena.

"But we'll save the fun for later," Frank continued.

"We've got to get everything ready first. The dweeb should be home anytime now. We've got to wait for him."

Ramon listened as the footsteps moved away. He'd thought that he was in the living room; it sounded like they were heading toward the kitchen. He knew he was right when he heard the refrigerator door open. Ramon moved his hands around, trying to get a grip on something, trying to feel what he was restrained with. He didn't have much time; he knew they would be back soon. He grasped some material in his hands. It felt like linen. As he inhaled he could make out a faint scent of laundry deter-gent — they'd tied him up with bedsheets.

He pulled on the fabric, looking for some slack, but his efforts only pulled the sheets tighter. He heard the pop-ping sounds of two beers being opened.

"You got the number?" Ramon could hear them talk-ing, their loud voices carrying. He flexed his shoulders and pushed out with his arms trying to loosen the ties.

"No, I thought you wrote it down."

"I didn't write it down. I told you to."

"Well, I didn't have a pen."

Ramon rolled his shoulders and stretched as he listened to them arguing. He could feel the sheets loosening. He grasped onto a portion of the sheet with one hand as he continued to move. It was working; he could feel the knots giving way.

The roommates voices were coming closer again and Ramon could hear their footsteps. He stopped moving, slumped down, and played dead.

"You are *too* stupid, dude. Why didn't you write it down?"

"Why's it my fault? You could have done it."

Ramon lay quietly, waiting for the fighting to start. But this time it didn't.

"OK, man, you're right. Let's not fight about it." It was

Frank's voice. "We can get the number. We just got to be cool and we'll be getting the cash."

"Yeah, you're right, Frank."

"Just call information and ask for the TV station. They'll have it." The footsteps moved into the room. "I just wish the dweeb would show up. Then we'd have the whole package."

There was a plopping sound as they flopped down on the couch. Ramon could hear the beeping of the phone as they punched in the number.

"Yeah, uh, I want the number for that TV station . . . uh, the one with the show about . . ."

"Give me the phone, moron."

Ramon listened as Frank talked with the operator, asking for the number of a TV station. Why were they calling a TV station? Something had happened—now they knew who he was. They had talked about money, was there a reward on their heads? He strained to listen as Frank repeated the number and punched it in.

"Yeah, I need the hot line number for that most wanted show."

It took about a minute before he got the number and hung up. Ramon tried not to move as Frank hit in the new number. Someone on the other line picked up, "What's it take to get the reward, man?" Frank barked into the phone. There was a long silence, then he said, "Well, I've got 'em. They're tied up in my living room right now." He talked a little longer, answering their questions and giving the address of the house and some quick directions. He ended the conversation with, "Yeah, it's them, there's no doubt about it. I got their guns and everything."

He slammed the phone down with excitement. "All right, Jelly boy! We got the cash. They're sending out a special team. They'll be here within an hour." Ramon could hear him shift his weight off the couch and on to his feet. "If we're gonna have some fun, we got to have it now."

Ramon listened to the footsteps as they moved toward him. He tensed, expecting contact. But nothing happened. The footsteps moved past him. For a moment he felt a sense of relief. Then Lena moaned.

"Shut up, bitch. You've been asking for this."

Ramon heard the slap of a hand on flesh, then the sound of ripping fabric. A surge of anger rushed through his body. He strained against his restraints, not caring if they saw him or not. The sheets were looser than before but he was still held tight.

"I dunno, Frank. We could get in trouble for this." Jelly sounded worried.

"Shut up. No one's going to do nothing. This bitch is a murderer. What are they going to do?"

Lena groaned again.

Ramon could feel the sheets slackening. He gripped an end in his hand and tried to move it through, searching for the knot. He could now move easily inside the sheets. He was ready to make his move—he was about to stand up and try to tear the sheets off, when he heard a noise from the other end of the house. The door was opening. He stopped moving and stiffened. Had the people from the TV come so quickly?

"Uh, hi. Is uh, anybody home?" It was Philip. Ramon stayed motionless.

"It's the dweeb. Let's get him."

They clomped past Ramon as they hurried out to the hallway. There was a thud. It sounded like they'd thrown Philip against the wall. They were yelling but Ramon didn't pay any attention to the words. He forced himself to his feet and shimmied his body as he tore at the sheets. It took a minute but he was able to get the whole tangled mess over his head. He was free.

Quickly he scanned the room. The roommates were in

the hallway screaming at Philip. Lena was on the floor in the corner. Her blouse was ripped open in the front and her arms and legs were wrapped tight with electrical cords. She was gagged and there was a small streak of blood running down from the corner of her mouth. He looked into her eyes. They showed fear mixed with relief. Ramon glanced behind him—it was still clear. He reached down and unraveled the cord. "Are you all right?" he whispered.

She nodded as she reached up to remove the gag. "We've got to get out of here."

"I know. Wait here."

The roommates were still yelling in the hallway. Ramon could hear Frank shouting, "You could've got us killed, you dumb shit! You brought killers into our house."

Ramon glanced about the room, looking for anything that could be used as a weapon. There was a fireplace against the far wall. It looked like it hadn't been used in years, but there was an old poker leaning against the hearth. It was black cast iron with a flat shovel at the end. He quickly moved over and picked it up, gripping it like a baseball bat.

The noise from the hallway was coming full blast. Frank and Jelly's yelling were punctuated with thuds and sobs.

"You're toast, dweeb!"

Ramon took a deep breath, then stepped into the hall. They swivelled their heads and looked at him in surprise. Ramon swung the poker overhand, coming down hard on Frank's arm. Frank cried out in pain and dropped to the floor, clutching his arm.

Jelly raised his gun. Ramon reacted by swinging again, aiming for Jelly's arm. Jelly moved in anticipation but the poker still caught him, hitting his huge stomach. *Thwack.* The gun went off as Jelly grunted in pain. The bullet missed Ramon, but Frank howled in pain again.

Ramon swung again. This time he hit the gun, knocking it out of Jelly's hand and sending it clattering to the floor. He tried to swing again but he didn't get the chance. Jelly came on him like a rabid dog. He grabbed Ramon's wrist and pried the poker out of his grip. His strength was amazing.

"You asshole!" Jelly flattened him against the wall, leaning in with his huge body so Ramon couldn't move. Ramon choked at the smell of the fat man's beery breath. Jelly locked his hands on Ramon's neck and started to squeeze. Ramon couldn't breathe. He sputtered, struggling, he tried to move—but couldn't. He felt the pressure in his eyes, and he thought his head would burst or he'd choke on his own tongue. Jelly smiled and squeezed harder. Ramon felt light-headed and knew he was about to pass out, when the expression on Jelly's face suddenly changed. There was look of disbelief. Then, his eyes glazed over, and he released his grip and fell to the ground.

Ramon panted for breath. It took him a second to realize what had happened. Philip stood in the middle of the hall, a shocked expression on his face and the poker in his hands. Philip smiled, then dropped the poker and stepped away.

Frank was propped against the wall, sobbing. His right arm hung limp and the bullet had caught him in the thigh. Ramon bent down to examine it. The pants were soaked in blood and the wound bled freely, but it wasn't spurting.

"We've got to get out of here." It was Lena, she'd moved into the hall holding their bag. "We don't have much time. They're already on their way."

"I know. This'll just take a minute." Ramon ran back into the living room and grabbed his sheet. As he walked back to the hallway he ripped a shred of it off. He bent back down and tied it tightly around Frank's leg. "This will hold for now. Twist on the knot if you need it tighter. You'll live."

Frank just moaned. Ramon looked down at Jelly. His chest moved up and down with regular breaths. "OK, let's move."

Philip stepped up. "I broke the code."

"What?" It didn't register.

"I broke the code. I deciphered the tape." He looked over at Lena with a strange smile. "It's just like you said, the proof is all there. I printed it out." He handed over a thick file and a copy of the computer tape.

Ramon took it. He wanted to look through it, learn its secrets. But they didn't have time. "We need to leave now. You've got to go, too. You're part of this now. If they find you you're dead."

"I'm sorry we got you into this," Lena said.

Philip smiled again, a serene smile. "No, this is cool. I've always believed in conspiracies, that things weren't what they seemed, and people always laughed at me when I told them. Now I know I was right."

"We've got to go, now," Ramon said. Frank was still staring off into space and sobbing, Jelly laid on his side, breathing deeply. "Where are the keys to their car?" he asked.

"They're in the kitchen. I'll get them for you."

As Philip moved quickly toward the kitchen, Ramon turned to Lena. "Are you all right?"

She nodded. "I'll be fine."

Philip returned. He handed them the key ring to the roommates' car along with a handful of cash. "Take this. You'll need some money."

They'd already taken too long. They quickly left the house and went to the cars. "Will you be OK, Philip?"

He just smiled and nodded as he got into his car and started the engine, and pulled away.

· · · ·

THE ROADS WERE clear and they made good time. On the interstate they blended in with traffic as they went through central Milwaukee, heading south. The street lights bathed the road in a yellow glow. Lena opened the window a crack to get some air. The yeasty smell of baking bread filled the car as they drove past a brewery.

They hadn't said a word since leaving Philip's. It was so sudden. In the time they'd been there they'd settled into a pattern. As strange as the situation was, it had started to feel normal. She knew it was an illusion, but she'd started to think they were safe. Now that feeling was gone. They were running again.

She knew how lucky they were. They were still being hunted and they'd probably escaped just in time. Somehow they'd beaten the odds again. Somehow they were still alive. But they were out of options. There was no way they could keep this up forever. They needed help and there was no one left for them to turn to. Lena took a deep breath and let it out slowly. She wasn't scared anymore. She was past that. Now she just felt sad and tired and wished the whole thing was over.

She glanced over at Ramon. He was intent on his driving, eyes focused on the road, both hands on the wheel. She wondered what he was thinking. Was he scared? He didn't seem to be, but who could tell? He'd never say if he was, but talk wasn't his strong suit anyway. He'd taken control again. He was a survivor—by force of will and quick response he always pulled through.

Traffic thinned as they moved away from the city. South of Milwaukee they began to see signs for the airport. Ramon checked the rearview mirror. "We can't keep this car much longer. They're probably looking for it by now."

Lena nodded. She didn't even have the energy to talk. Ramon turned off at the airport exit and followed the signs for long-term parking. At the gate they collected a ticket from the machine and drove inside. They moved through a long aisle, past row upon row of parked cars. Ramon found a secluded space at the far end of the lot and pulled in.

"If we get lucky they won't find this for a week," he said. "Let's grab our stuff. We need to go."

Lena didn't move. She couldn't. After everything that happened she just felt numb. It was too much effort to go on. She just wanted to sit in that spot and pretend that everything was all right—but she knew it wasn't. Tears welled up in her eyes. Without meaning to she let out a sob.

"Are you OK?" Ramon asked. He reached over and softly touched her arm.

The touch was reassuring. Just the brush of his fingers on her skin and she felt better. Lena took hold of his hand and squeezed lightly. That was the truth, she felt better whenever he was close. She hadn't realized it before. Since they'd been thrown together she'd been trying to deny the attraction. In her old life she wouldn't have given him a second thought—they were too different. But this attraction was too fierce to ignore. He was so strong, she needed his strength if she was to go on. And together they were so much stronger.

She squeezed his hand again and pulled him, ever so slightly, toward her. Their eyes locked. Ramon moved his hand up to the base of her neck, lightly caressing her with his fingertips, then pulling her in close. Lena squeezed him tight and rested her head on his shoulder. She felt better just holding him, smelling him, and feeling the texture of his skin against her cheek. As strange as it was, fate had thrown them together, and now, she realized, she needed him. She turned her head and brushed her lips against his neck, tasting the salt.

Ramon ran his fingers through her hair, then softly pulled away. "We've got to go," he said.

She nodded. She squeezed him again before they broke apart and moved out to find a new car.

THE DRIVEWAY WAS empty as Cain pulled up to the house. The porch light was on. It splashed a yellow glow that illuminated the front door but left the rest of the porch in shadows. Lights were on inside the house, but it seemed quiet. Cain breathed a sigh of relief as he stepped out of the car. On the trip up, he'd had visions of being too late; of arriving to find that the local police had taken the call and beat him to the prize. But the whole neighborhood was quiet. No patrol cars, no news crews. It looked like they'd made it before news leaked out.

Cain had three men with him—all that was left of his team, just Ortman and two sergeants that he hardly knew, one blond, one dark. It wasn't enough to do the job properly but it was all he had. But if the tip was right, if his targets were really inside, then it wouldn't matter anymore. He'd take care of everything. He'd do the job right this time. Then his reputation would be restored and he'd be back on the colonel's good side.

"All right, you check out the back and keep watch outside," he addressed the dark-haired sergeant. "I don't want any surprises. If it sounds like we're having trouble inside, then move on in. Otherwise just make sure the exits are covered and no one's able to come in or get out. Got it?"

The sergeant nodded and silently drifted back into the dark of the yard. Cain took out his handgun and moved toward the porch. He turned to Ortman and the other sergeant. "Let's see what's goin' on in there."

On the porch he prepared to bust the door open, but tried the knob first. It was unlocked. "Let's go!"

He threw the door open and came in low, his gun in front, the blond sergeant a step behind. Ortman was positioned in back of the door providing cover. There was a small foyer that led into a long hallway. The hallway light was on. Cain knew there was a problem as soon as he was in. In the dim light he could see two figures. Halfway down the hall, propped up against the wall, was a dark-haired man. His arms were hanging limply to his side, his leg was soaked with blood. Standing over him was a huge, obese redheaded man. Neither one was his rabbit. The fat man looked up blankly as they came through the door. The man on the ground looked over at Cain, a pleading expression on his face. "Help me. I need a doctor."

"Put your hands up and don't move!" Cain barked. The fat man instantly obeyed.

Cain sprinted forward, followed closely by the two soldiers. On the ground, right in front of the men, were a gun and a black fireplace poker. Cain scooped up the gun. A quick glance and he recognized it as a Glock pistol — it was his gun, the same one that the rabbit had stolen. A new surge of adrenaline kicked in. This was for real, they were at the right place. But was the rabbit still there?

While the other two covered him with their guns, Cain spun the fat man around and smashed him in the kidneys. The fat man howled with pain. "I didn't do nothin'."

"Shut up." Cain pulled a pair of handcuffs out of his back pocket and twisted the big man's arms as he slipped them on. He shoved the man's shoulders and kicked the back of his knees, forcing him to the ground. "Stay there until I tell you to move." Then he turned his attention to the other man.

Cain bent low over the bleeding man and quickly patted him down for weapons. He was clean. Ortman and the blond sergeant stepped in front and continued to move down the hallway to continue the search.

"Where are they?" Cain asked.

"I don't know, man. I need a doctor. I'm bleeding to death."

Cain quickly inspected the wound. There was a lot of

blood but the bullet had hit the thigh, it hadn't pierced an artery and the damage was relatively minor. "You'll live. Are you the one who called?"

"Yeah, but I need help."

Cain bent down to the man's eye level. He moved in close so his breath was in the man's face as he stared him down. "Where are they? Are they still here?"

"I don't know. But can you just call a doctor? Jelly couldn't find the phone."

"Jelly?" Cain glanced back at the fat man in handcuffs lying on the floor. "This fat piece of crap here? Is this Jelly?" He grabbed the chain between the handcuffs and jerked hard, pulling the fat man back up to his knees.

"I didn't do nothing."

Cain twisted the chains and propped him against the wall. It took all his strength to move the big man around. "What did you see, fat boy? Where's my rabbit?"

"Rabbit?" The fat man's pasty face was scrunched up in concentration.

"The Mexican, him and the girl. Where are they?"

Jelly looked dazed. "I don't know. I didn't do nothin' and the guy jumped me. He hit me with somethin', otherwise I could've taken him. He knocked me out cold. And I couldn't find the phone. Do we still get the reward?"

Cain heard a sound behind him. He turned to see Ortman making his way down the stairs and back into the hallway. "Um, Captain?"

"What?"

"Um, they're not here. We've gone through the whole house and they're not here."

"Shit!" Cain slammed his palm into the wall, punching a hole in the plaster. He'd missed them again. His head throbbed. The pressure was building, the pain intense. This was his last chance and he'd blown it. He took a deep breath to regain his composure. "Get out of here." His voice was a forced calm. "Search the house for any clues.

They couldn't have been gone long. I'll get the story from these two."

He waited a second for Ortman to leave, then he turned back to the injured man. He spoke softly, trying to control his anger. "I don't have time to waste. It looks like my rabbit fucked you up. What I want to know is where did he go and how did he get there. You understand? How long has he been gone?"

"I don't know, maybe twenty minutes," he moaned. "I don't know. You got to get me to a doctor."

"You're not getting this, my friend. I need your help and I need precise answers. Where did they go?"

"I don't know, they just went, man. You got to help me." There was panic in the man's voice.

Cain spun around and grabbed Jelly by the front of his shirt. "How 'bout you, fat boy? Where did they go?"

"I don't know."

Cain felt like an overfilled balloon. His head was throbbing and his eyes ached from the pressure. The anger and frustration of the hunt had reached a peak. He'd exercised control, he'd maintained discipline for so long. And for what? The rabbit had defeated him—these two morons in the hallway were a reminder of that. He reached down to the ground and picked up the fireplace poker. He gripped it tight and in one fast move swung it hard into Jelly's jaw.

Jelly screamed in pain and tried to stand. But with his arms behind his back and all his weight on his knees, he couldn't. Cain swung again, downward this time, bringing the poker down hard on the top of the head. Jelly fell to the ground like a bag of rocks.

"Last chance if you want your friend to live!" Cain yelled. "Where the fuck are they?"

The injured man was sobbing. "I don't know! I just don't know!"

Cain swung again. The poker came down hard on the

top of Jelly's head and split the skull this time. But Cain
didn't care. He swung again and again. The poker made a
squishing sound like a shovel hitting wet cement. After a
dozen swings Cain stopped. Blood splattered the walls.
He was breathing hard and his wrists were sore. But the
pressure in his head was gone. In a way he felt better.

He turned back to the injured man who was now sobbing on the ground. "Where did they go?" Once again
Cain's voice was low and in control.

The man didn't answer. He huddled with his head
down like he was trying to disappear. Cain drew out the
Glock, swung the barrel over to the man's forehead, and
pulled the trigger. *Thwack.* The top of the man's head was
reduced to a red mist.

He put the gun back in his holster and took a deep
breath. Now he'd done it. He'd crossed over the line. Before, whenever he'd killed a man, it had always been controlled and thought out. Necessary operations carried out
with strict discipline. And always under mandate from the
colonel. These were different. These just made a messy
situation messier.

Cain stepped over the bodies and made his way down
the hallway and up the stairs in search of his men. A
thought occurred to him. After this fiasco he was as good
as finished at the installation. Maybe he should make the
best of a bad deal. There were only three men with him—
it would be easy enough to take out the three of them—
they were no match for him. Then he could disappear. A
man of his skills could do well. There were other organi-
zations that would pay highly for his services. He gripped
the butt of the gun as he walked up the stairs.

He found Ortman and the blond sergeant in a room
across the landing at the top of the stairs. They looked at
him nervously as he moved into the room. Cain stroked
the gun's handle.

"Um, uh, Captain? I think we found something," Ortman said.

Cain hesitated. "What?"

"It's right here on the computer." He jumped aside to let Cain see the screen.

Cain quickly read the words on the monitor. He let go of the gun as he smiled. "They're goin' to Washington."

21 _____

IT WAS DARK when they pulled off the road. After driving the back roads through Ohio and Pennsylvania all day, they were exhausted and needed to find a spot to catch some sleep. They were in deep hilly country, miles away from the nearest town. Ramon turned onto a dirt road. It looked like an access road, maybe something used by hunters, but it was overgrown and didn't look like it got much use.

Ramon drove in and parked the car under a grove of trees. They were hidden from the road here, virtually invisible. He shut off the engine and they sat still for a moment with the windows open, listening. It was quiet, the only sound the hum of cicadas in the distance.

"We can stay here for a while," he said. "We'll go before it's light."

Lena nodded.

They got out of the car and walked to a clearing. The

grass was lush and long, and they had to raise their feet to get through it. A slight chill was in the air. Lena crossed her arms and hugged herself, trying to stay warm. They found an area where the grass had been flattened by the wind. Without talking, they settled down, lying close to share their warmth.

For a long time they lay together, so close he could feel her breath on his skin. It felt normal, though. After all they'd been through they had a connection; he couldn't imagine what life would be without her. After a while Lena's breathing became slow and steady. Ramon thought she might have fallen asleep. He turned to look at her and was surprised to see her eyes were wide open. She smiled at him.

"I thought you were asleep," he said.

"No. I was just thinking." She raised herself up on an elbow. "Do you think we'll get out of this?" she asked.

Ramon thought for a moment before answering. "I don't know. I'm not sure how we've made it this far."

They were silent again for a time. The air was still. A lone cricket chirped nearby. Ramon relaxed and looked at the sky. It was awash with stars, faint pinpricks of white splattered against the darkness. It reminded Ramon of his boyhood in Texas, far from the lights of the city. Looking at the heavens, feeling the calm, it was hard to imagine they were hunted. Staring at the stars, their troubles seemed far away.

Lena moved beside him. "What will you do if we do make it out?" she asked.

"I don't know. I don't think I can stay here. I haven't thought that far ahead." Feeling her body resting against his, feeling her breath and her warmth, a sense of regret overcame him; the thought of what might have been. He turned toward her. "I'm sorry I got you into all this. . . ."

"Shhh," she said. She reached over and touched his face.

The simple contact sent a buzz up his spine. Ramon moved his hand to her cheek and she turned her body toward him. Her eyes were bright and clear. Her soft hair glistened in the pale light. Her lips parted slightly and then his mouth closed over hers. The kiss started gently, but quickly built in intensity. As tongues tangled, their hands flew over each other with an urgency to touch skin. It was as if all they had been through together had brought them to this moment, this affirmation of life, of sharing something other than danger. Ramon cupped her breasts in his hands. "I've wanted you for so long," he said.

"I know," she replied.

She pulled at his clothes, as he unbuttoned her blouse and slid her skirt down past her hips. And then he was inside her. Together they moved in rhythm, fast and hard with a savage intensity.

When it was over, he held her tight as their breathing fell into a perfectly synchronized pattern.

THE SKY WAS overcast and gray as they drove into town. Lena thought of how different this was from the last time she'd been in Washington. It was just weeks ago, but the situation was so different then. She'd been about to start a new phase in her life, as the capital correspondent for the *Austin Star*. That was going to be the springboard to her career, taking her away from local news and putting her on the national scene. As she came off the plane that day, the sky was a clear, optimistic blue; the sun was dazzling in its intensity. The day was as bright as her prospects. So much had changed since then.

She looked away from the window and fought back a yawn as the fatigue began to overwhelm her. After leaving Philip's, they had decided to go to Washington. It was the only real option. Washington was the source of power. If anyone could help them, this is where they would most likely be. Besides, that's where the missing files were.

There was some connection between Colonel Pope and the restricted file. If they could find it, then they would find the answer to the puzzle and maybe a way out of their trouble.

They'd been extra careful on their way to Washington. Driving the back roads and secondary routes it had taken them two full days to get there. Lena was tired and hungry. The thought of a soft bed with fresh, clean sheets was an appealing fantasy. But the despair she had felt was now gone. She was just glad she wasn't alone.

Ramon, sensing her thoughts, glanced over. "Everything OK?"

She smiled. "Yeah. I'm fine."

He reached across and took hold of her hand. She gave a soft squeeze and held on as he turned his attention back to driving.

She looked back down to the file folder on her lap. The long drive had given her a chance to continue the investigation. She'd been reading through the files that Philip had taken from the computer tape. The file was huge. Printed out it came to over a thousand pages, a great mass of paper that was now separated into piles on the floor and in the backseat. A lot of what she'd guessed was now confirmed. From what she could see, it was clear that the primary objective of the installation was the development of vaccines. There were vaccines listed for a number of the more common BW agents.

And her guess about a super toxin was right also. It appeared that the installation had come upon a microbe, an agent that went beyond any other for use in germ warfare. The virus was code named CX471, and their tests showed a kill rate of almost 99 percent. It was for this toxin that they had been trying to develop a vaccine over the last three years. The records clearly showed that several hundred lives had been lost in the vaccine's testing and development. This was the same vaccine that had finally worked in Ramon.

But what was their plan? Why was it so important to have a vaccine for this virus? Were they developing this as a weapon of last resort? Something that would be put on the shelf and never used? Or were they really planning on using this toxin in battle conditions? If it was as deadly and communicable in the field as it was in the lab, they were truly playing with fire.

There was something else in the files that didn't make sense. It was under the code name Phoenix. The section was over a hundred pages, set in small type. It was a list—several lists really. Each one was headed by a city or location name, then a series of people's names and addresses were listed below. For each name there were a number of columns: occupation, age, health status, and IQ were all noted. Between all the lists Lena estimated that there were several thousand people accounted for. It didn't make sense. There was no pattern here. What did these people have to do with Pope and the installation? These were civilians—doctors, farmers, artists, technicians. Seemingly normal people. She could see nothing that tied them in to the plot. Another question without an answer.

Lena shifted in her seat. The car radio was tuned to an oldies station. An old Motown song came on. Lena turned the volume up and nodded along with the rhythm. The familiar sounds lifted her spirits. They'd come so far, she thought. It seemed that they should be close to the answer, but the full story still eluded her. They rounded a corner and the city came into view. Up ahead the Washington Monument rose up like a clean white finger against the dirty gray sky.

Ramon looked over again. "We're here. What do we do now?"

Lena thought for a moment before answering, "We need to find the archives."

The song on the radio ended and the fanfare for the news came on. *"This just in."* The voice of the announcer spoke with a sense of urgency. *"Two bodies were discovered today at a house in the suburbs of Milwaukee, Wisconsin. Authorities have identified the victims as Frank Abalone, age twenty-six, and George Schmucker, twenty-five. The men were brutally murdered. Investigators at the scene state that there is evidence linking these killings to two Texas fugitives, suspected serial killer Hector Ramerez and his companion, Lena Dryer. . . ."*

It was happening again.

THE ROOM ON the third floor down was a pure pristine white, so bright it hurt the eyes. The technicians on this level all wore breathing apparatus and stark white suits that blended in with their surroundings. The work here was physically easy but emotionally stressful. The lack of fresh air, repetitive work, and the monotony of the environment all took a toll. Requests for reassignment were more frequent here than anywhere else in the Johnson Installation.

Major Durmo stood outside the room, watching through a thick glass window as the technicians went about their work. Inside, four technicians were positioned at stainless-steel tables, each was working at a different piece of machinery. Durmo squinted, trying to see through the glare from the window. He studied each worker. He'd been told that Dr. Peterson, the project's director, would be in the room today. But in their white coats and masks the workers all looked alike. Durmo couldn't tell one from another. He rapped his knuckles on the thick glass, trying to get their attention. No one looked up.

Durmo tugged on his ear and breathed out sharply. His stomach had been bothering him all day; it was churning now. He wasn't sure if it was from something he ate or if it was his nerves. He'd been feeling more pressured lately. His plan was to take the day off and just relax, but this was too important to put off.

He rapped on the window again. This time one of the technicians glanced up, made eye contact, but then went right back to his work. Durmo sighed. About half of the technicians were civilians, and sometimes he wasn't shown the respect he deserved. Durmo looked around again and noticed an intercom panel between the window and the door to the room. He didn't know how he had missed it before.

Durmo pressed the red button. "Hello, hello, can you hear me?" There was no response, so he did it again. "Hello, can you hear me? Is Dr. Peterson in there?"

The technician who had looked over before now turned around and pushed the inside intercom button. "What is it now, Major?" There was irritation in his voice.

"I'm sorry to bother you, Doctor, but I was wondering how it was coming along."

The doctor adjusted his cap. "You already asked me that once this morning. Do you really think it's changed since then?"

"Well, no. I'm sure it hasn't. And I am sorry to bother you, Doctor, but I'm getting a lot of pressure from the colonel, and I was hoping you could get me some good news."

The doctor stood for a moment, thinking. "Hold on a minute, Major. I'll come out there."

It took nearly five minutes for the doctor to come out. When he did, his face mask and hat were off and he smelled of fresh disinfectant. He came right to the point. "You can tell the colonel that we're right on schedule. We'll be finished packing the vaccine by tomorrow. Over half of it's already been shipped. We're finishing the load for upstate New York now."

Durmo smiled weakly. "Well, good. That means we'll be done soon."

"The toxin's going to take longer. We've been growing the extra units and we'll have enough there. But packaging the aerosols is tricky. I have a crew setting up a new safety procedure before we even start. That will take another week before we're ready to run."

"Another week?"

"Yes. But once that's set up we should finish quickly. I think we can finish everything in about ten days."

"Well, good. I'm sure the colonel will be pleased," Durmo said, but now he was feeling really sick.

THE ARCHIVES WERE located in the basement of a federal office building down the street from the Capitol. Ramon parked nearby and waited while Lena went inside. Using a scarf and her makeup kit, she'd done her best to change her appearance. A quick glance at her reflection convinced her that she looked older, more world-weary than her usual self. She would pass a casual inspection, she thought. But if someone was looking for her it would be all over. Was that possible? Could someone know where they were?

Lena took the elevator down to the basement and crossed the hallway to the archives. Her stomach was doing back flips. She felt naked and exposed as she entered the room. She tried to empty her mind, forget about the fear, the guilt, and the anger. She needed to focus on what she had to do.

The archives were kept in a large room cordoned off into two sections separated by a long counter. The section closest to the door had ropes in place to direct the line up to the counter. No one was waiting. To the side, taking up the most space, was open area with tables scattered throughout. Behind the counter were row upon row of gray metal cabinets. The walls of the room were painted an industrial shade of green. The color was different, but for some reason it reminded Lena of the prison down in Huntsville. A handful of people were at the tables. No one even looked up. Behind the counter, several employees stood back by themselves talking. One clerk leaned against the counter. Lena walked over to him.

"I'd like to see file . . ."

"You've got to fill out a request," the clerk interrupted. He motioned down at a form on the counter.

"Oh . . . sure." Lena picked up a pen and quickly filled out the form. She wrote down the file number, but in the section asking for her name she wrote the name of a friend from high school, the first name that came to mind.

The clerk glanced down at the form. "I'll be back in a minute." Lena glanced around the room nervously while she waited for him to come back. It took close to five minutes, but he returned with a small box. "It's microfilm. Do you know how to use this?"

Lena nodded her head. "Sure. I've done it before." She accepted the package and headed over to a table with a microfilm viewer in the corner of the room. She threaded the film into the machine and flipped on the light. She turned the knob, advancing the film to its title page: *Strategic Arms Subcommittee—Armed Services Committee—U.S. Senate—October 1991.*

Still nervous, Lena looked up and scanned the room again. Nothing seemed unusual or out of place. The people in the room all appeared to belong there. They looked like academics or researchers, maybe reporters. No one was looking at her, though, and no one appeared to be a threat. She relaxed a little as she turned back to the file and began to read.

The file was a transcript of the subcommittee's investigation into complaints of Gulf War syndrome. The first part of the file was made up of interviews between the members of the committee and soldiers who had been healthy when called up for Desert Storm but had developed health problems since then. Symptoms included fatigue, memory loss, seizures, depression, and paralysis. Lena had read reports of this before. Even now, years later, veterans complained of the same symptoms, although the army had never acknowledged that there was a problem. Veteran's groups blamed their poor health on everything from germ warfare to environmental conditions in Iraq and Kuwait. Lena skimmed through this section; the examples went on and on.

The next section was taken up by interviews with physicians, restating the symptoms and testifying that there was no medically known basis for the problems. Some theorized that the disorder were mental, some type of stress-induced hysteria. Other doctors said that there was a medical basis for the complaints but they could only guess as to what had caused it. After the first few interviews Lena skimmed through the rest. There was nothing new here. At least nothing that related to her own concern.

Lena checked her watch. She'd been in the archives for over an hour. It felt dangerous to be in one place for so long. But if there was something in the file she had to find it. She ignored the queasiness in her stomach and continued reading.

The next section was comprised of interviews with army officers. It was in this section that she found what she was looking for.

Colonel Pope had been called before the committee to testify. The transcripts showed that the questioning was handled entirely by the subcommittee's chairman, Senator Randall Morgan of Wisconsin. The early part of the testimony was simply a rehash of Pope's record and what his duties had been leading up to Desert Storm. After that the transcript got interesting:

Morgan: So, Colonel, what exactly were your responsibilities as part of the invasion force?

Pope: I was not part of the invasion force, Senator. For this campaign I was assigned to the medical corps.

Morgan: The medical corps? Isn't that unusual, Colonel? Is it normal for a combat officer like yourself to work as a medical officer?

Pope: I am a soldier, sir. I do not waste my time thinking of whether an assignment is normal or not. That was my assignment and I carried it out to the best of my abilities.

Morgan: Yes, I'm sure you did. According to your records, you have no training in medicine. Is that correct?

Pope: Yes, that is correct.

Morgan: Well, I'm a little bit confused. Why would someone with no medical training whatsoever be put in charge of the medical corps for a full-scale military campaign?

Pope: That was not my decision to make. However, I do not feel that this is unusual in the least. You see, Senator, my position is to be a leader of men. There is little difference between leading infantry and managing doctors.

Morgan: Yes. I have another document here, Colonel. This is a transcript of a speech you gave to the War College at West Point back in December of '89. Do you recall that speech?

Pope: Yes, I do recall it, in a vague way.

Morgan: If I can refresh your memory of it, Colonel, the speech was in regard to biological warfare. You called for a program of, if I can quote you here, "prevention and containment." Your plan was to develop a series of vaccines. Is that correct?

Pope: That was what I stated in that speech. That is correct, Senator.

Morgan: Did you move forward with this proposal, Colonel?

Pope: That is entirely beyond the scope of this investigation, Senator. The issues you are bringing up are matters of strategic importance. I see no reason to discuss them further.

Morgan: Were you involved in any experiments with biological warfare at any time during this campaign?

Pope: That is an absurd question, Senator. Of course I was involved in nothing of the kind.

Morgan: Did you set up a program of vaccinations while acting as a medical officer during Desert Storm?

Pope: Vaccines were administered. That is standard procedure when operating in any foreign theater.

Morgan: Were you using a new vaccine tailored for the possibility of germ warfare in this conflict?

Pope: I have nothing further to add to these proceedings. Good day, Senator. Good day, gentlemen.

Morgan: Sit back down, Colonel. You haven't been excused. Colonel, sit back down or you will be ordered to— Colonel . . . let the record show that Colonel Pope has walked out of the subcommittee chamber. I would like to issue an official rebuke through his commanding officer and have him called back at the earliest possible opportunity.

Lena sat back in her chair and took a deep breath. She looked around the room again. Nothing had changed. She turned back to the viewer and quickly searched through

the rest of the file. Pope was never called back to the committee and his name wasn't mentioned again. She took the
film off the machine and got ready to go.

It was all starting to make sense.

RAMON WAITED OUTSIDE. At first he stayed in the car, but the
longer he waited the more anxious he felt. After half an
hour of sitting, he got out of the car and paced along the
sidewalk, trying to stay where he could keep an eye on the
building's entrance. Why was it taking so long? he wondered. The longer she was in there, the more dangerous it
was. Being out on the sidewalk was dangerous, too, but he
couldn't sit still. What would he do if they came for him
now? In their haste to leave Philip's house, he'd left the
guns behind. So now, they were completely defenseless.

Ramon took a deep breath and tried to relax, but he
couldn't. They were still alive, both he and Lena, but there
was a trail of blood in their wake. And it was all his fault.
If Lena hadn't called Philip, the two roommates would
still be alive. If Ramon hadn't contacted Lena, her editor
would still be alive and Lena would be free. In the end it
all came down on his shoulders. The blood was on his
hands.

But at each step along the way, it had seemed to Ramon
he'd had no choice. When he'd been a guinea pig at the
installation, all he'd wanted was the chance to be free. But
he'd found that his pursuers were determined to prevent
that. Something horrible was going on at the installation
and somehow he was at the center of it. He didn't know
everything but he knew too much. His tormentors
wouldn't let him disappear. In fact, he was sure now that
they wouldn't rest until he was dead and buried. Well, he
wasn't dead yet. If there was anything he could do to
bring them down he had to do it.

Ramon walked slowly at the edge of the sidewalk,
keeping his gaze down, avoiding eye contact. It had now

been two hours since Lena went into the building. He knew it didn't make sense but he had an urge to go inside, just to make sure she was safe. He was headed toward the building's entrance when Lena came out onto the street. Seeing him, she walked toward him.

"You've been in there too long. We need to get out of here," he said.

"I know."

They quickly made their way back to the car. Ramon started it and they pulled out in the street and blended in with traffic. It felt good to be moving again. Inside the car he felt safe and protected. He checked his mirrors; nothing seemed out of place.

"I was worried. You were in there a long time."

"I found what we were looking for." Her eyes sparkled with excitement. "There was a missing piece and I think I found it." She twisted around in her seat as she talked. "Colonel Pope had put forward a plan for a preventive vaccine program in a speech back in '89, I'd read that before. It looks like the army staff liked the concept. I think what happened was that Pope was the head of a vaccines program that they tried in Desert Storm—but something went wrong. Most of the soldiers who received the vaccine turned out fine. But a percentage of the soldiers developed a kind of neurological disease—Gulf War Syndrome."

Ramon nodded his head. "It came from the vaccine?"

"This was all hushed up of course. The army has never acknowledged the problem. But they sent Pope in front of this committee and let him take the blame. Pope was the scapegoat and that's why his career stalled. That should have been the end of it, only we know he's doing it again on an even bigger scale. That means the army brass must be behind it. This has to be a sanctioned project otherwise he'd never have gotten the funding to run the operation after the problems he had before."

Ramon kept his eyes on the road. "So we can't go to anyone in the army."

"No. That explains how they've been able to manipulate everything. There's a lot of power behind them."

"So we're still in the same place we were before. Who can we turn to?"

Lena hesitated for a moment before she talked. "The senator who ran the committee really seemed to have it in for Pope. He'd have the power to stop it. Maybe if we can get him to believe us. It's Senator Randall Morgan."

Ran-dall-Mor-gan. Ramon kept his eyes on the road as the Capitol building came into view.

22

THE SUN SILHOUETTED the dome in a blaze of orange. It was late afternoon and the grounds were crowded with people who had made this their last stop for the day. Families and small groups of sightseers clustered along the Capitol steps, posing for snapshots with the building as a backdrop. Charter buses were lined up on the street, dropping off loads of tourists. Uniformed policeman paced casually about, maintaining order and watching for signs of trouble.

As Ramon walked up the white stone steps leading to the east entrance, he felt as if a target were strapped to his back. Lena walked beside him; the look on her face told him that she felt the same way. It was crazy. They were back in the news—wanted for murders in two states—and here they were, walking out in the open, in the middle of a crowd, where anyone could see them. He felt a tickle at the back of his neck, a feeling that they were being watched. But that was just paranoid thinking — justified, but still paranoid. They were vulnerable out here in the open, but there was really no choice. If this was ever going to end they needed to take drastic action. And contacting Senator Morgan was the only option that made any sense.

And if people were looking at them, it was because they looked ridiculously like tourists. On the way over they had stopped at a souvenir stand. They were dressed in matching "I Love Washington" shirts and hats. They came to the top of the steps and queued into the line to get inside. Ramon glanced around; there were people of every race, age, and nationality there, dressed in every manner. Many of them had cameras hanging from their necks. Typical tourists. He hoped he and Lena fit in.

As the line fed through the doorway, everyone had to pass through a metal detector. Guards on each side eyed visitors as they came through. Ramon turned to Lena. She was nearly shaking. "Are you all right?" he whispered.

She gave a tight smile and nodded her head. "I'll be OK."

When their turn came, the guards hardly noticed them. They walked through the metal detectors and into the Rotunda, the great circular hallway that opened into the wings for the House and the Senate. Red velvet ropes cordoned them off along the side walls. Large oil paintings of historic events hung from the walls. The sounds of the people talking in the gallery seemed to echo, reverberating off the stone walls and marble floors. Ramon looked up. The Capitol dome towered above them. It was a huge space.

"His office is on the second floor," Lena said. "I found it in a map at the archives. We need to get up there without attracting attention."

A red-jacketed tour guide was moving forward, a string of tourists following behind. Ramon and Lena fell into line and joined the group. They walked through the gallery, pausing at different paintings or statues while the guide laid out the history of the building. A few people looked at them curiously, one person glared. But no one spoke and no one approached them. It wasn't long before the guide led the party up to the second floor. At the top of the stairs, as the group turned to go down a hallway, Ramon and Lena hung back. They were on their own.

The space here was a mixture of offices and meeting rooms. There were hallways leading off of hallways; the building had a chopped-up feel to it. The fixtures were old and ornate, with carved wood and chandeliers in the hall. It took a few minutes of wandering before they found Senator Morgan's office. The door was frosted glass and wood with Morgan's name printed on the outside. Ramon took a deep breath. This was it. It was time to come clean. He turned the knob and they went in.

As they opened the door they were greeted with the smell of fresh paint. The room was near overflowing, a cluttered office that had too many people and too much stuff in the small space. A dark-haired receptionist sat at a desk facing the door. There were two other desks off to the side. A tight-featured woman sat at the back desk, a thin man with a weaselly face sat at the front. He had a cigarette smouldering in a smokeless ashtray. A dropcloth with painter's equipment was piled up against the wall. One wall was freshly painted, the others sorely needed it. Papers and files covered every inch of the desks and were stacked haphazardly about the office. There was an aisle in between the desks that provided just enough room to walk through. Even with the computers and fax machines the office seemed old and inefficient. At the far edge of this room a wall jutted out to show the outline of a back office. Its door was closed.

The receptionist looked up. "Can I help you?"

"Yes, we need to see Senator Morgan," Lena said.

"Do you have an appointment?" The cool tone of her voice said she knew they didn't.

"No, but it's urgent that we see him."

"I'm sorry but the senator has a very busy schedule. He's not able to see anyone without an appointment."

"But this is important."

"Are you a constituent?"

The weaselly-faced man was monitoring the conversation closely and looked ready to jump in if there was any trouble.

Lena grasped her hands together nervously. "No, we're not. And I can understand how busy he is. But he needs to see us." She quickly jotted a note on a piece of paper and thrust it at the receptionist. "Could you please tell him that this is in regard to Colonel Pope and Senate document #91-45688b."

"Look, I'm sorry. . . ."

"He will want to see us." Lena spoke forcefully. The change in tone surprised Ramon. "Please give him that message."

The receptionist looked resigned and a little angry. "I'll give him the message. Who can I say is here to see him?"

Ramon cut in. "Just give him the message, please."

The receptionist went through the door into the back office. The weaselly man kept glancing in their direction but turned away as soon as they looked back, avoiding eye contact. Ramon's tension increased. Maybe this wasn't the right plan after all.

A minute later the receptionist came back out with an incredulous look on her face. "Please go on back. The senator will see you."

She escorted them to the door to the back office and opened it. Ramon stepped in first and Lena followed. This room was half the size of the outer office but seemed more spacious. It was furnished with only a large, paper-strewn wooden desk and several red leather chairs. Morgan sat behind the desk talking on the phone. As they came in he gestured for them to sit down.

Ramon recognized Morgan from the billboard he'd seen in Wisconsin. He had a full head of silver hair, a strong jutting chin and piercing steel-gray eyes that reminded Ramon of a hawk. He sat straight in his chair, but his attitude was relaxed, at ease with himself and his surroundings. He rubbed a finger over his thin nose as he talked. "The way I count it, Harry, you're still short by three votes, and some of that support is soft. . . ."

Lena and Ramon sat down to wait while he finished his conversation. Ramon could hear Lena's breathing, fast and shallow. Her chest rose and fell more quickly than normal. He sensed the stress she was feeling.

Morgan kept his eyes trained on them while he talked. ". . . Put me down as a yes. But I expect your help on the parks bill, Harry. I don't just want it to pass, I want to send a message. . . ." His voice was smooth and comforting.

Ramon looked around the room. The walls were plastered with so many awards and photographs that hardly an inch of paneling showed. Many of the pictures were of Morgan when he was younger. In one picture, Ramon recognized Morgan in a faded blue work shirt, standing with his arm around César Chávez of the United Farm Workers union. Another picture showed a younger Morgan in a suit, standing stiffly, shaking hands with President Johnson. One more recent picture that caught Ramon's eye was of Morgan, wearing hip-high waders, fishing in the middle of a stream. There were also awards of all kinds. Ramon noticed citations from the Wisconsin Dairy Products Association, the Sierra Club, and the National Education Association.

"No, Monday will be fine. . . . Good, I'll see you then." Morgan carefully set the phone down in its cradle, leaned back in his chair, and scrutinized their faces. "I understand that you have something urgent to see me about."

"Yes, sir." Lena cut in. "We're here because we had nowhere else to turn, and you're in a position to help. We have some information regarding Colonel Lucian Pope and the possibility of biological warfare."

Morgan slowly nodded his head. "Yes, Colonel Pope. I saw your note." He thought for a moment. "But first I need to know who you are."

Ramon glanced at Lena. She looked straight at the senator. "My name is Lena Dryer," she said. "I've been a reporter with the *Austin Star*. And this is Ramon Willis—they've been calling him Hector Ramerez on the news."

Ramon's stomach knotted. It was out in the open now. He waited for a shout or some sort of alarm. He tensed, waiting for the door to be thrown open and the authorities to burst into the room. But it didn't happen.

Morgan raised his eyebrows but spoke calmly. "I thought you looked familiar. You're the ones they have the manhunt out for. You two are wanted for murder."

"But it's not true! Everything they've been saying is a lie. We have proof."

Morgan was silent for a long time, thinking. Then, he said, "If Colonel Pope is involved that could be possible." He leaned forward in his chair. "Tell me what happened."

Lena took a deep breath, "I know how bizarre this sounds. I found it hard to believe myself, but it's true." She told the story, logically and clearly, starting with her visit to Ramon and how she had watched him die. She told Morgan how Ramon had been taken to the Johnson Installation and used as the subject of biological testing and how Lieutenant Green had helped him escape. She told of how Ramon had contacted her and how they had been thrown together. Lena detailed how they had been hunted, and explained that they hadn't turned themselves in because they didn't know who they could trust when everything said about them was a lie. She explained about

Philip and the computer tape, how it showed proof that Pope was not only using death row prisoners and others for biological experiments but had developed some kind of super toxin.

Ramon watched Morgan as Lena talked. He listened patiently, sometimes interrupting to ask a question or to have her clarify a statement. His expression stayed impassive throughout.

"We know that the purpose of the experiments was to develop a new vaccine," Lena said. "And we know the vaccine is for protection against a new super virus that the installation has developed. We have proof of all this. What we don't know is what Pope, or the army, whoever is in charge, is planning to do with it."

When she finished talking the room became quiet. No one spoke for over a minute. Morgan broke the silence. "That's quite a story."

"But it's true," Lena insisted. "Everything . . ."

They heard a knock on the door. Lena froze. Ramon could feel his muscles tense. If someone was here for them it was all over. He'd fight his best but they were trapped.

"Yes?" Morgan called.

The door opened and the weaselly-faced man stuck his head in the room. "Sorry to bother you, Senator. But it's six o'clock and we were about to lock up. I just wanted to make sure everything was all right."

"I'm fine, Jerry. I'll lock up when I leave."

"Yes, sir. Good night then." He glanced suspiciously at Ramon a last time before closing the door behind him.

For a moment it was quiet again. Morgan sat back in his chair and steepled his hands to his face in thought. "That's quite an interesting story." He raised a finger to stop any interruptions. "And I don't have any reason to doubt what you say, as extraordinary as it does sound. This proof you mention, did you bring it with you?"

Ramon answered, "We have it right here." He held up the bag, which contained the computer tape and the papers.

"Excellent," Morgan solemnly nodded. "You better let me have that. If I'm going to help, I need to have the evidence." He stood up and reached over to get the bag. "Don't worry; we'll make good use of it."

Ramon felt uneasy. This wasn't the reaction he'd expected. The senator was too calm, too willing to believe their story. And after all they'd gone through to get and keep the evidence, it was hard to give it up. Ramon glanced at Lena. She seemed puzzled, too. Ramon hesitated, then handed it over.

"Good. Let me see what I can do." Morgan picked up the phone, he glanced up as he hit a number. "I'm calling someone that can help." He turned his attention to the phone. "This is Morgan. I have something for you. Something sensitive. Come on up and we'll discuss it." He hung the phone up and glanced at his watch. "We've got a few minutes yet."

Ramon shifted anxiously in his chair. He didn't know what he'd expected to happen but this wasn't it.

Morgan moved around the desk toward the door. "We need to get you out of here and find you someplace safe," he said. He opened the door and they followed him into the outer office. The room was now empty. All the workers had left for the night. Morgan glanced at his watch again, seemed to think for a moment then sat down on the corner of a desk.

Ramon and Lena hesitated, standing in the open, waiting for Morgan's cue.

"I have to tell you, nothing surprises me anymore." Morgan smiled at them. "While we're waiting, let me tell *you* a story. Do you know anything about Easter Island?"

Ramon shook his head but Lena nodded. "Yes, it's the place with the statues of giant heads."

"That's right, the place with the giant heads. The island is just a speck of land in the middle of the South Pacific, thousands of miles from anywhere. It's one of the most remote places on earth. If you visited the island now, you'd find it rather bleak. It's almost a desert. Just scrub vegetation, and a small population that up until recently was living at subsistence level—right out of the Stone Age.

"But at one time it was very different." Morgan leaned forward as he talked. "At one time they were very prosperous. You see, the islanders were a strong, resourceful race, and the island was graced with a forest of large palm trees. The natives used these trees to make a type of canoe. They could navigate by the stars and the ocean currents. They'd travel thousands of miles in these canoes, trading, picking up the resources they needed. And the island was fertile, they planted crops and the people thrived."

Ramon tried to focus on the words but he couldn't. His stomach was tight and his breath came short. He couldn't place what it was that made him nervous. He turned toward Lena; she was listening intently but looked uncomfortable.

Morgan stood up and began to pace across the office. "They lived a good life. This went on for hundreds of years and the population grew. It reached a peak of nine thousand people on that island. But that's where the problems came in. You see, the island couldn't support that many people. As the population grew, they had to cut down more and more of the trees in order to make more land for agriculture." Morgan shook his head slightly. "Eventually they cut all the trees down. But even then, there still wasn't enough to feed everyone. A famine ensued. They ate all their crops, they ate all the animals on the island. The people were reduced to foraging. They ate all the bushes and even the grass, but it wasn't enough.

And with all the trees gone they were stuck. They couldn't build the canoes anymore. . . ."

"I don't understand. . . ." Lena tried to cut in.

"In the end they became cannibals. Eating each other to survive." He spoke slowly in a controlled monotone. "Do you see the parallels, Ms. Dryer?"

"No, Senator. I don't—"

"Our planet now has six billion people. We're so insulated here we don't see the problems. It amazes me how complacent we've become. The lowest among us live like kings. We have it all. But it doesn't matter what we have. It's never enough. We want more, always more. We live with our SUVs and our disposable razors, fouling the air, making mountains of garbage, and sucking the earth dry. You think there are no repercussions for what we've done?"

Ramon nodded to Lena and took a step toward the door. His internal radar was beeping like mad. He felt confined and closed in.

"It seems that man's capacity for evil knows no boundaries. Here in America we talk about freedom, but are we really free? What we have now is the freedom to choose Coke over Pepsi; the freedom to consume and rape the earth.

"An interesting fact—did you know that deformed frogs are being born at an alarming rate? It's happening all over the world. I've introduced a bill to officially look into it. Scientists don't know why it's happening. They have some theories. It could be radiation from a hole in the ozone; or it could be the residual of pesticides that we've sprayed in their habitats. Either way the blame is the same: It's due to the acts of man. These mutations are said to be significant because frogs react to changes in the environment quicker than we humans do. We can put a man on the moon but we can't figure out what we're doing to the earth. We're doing our best to kill off the whole damn planet."

Ramon caught Lena's wrist as he moved to the door. There was something close to panic in her eyes. "I think we made a mistake, Senator." He held out his other hand. "Please give me back the bag, then we'll be out of your way."

Morgan moved the bag defensively to his side. "I'm afraid that's not possible."

Ramon let go of Lena and lunged toward Morgan, grabbing him by the collar. He reached down and pried the bag out of his hands. Morgan didn't even struggle. Ramon took the bag and turned back to Lena. "Let's go."

Morgan stayed where he was, up against the desk. "It isn't like you think," he called.

They were nearly to the door when the knob turned. They froze. The door opened and a man stepped through. Ramon recognized him immediately. He had a broken nose, mirrored glasses, and a gun.

LENA FELT LIGHT-HEADED and disoriented. It was like she was seeing through gauze. It didn't seem real. Somehow she'd convinced herself that once they got to Morgan everything would work out right. She'd been sure that because they were innocent they would be able to beat the forces at the installation and clear their names. Up until the man walked in the room, she was sure they would stay alive. Now she knew that was just a dream. They'd come so far—further than anyone could have expected. But it wasn't enough. She'd put so much hope on Morgan. In theory it had been so clear. The logic pointed to Morgan as their salvation—but it all had been a trap. She hated herself for being so stupid.

The man in the mirrored glasses came into the room followed by a huge, muscular black man. They both wore military uniforms; the man with the glasses had captain's bars and a name tag identifying him as Cain. The other wore lieutenant's insignia. Cain closed the door behind him and gestured menacingly with the gun. "All right, be good little rabbits and hop on over there." He pointed toward the far wall.

She looked at Ramon. His eyes were fiercely set. He nodded at Lena, then slowly backed toward the wall near the dropcloth. Lena did the same.

Keeping his gun in position, Cain pulled out a walkie-talkie and hit the send button. "All units, this is Alpha. Hold your positions, we've got 'em right here. It looks like we got a wrap." He released the button and pocketed the device. "Nice work, Senator. You handled it fine. Now we can get rid of this last loose end."

Morgan turned and looked at Lena. "I'm sorry it has to be like this. This is truly a sad occasion. But it's unavoidable."

"Quit your talking, old man." Cain turned back to the lieutenant. "Cover me, Rev. I don't want this guy to try anything cute." He kept the gun in front as he walked straight toward Lena and Ramon. She couldn't see his eyes through his dark glasses, but there was a slight curl to his lips. "You two have caused me a *hell* of a lot of trouble." Without warning he snapped his wrist, knocking the gun barrel into Ramon's face, smashing his nose. Blood gushed out. Ramon instinctively jerked his head back, hitting it on the back wall.

Lena cringed. She wanted to look away, but she couldn't. She felt she had to watch. Ramon brought his hands to his nose. His muscles tensed. It was obvious that he was in pain but he wouldn't acknowledge it. He didn't cry out or say a word. He stared hard at Cain.

"So how does that feel, tough guy?" Cain brought his knee up sharply, smashing Ramon in the groin. Ramon doubled over in pain but he still didn't make a sound.

"Captain, please, there's no need for this." Morgan stood up from the desk.

"Not now, Senator. This is old business." Cain hit Ramon again, driving him down to his knees.

Morgan kept talking. "Really, Captain, this is unnecessary. I know it has to be done, but it doesn't have to be painful and you don't need to do it here."

Cain ignored him. He looked back at the lieutenant. "How 'bout it, Rev? You wanna take a couple of whacks?"

The lieutenant looked uncomfortable. He shook his head. "No."

Lena took a deep breath and tried to cleanse her mind. Her knees felt weak and her stomach was churning. She knew that soon the gun would turn her way and the bullet would follow.

Morgan turned to Lena. "I'm sure you don't see the reasoning for this but you've got to look at the big picture. It's truly a difficult choice. This is a form of radical surgery. Millions—no, billions will die—"

The lieutenant appeared confused. "What's he talking about?"

Morgan continued, "But these people have to die if the earth is to live."

Cain turned away from Ramon, toward the senator. "Senator, it's time to shut up."

Morgan kept on talking. "You see, by reducing the population now we're really saving the species. What may seem like evil is being done for the greatest good. . . ."

The lieutenant stepped closer. "What the hell's he talking about, Parker?"

"This isn't your concern, Lieutenant. The colonel has it all figured out. You just do your job and follow the orders and we'll all be fine." Cain turned back to the senator. "And I told you to shut the hell up—"

"Most people would consider Abraham Lincoln to be

our greatest president." Morgan kept talking, ignoring the captain, looking straight at Lena. "Yet thousands of citizens, the nation's best, died in order to achieve the greatest good. Like then, history will show that this is the proper path. This will be a new start. A rebirth, a chance to get things right."

"Parker, this is crazy." The lieutenant's voice was a booming baritone.

Cain's face was red with anger. "I tol' you to shut the hell up!" In one fast move he raised the gun, pointed it at the senator, and pulled the trigger. *Thwack.* Morgan staggered backward, his chest stained red.

"What the—" The lieutenant recoiled in shock.

Lena gasped. Ramon staggered to his feet.

Suddenly Cain was cool again. "Be cool, Rev. He was a loose end. Eventually he'd be a thorn in the colonel's side. It's better this way." He pulled a handkerchief out of his pocket and quickly wiped down the gun.

"This is insane—"

"We'll talk about this later. Now isn't the time." Cain finished wiping the gun, turned toward Ramon, and tossed him the gun. "Here you go, killer, you're about to make the news again."

Ramon caught it instinctively. His nose was bleeding, his face a mess. He stood unsteadily on his feet, pointed the gun at the captain, and pulled the trigger. *Click.* Again, *click.*

Cain laughed. "I'll bet you wish you'd a done that the last time. There were bullets in it then." He reached down to his holster and pulled a second gun.

"What the hell is goin' on, Cain?"

"Relax, Rev, we just caught ourselves a couple of assassins. It all wraps up nice and saves the colonel some problems later."

Lena felt weak and dizzy. The whole scene was surreal. She leaned over, bracing herself on the desk. She closed her eyes as she tried to clear her head. The lieutenant was in Cain's face yelling now. It was obvious that the plan had come as a shock to him, too. Lena opened her eyes again, her nose puckered. She smelled the strong odor of dead cigarettes—her nose was nearly planted in the weaselly guy's smokeless ashtray. And right next to it was a cigarette lighter. She palmed it as she stood back up.

"When were you gonna tell me, huh?" The lieutenant was in Cain's face shouting. "I should've been told a long time ago, Cain."

"Calm down now, Lieutenant—"

"This is bull, Cain!"

Lena looked at Ramon. Though shaky, he was back on his feet. He'd been beaten but he was still defiant. She could tell by his eyes that he was looking for a way out. They were too far from the door. Even with the argument going on they wouldn't stand a chance if they tried to run. Cain could turn and cut them down before they reached the door. Ramon had seen her grab the lighter. He slowly crouched back down. The dropcloth at his feet was piled with the painter's equipment, including a metal can of paint thinner. Moving slowly so he wouldn't attract attention, he unscrewed the can's top.

"The end of the freakin' world and you weren't going to even tell me about it?"

"This ain't the time to discuss this, Lieutenant." They were still going at it hard.

Ramon tipped the can spilling the contents on the floor. The puddle flowed toward the door, making a line across the room, slopping onto the piles of files. Ramon nodded to Lena, motioning toward the door. She nodded and started edging over.

Moving slowly, they were halfway to the door when Cain stopped in mid-sentence, wrinkled his nose in recognition, and turned toward them. He knew something was wrong. He swung the gun at them. "Get the hell back—"

Lena flicked the lighter and the fumes ignited. With a *whoosh* the flames shot up, cutting the room in half with Ramon and Lena on one side and their captors on the other. They dove for the door as the room quickly filled with smoke. Ramon was fumbling with the door handle, trying to get it open when Cain fired. The bullet hit the glass of the door, shattering it. The door opened and Ramon burst through with Lena a step behind. They stepped into the hall and ran as the fire alarm began to scream.

23

RAMON'S NOSE WAS still bleeding, making it hard to breathe. Blood dripped out steadily, and the membranes were swelling, closing up. He tried to breathe through his mouth but it felt unnatural and limiting. It made it harder to run. He was at full throttle now. But with his shortness of breath he didn't know if he could keep it up. Once again they'd faced death and won. It was a miracle that they were still alive. But the odds always evened out in time. He wondered if their luck could last.

His head throbbed from the beating but an adrenaline rush made his pain irrelevant. His body was on automatic, taking opportunities and responding when it had to. With one hand he held the canvas bag, with the other he gripped Lena's wrist, trying to keep her in step with his pace. They raced down the hallway, away from the senator's office. The fire alarm blared. People were coming out of the offices and rushing for the exits. Ramon and Lena had a head start but that would only help for a few seconds. The pursuers would be after them soon. If they continued running straight ahead it would be over in no time. Cain would be coming soon, and he had a walkie-talkie. He was probably calling his reinforcements now.

They turned at the end of the hall into a new passageway, past two closed office doors. The next door they came to was a Senate meeting room. Its door was ajar. Without hesitation Ramon swung in.

"Come on. We've got to move." He tugged on Lena's wrist as he pulled the door shut behind him. The room was long and narrow with a large oak table at its center. It looked as if that a meeting had just broken up; there were dirty coffee cups and used notepads scattered throughout. At the opposite end of the room was another door. They sprinted across the room and out the other side. On the way out Ramon pulled the door shut.

Now they were in a different hall. Ramon stopped to consider their next move. His nose gurgled as he breathed, spraying a mist of blood into the air. He wiped his nose on his sleeve and looked both ways down the corridor. There were a few people at the end of the hall, moving rapidly away. Lena squeezed his hand tightly, her hands were trembling.

"Which way should we go?" There was a quiver to her voice.

"I don't know. Maybe this way." He picked a direction and they started up again. His sense of direction was off. He thought they were on the west side of the building but he wasn't sure. He didn't know where they were or how they could get out. By now all the exits would be covered. They were as good as trapped. But maybe in the confusion they'd be able to slip out. For now it was important to keep moving.

At its end, the hall opened out to the landing by the Rotunda, close to where they had been before finding the senator's office. The Rotunda was walled off. Ramon remembered that the stairs to the ground floor were just around the curve.

"Let's check the stairs." Their footsteps echoed off the tile floor. The landing was now empty. Their luck still held.

They were around the curve and about to start down the stairs when they heard the staticky burst of a walkie-talkie and a voice responding. Someone was on the stairs, waiting right below them. Lena's eyes were wide with fear as they backed up and retraced their steps around the curve. They couldn't go down and they couldn't go back. Cain and his men would surely be on them in moments. Around the curve on the other side, the building opened up to the House wing. There would be halls to run through and places to hide in there. But they didn't have enough time. By the time they got across the landing it would be too late. In the middle of the curve, a wooden door was built into the Rotunda wall. The sign on the door read Restricted. They had no choice.

Ramon kicked the door. It was solid. It didn't budge. The adrenaline was singing in his head. His heart banged in his chest; he knew he had to do something. He crouched down, then shot forward, hitting the door hard with his shoulder. He felt a jolt of pain as he connected. The door shook but held firm. He did it again. The wood splintered by the lock. He hit it a third time and this time the door caved in, swinging inward.

He gripped Lena's hand as they stepped through onto the balcony of the Rotunda.

THE SPRINKLER SYSTEM had kicked in and quickly doused the flames in Morgan's office, but the room was still heavy with smoke.

"God damn it." Cain stepped over the smouldering piles as he moved toward the door.

Tanner's face was set hard. "I want to know what's going on, Cain."

Cain opened the shattered door and stepped into the hall. "We'll discuss this later, Lieutenant. But now we have a job to do and I expect you to do it." He glanced down the hallway in both directions before setting out. He chose the path to the right. It was already clear of people. "Take the other way. The colonel will fill you in later."

Cain moved down the hallway as the fire alarm shrieked chaotically. His clothes were soaked. He couldn't believe it had happened again. He held his gun in one hand and the walkie-talkie in the other. He moved at a trot, trying to get a feel for where his rabbits would have run. Without stopping, he hit the button on the radio. "All units, this is Alpha. We got a problem here. Initiate plan B. Targets are loose in the building. If you make contact, shoot to kill. We're not gonna take no prisoners."

He released the button and stuck the unit back in his belt. His men were scattered through the building on the lower level. They'd cover the exits first and then begin search procedures, starting at the bottom and working their way up. The rabbit had gotten away again but this time he wouldn't get far. With the manpower Cain had, there was no way his prey would get out alive. He hadn't expected this. This target was tougher than he'd expected.

Cain came to the end of the hallway. It branched out so there were three possible choices, left, right, or straight. It had taken less than a minute for him to get out of the office, but it was enough time for them to disappear. They could have gone in any direction. He stopped and listened. All he could hear was the alarm's blare. If he took the wrong path, it would kill valuable time. He backed up and looked around. Then he saw it. The carpet was a pattern of blue, silver, and gold. But looking closely he saw specks of red. Fresh blood. The rabbit had left a trail of blood for him to follow.

Cain smiled and followed the tracks. Now he felt calm and in control. This was the end game—the most enjoyable part of the hunt. He turned and traced the blood down the new hallway. He walked past the meeting room before he realized that he'd gone too far. He backtracked until he found the trail again, went through the room and into the other hall. The blood was heavier here. It looked like they'd stopped, maybe to plan their moves or collect their thoughts. Then the trail turned and went back toward the center of the building. He picked up his pace as the noise from the fire alarm suddenly stopped.

He was near the end of the hall when he heard a banging noise. *His targets were up ahead.* Gripping his gun in his hand he broke into a run. He heard another bang and then a crash. He came out at the landing by the Rotunda just in time to see his prey step inside, onto the balcony leading upward. He sprinted the few yards and went in himself. They were around the corner, moving up along the curving stairway.

Cain smiled. This was perfect. The Rotunda had at one time been a popular attraction. But with the steep, winding stairs it was a potential health hazard. They'd closed access years ago. There were no other exits. To get down they'd have to get past him—they were trapped.

LENA HAD THE urge to laugh. She didn't know why. It wasn't funny. They'd nearly been killed and probably still would be before too long. In the senator's office she'd nearly wet her pants from fear. She'd been expecting the bullet to take her; she'd been waiting to die. And now they were out again. She was still scared, almost terrified. But in some sick way it struck her as hysterically funny. Or maybe it was just hysteria.

They'd rounded the curve and were climbing higher. She glanced out as she ran. They were on a winding staircase adjacent to the balcony of the Rotunda. She looked across the chasm; the balcony wound around several more times before it ended. There had to be an exit somewhere along the way. But where? She glanced down and had to quickly look away. They were higher up than she thought. Even now the ground was far below.

The stairway was impossibly steep. She was panting and her chest burned. The muscles in her legs tightened with fatigue, and her heart was like a drum in her chest. There was no way she could keep up the pace.

"Stop . . . can we rest for a minute?" she wheezed.

Ramon looked back. His face was smeared with blood, his eyes were wild. His breath came fast, he was breathing through his mouth. "We can't. You've got to keep going." He tugged on her wrist again, pulling her along.

But it was too much. She couldn't keep up. She needed to rest—just for a minute—then they could go on. She stopped. "No . . . I just need a minute. . . ."

Ramon stopped and glanced back nervously. "Okay, just for a minute."

That's when they heard it, a voice, calling, "Hello, rabbits. Wait for me." It was Cain's voice, taunting them. It came from the stairway just below them.

Lena moved forward. It didn't seem funny anymore.

CAIN FELT ENERGIZED and alive. After the frustrations of the last months this was a thrill. It was better than he'd imagined. It all tied up so nicely, he thought. The way it laid out he would have a clean kill by the time they reached the top of the stairway. And he would come down a hero and get back in the colonel's favor at the same time. These were wanted killers here—they'd just killed a U.S. senator. He'd probably get a medal for catching them. Not that it mattered. Medals wouldn't have much value in the near future.

He stopped and listened. They were around the curve,

almost above him. He could take his time now. They weren't going anywhere.

"Hey, rabbits," he yelled. "You can run, but you can't hide." He heard the sound of scurrying feet above him. He smiled. It was perfect. He could almost imagine the looks of fear on their faces. Fear and the knowledge that it was over. They were about to die and he had won.

He turned to the railing, aimed his gun out across the chasm, and waited for his targets to come into view. A second later he saw a flash of movement across the way on the balcony above him. He had a clear shot. It was a long distance for a handgun, but he thought he could make the shot. But that would ruin the fun. It would be much more satisfying to get them close up.

He turned back to the stairway and continued his climb up.

A NEW WAVE of fear washed over Lena. She wasn't tired anymore, her head buzzed with adrenaline. She felt light-headed and could taste the metallic tang of panic in her mouth. She couldn't run fast enough. Hearing Cain's voice made it so much more real. He was treating it like a joke. He wasn't chasing them, he was coming up slowly. Taking his time. Now she knew it. There were no other exits. They were trapped.

Ramon ran a step ahead of her, scanning the balcony in front. They'd nearly sprinted around the curve, taking the steps two at a time. Maybe they could put some distance between themselves and Cain. But it wouldn't matter. If they couldn't find an exit, it was over.

They heard him again, his voice mocking. "Hey, rabbits, what's up, doc?"

Lena gulped in air. Without slowing down, she glanced past the edge of the balcony. They were over a hundred feet up. The people below looked like tiny dolls. An image flashed through her mind. She pictured herself stepping onto the edge of the balcony and launching herself into space, falling down to the floor of the Rotunda. She shuddered. No matter how hopeless their situation looked she couldn't give up. She blinked her eyes, trying to get the image out of her mind.

The rise in the flooring here wasn't as steep, but was on a steady incline. Lena stepped forward but misjudged the step and twisted her ankle. "Ooww!" she cried.

Ramon stopped and bent down to her. "Are you all right?"

"It's my ankle."

"Can you walk?" Ramon put his arm around her, supporting her, as he helped her to her feet.

"I think so." They moved forward again. Slower now. She leaned on Ramon, keeping most of the weight off her ankle.

"I'm comin' to get you, rabbits." Cain's voice sounded closer.

THE WALKIE-TALKIE ON Cain's belt buzzed with noise. He yanked it out and hit the button. "Yeah? This is Big Dog."

"Hey, Captain, can you hear me?" It was Ortman.

Cain felt a flash of irritation. "Of course I can hear you. What's up?"

"Well, we've got the first floor secured, but there's no sign of the targets."

"I've got that under control. They're as good as got."

"Oh, well, good. But we got another problem here, sir." Ortman's voice came out in a conspiratorial whisper. "The Senate police are here and they kind of resent that we're taking over. And there're a couple of senators that are asking questions, too."

"Don't worry about it. We'll smooth it all out later. I'll get the colonel involved." He replaced the radio on his belt. He didn't have time to worry about details. It would all sort out in time. But now he had to finish his hunt. He stopped again and listened. He could hear them running, up ahead, somewhere around the corner. There wasn't much space left for them. They'd be at the end soon. Slowly and deliberately, he moved forward.

It should be easy, Cain thought. His targets would come to the top and have nowhere left to go. He'd have a clear shot. But the Mexican was crafty. He wouldn't go down without a fight. Cain knew that if the positions were switched, if *he* were being pursued, he would try to set a trap. He'd do something to equalize the situation. He'd underestimated the rabbit before with disastrous consequences. He wasn't going to let it happen again.

Cain reached down, rolled up his right pant leg and took out a short-handled combat knife. The grip was tailored to fit the hand and the blade was razor sharp. He expected to have a clean shot. But there was no sense taking any chances. He kept walking, around the curve, moving up.

He listened again. He couldn't hear any sign of movement. They'd stopped. There was no more room. That would be where the rabbit would make his stand. Gripping his knife in one hand and the gun in the other, Cain continued forward.

HELPING LENA, RAMON rounded the corner. They moved slower now. Too slow. It wouldn't be long before they were caught from behind. Besides, it looked like there was nowhere left to run. The balcony curved around for one more turn, but that was it. There were fewer steps here and the incline leveled off. They were as close to the top as they could get and he'd seen no exits along the way. It looked like this was the end of the line.

"He'll be here soon. We can't keep running," Ramon said.

Lena nodded. "I know."

He looked both ways, up and down the balcony, "Can you walk by yourself?"

She nodded her head. "I think so. I can walk."

"I want you to get around the curve ahead. As far as you can. Can you do that, or do you need help?"

"No, I can do it."

"Good. Get back as far as you can, then get down low and out of sight."

Lena nodded, then gripped the railing for support and pulled herself along.

Cain called out again, "Ready or not, here I come." He was still a ways back. It sounded to Ramon as if his voice came from the area a full curve down. That meant they still had some time. At the pace Cain was coming, it would take another minute before he was on them.

Ramon quickly surveyed the area one more time. Cain knew they were here, and would be expecting a fight; but he wouldn't know exactly where. Their only hope was to take him by surprise. But that would be hard by itself, and impossible in an area as bright as this was. There were light fixtures along the outer wall spaced every five feet or so. Ramon pulled off his shirt and wrapped it around his fist for protection. He smashed his fist into the glass housing of the lamp closest to him. The housing shattered. Being careful not to cut himself he did the same with the bulb. He repeated the process at each of the five lamps positioned around the curve. Looking back he still didn't see Cain.

He panted heavily. His nose had stopped bleeding and was beginning to clot. He had to breathe through his mouth now. At the edge of the balcony, rectangular columns of dark wood were spaced between the railings, three feet apart. There was a ledge on the railing just wide enough for him to stand.

He looked back. Still no sign of Cain. He bent down and picked up a piece of the shattered glass. He wrapped it in his shirt and put it into his pocket. Then, moving back in the curve, into the shadows, he stepped up onto the railing. The ledge was narrower than he'd thought. He barely fit. Suddenly he felt unsteady. He had to bend forward so he wouldn't fall back. He wanted to grip the outer column and hold on tight. But then Cain would see his fingers. He had to stay still, maintain his balance and hope for a chance to attack. He took out the glass shard and gripped it in his shirt. Now it was time to wait. He took a deep breath and tried to relax and not think about falling.

CAIN SMILED WHEN he saw the broken lights. It was so transparent. He'd expected more. The attack would come as soon as he walked around the corner. The rabbit would be waiting for him in the dark, crouching down; he'd jump out of the shadows in a kamikaze hit. A suicide strike. Cain savored the thought of it. It would be too easy.

He stopped for a second to take off his mirrored glasses. He was in full hunter mode now. He lightly gripped his weapons as he walked, his senses tuned to anything out of the ordinary, any movement, sound, or even smell. He was by nature a predator. It was second nature, probably something in his genes. This was his element. This was fun.

Taking his time, he walked forward. As he reached the dark area where the lights had been broken, the hair on the back of his neck stood up. It was time. It would happen now.

He stepped into the shadow squinting to see better. There were layers of shadow and light. He tried to make out the shape of a body in front of him. Then he heard the sound of a heavy breath escaping. It came from behind.

RAMON HELD HIS breath as long as he could. He listened to the sound of approaching footsteps. It was almost time. He stood still as stone, trying not to move, not to breathe,

not even to think. Any motion and Cain would be on him.
The ledge was too narrow for comfort. It was hard to keep
his balance, knowing that just a shift backward and he'd
be off, plummeting down to the ground below. The footsteps came closer.

He clutched the glass shard in his hand, keeping it
down by his side, waiting. The footsteps were louder now.
He tensed as Cain stepped into his field of vision, his head
tilted slightly forward as he searched the passageway.
Ramon had the urge to back up, to move away from the
threat, to get outside Cain's field of vision. He fought the
urge and remained still. He couldn't hold his breath much
longer. His chest constricted; he wanted to let go and gasp
in the air. He held still. It seemed like the moment lasted
forever. Cain stepped past without seeing him.

He couldn't hold it any longer. He let out his breath.
With the reflexes of an animal, Cain turned. Ramon leapt
toward him, the shard of glass in his hand.

CAIN SPUN AROUND—the rabbit was lunging at him. *How
did he get there?* Cain reacted by instinct. He swung the
gun into position, his finger tensing on the trigger. But his
attacker hit before he got the shot off. Cain grunted. He
was driven back, his breath knocked out of him. A jolt of
pain flashed through his arm, the rabbit had cut him somehow. He felt his grip on the gun loosen. The attacker
seized the advantage and smashed Cain's arm against the
wooden column. Cain tried to grip tight, but he couldn't.
The gun slipped out of his fingers, clattered onto the balcony ledge and bounced over. Out of the corner of his eye,
he saw it fall out of sight. There was a metallic ping as it
hit the tile floor far below.

He'd underestimated the rabbit before and regretted it.
Now he was pressed against the balcony, off balance, the
rabbit's hot breath in his face. He was stronger than Cain
had thought. Cain's right arm stung; there was a gash

where the forearm had been sliced open. He felt his anger bubble up. These last months he'd been obsessed with revenge, finishing the job and making it right. He'd lost so much in the hunt. And it was happening again.

They were in close, pressed body to body, but Cain still had his knife. His arm was locked down by his side. He took a deep breath and brought his knee up sharply. The rabbit anticipated and turning slightly so the knee just grazed his thigh. But it was enough. The rabbit loosened his grip just enough so that Cain could break his arm free.

He thrust with the knife and hit home, sinking into the rabbit's shoulder. Blood spurted. Shocked, the rabbit released his grip. Cain twisted his body and pushed in, driving the knife farther and turning the rabbit's back hard against the ledge of the balcony. He had the advantage again. It was time to end it all.

With one hand gripping his opponent's throat and the other the knife, he leaned in hard. He pushed the rabbit back hard against the ledge so his head was over the balcony. Cain aimed for the throat. But the rabbit still gripped the wrist of his knife hand, trying to put off the inevitable. Cain pushed down, but could bring the blade no closer. His opponent's arms were locked firm against the pressure.

Cain's head pounded. He felt the rage taking control— he wouldn't be denied. His strength surged. He pushed down hard and felt the rabbit's elbows bend, breaking the lock. He pushed the knife closer, the resistance slowly breaking down. He forced the tip of the knife down to the rabbit's neck. But the rabbit didn't give up. He still pushed back, his eyes registering defiance. Cain smiled. This was a tough one, a worthy opponent. He pushed a little harder; the tip broke skin and drew blood. Another second and it would all be over.

• • •

RAMON KNEW HE was going to die again, and it didn't feel
any better than the first time. The knife cut into his skin,
and Cain's other hand squeezed his throat, making it hard
to breathe. He strained with all his strength to keep the
blade away. But Cain's eyes showed triumph. They both
knew it was over.

Ramon's shoulders were jutting past the ledge now. As
Cain pushed harder he leaned over more, using the full
leverage to his advantage. His center of balance was high,
he was leaning too far. Ramon strained against him and
Cain moved just a little higher to push in the killing thrust.
Ramon tasted blood. This was it. He set his feet and
kicked up with all his strength, arching his back and
thrusting his pelvis out. He waited for the blade to plunge
in deeper but instead it was quickly pulled back as Cain
dropped the knife and waved his arms, trying to regain his
balance. Ramon saw it in Cain's eyes. Surprise—panic.
His balance had shifted and he was trying to pull back to
safety—but couldn't.

They both toppled. Cain went over first, clutching at
Ramon's throat to right himself. It was too late. His fingers couldn't grasp, and he was falling. Ramon shot out
his arms and grabbed at the ledge. He clawed at the wood
and clamped on tight, his legs dangling. Without meaning
to, he looked down. Cain fell faceup, screaming all the
way down. Ramon winced at the sound when he hit. There
was a commotion below as people ran to the body. The
floor was crawling with men in uniform. He didn't know
if they were police or soldiers. It really didn't matter.

It was all Ramon could do to just hold on to the railing.
His shoulder throbbed with pain; his arms ached with the
effort. It hurt to breathe. He knew that he'd lost a lot of
blood, from both his shoulder and his nose. He beat Cain
by outlasting him, he thought. But he couldn't last much
longer. He was bone tired and his fingers would soon lose
their grip. He closed his eyes and pictured how it would

be if he let go: The air would rush past as if he were flying, his stomach would rise up to his throat like on a roller coaster, then he'd hit and it would all be over. No more thought. No more pain.

"Ramon, I can help you up, but you've got to pull." It was Lena. She looked so beautiful looking down at him.

"I can't," he said.

"You've got to." She leaned over the balcony and grabbed onto his arms. "You've got to try."

Ramon sucked in a deep breath. If he let go, then they'd win. He'd come this far, he couldn't quit now. His fingers gripped onto the ledge and he pulled. He closed his eyes and strained as Lena pulled from above. With effort he gained a few inches and a new fingerhold. He focused his mind and worked through the pain. There was shouting down below. He tuned it out and pulled harder. The only thing in life was the other side of the ledge. Lena pulled from on top and he was there. His chest landed on the ledge; he shimmied forward and over the ledge where he collapsed on the floor.

He lay there for a minute, gasping for breath. Lena picked up the canvas bag. "Come on. We can't stay here. You're bleeding too bad. We need to get you some help."

Ramon nodded and pulled himself up. They leaned against each other for support and started back down the stairs.

24

TANNER FELT LIKE a traffic cop as he paced outside the broken door leading to the balcony. He'd kept the position staked out even as the floor swarmed with people. The Senate police had come on the scene within minutes of the fire alarm going off. The firemen arrived soon after, and two senators and their aides were still on hand, waiting for the all clear sign. By now the media would surely be camping outside. It was a zoo. Under authority of the Office of Homeland Security, his men were still involved in the search. But that wouldn't last long. Someone was bound to ask questions.

The whole situation was crazy, he thought. Cain had known the rabbits would show up eventually. He'd set the bait to make sure they came. The plan was to wait for the phone call, pick up the targets, and quickly leave the area. The plan called for a quick entrance and a quick exit—no one had said anything about killing a senator. Now everything was fucked up. The situation had started out bad and quickly deteriorated.

But the thing that really infuriated him was that they'd done it to him again. All along he'd been told he was part of the inner circle, in the know. After the test in the desert he'd had it out with Major Durmo. Durmo came up with some lame excuse, but he apologized and assured Tanner they wouldn't put him in a situation like that again. They promised that they'd tell him everything he needed to know. And now, they blindsided him with *this* news. He'd been played for a fool all along.

Tanner checked his watch; it had been twenty minutes since Cain had followed the targets up the balcony. He'd be back soon and then Tanner had a decision to make. Up to now, he hadn't really considered what he was involved in. He knew they were dealing with an illegal program, there was no denying that. They were carrying out prohibited germ warfare agents, they had used humans as subjects for testing the vaccine, and they had killed innocent people in the desert while proving the toxin. But in his mind, he'd been able to rationalize it all away. They were working toward a higher cause—the ends justified the means. Besides, the people they used were expendable, losers. Society was clearly better without them.

Tanner believed in the colonel. He had faith that the colonel saw the big picture and that what they were doing was necessary and, in the end, honorable. But after listening to the senator, he was shaken. This plan was flat-out crazy.

Tanner heard a commotion from down below. Something was going on. He thought about using the walkie-talkie to check but thought better of it. With all the other people involved, it was best to stay out of the way. He glanced back across to end of the hallway to where a group of middle-aged white men were clustered. They all wore suits and ties and spit-shined black wingtips. Before he could look away one of the men made eye contact and started walking over. The others followed at a distance.

"Lieutenant. Would you tell me what in hell is going on here?" the man asked.

Tanner recognized the man's face but couldn't place his name. He knew he was a senator from one of the western states. Tanner hesitated before answering. "We believe there is an assassin in the complex. The situation is—"

"An assassin?"

"Yes, sir—" He heard a sound behind him and spun around. It came from the stairway. He raised his gun and waited. He expected Cain to step out, and then what would he do? He didn't know, but he gripped the gun firmly as he waited. A second later they came through the doorway—the two rabbits. Ramon was soaked through with blood, his eyes half closed, his face twisted with pain. The girl leaned against him, staggering as she tried to support his weight.

Tanner reacted with shock. "Where's Cain?"

Lena stared into his eyes. He saw a strength there, a resolve. "You heard what they were saying," she said. "Is that what you want?"

Tanner motioned with the gun. "Don't say another word. Step all the way out and show me your hands."

She didn't hesitate. "Are you part of this? Can you picture what life will be like? They've been planning the end of the world. The end of the world! And if you go along with it, you're as much to blame as they are."

Tanner didn't move. She was right. They'd played him for a fool and he was part of it. It was all crazy. It had gone too far and he was part of it. He kept the gun on them, but he knew she was right.

Lena stared at him. She could see the change in his eyes. "You know what's right." She stepped forward, ignoring the gun. "He's lost a lot of blood. I need to find a doctor." Tanner stood rooted to the ground as she stepped past him, heading for the stairs. He dropped the gun to his side and let her pass.

"What the hell is going on?"

He'd forgotten the senator was behind him. He turned to respond. "Senator, I need—" He heard the clatter of someone running up the stairs. Out of the corner of his eye he saw it was Ortman. Tanner spun toward the stairway to see Ortman raise his gun. Tanner sprang forward. "No. Stop!"

It was too late. Ortman fired, hitting Ramon, who crumpled to the floor. Tanner rushed ahead and slapped the gun out of Ortman's hand. "It's over. You hear me? It's over."

Ortman stepped back, shaken. Tanner's shoulders slumped as he turned away.

Lena was bent over Ramon's body, sobbing. The canvas bag they'd brought in was at her feet. Tanner reached down to pick up the bag. Then he took a deep breath and straightened his shoulders. The senators were frantic. He marched over to them, straight and proud.

"Sirs, there is a conspiracy to commit treason. I am involved and I have firsthand knowledge of the plan." He handed over the canvas bag. "This tape contains additional proof."

It was over.

MAJOR DURMO CROSSED his arms to hold in his warmth, but it didn't help. He'd never felt so cold. The room was cold and dark, as always. But it had never bothered him as much before. Today it felt like a morgue. His mind reeled with images of death; deaths to come and death averted, and ultimately his own death. This was clearly the end; all their plans were now laid to rest.

In a small way he was glad that it was over. He'd never

felt comfortable with the plan—it was too drastic. These past weeks he'd been watching with dread as the plan moved closer to completion. But he'd felt impotent. There was nothing he could have done to stop it. It would have been unbearable to go against the colonel. And besides, he was already in too deep. So in that way he was relieved that it was at an end—but mostly he felt terrified. Now came the accounting. Now they'd be pointing fingers and laying blame. They'd point at the colonel first, and surely they would point at him next.

The colonel sat back in the dark. His glasses reflected the images from the monitor behind Durmo's right shoulder. The colonel calmly watched, not saying a word. Durmo didn't turn around. He knew what the picture showed. The tanks were rolling, the first wave had already moved inside the installation's gates. His men had laid down their arms and had given no resistance. Who could blame them? This was unprecedented. The United States had never had to bring force against its own before.

Durmo cleared his throat again. "You've got to tell them, sir. I didn't do anything wrong. I was just following orders."

Pope remained quiet. He hardly moved.

"Please, sir. You've got to tell them. It's not my fault." He tried not to whine, but panic was getting the better of him.

Pope stirred as if wakened from a trance. "I heard you, Major." He took a deep breath and leaned back in his chair. "I heard you clearly. But you are being a nuisance. I need to think."

Durmo fidgeted in his chair.

Pope steepled his fingers together in thought. "There are always options, Major. For a man with resolve, there is always a way to regain the advantage."

"Yes, sir." Durmo was puzzled. The situation looked

pretty bleak to him, but he didn't have the colonel's vision.

Pope pulled open the top desk drawer and removed a fresh deck of playing cards. Deep in thought, he pulled off the cellophane and shook the cards out into his large hands. He gave a quick shuffle and set the deck down on the top of the table. "We need to maintain control, Major. A true leader keeps his head, even when those all around him are losing theirs."

"Yes, sir."

"The turn of events has been unfortunate." He picked up the first two cards, turned them on their sides and leaned them against each other. "But there has to be a way to turn the tide, to regain the advantage."

"Please, sir—"

"If only we had another week. If the colonies were in place it would make all the difference." He pulled another card from the deck and set it atop the first two, but his touch was too heavy and the cards fell down. He started again, setting the cards against each other, and this time it worked.

Durmo shifted uncomfortably. His stomach was in knots. Despite the coolness of the room he had started to sweat. Pope pulled two more cards from the deck and tried to place them adjacent to the first structure. But his touch was heavy and it knocked everything down. Durmo saw that the colonel's hands were shaking.

Pope placed his hands heavily on the desk. "There's only one way, Major. The toxin is in place. We need to release it now."

Durmo looked down at his feet. It felt like his stomach had moved up to his throat. "Uh, no, sir. We can't do that."

"I was not requesting, Major. That's an order."

"Uh, no, sir." He looked up. It took all his willpower to meet the colonel's eyes. "We can't take this any further, sir."

Pope swept his arm across the desk, knocking the cards to the floor. He jumped to his feet and towered over Durmo. Pope wore his full dress uniform; his chest was plastered with medals, his holster and side arm on his hip. His face swelled with anger, his breath came heavy. Durmo slunk down in his chair and waited for the explosion. But it didn't come. After a long moment the anger passed. Pope's shoulders fell as the energy drained from his body.

"That will be all, Major. You're dismissed."

"But, sir—"

"That is all." The colonel turned his back to Durmo.

"Yes, sir." Durmo said. He rose to his feet and quickly headed out the door, closing it behind him. This was it, he thought. What would they do now? He assumed there would be a court-martial. All the details would come out and people would look at him like he was some kind of monster. And after that it would be life in the brig, or more likely, the firing squad. People would see him and they wouldn't understand. It wasn't his fault. He was simply following orders. He would have done something if he could. But it just wasn't his fault.

Durmo's heart was racing. He felt a wave of panic rise up and flood his body. It wasn't fair. What they were doing to him was so unjust. He'd walked across the outer room and was almost out the door when it occurred to him. He needed to talk with the colonel again. If he talked with him one more time, he could convince him. The colonel would make sure that everyone knew that it wasn't his fault. Durmo turned around and paced back to the room.

His hand was on the doorknob, starting to turn, when he heard it. A single gunshot followed by the sound of a large body dropping to the floor.

Durmo shivered as he imagined what the colonel had

done. The final betrayal. Now the fingers of blame would shift. Now they would point straight at him.

THE DESERT FLOOR was ablaze with color. Golden poppies, pink and blue lupine, primrose and cactus flowers. Just days before, the desert had seemed dead and barren. After months of dry weather the sand was baked as dense as concrete. All signs of life lay dormant. But then, a spring rainstorm had passed through, drenching the earth. The heavy rain pounded the hard-packed ground. The rain came in a deluge, fast and strong. The water couldn't sink in and it had no path to run. Flash floods raced through, then fanned out and paused as the rains stopped. Soon the ground was again baked dry. But the water had done its trick. Springtime had come to the desert.

The jeep kicked up a cloud of dust as it moved across the sand. Lena rolled her window farther down. The musky scent of creosote bush filled the air. She breathed it in deeply. She knew she'd remember the smell later when she thought back on this day.

She glanced over the console to the passenger seat. Ramon leaned back, relaxed, a smile on his face. It was a wonder he was alive. The bullet had ripped through his intestines leaving a gaping hole. The ambulance picked him up quickly and rushed him to Georgetown University Hospital, where they operated on him for over six hours. The surgeons had to cut out sections of his intestines as they pieced him back together. After they were finished, it still looked grim. He'd lost a lot of blood and the risk of infection was high. It was touch and go for nearly a month. But Ramon was a survivor. He'd pulled through.

Ramon caught her glance and reached over to take her hand. "Beautiful, isn't it?"

"Yes, it is," she said. He squeezed her hand tightly as she drove. It felt so good to be outside and on their own. At the Capitol, after Ramon had been shot and Tanner sur-

rendered, Lena had been handcuffed and taken to a holding cell at the Senate police complex. They fingerprinted
her and took her mug shot. But she was there less than an
hour before being released to the FBI. Over the next three
days a full team of agents interrogated her. They grilled
her on everything from how they had managed to hide out
for so long, to what she really knew about the Johnson Installation. They wouldn't tell her what had happened to
Ramon, or what they intended to do with her. It was emotionally draining.

Eventually they turned her over to an agent named Jacobs, a senior administrator from Washington. "From all
the evidence we've obtained, it's apparent that you are
completely innocent. The charges have all been lifted," he
told her. "The official line is that this entire situation was
a bizarre case of mistaken identity. We've worked some
angles so that the press has bought the story."

"So I'm free to go?"

"Technically. But we're in a ticklish situation," he explained. "We have a problem. This story is too explosive.
We can't let the public find out what really happened. It's
a case of national security. If people find out about this
they'll question everything. We need citizens to have faith
in the government if it's to survive. We're still trying to
figure out how to treat the two of you. The last thing we
need is for you to cause a fuss by writing some story about
all this."

"So what are you saying? I can't write the story?"

"I'm not saying anything of the sort. I'm appealing to
you as a citizen and a patriot. You don't realize how dangerous this information is."

"Well, even if I don't say anything, the press will never
go for that. They won't buy some made-up story."

Jacobs smiled. "Ms. Dryer, you are being naïve. The
press—the media—is nothing more than a group of corporate interests. They rely on us for assistance in a myriad

of ways. It's all about profits. If they make it difficult for us, we can make it very difficult for them. It's not a matter of if they will cooperate, they already have. Even if you do write the story, no one will print it."

Lena thought for a moment before replying. "And what if I go with it anyway?"

Jacobs smiled and paused for effect. "I guarantee you don't want us for enemies."

So in the end it really wasn't a matter of choice. The first week, Lena granted scores of interviews and went on all the news shows, telling a sanitized version of the events—how she was just in the wrong place at the wrong time and everything was coincidental. There was an implication that what happened was tied to the war on terrorism, so some specific details couldn't be released. To Lena, the explanation seemed bizarre, but the press bought it and the authorities confirmed it. It didn't take long for the frenzy to die down. She was offered positions at *Newsworld* and several other publications. But she declined. Her career didn't seem important anymore.

Ramon's situation was a bigger problem. After all, right or wrong, he'd been convicted of murder and was supposedly executed for it. His very existence was living proof of the conspiracy. There'd been a discussion about giving him plastic surgery to alter his appearance, creating a new identity, and placing him in the witness protection program. But that was too risky in its own way. In the end it was Ramon's decision. There was no way they could do an official deportation, but they furnished him with a Mexican identity and some money, and encouraged him to disappear. Again, there was the underlying threat of what would happen if he didn't.

And now they were out. Together again, as free as they could be. They held hands as she drove, both lost in their own thoughts. They didn't talk but enjoyed a comfortable silence. They were in the desert west of Brownsville, miles from any town. Lena crested a rise and the topography changed. It was hilly now, gently sloping upward.

"Just a little farther. We're almost there," Ramon said.

The elevation increased; a mile farther it began to peak. "This is good." Ramon said.

Lena pulled the jeep to a stop and set the brakes. They both climbed out and walked around to the front. A light breeze blew through, rustling Lena's hair. The sun was straight up in the sky, shining bright and strong. The only sound was the whistle of the wind. Down below, the river curled like a ribbon, the water reflecting back diamonds.

Ramon reached over and took her hand. "What are you going to do now?" he asked.

"I don't know. A lot has happened and I just need to do some thinking, let it all sort out and figure out my options. I can't write about what happened to us—everything would have to go through the censors. But there are other issues. I can still go back and look at your case, and some of the others. I'm sure you weren't the only innocent man sentenced to death. There's a lot of injustice in the death penalty and the prison system. And I might want to do some environmental reporting. If people have the true information, maybe things can change." She flicked her hair back. "I'm hoping something good can still come out of this."

"It'll work out. I know you. You're going to make something happen."

She smiled at him. He touched her neck and pulled her close. They kissed, long and tenderly. Lena held him close, trying to feel the rhythm of his heart. It felt so natural to hold him, to touch him. Being with him she'd felt the desert bloom inside. But there was no way they could stay together. Ramon wanted a simpler life; he wanted to go somewhere and blend in—disappear. Lena wasn't sure where her life would lead, but there were still things she needed to accomplish. She gently pushed him away. "You better get going."

Ramon smiled. "I'll always remember you." He picked up his backpack and canteen, slung them over his shoulder, and started down the hill toward the Rio Grande. Lena watched as he descended the hill, made his way to the river, and crossed over.

He didn't look back.

Epilogue _____

THE METROPOLITAN HOTEL anchored the corner of Providence and Western, down the block from Cy's cut-rate liquor and St. Mary's Catholic Church. In its glory days, it was a working man's hotel, providing bare-bones lodging at reasonable prices. The clientele then was a mix of immigrants and displaced country boys, new to the city. But its glory days were long past. The hotel, like the neighborhood, had fallen on hard times. The taped-over marquee sign advertised rooms available at weekly and monthly rates.

From across the street, the man studied the hotel. His clothes were dirty and his shirt soaked with sweat, his body lean and hard-muscled from months of heavy labor. He rubbed his glasses on the cleanest section of his sleeve as he took in the scene. The teenage gangbanger stood watch at his post against the streetlamp; two bums leaned against the building, clutching their bottles in paper bags;

an old Hispanic woman waited at the bus stop. The scene was normal. Nothing out of the ordinary to set off his radar. He glanced both ways as he set off across the street and kept his eyes down, avoiding contact as he climbed the steps to the hotel.

The lobby smelled stale, a mix of dirty laundry, damp wood, and bug spray. The man wrinkled his nose in distaste as he moved through. He'd almost crossed over to the stairs, when the clerk behind the counter yelled out, "Hey, O'Brien."

The man turned back and slowly walked to the counter. He gave the fat-faced clerk a hard look. "Yeah?"

"Your week's up tomorrow. You plannin' on stayin' longer?"

"No. I'll be gone tomorrow." He turned and headed back toward the stairs.

"I'll need that key back," the clerk called after him. "And if you're here past twelve, you gotta pay for another night."

The man ignored him as he headed up the stairs. He stopped at the second floor landing. He waited in the shadows for a moment to make sure the hall was clear. The hallway was dimly lit with peeling green paint and grayish brown carpet that had been shredded by wear. Pairs of doors fed off on each side, with a door at the end for the shared bathroom. Here, the smell of bug spray was more intense, but it wasn't enough to overpower the stench of urine and soaked-in beer. As he walked down the hall he listened to the sounds of TVs, radios, and an old man coughing.

He used his key to open his room and quickly went inside. The room was small and dingy. The bare lightbulb sent a harsh glow on the dresser and unmade bed. He pulled his backpack from beneath the bed, and took out a towel, some soap, and a fresh set of clothes. He left the room, locking the door behind him, and went down the hall to the communal bathroom. He was in luck tonight. It was empty.

He locked the door behind him, stripped down and stepped into the shower. The water didn't get more than lukewarm, but it still felt good to get wet and rinse off the grime. As he rubbed the soap over his head, he could tell his hair had grown out some. It was probably time to shave again. He'd only been in the shower for a minute when someone banged on the door. He finished up and took his time getting dressed. The freshly washed clothes were a luxury. He wrapped his soiled clothes in the wet towel and opened the door.

"Whatcha hoggin' the bathroom for, man?" It was a short Mexican with tattoos on both arms.

The man felt a momentary surge of panic. He felt like flapping his arms and moving away. Instead, he kept his gaze straight. He didn't say a word as he coolly walked past. He dropped the old clothes in the room, went down the stairs and out of the hotel. On the street he headed east. Walking at a leisurely pace, he scanned the faces of those going by, watching for danger. He passed bodegas and taco stands, taverns and graffiti-sprayed buildings. A few blocks down he turned onto a cross street. This block was residential. The houses were large brown-brick boxes with wide porches. Some of them were gutted and abandoned, with plywood sheets where the windows should be. Others had well-tended lawns and showed pride of ownership. It was early spring and the neighborhood was alive. People sat on their steps and yelled out to their neighbors. They all stared at the man as he passed, but he kept his eyes forward and didn't stop.

Two blocks down the area began to change. The houses here were the same construction but had been recently rehabbed. The brick was sandblasted clean and there were ornamental steel bars on all the windows. No one sat on the steps here, and the cars parked in front were all newer imports.

Another block down he came to a commercial street. He paused for a moment, then turned down it. The stores here were newer with colorful awnings and tasteful signs. He passed a Starbucks, a copy center, and several small ethnic restaurants. Halfway down the block he went into a storefront with a sign marked The Cyber Café.

Inside, the shop had bare wood floors and bold colors on the wall. Computers were stationed throughout the space, some on long curving counters, others in more recessed cubes. A coffee bar was off to the side. A menu board hung above it, presenting prices for computer time and assorted coffee drinks. The girl behind the counter had short red hair and a ring in her nose. She smiled as he came up to the counter. "Hi," she said.

"Hi." He pulled some cash out of his jeans and handed it over. "I guess I'll need about three hours."

"Want anything to drink tonight?"

"Maybe later. I'll be over there." He motioned to a cube in the corner.

"Sure. See you then." She smiled again as he walked away.

The man sat down at the monitor, and opened an Internet browser. The connection was fast and it came up quickly. He keyed in the address for the site and waited as the connection was made. Then he took a deep breath, logged on as TRUE BELIEVER, and began to type.

It was time to tell the truth.

Robert Kelly Studio

Peter J. Thompson lives near Chicago with his three sons. He's currently working on his second novel. You can contact him through his website, www.peterjthompson.net.